The story of Josephine Cox is as extraordinary as anything in her novels. Born in a cotton-mill house in Blackburn, she was one of ten children. Her parents, she says, brought out the worst in each other, and life was full of tragedy and hardship – but not without love and laughter. At the age of sixteen, Josephine met and married 'a caring and wonderful man', and had two sons. When the boys started school, she decided to go to college and eventually gained a place at Cambridge University, though was unable to take this up as it would have meant living away from home. However, she did go into teaching, while at the same time helping to renovate the derelict council house that was their home, coping with the problems caused by her mother's unhappy home life – and writing her first full-length novel. Not surprisingly, she then won the 'Superwoman of Great Britain' Award, for which her family had secretly entered her, and this coincided with the acceptance of her novel for publication.

Josephine gave up teaching in order to write full time. She says 'I love writing, both recreating scenes and characters from my past, together with new storylines which mingle naturally with the old. I could never imagine a single day without writing, and it's been that way since as far back as I can remember.' Her previous novels of North Country life are all available from Headline and are immensely popular.

'Bestselling author Josephine Cox has penned another winner'
Bookshelf

'Hailed quite rightly as a gifted writer in the tradition of Catherine Cookson'
Manchester Evening News

'Guaranteed to tug at the heartstrings of all hopeless romantics'
Sunday Post

'Impossible to resist'
Woman's Realm

JOSEPHINE COX

The Woman
Who Left

headline

First published in hardback in 2001 by
HEADLINE BOOK PUBLISHING

First published in paperback in 2002 by
HEADLINE BOOK PUBLISHING

20 19 18 17 16 15 14 13 12

ISBN 0 7472 6634 4

Typeset by Palimpsest Book Production Limited,
Polmont, Stirlingshire
Printed and bound in Great Britain by
Clays Ltd, St Ives plc

HEADLINE BOOK PUBLISHING
A division of Hodder Headline
338 Euston Road
London NW1 3BH

www.headline.co.uk
www.hodderheadline.com

TO MY READERS
(and Brenda!)

If any of you are thinking of travelling on British Airways, watch out for Brenda (she's the little one who smiles at you as you enter the plane).

The hostesses are wonderful. The service is exemplary (as you would expect) and the food on our particular flight was superb – hot and delivered with a 'Brenda' smile.

But our little Brenda is somewhat over-enthusiastic, so keep your eyes peeled for her, especially as she prefers to deliver your food right into your lap – and in your face, and your shoes, and seat (in my case it was piping-hot mushroom stroganoff).

But she does it with 'that' smile, bless her cotton socks, and afterwards loses no time in delivering you to the loo where she'll despatch handfuls of tissues.

If British Airways gets rid of our Brenda, I'll never fly with them again!

Keep it up, Brenda – you're a little gem. (You made my day, anyway.)

Out with the stroganoff and on with the smile, that's what I say!

CONTENTS

PART ONE

SUMMER, 1952
THE LEGACY

Chapter One

The Vale of Salmesbury, Blackburn, Lancashire

THE OLD MAN'S voice carried on the summer breeze. 'There'll be blue skies over . . . the white cliffs of Dover . . .' he sang. When the song was done he took to whistling, for he was a fine whistler and proud of it.

'You there! Stop that dreadful noise!' the woman shrieked at him from her bedroom window, but he didn't hear. He was too engrossed in his whistling. It was a fine day and he was a fortunate man to be carrying on this trade, when others out there trudged the streets to work that brought them no joy.

For more years than he cared to remember, Mike Ellis had brought his horse and cart along Scab Lane, delivering milk to the isolated families who lived hereabouts. It was a job he had loved, and would be sad to leave.

3

All too soon, it would be time for him to put his feet up and let some other poor devil climb out of his bed at four in the morning. But that was a small price to pay for the sights you saw before the world came awake: foxes scurrying for their dens, hares leaping across the horizon, and every kind of night animal imaginable making for home and safety. At four o'clock on a summer's morning like this, the skies were unbelievably beautiful . . . shot with wide, scintillating swathes of colour that few men were privileged to witness. Enthused by his happy lot, Mike began singing again, this time in an even louder voice.

Exasperated, the woman bawled, 'Damn and bugger it, Mikey Ellis! Will ye stop that confounded racket!'

Hair on end and the sleep still on her, she hung out of the bedroom window. 'You know I can't be doing with all that noise first thing of a morning.'

'Away with yer, Mabel, ye old misery,' Mike replied with a grin. 'You'll miss me when I'm retired. Happen you'll get a young fella-me-lad as couldn't sing even if he tried, an' it'd serve ye right, so it would.' He drew the horse to a halt outside the white picket-gate. 'So, what'll it be today, then?' Climbing down from his seat he patted the horse and gave it a knob of hay from his pocket. 'Come on now, missus, let's be having ye. I ain't got all day.'

Gathering her wits, Mabel Preston gave a lazy yawn. 'Just you wait there,' she replied with a coy grin. 'I'll be down in a minute.'

While he waited, Mike talked to the horse, like the old friend he was. 'She's a bit of a sourpuss,' he confided. 'By rights, I should be on my way to Maple Farm instead of hangin' around here to be pounced on. Oh aye! I'll get a smile from Louise Hunter, so I will – and a slice of cherry cake with a mug o' tea to wash it down.' He thought of Louise, and his expression softened. She was a good woman. Over the years she had faced some hard times and seen them away like the fighter she was.

He glanced warily at Mabel's door. 'This one's different – fancies herself as every man's pin-up, she does. She'll be down here any minute now, hair combed and lipstick on, an' with a smile on her face that'd put the fear o' God into any man!'

The very thought made him shiver. 'By! She thinks I don't know that she's got her sights set on me. I'm telling ye, that there Mabel Preston's got it into her head that I need a wife now I'm on the point of retiring, but she's got another think coming. What! She'd be after me every minute of the day. "Do this, do that. Out the bed with ye, Michael, there's work to be done!" I can hear her now, God help me.'

A terrible thought suddenly occurred to him. 'Jesus, Mary and Joseph!' He turned every shade of pink. 'I wouldn't put it past her to demand her marital rights an' all.' His eyes rolled with terror. 'By!' he shuddered to the horse. 'It don't bear thinking about.'

Preparing to make his escape, he was brought to a sudden halt when she hissed in his ear, 'Right then, Mikey, show me what you've got to offer.'

Swinging round, he gasped in dismay; Mabel Preston in full sail was a sight to daunt the bravest of men.

'Well?' When she smiled, he instinctively took a step backwards.

'Well *what*?' Mesmerised by her false teeth which flashed blindingly in the bright sunshine, he found himself rooted to the spot.

'Oh, really!' Spreading chubby hands over ample hips, she gave an unexpected twirl and almost knocked him over. 'Don't pretend you haven't noticed my new dress.'

Hanging like a sack at the waist and so tight round the neck it made her eyes bulge, the dress in question was sickly-brown with great yellow sunflowers all over.

'Well, what d'you think?' She had no intention of letting him off the hook!

At that moment in time, with Mabel's fat face plastered in make-up and her lips plumped out by those dazzling but ill-fitting teeth, poor Mike didn't know *what* to think; however he knew he had better compliment her, or his life wouldn't be worth living. 'It's . . .' He gulped. 'It's lovely,' he muttered lamely. 'Just lovely!'

'I knew you'd like it.' Beaming with pleasure, she dared to give him a juicy wink. 'Now then, you didn't answer me.'

By now, the milkman was shaking. 'Sure, I can't for the life of me recall what ye said.'

Sidling closer, she murmured, 'I asked what you had to offer.' Her bushy eyebrows went up and down, like a couple of ferrets ready to pounce.

When Mike was nervous he always stuttered. He stuttered now. 'I . . . don't know what . . . ye mean!'

The woman tutted loudly. 'Really, do I have to spell it out? *What have you got on your cart today?*'

Giving a great sigh of relief, Mike led the way to the back of the cart, where he threw off the tarpaulin to reveal a dozen sacks of potatoes, piled-up crates of milk, numerous boxes of freshly picked early plums and some large wicker baskets filled with newlaid eggs. 'You'll not get better wherever ye look,' he told her, and she knew it was the truth.

Mabel quickly selected a dozen brown eggs, four large potatoes and a bottle of milk. 'Will you come in for a cup of tea before you go?' She made one last, valiant effort to interest him in what she herself had to offer. 'I've a home-made apple tart just waiting to be sliced.'

Before he could reply, the sound of voices raised in anger made them turn their attention towards the spinney. 'Sounds as though somebody's squaring up for a fight.' Losing no time and glad of the opportunity to escape her attentions, Mike ran towards the hedge. 'Stay back, Mabel,' he ordered, though not for one minute did he expect her to heed his warning.

Forcing his way through the bramble-hedge, he broke into the field behind her house. Mabel might have done the same but for the considerable width of her hips, not to mention the fact that the brambles could tear your skin to shreds.

'It looks like the Hunter brothers.' Keeping her distance, she peered through the hedge.

'*Stay back!*' Mike repeated, and this time she obeyed. 'I'll see what I can do. You away up to the farm . . . tell Louise her husband and his brother are out to kill each other.' When she hesitated he bellowed at her. 'Away with you, woman. *Now!*'

Trying her best to hurry, the poor woman slipped and fell right into a run of cowpats. Mike made no move to help her. This was no time for sympathy, he decided, not when the two men were already stripping off their shirts to settle the argument with bone and knuckle.

'Get on with ye!' he roared, and get on she did

until, red-faced and fighting for breath, she stumbled to the bottom of the hill leading to Maple Farm. Here she paused to gather her strength before continuing at a pace more suited to a woman of her generous size and years.

While Mabel made haste to break the news to Louise, Michael ran across the field to try reasoning with the two brothers.

'Clear off, you! It's none of your damn business.' That was Jacob, the eldest. Tall and thickset, with piercing blue eyes and long, untidy brown hair, he had already attracted a reputation for trouble.

The other young man was called Ben; shorter in stature than his brother, he had the same sturdy physique of their father before them. Dark-haired, with serious brown eyes, Ben was the more responsible of the two. 'Best do as he says,' he advised the old man. 'There's no reasoning with him. It's gone way beyond that. Me and Jacob . . . we've a score to settle. It's best we get it over and done with.'

The score he spoke of had to do with their late father and the accumulation of his life's work.

In spite of his years, Mike was not easily dismissed. 'The pair of youse should be ashamed of yerselves,' he raged, 'fighting and arguing, with your poor father lying in the chapel of rest not two miles away!'

When he took a step forward, Jacob suddenly

rounded on him with clenched fists. 'I warned you you old fool!' Rushing at him, he took the milkman by the throat. But then he was suddenly fighting his own corner, when Ben marched up behind him and, spinning him round by the shirt collar, landed a crunching blow squarely on his chin.

Enraged, Jacob ran at him, head down like a battering ram. When his head collided hard with his brother's mouth, the blood from Ben's split lip sprayed out like a crimson shower. 'Come on then, let's have you!' Beckoning with both hands, Jacob backed off, laughing and taunting as Ben wiped his mouth with the back of his hand.

Glancing towards the old man to make sure he wasn't hurt, Ben made one last plea to his brother. 'Mike is right,' he said. 'We shouldn't be fighting. Not now.' His sorry gaze went to the hills and the town beyond. 'What would *he* say?'

Jacob was like a crazy thing. 'I don't give a stuff for what he'd say. Happen he'd see you for the coward you are.'

Anger lit his brother's eyes. 'I've never been a coward in my life, and you know it!'

'You've *allus* been a coward. Only *he* wouldn't have it, would he, eh? Oh no! He thought the sun shone out of yer arse! Oh, but you were clever, I'll give you that . . . toiling the land and working with him hand in glove. The poor old sod didn't know what you were up to, but I was wise to you.' The words spat out.

'What are you saying?' Ben's voice was tight with rage.

'What normal man would prefer to break his back working the land when he could be out in the big wide world, making his mark?' Jacob sneered. 'You stayed because you had in mind that one day all this would be yours.' Flinging wide his arms he embraced the land about them. 'You're a cunning bastard, Ben Hunter, but don't think you've done me out of what's rightfully mine, because I'll fight you tooth and nail all the way!'

'Out with it.' Knowing his brother from old, Ben sensed that Jacob was up to no good. 'What's your game, eh? *You* were the one who chose to leave all this behind. You didn't want it before and you don't want it now. I'll never see the day dawn when you roll up your sleeves and bend your back to hard work.' He shook his head in disgust. 'What you're after is selling it to the highest bidder, isn't that right?'

'None o' your business what I want with it. It's *mine* – that's all you need to know.' Ben had hit the nail on the head and that rankled. 'If you want a fight, I'll give you one, any way you like.' Though he feared his brother was more of a man than he would ever be.

Shamed by the whole sorry business, Ben gave

it one more try. 'Why can't you understand? Dad really loved this land,' he said softly. 'It was his whole life.'

'Pity!'

Ben knew there would be no peace until this was settled, so he laid down the terms. 'I love it, too. I don't know what Dad put down on paper, but I'll tell you this. If he's left it all to Mother, I'll stand by her, the same way I stood by him. And not for any reward, but because like Dad, I love the land and the way of life here. And I swear to God . . . if he's left me any part of this wonderful place, *you'll* never get your hands on it, not unless you're prepared to dirty them, the same as he did.'

Jacob laughed harshly. 'D'you really expect me to believe that you don't know what he put in his will? Liar! He'll have left you the lot, make no mistake; God only knows you've had years enough to persuade him. He thought I could never compare with you, so I never tried. There was no point.'

'You're wrong, Jacob. He knew you didn't like working the land and he came to accept that. Why d'you think he set you up with that delivery business? Good God, man! He even borrowed money against everything he owned, just so's you could have your big chance.'

'He wanted shut of me, that's why.'

'Don't talk stupid.' His heart heavy with emotion,

Ben lashed him with the truth. 'How many times did he beg you to stay? He even promised to build you a house here, but what did you do? You threw it all back in his face. "I want out" – that's what you said, and you broke his heart. But he did what you asked. He gave you a business of your own and asked for nothing in return. Farming never made any man rich. You either love the land or hate it. I loved it and you couldn't get away fast enough, that's the truth of it.'

'I told you . . . he wanted shut of me. He owed me a living, and that's all there was to it.'

'Did you ever wonder where he got the money from to set you up with delivery wagons and a warehouse right smack in the centre of town – not to mention contracts with the locals to get you started? O' course not! Well, I'll tell you. He mortgaged his home and his farm; something he swore all his life he would never do. Afterwards, it played on his mind. He couldn't rest until it was paid off. Morning, noon and night, he worked like a dog, until every penny was repaid.'

Tears filled Ben's eyes. 'And yes, you're right. I *did* work alongside him and was proud of it. And shall I tell you why? Because I loved that man, more than you could ever know. And if he's thought to leave me here, where I'm content, I'll thank him to my dying day.'

'That's 'cause you're a coward,' Jacob repeated viciously. 'A cissy who'd rather hide away in this godforsaken place than get out and face the real world. You and him, you were just the same – both cowards. Both afraid of the world beyond these fields. At least I went out and did my best.'

'No, you didn't! You threw it all back in his face . . . wasted all his efforts to look after you. Women, boozing, driving flash cars, up to your ears in every shady deal that comes along – that's you, Jacob. That's why you want to get your hands on his land . . . to get your business out of trouble and finance your high-living. And when this land's gone, and all the money with it, you'll find a way of cheating somebody else out of everything they cherish. Dad had you down for what you are: a user. You'll never change.'

His brother laughed in his face. 'Well, you see, I always did know how to enjoy myself. But I'm back now, and like I say, I intend laying claim to what's rightfully mine. I *am* the eldest, don't forget, and it's time I put you in your place. Since I've been gone you seem to have taken over.'

'If you think that, why didn't you make your way back when Dad was alive, when he needed you? When we *both* needed you.'

'You know why – because he would have sent me packing. But he's not here now, is he?' His face contorted with loathing. 'And I can't say I'm too sorry about that!'

His cruel taunts hit hard. With a roar, Ben lunged at him, and each time he was thrust aside, he came at him again. For his part, Jacob gave as good as he got; and though the fighting was terrible to see, there was no victor, for one was as strong as the other.

Helpless, Mike Ellis watched until he could bear it no longer. Torn and blood-spattered, the brothers were locked in a struggle so vicious it would take more than one old man to separate them.

Taking to his heels, Mike ran to the hedge and scoured the horizon. 'If anybody can stop them, it's Louise,' he said aloud. But there was no sign of her. 'Where the devil *is* she?'

Convinced they would kill each other if they weren't stopped, the old man set off at an awkward run towards the farmhouse, to find the only person who might make the brothers see sense.

━━━━◆━━━━

IN THE GARDEN, Louise hung the last of the washing on the line. Turning to push up the prop, she didn't see the old mongrel dash out and grab the bloomers off the line. It was only when she heard his playful growl as he dashed about, that she realised what he'd done, '*Hey!* Come back here, you devil.

Them's me mother-in-law's bloomers. She'll have my guts for garters if they get torn.'

The more she chased the mongrel, the more he enjoyed it . . . diving in and out of the line, off down the path one minute and into the shed the next.

That was where she cornered him – in the shed. 'You little sod!' Breathless and laughing, she persuaded him to drop Sally's bloomers, which by now needed a second wash. 'You rascal, you.'

Even so, she had to laugh at herself. 'You had me running a right old dance.' Stuffing the bloomers under her arm, she confided, 'If it were up to me, you could have these awful bloomers for dinner, but they're Sally's, not mine, thank God, and I've been entrusted with their safekeeping, so you're not having them, however much you might wink your little eye.' Boris had a habit of closing one eye and laughing with the other, which gave the appearance of a mischievous wink.

Making her way back to the washing line, Louise kept a wary eye on him. 'Don't you dare!' she threatened when it seemed he might make a bee-line for the washing basket. Wagging a finger, she dropped the bloomers into the basket and afterwards, hoisted the prop as high as she could get it to keep the washing out of his reach.

With the washing safe and the basket tucked securely under her arm, she took a moment to look out across the valley, the magnificence of it taking her breath away, as always.

It was a beautiful scene, with the valley sweeping away to the river, seeming to merge with the skies when it climbed away up the other side. The recent showers had quenched the parched earth and now the fields spread out before her, like velvet patchwork beneath the blue, sunny skies. There was content-ment here in this lovely place, she mused. It had an uncanny way of quieting the soul.

Her thoughts turned to her father-in-law, Ronnie Hunter, a man she had loved and respected. 'This was his little piece of heaven,' she sighed. 'We'll miss him, that's for sure.'

Blinking away the tears, she let her mind picture him in the field; she could see him clearly now – a short, round figure, strong and solid, though slightly stooped at the shoulders from his many years working the land. He would always walk his dog along the same track, stopping every now and then to pick a flower for his beloved wife, Sally. 'Aye, she'll miss you an' all.' Glancing towards the cottage, Louise gave a wistful little smile. 'Sally's tekken it badly. But we'll help her through,' she promised. 'God willing, we'll help each other.'

From inside the cottage, Sally looked out the window to see her daughter-in-law in deep thought. 'You're a good lass,' she whispered, her fond gaze taking in Louise's slim figure and strong stance, and the way her long brown hair lifted in the breeze. 'Eh, love, it's been a sorry few days. God only knows what I would have done without you.'

She ambled away from the kitchen window and eased herself into the rocking chair beside the empty firegrate. She looked up at the mantelpiece, and at the photograph of her late husband – a jolly-faced fellow with bright blue eyes. 'You silly old fool!' she chided him gently. 'What did you want to go and leave me for, eh?'

The tears trembled in her smile. 'We had some good years together, you and me,' she murmured. 'I wouldn't change one day of it.'

Then the smile slipped away, and the aging features stiffened. 'Except for that lazy, no-good son of ours!' She recalled the day she had brought her firstborn into the world; such joy and high hopes, only to be dashed the minute he could decide for himself.

Thinking of him now, she felt heavy-hearted. 'Jacob was born bad,' she whispered. ''Tweren't nobody's fault. He could have shouldered his responsibilities like a man. Instead he turned his back on all of us. A waster and a liar, that's what he is, and I rue the day I ever gave birth to him.'

Her voice shook with emotion. 'Even when he'd been told you were so poorly, he made no effort to come home, to say his goodbyes.' She paused, unable for a moment to go on.

Taking a deep breath, she smiled wryly at the photograph. 'Oh, he'll show up for the reading of the will all right, you can be sure o' *that*! Truth be told, I'm surprised he's not already sniffing about, looking to cause trouble, like always.' She shook her tiny fist in the air. 'Let him try, that's all. Just let him try!'

A moment or so later, her fast-beating heart had quietened. She closed her eyes and was beginning to nod off, when Louise's urgent voice woke her up. 'I've to get off down the bottom field,' she cried. 'Mabel's here – she says them two buggers are down in the valley, looking to kill each other, by all accounts!'

Her face drained white, Sally clambered out of the chair. 'I knew it!' she gasped. 'I *knew* he'd be back to cause trouble.'

'Don't you worry,' the younger woman consoled her. 'He'll not get the best of our Ben, you know that. An' he'll not get the better o' *me* neither.'

Ushering Mabel in, she explained, 'Mabel's agreed to sit with you till I get back.' To their visitor she said, 'Put the kettle on, won't you. Mek the pair of youse a brew, an' I'll be back afore you can say Jack Robinson.'

Leaving the women to settle themselves, Louise

lost no time in making for the bottom field. 'Sal was right,' she muttered. 'It was only a matter of time before *he* came back here, looking for trouble. With his dad out of the way, he'll have his mind set on taking over, or so he thinks.'

She quickened her steps. Jacob was well known to be a bad lot. When he wanted something badly enough, he usually got it one way or another. But not *this* time, she thought bitterly. If there was any justice, he'd not get his mucky hands on this farm . . .

She paused, catching her breath and thinking back over the years to a time when Jacob had had a yearning for her. 'An' if he thinks he can get his hands on me after all this time, he can damned well think again.' Ten years ago, she had rejected him in favour of Ben – a decision she had never regretted, and one for which Jacob had never forgiven her.

'Hurry, Louise!' Mike Ellis had seen her making her way down and ran to the hedge to urge her on. 'For God's sake hurry, afore they kill each other!' He had never been more thankful to see her.

In a matter of minutes she was beside him. 'There!' Pointing to the river, he told her, 'Jacob's got yer man under the water. You've got to stop 'em, lass, or there'll be murder an' no mistake.'

With the little milkman stumbling behind, she

went like the wind across the field towards the river; and on the way taking a precious minute to retrieve a shovel from the old barn.

With the shovel secure in her hands she rounded the bank and there they were, as Mike had said, intent on killing each other. Jacob had Ben by the throat and was about to duck him in the water again, but Ben was too quick for him and, grabbing him by the legs, he pulled him under. Once he had him at his mercy, it seemed he might keep him there until the last breath was gone. 'Stop it!' Louise screamed out. 'Have you both gone mad or what?'

Startled, Ben glanced up. As he did so, Jacob took his chance. Knocking Ben off his feet, he first smashed his fist into his face, before thrusting him beneath the water and holding him there; the more Ben struggled, the harder Jacob pressed him down. By the look on his face, he meant to finish his brother off, once and for all.

Horrified, Louise ran at him; swinging the shovel she landed it smack on the centre of his back. 'You little bitch!' With a roar he grabbed at the shovel and when she clung to it, he drew her towards him, the scowl on his face turning to a leer and leaving her in no doubt as to what he intended.

'Leave us alone, Jacob!' she demanded. 'Nobody wants you here!' Defiant as ever, she warned him,

'If you've come back for the farm, you'll be sadly mistaken. Did you really think your father would leave it to you, after what you did?'

'Whether he's left it to me or not doesn't matter. I'm the eldest. I'll get the farm, one way or another.' Close enough to reach out and take her, he grinned wickedly. 'Besides, it's not just the farm I've come back for. I want you with it.'

'Never.' Throwing the shovel at him, she ran to where Ben was lying on the ground, half in, half out of the water. Before she could help him, she felt herself being lifted up by the waist, Jacob's evil laughter assailing her ears. 'Leave him,' he murmured, drawing her to him. 'It's me you want. Why don't you admit it?'

Grabbing her by the hair, he yanked her head back, and was bending to steal a kiss when two things happened all at once. First, Louise kneed him hard in the groin, making him cry out in pain, and while he was bent double, cursing and threatening, Ben leaped on his back.

Though dazed and half-drowned, he had seen his wife in danger, and mustered every ounce of strength to protect her.

Beaten and humiliated, Jacob was soon flat on his back, moaning softly.

'Clear off out of it – go on, get out of my sight!' Standing over him, Ben watched his brother scramble up and make his escape, though as he went, Jacob turned to shout out defiantly, 'You've not seen the last of me yet!'

When his brother was far enough away, Ben held out his arms and Louise came running. 'Let's get you home,' she murmured. The deep gashes on his face and neck were evidence of the fierce struggle between these two. 'We need to clean you up,' she observed, 'but I don't want your mam to see you like this. She's got enough to contend with.'

The very same thought had crossed Ben's mind. Turning to Mike, who had seen the whole terrible scene unfold, he asked, 'D'you think I might tidy myself up at your wagon?'

Mike had been on the point of suggesting the same idea. 'As if yer need to ask!' he chided and, without delay, the three of them made their way there.

As they went across the field and on towards the lane, Mike leading the way, the couple talked of Jacob and what he might be planning. 'Did he mean what he said,' Louise asked anxiously, 'about us not having seen the last of him?'

'No, he's all mouth,' Ben reassured her.

'I hope you're right.' With her arm round his waist, Louise felt safe and secure.

Suddenly he paused and, taking her by the

shoulders, he asked intensely, 'What he said – about you wanting him . . .'

His wife had half-expected him to mention that. She shook her head. 'You know what he's like, how his pathetic brain works. Just because we had a brief fling before I met you, he thinks he has a claim on me.'

'You do know he's mad about you, don't you?'

'I really thought he'd have got over all that by now.'

'Judging by what he said, he still feels the same towards you.'

'I'm sorry, Ben, but I can't help how he feels.'

His quiet gaze penetrated her soul. 'And what do *you* feel?'

She met his look with honesty. 'Contempt – *that's* what I feel for him. I was just a kid when I met him, but it didn't take me long to see him for what he was.' Her brown eyes crinkled into a smile. 'It's *you* I love.' The kiss she gave him allayed his fears. 'Jacob means nothing to me, and never will. That was all done with a long, long time ago.'

Ben was satisfied. 'I'm sorry, but I had to be sure. I don't know what I'd do if I ever lost you.'

'And are you sure now?'

He nodded. 'My God, lass. I'd break every bone in his body if he ever touched you.'

'He won't.' She would die first.

With the atmosphere less tense, Ben even managed a grin. 'I never knew you had such a way with a shovel.'

Louise laughed. 'Neither did he, I shouldn't wonder.'

Mike, who had waited for them to catch up with him, heard the last two remarks and quipped, 'Remind me never to get on the wrong side o' you, young lady!'

<hr/>

MIKE KEPT ALL manner of things in his wagon; a car was impractical to use in the narrow cobbled byways and country lanes of Salmesbury. He dug out a clean old towel and a screw-top bottle of water he'd brought along to quench his thirst. Despite his trade, the little man had no liking for milk.

It took all of ten minutes to tidy Ben up and bathe the cuts and bruises. 'You still look like you've been in a fight.' After swilling the dirty water into the ditch, Louise rolled down her sleeves. 'Unfortunately, your mam knows the two of you have been fighting. I had to explain why Mabel was at the cottage you see.'

'Well, at least she'll be pleased to know he's gone. After what's happened today, he won't want to show his face round these parts again. There's nothing here for him. He knows that now.'

Before they left, Mike spoke up: 'You don't reckon on him being at his da's funeral tomorrow then?'

His pointed question caused Louise and Ben to look to each other for the answer; in the event, it was Ben who spoke. 'He's got nerve enough, Mike, I won't deny that. Mind you, as he said himself, he *is* the eldest son, and by rights he should be there. Whether we like it or not, it's his duty to stand beside our mam and lead us into church.' He shook his head in dismay. 'God help us!'

Louise intervened. 'That might be true enough, but Jacob and duty don't exactly go together, do they?'

Her husband agreed. 'There'll be nobody more surprised than me, if he shows up tomorrow. My brother came here with a prime purpose – to cause mischief. Well! He managed that an' no mistake. All in all, I don't suppose we'll ever clap eyes on him again.'

In a hurry to get back to Sally, they bade Mike Ellis cheerio. 'Tell yer mam I'll be there tomorrow, to pay my respects,' he assured them. 'Yer father was a good man, so he was.'

As they hurried away, shaken by events but ever content in each other's company, he watched them climb the brow of the hill. 'Yer wrong, me laddo.' Shaking his head despondently, he recalled Ben's parting words. 'I wouldn't be so sure about not clapping eyes on yon Jacob again.'

Shifting his gaze to where the young man had already gone from sight, he voiced his own, disturbing thoughts. 'Jacob Hunter is a law unto himself. He ain't done yet, not by a long chalk. If you ask me, he'll be gone long enough to lick his wounds, then he'll be back, bad as ever.'

Returning his sorry gaze to Ben, he commented, 'Oh aye, he'll be back all right. And when he is, you'd best keep a sharp look over yer shoulder, 'cause if I'm any judge of character, that brother o' yourn won't rest till he's got what he wants.'

Just before she disappeared from view, he caught sight of Louise; a slender, strong figure, she was bunching her long hair into a fist but it made no difference; the breeze took hold of the flailing tendrils and blew them about her pretty face.

The old milkman smiled. 'Yer a lovely lass, Louise Hunter, an' that husband o' yourn would walk over hot coals to please yer. But he'll need to be wary, I can see that. It's *you* Jacob wants . . . more than the farm or the money – more than anything else.'

He had seen the look on Hunter's face when he had Louise in his arms. And he had never seen a man more determined to take what he believed to be his.

27

Preparing his wagon for off, the old man continued to mumble, 'How can a good man father two sons so unalike? One out of his own mould, and the other akin to the divil?'

When the horse gave him an impatient nudge, he remarked with a twinkle, 'And how would *you* know, eh? You're nobbut a four-legged animal, with a mind for a bag of hay an' a sight of them pretty mares in Farmer Shaler's field!'

Going to the back of the cart, he threw the canvas over his precious wares. 'Don't want the sun to ruin me market-stall, do we, eh?'

Once his precious cargo was secured, he climbed on to the seat and took up the reins. 'Let's be off, me ol' beauty,' he urged with a tickle of the reins. 'We'd best mek tracks, afore Mabel Preston comes after us at the gallop.'

He laughed aloud. 'By! If ever there's a woman on the face of this earth who puts the wind up me, it's Mabel Preston an' 'er painted face. Like some bloody Indian on the warpath, she is!'

The sound of his laughter rang out above the clip clop of hooves as they went at a fair lick down the lane; as far and as fast as the old horse could carry him.

Chapter Two

SEATED ON THE doorstep of the farmhouse, Ben Hunter looked a sorry, lonely man. Finding a small degree of comfort in the stub of a cigarette, he held it between his fingers until it scorched the skin and made him cry out.

Unthinking, he flicked it into the shrubbery. Preferring to smoke a pipe in times of stress, he was never a lover of cigarettes but, having found the stub in his coat pocket and matches to go with it, he had lit it, taken two drags from it, and quickly lost interest.

After a bad night, twisting and turning in his bed and woken by dreams of his father, he felt worse for wear. Louise was the same, for if he couldn't sleep, then neither could she. And what with Sally walking the bedroom floor through the early hours, it seemed none of them would be going to church looking their best.

Not for the first time that morning, Ben's thoughts turned to his brother Jacob. Involuntarily, his fists clenched. 'Don't do it, Jacob!' he warned softly. 'Don't make this day harder than it is, especially for our mam. By! If you turn up and cause trouble at the church, you'll answer to *me*!' He had hoped Jacob would keep his distance after yesterday's humiliation; now though, he knew in his heart that his brother had it in him to turn up and break their mother's heart all over again.

Wearied by his own thoughts, and blinded by the bright sunlight, he closed his eyes. Rubbing his hands over his face, he leaned back against the door and shut out all thoughts. He needed to breathe. He needed to clear his mind, before the ordeal ahead.

But there was no peace. Try as he might to rid himself of bad thoughts, he remained a troubled man. Not just because of Jacob and his uncanny ability to wreck other people's lives, but because he knew how difficult this day would be for his mother. On the surface, Sally had been so brave, but Ben knew that underneath she was grieving for her beloved Ronnie, more than she would ever say.

'I know how you feel, lad. This is allus the worst day.'

Startled by the intrusion, he blinked against the bright sunlight. 'Oh, it's you, Auntie Edie.' A distant relative of Louise's, the woman had always been known hereabouts by the fond title 'Auntie Edie' whether or not she was related.

Here to offer support to them as needed it, she gave him a warm open smile. 'Now then, lad. What can I do to help?' A wise, kind soul, Edie was as reliable as day following night.

About fifty years old, though never admitting her age, Edie must have been pretty in her youth, for she had the softest green eyes and clear skin. That skin now hung loose round her jowls and her shoulder-length hair was fast beginning to grey. Scraped back from her face, it was tied up with a wide, scarlet ribbon – the 'ribbon' being a strip torn from her best, slowly diminishing tablecloth.

Ben returned her smile. 'Thanks, but you'd best see Louise.' He gestured to the front door behind him. 'You'll find them both in the kitchen.'

'Coping, are they, yer mam and her?'

'Well enough.' Much as he liked her, he wasn't in the mood for a long conversation. 'I'm out here keeping watch for the cars.'

'Right ye are then, lad.' Edie understood. 'I'd best go in – leave you to it, eh?' Wide and comfortable as an easy chair, she had no airs or graces, and possessed the wickedest sense of humour. But not today. Today was occasion for reflective thought.

Quickly on his feet, Ben moved aside to let her past, and as she did so, he gave her a welcoming hug.

'Our mam's getting herself in a bit of a state, if you know what I mean,' he confided. 'Have a word with her, will you?' he pleaded.

No sooner had Edie gone in, than the cars could be seen arriving in the distance. In what seemed no time at all, they were drawing up outside – two smart black Austin saloons. One carried his father, the other would carry them.

At the sobering sight, Ben's heart sank to his boots. This was the moment he had dreaded.

In that same, memorable moment, the young man had mixed feelings.

Relieved that his father's last journey would soon be over, he was also saddened by the fact that it was happening at all. These past years he had been especially close to his dad, having worked with him from early light to late evening. Without him, life would never be the same again, he knew that.

But he must put aside his own feelings for now, he chided himself. There was his mother to think of. And today, she was foremost in his mind.

Like a dutiful son, he tended the family one after the other. First his mother. 'Take your time, Mam.' Helping her to the car, he was shocked to see how small and frail she seemed. When she was got safely into the car, he helped his wife in, then Auntie Edie. Finally, after making sure the house was secure, he too climbed into the car.

As was the custom, he and his mother, as nearest kith and kin, sat in the front of the car, while Louise and Auntie Edie sat in the back.

It was a good fifteen-minute drive into Blackburn town; fifteen minutes that seemed like a lifetime. Along the way, there was talk of Ronnie and how so many of his mates had called at the house to pay their respects. Auntie Edie asked if there was anything else that needed doing back at the house. 'There's bound to be a lot o' folk who'll return for the tea.'

Louise reassured her. 'It's all done, love. Me an' Sal kept ourselves busy all morning getting it ready. But thank you all the same.' Grateful for the offer, she squeezed her hand.

Throughout the journey, Sal and Ben spoke not a word. Instead they sat hand-in-hand, steeped in quiet thoughts, each concerned for the other.

'I allus reckon this is the worst part,' Auntie Edie whispered to Louise. 'After today, it'll get a bit easier. It's final, y'see, once he's tekken into the Lord's care.'

Her well-meaning words brought tears to the younger woman's eyes. 'I'm sure you're right,' she replied in a whisper, hoping Ben and his mam hadn't heard.

But they had heard – and somehow felt better for it.

———◆◇◆———

ON ARRIVING AT St Peter's Church, Sal gasped at the large gathering waiting outside. 'By!' The sight of it filled her heart. 'I knew he were well-liked, but I'd no idea so many folks would turn out.'

Louise's relatives stepped out ready to line up behind the procession. First came her kindly parents, Patsy Holsden, a little woman with a homely face, and Steve, small and wick, wearing his best flat cap and stiff collar. Then came her younger sister, Susan. An attractive young woman with a good figure, baby-blue eyes and wonderfully thick, shoulder-length auburn hair, in her new, short-skirted brown suit and navy court shoes, she made a stunning sight.

Unfortunately, in her early twenties, Susan was irresponsible, and something of a heartache to her parents. She was not considered to be bad however, just wayward and rebellious. As her dad was fond of saying, 'She's never bloody well grown up, that's the trouble!'

Behind the Holsdens came farmers Ronnie had known, several neighbours, and other folks that Sal didn't even know, but who had come to pay their respects all the same.

On seeing Ben's bruised face, they were assured

of the trouble between him and Jacob. There had already been talk of it down at the pub last evening; Mike Ellis had oiled his tongue with too much booze and it got loose enough to tell the tale. 'Knocking hell out of each other, they were.' He related the shameful incident – 'And their daddy not yet put to his rest.' Then he wept into his beer and they had to carry him home.

Ignoring their obvious embarrassment, Ben greeted them all with a nod, before linking his arm with his mother's. 'All right, are you, Mam?'

Sally didn't hear him. Her attention was taken by someone approaching from the other side of the churchyard. Following her gaze, Ben was not altogether surprised to see Jacob striding towards them; in dark suit and trilby, he looked almost unrecognisable.

'Don't worry, Mam,' Ben murmured. 'He knows better than to cause trouble here.'

The entire gathering watched as Jacob made straight for his mother. 'I'll take you in, Mam.' Crooking his elbow he waited for her to accompany him.

There was a long, poignant moment when Sally looked him in the eye, her face set like stone as she locked her gaze with his. All around them, the silence thickened.

Unnerved by the hardness of her stare, Jacob

asked again. 'Mam, it's my place to lead you in. You need me!'

Sally smiled at his words. 'Your father needed you,' she reminded him. 'Where were you then, lad?'

When he seemed lost for words, she turned to her younger son. 'I'm ready,' she said, and together they walked into the church. Behind them came the family and friends and all those who had attended in a spirit of affection.

When they were all gone inside, only Jacob remained – a solitary figure, seething with rage. The rage soon dissipated and in its place came defiance. He had not gone to all that effort only to be shut out.

Making a noisy entrance so they would all know he was not yet defeated, he entered the church. Walking boldly to the front, he then squeezed himself between his mother and his brother.

To his annoyance, neither of them acknowledged him.

When, a short time later, the service was over, he led the way to the churchyard and took his place at the head of the family. But, for all the notice anyone took of him, he could have been a stranger; even when he went about shaking hands and thanking everyone for attending, they merely nodded and moved away as quickly as possible. They all knew his badness. And because of it, not one of them had an ounce of respect for him.

UNDAUNTED, HE FOLLOWED the mourners back in his own car to the farmhouse. 'It seems you've got no shame at all!' Louise saw him arrive and went to intercept him. 'Can't you see nobody wants you here?'

He smiled, a wicked, blatant smile. 'I can't recall being told to leave.'

'Very well – *I'm* telling you to leave. Go away and leave us be, Jacob. Like I said, nobody wants you here.'

'Not even you?' he said in a low, intimate voice.

'Especially not me.'

'I don't believe that, Louise. I know you still want me, only you're afraid to say it.'

'You're mad.' Realising she could never reason with him, Louise swung away, sighing, 'I'm not arguing with you, Jacob. You're not worth it.'

'*Hey!*' Reaching out, he caught her by the arm. 'I'm not done with you yet.' Before she could stop him, he slid one arm round her waist and the other over her mouth and face. Hustling her into the shrubbery, he fought her to the ground. Like a crazed animal, he tore at her underclothes. He meant to claim her; whether she wanted it or not.

'Come away with me, Lou,' he pleaded, his mouth against hers, his hands all over her. 'I'll forget the farm . . . *he* can have it. It's you I want. We'll have a good enough life, you and me. I'll work hard, you'll see.'

His words tumbled one over the other, and all the time she tried to cry out, but he was too quick for her, stifling her cries with the flat of his hand, while she twisted and fought to throw him off.

Later, when she thought about it, Louise could not imagine where she got the strength to free herself from him. It might have been the awful prospect of him taking her like that, or maybe she was afraid of what would happen if Ben suddenly came round the corner and saw what his brother was up to. Murder would have been done. Or it might have been the awful realisation that she had not yet been missed from the gathering, so help would not arrive in time.

One thing was certain: someone 'up there' was looking after her because, before he could defile her altogether, she managed to get the better of him. Reaching out her arm, she fumbled about on the ground, her long sturdy fingers searching, until suddenly they were curling about the small, heavy stone.

Clutching the stone tightly in her fist, she raised her arm and brought it down on his head as hard as she could, rolling away as he cried out in pain. 'Jesus!' Though he wasn't badly hurt, Jacob was shocked enough to release his hold on her. 'Bitch!'

His face contorted with rage, he stared up at her. 'Filthy bitch!'

Groaning, he put his hands to his head and seeing the blood trickle through his fingers, he gave an agonised cry. 'You'll pay for this, mark my words!'

As she ran, his voice followed her. 'You got away this time, Lou.' Then his laughter, low and devilish. '*But we're not finished yet. You think on that.*'

FROM A DISTANCE Louise heard her husband's voice calling. 'Sweetheart, where are you?'

She hurriedly tidied her clothes and smoothed her hair. 'I'm here,' she called back, trying to sound normal and unflustered. Doubling back onto the path, she glanced out of the corner of her eye, to see Jacob making a hasty retreat.

'I've just been outside for a breath of air,' she told Ben, and there was no reason for him to doubt her word.

Taking her into his arms, he swung her round. 'I began to think you'd run off,' he teased.

Smiling, she retorted lightheartedly, 'Now how could I do that when there's washing-up to be done?'

Teasing subsided as Ben answered in a more serious tone. 'To tell you the truth, sweetheart, I'll not be sorry when this day's over.'

'I know,' she agreed sympathetically. 'Maybe Auntie Edie's right. Maybe this really is the worst day of all.'

As they walked arms linked into the farmhouse, Louise peered back towards the shrubbery. There was no sign of Jacob. Good riddance, she thought. Remembering his frustrated intent, she shivered.

'You're not cold, are you, lass?' Ben had felt the shudder right through his body.

'A little,' she murmured, and clung to him all the more.

<hr />

AFTER MAKING HER apologies, Louise set about helping Auntie Edie. First there were the empty cups and plates to clear, and after that a fresh supply of tea to make for the women and stronger liquids for the men; and sandwiches piled so high they would keep them all going for a week.

Patsy Holsden noticed her daughter's pale face and was concerned. 'Are you all right, lass?'

Louise's mind went straight to the shrubbery and what had happened out there. 'What d'you mean, Mam?' Frantic that she might have left her blouse hanging out, or a wisp of hair that told a tale, she instinctively ran her hands over herself.

Patsy shook her head. 'I don't rightly know, but

you seem a bit flustered.' Louise was her favourite daughter though she would never admit it to anyone, least of all to Susan.

Louise gave an inward sigh of gratitude. 'Oh, is that all?'

'You don't take enough care of yourself,' her mother chided. 'You always did have a tendency to run yourself ragged.'

Susan's voice cut them both short. 'It's a good job she hasn't got kids, that's all I can say.' Sipping a glass of elderberry wine, she was decidedly unsteady on her feet.

Louise couldn't let the comment go unchallenged. 'What's that supposed to mean?' she demanded, her hackles rising.

'Well, if you can't even organise a funeral tea without looking like summat the cat dragged in, God only knows what state you'd be in with a couple o' kids round yer arse.'

Before Louise could retaliate, Edie came between them. Taking the half-filled glass from Susan's hand, she wagged a finger. 'I think you've had more than enough, my girl! The strong drink is for the men. There's a pot of fresh-brewed tea on the table over there, if you're thirsty.' With that she nodded to one and all, before making her way back to the kitchen.

'Old cow!' The young woman didn't take kindly to being disciplined.

'I'd best go and mingle for a while,' Louise suggested. 'I'll see you later, Mam.'

In sullen mood, Susan hadn't finished yet. 'Who the devil does that Edie think she is, taking my drink like that? I'm twenty-five years of age. I can drink whatever I fancy.' She swayed as she spoke, her face flushed.

'Now just you stop that, young lady! Remember where you are.' Patsy took her aside. 'Have you no respect?'

'Hmh! It's a pity folks don't have more respect for *me*, snatching my drink away before I'd even finished it.'

She made to leave but her mother wasn't done with her yet. 'And what was the idea of that nasty remark to our Louise?' she hissed. 'You know damn well how desperate she is to start a family. Nothing would give her greater pleasure than having "children round 'er arse", as you so crudely put it.'

'Go on, that's right.' All the old bitterness rose to the surface. 'Take her side. You always do!'

'That's nonsense and you know it, Susan. I don't love either one of you more than the other. You're both my daughters and you're treated the same – you always have been. The difference between you is that Louise minds her own business, while you look for every which way to drag her down. If you're jealous because she's got herself a good man and a stable life

42

– well, there's nothing whatsoever to stop you doing the very same, is there?'

'We want different things, me and her. I've no intention of being shackled to one man . . . working on a farm and running round at everybody's beck and call. She can have it, for what it's worth.'

'There's nothing wrong with wanting something different. You're entitled to live your life as you see fit. But you are *not* entitled to blame Louise, or me, or anyone else for that matter, for what you want, or don't want.'

Realising the truth of what her mam was saying, Susan reluctantly apologised. 'It's just that she always seems to land on her feet, Mam, while I can't ever get anything right.'

Patsy knew her daughter's failings, and she sympathised. 'Aw, lass, happen you're wanting too much, that's why.' Gesturing to where Louise was handing out sandwiches, she appealed to the girl's innate decency. 'She's a good lass . . . you both are. And what's she got when all's said and done, eh? Like you said just now, she's out on the fields most of the time; she wants children and it never seems to happen for her. When Sally has her bad days, it's Louise who's called on to care for her. But she does it all with a good heart. What's more, if we ever need her, she soon comes running. Look at last winter when you were down with the flu. Never a day went by when she didn't come to see how you were.'

'That's what I'm saying – she's at everybody's beck and call. It's not what *I* want out of life.'

Patsy began to see what lay beneath Susan's bitterness. 'What is it, love? Why do you torment her every time the two of you get together?'

'I don't know. Maybe it's because she seems to be so happy.'

'Are you saying you want her to be miserable?'

'No.'

'It's not because of Ben, is it?'

Susan was taken aback. 'Why should it be?'

'Well, to be honest, there was a time when I thought you and him . . .'

'Well, you thought wrong!' Her mother's observation had put her on the defensive. 'Ben always had eyes for Louise, you know that. And anyway, I've never been serious about any man in my life. They're not worth it!'

'I see.' Susan had confirmed her mother's suspicions. Suddenly it all seemed to fit.

When Louise and Susan were both footloose and fancy-free, they were friendly with the Hunter boys, Jacob and Ben. For a time it seemed as if Louise and Jacob might get together, but then Ben captured her heart and they fell head over heels in love.

Susan and Jacob, it seemed, had no time for each

other. The friendship broke up and soon after that, Louise and Ben were wed. It was then that Susan became hostile towards her sister.

Patsy had to know. 'Be honest with me, love,' she said. 'You're not still hankering after Ben, are you?'

Feigning horror, Susan laughed in her face. 'Don't be stupid, Mam. I've got ambitions. I'm after somebody who can show me a good time. What would I want with a *farmer*?'

Glancing up, she saw Ben at the far end of the room. Catching her eye, he gave a friendly wink. 'No, Mother, he's nothing to me.' Though her heart leaped in her breast at his warm, innocent wink.

'I hope you're telling me the truth.' Patsy was well aware of her daughter's ability to lie when it suited her.

'Louise is more than welcome to him!' That said, Susan smiled sweetly and flounced off towards the drinks table, and a large glass of sherry.

FOR THE NEXT half hour, Louise was kept busy, chatting and commiserating, and taking round refreshments. 'You look worn out, love.' It had not missed Ben's notice that his wife was beginning to flag. 'Look, you go and sit down. I'll see to that.'

Reaching out to take the tray from her, his arms

fell to his side when he followed her horrified gaze. Sensing someone enter the room, Louise had looked up and was shocked to see Jacob there.

Fists clenched by his side, Ben stood quite still as Jacob made his way across the room towards them. This time, Ben was ready for him. 'I wondered how long it would be afore *you* showed up!'

Bold as ever, Jacob smiled from one to the other. 'Sorry I'm late,' he apologised, 'only I had a bit of an accident.' He paused, just long enough for Louise to worry. 'The damned car broke down and I got a bit messed up, y'see. I had to go back to the hotel and change.' In green corduroy trousers and brown tweed jacket he looked jarringly out of place among the sombre suits and dark hats.

Clasping the tray so hard her knuckles bled white, Louise excused herself. 'I have things to do,' she told them. The look she gave Jacob was darkly hostile. For a moment it actually silenced him.

Ben issued a quiet warning. 'These people are friends of Dad's,' he pointed out. 'If you mean to stay, you'd best show some respect.'

'So long as it's not to *you*.'

Ben gave a wry smile. 'A bit late for that, wouldn't you say?'

'If you're asking me not to sully Dad's name, I think I know how to conduct myself when the occasion demands.'

'You don't say.' Discreetly pushing Jacob back towards the wall, he hissed, 'You've already upset our mam once today. Try it on again and you'll be through that door on the end of my boot.'

'Oh, you reckon, d'you?' Prodding Ben in the belly, Jacob taunted, 'I think you must have forgot who were coming off worse out there at the river. As I recall, I were on top and you were fighting for your life. If that gutsy wife o' yourn hadn't turned up, who knows *what* might have happened.'

Ben's face drained of colour. 'You'll not get the better of me a second time. Think on. You upset our mam, or show this family up once more, and you'll be sorry, Jacob. That's a promise.'

Knowing when he had pushed far enough, Jacob grinned. 'What makes you think I'm here to cause mischief?'

'Because it's second nature to you.'

'I'm here for the same reason you are . . . to comfort our mam, and welcome Dad's friends.' Throwing out his arms he gave a mock gesture of frustration. 'I mean, where else would I be on a day like this?'

Wanting to shake him, Ben instead took quiet stock of this man who was his brother. He saw nothing that might endear Jacob to him. Instead he saw a grasping, scheming devil who would stop at nothing to get what he wanted.

'Well?' Jacob taunted. 'You must see I'm as concerned as you about our mam.'

Ben gave no answer. A searching look, a shake of the head, then he simply walked away. It was obvious that Jacob was trying to goad him, but this time he would not be such easy prey.

Defiantly, Jacob walked from group to group, smiling and shaking hands, though no one smiled back. Instead they huddled and whispered, and like Ben, Louise felt ashamed.

Sally had seen her eldest son parading about, and wondered how she could have given birth to such a devious, scheming creature.

'I've never known two lads be so different.' Old Jack Donaldson was a tenant on the neighbouring farm. A wizened fellow with flat cap and highly polished boots, he was a character known and liked hereabouts. 'You'd never think they were brothers.'

From her chair by the window, Sally looked sadly up at him. 'They were always different,' she confirmed, 'even when they were lads at school. When the School Inspector knocked on my door, I allus knew which o' the lads he were complaining about. Jacob were the one who'd land himself in trouble, and Ben were the one who'd get him out.'

Her tired gaze shifted to the photo of her husband on the mantelpiece. 'He'd tell you if he were here now,' she said, the tears smarting in her eyes.

'Oh, aye! Many were the time Ben came home with a black eye . . . all got through fighting our Jacob's battles for him.'

Now, when she saw him heading towards her, she was aware of everyone's eyes on her. With that in mind, she raised her face and let him kiss her on the cheek. 'How are you, Mam?' he asked, bending to stroke her face with the tips of his fingers.

When, repulsed by his touch she leaned back in the chair, he smiled and said, 'I expect you're tired.' Deliberately turning his back on her, he began a conversation with old Jack who, like everyone else in that tiny parlour, felt decidedly uncomfortable in Jacob's presence.

Unaware of the incident, Louise made her way into the kitchen, where Auntie Edie had a new-poured cup of tea waiting for her. 'I saw yer coming,' she explained, when the girl remarked how she must have read her mind.

Having been ensconced in the kitchen this past half hour, Edie was glad of the company. 'Sit yerself down, lass. I reckon you deserve a few minutes' rest.'

Doing as she was bid, Louise gulped down the scalding tea, afterwards leaning back in the chair with a groan of pleasure. 'Ooh! Thanks, Auntie Edie. That's just what I needed.' Kicking off her shoes she rubbed the soles of her feet.

'Sore are they, lass?'

Even the touch of her own hands on her aching feet was agony. 'Honest to God, it feels like I've walked ten miles there and back.'

After pouring another cup for Louise, Edie sipped at her own tea, her gaze drawn to the parlour and two departing figures. 'I see they've started leaving.'

The young woman nodded. 'I've done my thanking. Ben's outside now, seeing them all off.'

'Where's his mam?'

'By his side.'

'And that bugger, Jacob?'

'Oh, he'll not be far away, you can be sure of that.' Standing up, she slipped her shoes back on again. 'I'd best go.'

'Louise?'

'Yes?'

'Is everything all right?'

'In what way?'

Edie lowered her voice. 'When you came in earlier, I thought you looked . . . I don't know . . . upset, like.'

'Oh, I'd been for a walk – I needed to think. You know what it's like, Auntie Edie. Sometimes you need to be on your own.'

'And *were* you on your own?'

Edie must have seen her, Louise realised, and being the shrewd woman she was, must have put two and two together and guessed at the incident with Jacob. 'You know, don't you?'

Edie nodded. 'Yes. You looked most upset and dishevelled. If Ben hadn't been so taken up with other events, he'd have noticed it too.'

Louise's voice shook. 'You won't say anything, will you? It'll only cause trouble.'

Edie smiled, a quiet, reassuring smile. ''Course I'll not say owt, lass. What d'yer tek me for?'

'It was my own fault really.'

Lowering her voice to a whisper, Edie offered kindly, 'What happened, lass? Did yer ask him to keep away and he took it as an invitation to force himself on yer? Is that the way of it?'

At the memory, the young woman's hackles rose. 'He got no change out of me, I can tell you that!' She didn't want Edie thinking he'd had his way with her.

The older woman gave a low chuckle. 'Eeh, lass, yer don't have to tell me. I've known all these years it's allus been Ben for you. Jacob's one o' them fellas as thinks every woman's his for the taking.' Her expression hardened. 'Yer did right to put him in his place.'

'Hmh! I just hope it's enough to keep him at arm's length.'

'If it isn't, lass, you'll have to let Ben loose on him. Sometimes a man's fury is the only language a bad bugger like Jacob Hunter can understand.' Taking a deep breath, she advised, 'You've done all you can for now. If he comes back at yer, then you've to let Ben deal with it. You do understand that, don't yer?'

Louise nodded. 'I don't want any more trouble.'

'Don't you worry, lass.' Pointing to the parlour, Edie lightened her mood. 'Off with yer, then! You'd best show yer face out there. Your husband's probably looking for yer.'

As Louise made her way to the front door where folks were already gathering, Edie pushed back and forth in the old rocking chair. 'By! That Jacob's got a lot to answer for,' she muttered. 'His day'll come. What goes around comes around, and afore so very long, it'll be *his* turn to pay.'

<hr />

To LOUISE'S DISMAY, Jacob had made a beeline for her sister, Susan.

While everyone else was giving their goodbyes and solemn good wishes, Susan and Jacob were standing by the corner of the house, giggling like two schoolkids.

Suddenly, Jacob kissed Susan hard and long on the mouth. They exchanged words and he strode away, turning once to see the look of disgust on Louise's face. It made him smile. 'I told you I wasn't finished with you,' he muttered. 'And I meant it!'

When all the visitors were gone, Louise waylaid her sister. 'For God's sake, Susan! What do you think you're playing at?'

Having drunk too much elderberry wine followed by too much sherry, Susan sniggered. 'What's up with you?' she asked tipsily.

'You and Jacob. I saw you, kissing and cuddling, in full view of everybody!'

'So?'

'Do I have to spell it out? Jacob isn't interested in you, and you know it. You're not interested in him either. So why make a spectacle of yourself in front of all those people?'

'Mind your own business!'

'It may not be my business, but I reckon you owe Sally an apology.'

'I'm not apologising to nobody.'

Louise was shocked. 'I hope that's the drink talking.' Grabbing her sister by the shoulders, she shook her hard. 'That poor woman buried her husband today. The last thing she wanted was you and that conniving son of hers making fools of yourselves right here, in full view of everybody!'

Susan laughed. 'You can't fool me. You're not angry because of Sally or Mr Hunter, nor them as saw us. It's got nowt to do with them. It's to do with *you*!'

'What are you talking about?'

'Jacob wants nothing to do with you any more, he told me that. But you still fancy him, don't you, eh? But you're tied to his brother, and you can't do a thing about it. You're trapped, good and proper! That's why you're so angry with me . . . 'cause you want Jacob, and you can't have him.'

'You're mad!' How could she even *think* such a thing?

'Oh, mad, am I? So what were you doing in the shrubbery, you and Jacob? He told me how you followed him out there, making big eyes at him, saying how you'd made a mistake in marrying Ben.'

Louise could hardly believe her ears. 'He told you that?'

'Huh! You want him but he doesn't want you. Don't worry, I can keep my mouth shut when I want. But don't you ever lecture *me* on how to behave!'

Swaying dangerously from side to side, she made her way back to the waiting car and clambered inside. As the car drew away, she leaned out. 'Behave yourself, sis,' she called out. 'Don't do anything I wouldn't do.'

DEJECTED, LOUISE RETURNED to the farmhouse. 'All right are you, sweetheart?' Ben slid his arms round her waist, his thoughtful brown eyes looking down into hers.

'She's done too much.' Sally returned from the kitchen where she'd been thanking Edie. 'I'm grateful to you, lass,' she told Louise. 'Sit you down and we'll think on what to do next.'

Just as they all sat round the table, Edie came in with a tray, piled high with cakes and sandwiches. 'No use wasting 'em,' she declared, and set the tray down on the table.

Louise's mind was still on Susan's misguided accusations, when her thoughts were interrupted by Sally. 'You'll be there, won't you, lass? I'd like you to be there.'

Mentally shaking herself, Louise asked, 'Sorry, Sal, I was miles away.'

'The reading of the will. I'd like you to be there.'

'It won't be for a while yet, Mam,' Ben assured her. 'There's still a few papers to take over to Mr Bryce.' Pointing to a drawer in the dresser he explained, 'They're all ready. With a bit of luck I'll get them to him first thing in the morning.'

Sally sighed. 'Thanks for taking care of all that. Mr Bryce will do us proud. He's a good solicitor. Your dad allus used him.' Her voice broke. 'I hope to God Jacob stays away.'

'You know he won't, Mam, so you might as well resign yourself to the fact.'

Sally lapsed into deep thought. 'It might be as well,' she murmured. 'I've a feeling we're all in for something of a surprise.'

Nobody knew what she meant by that.

Not even Sally herself.

Chapter Three

KEEPING WELL HIDDEN, Jacob watched from nearby.

Waiting until the family had driven away in the car, he made sure there was no one to see him, as he went stealthily towards the farmhouse.

Just as he had suspected, the key was left in its usual place, underneath the loose step by the back door. 'Hah!' he laughed softly. 'Habits die hard, don't they, old fella?'

Once inside the cottage, he went straight to his parents' bedroom. Standing at the door he scratched his chin and stared around the small, plain room, with its double bed and dresser and large wardrobe set against the back wall. He looked at each item of furniture in turn, his face a study in concentration. 'Now then, old man, where would you hide it?'

He tried to think like his father. 'If you *had*

borrowed money to set me up, you'd have been so ashamed, you'd hardly want all and sundry to clap eyes on how much it was costing you. And, according to what Ben said, you didn't want our mam to know. "Didn't want her worryin'" . . . that's what he said.'

Resentment filled his dark heart. How like his father that was. Taking it all on his own shoulders, yet confiding in no one but his younger son. Seeing the photograph of his father he seized on it, his eyes narrowing as he studied the honest, familiar face. 'I never asked you to borrow money!' he hissed. 'It was *your* decision, not mine, and I won't take no blame for it. D'you hear, old man?' His voice rose to a crescendo. 'I WON'T TAKE NO BLAME!'

Realising he was letting his emotions run away with him, he lowered his voice. 'See? You're getting me all worked up, just like you always used to. Me an' you, we never saw eye to eye. My God! I'd rather die than be like you.'

Replacing the photograph exactly as it had been, he studied it a while longer, his lip curling with contempt. 'I expect you're wondering what I'm doing here? Well, I'll tell you, Father dear, I've come for what's mine. I've a bad feeling that when that will o' yours is read today, you'll 'ave taken care of everybody else but me.'

Looking away, he glanced furtively round the

room. 'I'll need to look after meself, I can see that now.' He went to the window and stared out. Satisfied that all was quiet, he returned his condemning gaze to his father's photograph. 'I'm here to find out what you borrowed, and how you managed to pay it back. As our Ben said, farming never made a man rich.'

His laughter echoed through the room. 'Don't tell me you lied to your precious Ben an' all. Told him you'd paid it back when happen you hadn't paid it up at all! I'm sure o' one thing. He doesn't know where the documents are, any more than I do.' A discouraging thought struck him. 'Unless o' course it's been told in the will?'

Anxious now, he rubbed his hands together. 'I must find them documents afore he does.'

He glanced furtively about. 'It seems nobody, not even Ben, knew who you borrowed the money from, nor how much, nor even whether it were all settled. You were such a secretive old bugger, I'd be surprised if *anybody* knew what you were up to – with the exception of the fella you borrowed it from.' That stirred another thought. 'An' who might that have been, eh? Not the bank, I'm sure of it.'

Delighted with the plan already formulating in his mind, he paced from one end of the room to the other, his brain working feverishly. 'So! Where would you have kept all the necessary paperwork . . .

receipts and such?' He began to doubt whether his father would have risked hiding such information in his bedroom, for fear of his beloved wife coming across it. 'Not in here, no. Not with our mam in every nook and cranny.'

Going downstairs, he stared round the scullery at the two small cupboards and rows of shelves. 'Hmh. You couldn't hide a farthing in here, never mind a wad o' papers.'

In the parlour, he scoured every drawer and cupboard, just to be sure; he even looked up the chimney and under the rugs for loose floorboards. 'Nothing!' But then, deep down, he had not really expected to find them in the house at all.

Just as he had done upstairs, he made sure that everything was left exactly as he had found it. 'We can't have them knowing I was ever here,' he muttered.

Then, following a sudden instinct, he went outside to the little wooden shed where his father had spent many a quiet, contented hour. 'Are they in here, you cunning old rascal?' Flinging open the door, Jacob reeled at the smell of must and damp. It was obvious no one had been in here since the old fella had taken sick and died.

'They're here somewhere, I know they are.' Chuckling like a lunatic, he rummaged through his father's belongings: the box of old newspapers in the corner; the rafters lined with tools. Finally, prising up the floorboards, he felt along every rim and hidey-hole but came up with nothing.

'Damn and blast it!' Sweating from his frantic efforts, he sat back on his heels. 'Think, man,' he urged himself. 'Think like yer father!'

And when he had thought, he realised he might well have missed something – something so obvious it could have smacked him in the face and he wouldn't even have noticed. 'Of course!'

Returning to the box of old newspapers, he took them out carefully, one by one, whereas before he had flung them out in handfuls.

When there was only one newspaper left, he tugged at it, careful not to tear it, but couldn't get it to shift. Only then did light dawn. 'Ah! This one was never meant to be taken out and used, was it, eh?'

Prising it from the four corner nails that held it down, he opened it out and there, cunningly wrapped inside, was a long brown envelope.

For a moment he simply stared at it, his heart beating fifteen to the dozen. 'By! You cunning old swine! I couldn't see the forest for the trees, could I, and that's exactly what you hoped. You knew how everybody put the old newspapers *into* the box, but only you ever took them out.'

Rising up through his loathing of that quiet man, sneaked the smallest measure of admiration. *Though not enough to put the envelope back where he had found it.*

With trembling fingers he opened it. Sliding the contents onto the floor, he perused the papers one after the other. As he had suspected, the contract of loan was not with the bank, but with a business acquaintance of his father's . . . a man by the name of Alan Martin. Though they didn't always agree, he and Ronnie Hunter had known each other for many years.

They had gone to school together and afterwards, while Ronnie followed his father into farming, Alan started a business, supplying farmers and hauliers with whatever they needed.

Of the two, it was Alan who made the fortune, though he never found the same level of contentment as Ronnie, whose love of the land and deep affection for his family gave him all the peace of mind he needed.

That was, until Jacob grew to be a burden on him, and even then he went out of his way to help his eldest son, because however headstrong the boy had become, his dad still loved him. Sadly, it was not a love that was returned.

Surprised at the name on the contract, Jacob began to put two and two together. 'By! The canny old sod! Alan Martin was the one who supplied most of my contracts . . . all part of the conditions, eh?

"I'll lend you the money if your son delivers to my customers".'

It was beginning to make sense. The loan was for the tidy sum of two thousand pounds, payable at monthly instalments of sixty pounds. 'Bloody hell!' Jacob whistled. 'That were a bit steep, weren't it? What with everything else, the old sod must have found it crippling.'

It took only a moment of contemplation before he was grinning craftily again. 'What do *I* care?' he said to the walls of the shed. 'Serves the old bugger right. Besides, if he did manage to pay it all back as Ben claims, the farm is bound to come to me. Dad may not have agreed with the way I did things, but he would never have cut his eldest son out of the picture altogether. He were too bloody decent for that.'

He chuckled. 'Not like me, eh? Once I get my hands on this place, I'll have 'em out on their ear so fast, their feet won't touch the ground.' With one exception, of course. 'But not my Louise. She'll be with me. I'll look after her an' no mistake.'

The thought cheered him up no end.

Eagerly, he rummaged through the receipts. 'By! Every one signed and filed away, and never a month missed.' Throwing them aside as they passed through his impatient hands, he was thrilled by the discovery that his father had dutifully repaid it all, right up to the very last payment.

The latter was dated 16 May, 1952. 'So, you managed to finish it only a few weeks back, then, you poor old bastard.' Even to a hard-hearted villain like Jacob, it seemed like a cruel jest. 'Finish the loan and drop dead. That weren't very clever, were it?' He shrugged his shoulders. 'Still that's the way it goes. Here one day, gone the next. That's why I mean to enjoy every bloody minute!'

Gathering the receipts, he folded them back into the envelope and tucked it safely into his pocket. That done, he replaced the old newspapers in the box. 'Mustn't mess up your precious little shed, must we, eh?'

At the door, he glanced around for the last time. 'It's a pity it's all got to go.'

Slamming shut the door, he strode at a fast pace to his car, brushing off the dust and tidying himself as he went. 'I can't turn up to the reading of the will looking like summat the cat dragged in, can I?'

Pleased with his morning's work, he climbed into the small black saloon; in a matter of minutes he was off down the lane at a fair lick. 'I'm going to be late,' he muttered. 'Still, it won't really matter if they start without me, so long as I'm there at the finish.'

Confident it would all go his way, he patted his top pocket. 'I needed to know the old man had paid every penny he owed. I mean, I wouldn't want it to end up being *my* debt, now would I?' But having found the receipts signed, dated and complete, there seemed little likelihood of that.

He glanced at his watch. 'There you are, Jacob, my boy. By the time the solicitor's gone through the rigmarole at the beginning, you'll find you've missed nothing at all.' And so full of himself was he, that he whistled all the way into town.

———※◦◈◦※———

IN AINSWORTH STREET, the family had already arrived.

Greeting them with a restrained smile to fit the occasion, Mr Bryce ushered them into their respective seats. 'You might like to sit here, Mrs Hunter.' Addressing Sally rather more formally than he otherwise might have done, he gestured for her to sit in the low, more comfortable armchair.

'Aye.' Sally nodded appreciatively. 'I reckon I would an' all.' On entering this tiny, fusty room with its faded pictures hanging on the wall and the well-worn rugs beneath their feet, Sally had taken wary note of the hard, high-backed chairs placed in a ring about the desk. 'I expect we'll be sitting for some long time, won't we?'

Pushing the chair under her as she sat, he gave her a reassuring smile, but not one that would deviate from the seriousness of the situation. 'It shouldn't take that long. Your husband was a very meticulous man, my dear lady. I've gone through his papers and they're all in tip-top order.' He glanced at the mound of papers pushed to one side on his large, leather-topped desk. 'In fact, he makes me feel ashamed.'

Gesturing at the papers scattered across his desk and every other available surface, he sighed wearily. 'I'm afraid the paperwork seems to fall about me until I can't see head above shoulders. Still! All in good time, eh?' His bright eyes embraced one after the other. 'Right. Let's make a start then.'

Losing no time, he rounded his desk, drew the pile of papers before him and, glancing up to see they were all seated, satisfied himself that the correct number of people were present. 'Let me see now . . . we should have Mrs Sally Hunter, her sons, Benjamin and Jacob, and her daughter-in-law, Mrs Louise Hunter.' He paused. 'There seems to be someone missing.'

Suddenly there came a tap on the door. 'Yes?'

The door opened to admit Mr Bryce's secretary and Jacob Hunter. 'Ah!' Assured that everyone was now present the solicitor quickly ushered Jacob into a chair.

It did not escape his attention that every other person in the room ignored this young man's presence. And to tell the truth, he could not blame them.

Jacob Hunter had been his father's greatest disappointment. With his devil-may-care attitude and lack of respect for anything and everyone, Jacob had been in and out of trouble since the age of fifteen, with no remorse or regret for the pain and humiliation he had caused his good parents over the years.

Impatient now to have it over and done with, Mr Bryce settled himself comfortably, opened the first page of the will, and in sombre voice, addressed them. 'If you feel the need for clarification of any points raised here, perhaps it might be best to leave it until after the reading?'

Duly noting the affirmative nods, he had one more observation to make before he began the business of reading the will. 'As far as we know, there is no part of the land or building under mortgage.' He instinctively looked to Ben. 'I understand there was a loan but that it was repaid?'

Ben reaffirmed what he had previously discussed with his father's solicitor. 'The loan was repaid to the last penny. My father told me that himself.'

'And do we not yet have a sighting of the receipts?'

Ben shook his head apologetically. 'Not yet, but I'll find them. He kept every single one, I'm sure of it. As you yourself pointed out, sir, my father was a man who kept his papers in good order.'

'I must say I find it very intriguing as to why your

father did not mention this loan against the property when he came to make his will. Also, I've been to great pains to check, and I find no registration of a mortgage against the property.'

One thought had occurred to him. 'Could it be that your father took a loan from an old friend, who simply did not find it necessary to register the loan against the farm?'

'Yes, it's possible. My father was known to be an honest man. Whoever loaned him the money would have no fears about it being repaid.'

'All the same, it's a pity he never saw the need to discuss it with me.'

'I think I can explain that,' Ben offered. 'Y'see, he were a very proud man. I reckon the shame of having to borrow money against his hard-earned property was summat he'd have found hard to discuss with anyone, even you, sir.'

'Nonetheless, I must have a sight of these receipts. Please keep on searching. They *must* be found before the will can be executed. Especially as none of you seems aware of who lent the money.'

'I'll find them.' Ben was sure of it.

At this point, having followed the conversation with amusement, Jacob was about to reveal that he had already found the receipts. He even put his hand to his pocket to take out the envelope. But then, being the cunning fellow he was, he decided to let them sweat a while longer. He simply smiled and let the matter go by. Let them search high and low, he thought. I'll put the buggers out of their misery when I'm good and ready.

As it turned out, the receipts were even more important than Jacob could ever have envisaged.

Bending his head to the task, Mr Bryce began to read:

'. . . I have always cherished my family above all else. Bearing that in mind, I believe and hope that I have made a fair and reasonable legacy. If by my decisions I have hurt anybody's feelings, I promise it was not meant to be that way. Making a will is not an easy thing. The truth is, I thought long and hard before putting these decisions to paper, and I am convinced that I have acted in the best interests of my family as a whole.'

Mr Bryce summarised that particular paragraph. 'I can confirm that Ronald Hunter spent many an hour discussing such matters with me. He came to his own conclusions and acted upon his own instincts. And what I have to say is that in all our talks his strong commitment to family was paramount.'

On hearing this, Jacob made an approving sound,

causing Louise to turn and scowl at him. When he smiled on her, she abruptly turned away.

Regarding the young woman from over his spectacles, Mr Bryce cleared his throat and continued.

'I leave my carved animals, and my sketches of the valley, to my grandchild. At the time of writing, I realise I have no grandchild, though I know how desperate Louise and Ben are to have a child. I believe in my heart, the day will come. Meanwhile, I leave the cherished items stated above, in Louise's tender care . . .'

At this, Ben took hold of his wife's hand, and when he gazed on her through tearful eyes, she knew she would never love him more than she did at that moment.

Jacob saw the gesture, and was quietly seething, his fists working feverishly, one into the other.

Disturbed, Mr Bryce went on. He too had seen Ben's gesture, and had witnessed Jacob's reaction. Suddenly, in that small, quiet room the atmosphere was thick as night.

'My father's treasured gold crucifix, and the grandfather clock left me by my mother, I leave to my beloved wife (if she has been fortunate enough to outlive me). Also, any

money which I may leave, after honouring
various commitments. (As always, Ben is in
my confidence.)

'I realise now that your father must be referring to
the loan.' Mr Bryce looked to Ben for a nod of the
head. When it was delivered, he went on.

'But much more than that, I leave my everlast-
ing love and gratitude for the wonderful years
we have shared together. Without my Sally, life
would not have been so very beautiful.'

On hearing these words, Sally softly cried, the tears
falling freely down her face, and her heart filled
with love for that dear, kind man she would never
see again. Silently, tenderly, Ben leaned aside and
stroked her face. It was enough to pacify her.

Cold and impassive, Jacob looked on. When
Louise put her arm round the old lady, he felt a
twist of envy. But then the solicitor was reading once
more, and he must listen.

'To my lovely daughter-in-law Louise, I leave
the mantelpiece-clock she has always admired.
Unlike my Sally, Louise took to its odd character as I did. I have a sneaking suspicion that
Sally will be pleased at my decision.'

Here he glanced up yet again, to learn from Sally's smile that Ronnie's joke had, indeed, been happily received.

'To my son, Benjamin, I leave my heartfelt thanks for all he has done to ease my work-load and continue the tradition of farming, as did his father and grandfather and his great-grandfather before him. If it had not been for my youngest son, I would not have been able to carry on in my old age. Therefore, I leave to him all my work tools; the cart and tractor, and any equipment he might think fit to retain.'

At this, Jacob sniggered. 'Work tools?' His brother was welcome to them! Though what he would do with them when the farm was sold from under him was another matter. Either way, Jacob didn't give a toss.

Ironically, when he next concentrated on what Mr Bryce was saying, the smile vanished from his face, and he was momentarily lost for words.

'. . . and I can make no greater thanks to Ben, than to leave him the farm itself, knowing that he will always take care of Sally. My wife and I discussed this, and she is in full agreement.

'For my eldest son, Jacob, I wipe out any

debt he may have owed me. I also leave him our handsome family Bible. In there, he will find our entire ancestral tree. From this, I hope he will learn of his roots and, God willing, may come to respect them.

'I bear you no grudges, son. For my part, all is forgiven.'

As Mr Bryce's voice faded, Jacob's voice returned. At first he could only make a small choking sound, but soon he was screaming, 'No! It's my farm, my land! I will have what belongs to me! I won't let you buggers cheat me out of my inheritance!'

Throwing aside his chair, he stumbled through the room and flung open the door. He paused on the threshold a moment to stare at his brother, and spoke, his voice low and trembling. 'You will never see the day when that farm is yours.'

Breathing hard, he stood a moment longer, staring from one to the other. 'I'll be back. You can count on it.' Then he was gone, and for a long time, there was an awful silence.

'I'm sorry.' Mr Bryce finally broke the silence with a sobering remark addressed to Ben. 'I think we have to be prepared. It looks like your brother means war.'

'Oh, I'm sure he does.' Ben had expected trouble, but even he was surprised to have been left the entirety of his father's estate. 'No matter,' he answered quietly. 'Let him do his worst. I'll be ready.'

On seeing the firm set of his jaw, Louise and Sally exchanged worried glances. One thought ran through both their minds.

Jacob would move heaven and earth to take possession of what he believed to be his. Even with his mother involved, he would show no mercy.

For Jacob Hunter was an unforgiving man.

Chapter Four

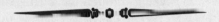

LOUISE EMERGED FROM a restless sleep. Something or someone had disturbed her and for a while, until her senses gathered, she could not think what it might have been.

Rubbing her eyes, she glanced at the bedside clock, an old relic of Ben's late father which occasionally seemed to have a mind of its own. 'Four o'clock!' She instinctively glanced round at the place beside her, where her husband would normally be stretched out fast asleep, one arm above his head and the other across his chest.

Not this morning though, because this morning, he wasn't here.

'Ben?' she called softly. 'Where are you?' In the half-darkness she thought she saw him by the window, but it was only shadow, created by the summer mist that sometimes rose up from the valley to block the coming daylight.

Scrambling out of bed, she threw on her robe and, crossing to the window, drew aside the pretty net curtains that Sally had made with her own fair hands.

Something below caught her attention. 'Why, it's Ben.' He was walking through the yard – she could see him clearly. 'What the devil's he up to at this hour of the morning?' She was used to him getting up early when there was work to be done, but the fields were clean right now and the harvest not yet ready. The chickens were still abed and even the cockerel was silent.

As he came out into the clearing before the field, she saw Boris at his heels, and tucked under his arm a shotgun.

Anxious now, she quickly drew the robe about her and tied it at the waist; in these old farmhouses the air was chilly of a night. Collecting her blue slippers from beside the bed, she kept them safe in her hands, and softly made her way downstairs. Going past Sally's room she was extra careful to make no noise; there was no point waking the old lady. One way or another, she had been robbed of enough sleep these past weeks.

Once downstairs, Louise grabbed a long-coat from behind the door and, flinging it over her shoulders, took the big iron key from the nail and gingerly opened the door. She shivered as the cool, damp air wafted in, taking her breath away.

Closing the door behind her, she went at a run, across the yard and down towards the big meadow, where she had last seen Ben. Reaching the stile, she paused to get her breath back, her anxious gaze scouring the land. 'He can't have gone far,' she said aloud. Wrapping her two arms about her to keep out the chill, she recalled the direction in which he was striding. 'I know he was headed this way.'

Suddenly, there he was. His familiar, comforting figure was silhouetted against the skies; the dog beside him and the slim, deadly shape of the shotgun clearly visible. 'Whatever he's up to, he means business,' muttered Louise. The first thought to leap into her head was – *Jacob!*'

But her brother-in-law wasn't here. He hadn't been seen or heard of these past four days, not since the reading of his father's will.

In a moment, Ben was joined by another man; Louise recognised him at once as the gentle giant, Eric Forester. As well as his job as gamekeeper on the estate of Salmesbury Manor, where he had a tied cottage, Eric was also a contract farmer. One of a handful hereabouts, he came to cut the corn when ripe, and in return take a percentage of the profits.

It was a common arrangement amongst the

farmers, and it worked well on both sides. One man would concentrate on contract farming and invest in the big, expensive machinery necessary for the job. This meant that small farmers such as Ronnie Hunter would have no need to put themselves in debt for machinery they did not need and could not afford. Instead, it was much more rewarding for them to turn over a small part of their profits to the hire of the contract man.

As the two men stood talking, Louise lost no time in going after them. Hurrying across the field, she called out her husband's name. 'Ben!'

He heard her and was startled. 'What in God's name d'you think you're doing, lass?' Taking her by the shoulders he held her at arm's length. 'By! It's a wonder you don't catch your death o' cold.'

Breathless, she took a minute to gulp in the cool air. 'I woke up and you weren't there,' she explained. 'I saw you out the window . . . you and the dog.' Her anxious gaze went to the shotgun tucked securely under his arm. 'Why do you need that?'

She noticed the covert glance that passed between Ben and Eric. 'What is it?' she asked. 'Are the foxes on the hunt again?'

Ben slid his arm round her and drew her away. 'That's right, sweetheart,' he lied. 'Eric knocked on the door early on. Apparently, some of the farmers had their chickens savaged late last night, so me an'' him thought it were time to do a bit o' hunting of our own.' Looking up at Eric, he gave a little wink. 'Ain't that right?'

When Eric assured her that was the case, Ben added, 'The best time to catch the beggars is early light when they're skulking back to the den.'

On that, Eric agreed wholeheartedly. 'Aye, that's right enough.' Addressing Louise in softer tone, he suggested, 'If you don't mind me saying, missus, I reckon you'd be better off back in the warm, aside a cosy fire.'

On reflection and with the early morning chill playing round her bare legs, she tended to agree. 'I'll get back then, Ben.'

'Mind how you go, sweetheart.' Reaching down he swung her into his arms and kissed her on the mouth. 'And mind you lock yourself in once you're inside,' he reminded her.

Louise gave her word. Locking the door at this time of morning came as second nature to her now. They lived in an isolated place and right from the start, Ben had taught her never to take chances.

The two men watched as the young woman made her way back. When she was at the top of the valley, she turned to wave, but they were gone.

Having seen her safely out of the valley, Ben and Eric had moved on. 'I've never had to lie to our Louise afore.' Ben felt bad about that.

'Why didn't you tell her the truth – how Jacob had got word to you through me? If he really means what he says, that he'll destroy you, then surely Lou would understand how you've to keep vigil?'

'She'd understand all right,' Ben answered. 'The main income is from these crops.' He marvelled at the corn blowing in the breeze.

How Jacob could deride this way of life he would never understand. But then he and his older brother had never had anything in common. That was something Ben had bitterly regretted.

Eric understood what was running through his pal's mind, even before he said it; Ben spoke with such emotion his voice shook. 'If Jacob were to set fire to these crops, he'd destroy us good an' proper. The income from the land is what keeps the roof over our heads, an' he knows it.'

'Is that why you didn't tell Louise . . . because you didn't want to worry her?'

'Summat like that, yes.'

'D'you think she might have tackled him about it?'

Ben smiled at the thought. 'She's a fiery one, is my lass,' he replied softly. 'Who knows *what* she might do?' He grew serious. 'I reckon it's best if the women don't get wind of what Jacob said to you in the pub.'

'It could have been the drink talking.'

Ben shook his head. 'Drunk or sober, Jacob would like to see me ruined. Since the day at the solicitor's, I knew he'd cause trouble one way or another.' He wasn't certain what Jacob had in mind, but, 'One thing's for sure. He's up to summat, you can depend on it.'

Striding on, he and Eric checked all the boundaries. 'Well, there's nobody been here that I can see.' As gamekeeper for Salmesbury Manor, there was little Eric didn't know about tracking intruders.

Ben was pleasantly surprised. 'We'd best check the chicken houses next.'

A quick examination showed that nothing had been touched, though they had woken the cockerel and he was shouting, as Eric said, 'like a good 'un!'

Ben looked up; the sun had risen, and the skies were lit the most wonderful shade of cornflower-blue. 'We might as well let the chucks out while we're here,' he suggested.

It didn't take long with the two of them, and soon the chickens were running about, clucking and fighting in the early morning light. 'They've put me in the mood for eggs and bacon,' Ben joked, and when Eric smacked his lips, that was the incentive to make their way back to the farmhouse, their empty stomachs urging them along at a quickening pace.

'I should think you're relieved there's no damage been done.' Eric continued to be wary; his quick eyes searching the ground for any signs of strangers.

''Course I am.' Though, like Eric, Ben was not altogether comfortable.

'Happen he were just mouthing off and nowt'll come of it.' Eric was ever the optimist.

'Happen.' Ben was not convinced. 'I'll have to watch my back,' he remarked thoughtfully. 'If I know Jacob, which I do more than most, I've a feeling it won't be too long afore my precious brother shows his face round here again.'

———⟫•◦•⟪———

CAREFULLY UNLOCKING THE back door of the cottage, Louise was surprised and dismayed to see her mother-in-law waiting in the passageway. 'What are them two doing at this time of a morning?' the old lady wanted to know.

'What are *you* doing?' Louise smiled at the picture before her. Sally was dressed in her old blue gown and ragged red slippers. The tin curlers in her fine hair had fallen partway out and there, clutched loosely in her fist, were her false teeth.

Fondly, the girl reprimanded her. 'I thought I'd left you safe in bed, fast and hard asleep.'

'You probably thought you were tiptoeing past

my room, but it didn't work, lass. In truth I thought there must be a herd of elephants on the loose!' Sally broke out laughing. 'I'm sorry, Lou, but you were never a twinkletoes.'

'Huh.' The young woman joined in the laughter. 'You speak for yourself, Sally Hunter!' Taking off the long-coat she flung it over the back door nail. 'By! It's a bit sharpish out there, I can tell you.'

When she shivered loudly, Sally grew concerned. 'Come inside, love. Sit yerself down at the fire an' I'll put the kettle on.' As she made her way to the scullery she added, 'Then you can tell me what's been going on.'

While Louise warmed herself at the fire which Sally had made in her absence, the old lady washed her false teeth under the tap and promptly popped them in her mouth. She then boiled the kettle and made the brew and in no time at all, brought two mugs of steaming hot tea through to the parlour. 'There y'are, lass. Just what the doctor ordered.'

Handing Louise one mug, she took the other and sat herself in the old rocking chair. 'Now then, what's that son o' mine doing out there at this time of a morning?'

Sipping at the tea, Louise shrugged her shoulders. 'Checking boundaries . . . making sure everything's all right. It seems the farmers were raided by foxes last night, and some of the chickens were taken.'

'Were that Eric Forester with him? Only I thought I recognised his long, lanky frame.'

The young woman nodded. 'He's a nice fella. Always polite and well-mannered.'

'Hmh.' Sally nodded. 'Good-looking too, in a skinny sort o' way.' In the mood for a bit of nostalgia, she indulged herself. 'I've known Eric since he were a lad,' she mused. 'Me an' his mam both had us fat bellies at the same time. If I recall, Eric were born four days afore . . .'

It stuck in her craw to say Jacob's name, so she wagged her head and pursed her lips and swiftly added, 'I followed that lad through his schooling and after when he were all grown up. And when he got wed, oh, I were that pleased for him.'

A deep scowl marred her weathered old face. 'It only lasted for two years. When that wife of his ran off to sing for a living in the clubs o' London, it were the best thing that ever happened to that young man.' She gave an almighty sigh. 'They got divorced soon after. By! It were a shameful thing. His poor mam couldn't hold her head up in the town for some long time.'

'She did well though, didn't she?' Louise recalled being told. 'Ben said Sharon Dewey made it good and married some rich Cockney fella.'

'Aye, an' I'll bet she's left *him* long since.' Sally found it hard to forgive. 'A bit of a slapper she were . . . game for owt, if you ask me.'

'Why did Eric never remarry?'

'Can you blame him?' Sally chuckled unexpectedly. 'I should think he had his fair share the first time round, poor bugger.'

Louise thought it a real waste. 'It's a shame. He's such a lovely bloke.'

'Away with yer, lass! He's got his parents and his sister, and he works all the hours God sends, so I'm sure he hasn't got time to be lonely. Besides, they say he's worth a bob or two, what with no wife to spend it on.'

With Ben in mind, and tired now of the chit-chat, Louise gazed out the window. 'I wonder if they're on their way back?'

Sally looked her daughter-in-law in the eye. 'I don't reckon they were chasing a fox at all. Not the four-legged kind, at any rate.'

'Whatever d'you mean?'

'I mean Jacob, that's what I mean.' Gesturing to the window, the old lady went on solemnly, 'You don't think for one minute that he's given up, do you?'

'But what can he do? The farm was left to Ben fair and square, all legal like. That's what the solicitor said.'

'Mr Bryce doesn't know him like we do. Oh no! He'll be out there, planning summat nasty, like the bad devil he is. I'm telling you, lass, Jacob has his sights set on this farm and if I know him he'll not rest till he's done all he can to get us out.'

'So you think they were out there looking to see if Jacob was around?'

'No doubt in my mind at all. That's what they were doing all right.'

'If that's the case, why would Ben lie to me?' Anger surged through her.

'Same reason as he wouldn't tell me neither.' Sally gave a mischievous wink. ''Cause they're men and we're women, and they're of a mind that women shouldn't be told everything. They think we'll worry and fret and get in the way.'

Louise grinned reluctantly at her words. 'You mean we're good for getting their meals and washing their socks and rolling about the bed naked when it suits 'em?'

'That's men for yer.' Making a frantic sign of the cross on herself, Sally gave a nervous little giggle. 'My Ronnie excepted, o' course.'

'O' course.' Louise was reading Sally's mind and it made her chuckle. 'You naughty thing, are you saying what I think you're saying?'

'Depends on what you *think* I'm saying.'

'They'll be here soon.'

Sally's eyes twinkled. 'Any minute now, I'd say.'

'Teach 'em a lesson, eh?'

Sally made a face. 'Why not?'

'After all, he did lie to me. Thought I couldn't handle the truth.'

Taking the two empty mugs, Sally rose from her chair. 'It would be a pity if they caught us here like this, wasting time sipping and chatting . . .'

Louise finished the sentence. '. . . Like two useless women!'

Sally went off to put the mugs in the sink, while Louise made sure the back door was well and truly locked.

Then they each went upstairs to their respective rooms and climbed back into bed.

———⟡———

WHEN THE MEN let themselves in, they found the fire crackling in the hearth, two empty pots in the sink, and on checking, Ben discovered both women fast asleep in bed. 'I'm sorry, mate,' he told Eric. 'Looks like we'll have to make our own breakfast.'

Seeing the funny side of it, Eric suspected Louise had played a trick on them. 'I thought you said the women would have the fire going, and the breakfast sizzling away by the time we got back?' He couldn't take the smile off his face.

Ben laughed out loud. 'The cheeky buggers!' But he too saw the funny side of it, and they ate a hearty breakfast all the same.

Upstairs, Louise heard them fumbling about in the cupboards. She wasn't really asleep. Instead she lay there, her stomach growling at the delightful smell of bacon. She heard the door close behind Eric. Then the bedroom door opened and there was Ben. 'Come here, you.' Opening her arms, she took him to her.

It thrilled her to take the shirt from his back and stroke the tips of her fingers down his spine. A moment or two of intimate fondling and lingering kisses, and then she gave herself to him.

Because more urgent matters were always demanding their attention, this was the first time they had made love for some weeks. And it was incredible; leaving them both breathless and fulfilled.

Afterwards they lay in each other's arms and spoke of their deepest thoughts. 'Do you really think Jacob will come after the farm?' Louise needed to know. 'Even though it was legally left to you?'

Ben thought on it for a minute, one arm over his head as always when resting; the other was round her shoulder. 'Yes,' he answered at length. 'He'll come after it . . . if only *because* Dad left it to me.'

Turning to face her, he kissed the tip of her pretty

nose. 'He won't get it,' he promised. Suddenly his voice dropped to a whisper, almost inaudible to his wife. 'I'll kill him first!'

Louise had heard and was afraid.

For a long time after he had gone to sleep, she lay awake, wondering what to do. Should she plead with Jacob to leave them in peace? There would be no point, she decided. He would only laugh and think she was offering herself to him.

Then she looked at her husband, sleeping the sleep of the innocent, and she felt her love deepen. 'We'll fight him,' she whispered. 'Let him do his worst. Whatever happens, I'll be there by your side where I belong.'

~>•<~

IN THE OTHER room, Sally too was unable to get back to sleep.

Just now, because there had been too many serious issues these past weeks, she and Louise had made light of Ben not telling them the truth. But that was like Ben, wanting to protect them. She couldn't blame him for that. He was a good son. He was all she could have hoped for.

Ben was warm and caring.

Jacob was cold and dangerous. He knew something, but wasn't telling.

And where *were* those receipts her husband had collected?

———◦———

F OR THE UMPTEENTH time these past few days, Jacob left his car parked halfway down Montague Street, where the traffic was less crowded. He then made his way across King Street to the official-looking building opposite.

Being a Friday, the streets were busy with women with babies and young children, hurrying home with their high prams and bags of shopping; white-collared men driving home in their little black Ford cars after a day at the office, and hordes of children, kicking and shouting their way home from school and causing uproar in the process.

Then there were other men, flat-capped and booted, and women of all age and type, all teeming out of the cotton mills, still wearing their pinnies and turbans, headed for home and a chance to kick off their shoes and put their weary feet up for a while.

In his ignorance, Jacob looked down on such people. These were mere workers who danced to another's tune and knew nothing of life. They trudged to work and trudged home again, and found nothing worthwhile in between. They were no better than worker bees, or sheep, he thought, and when he bumped into one, he would wipe himself down as if he had touched something contagious.

One woman, a winder at the local mill, had seen him before and knew him for what he was. 'I'm not bloody surprised you can't see where you're going,' she told him when he collided with her on the pavement. 'Your nose is so far stuck up in the air, you can't see your hand in front of your bloody face!' With that she strode on, leaving Jacob staring after her with his mouth wide open. He had been deep in thought and for once, had been caught unawares.

Spitting abuse at her, he took a moment to compose himself.

Afterwards, turning his attention to the building in front of him, he brushed himself down, straightened his tie and lifting the knocker on the door, let it clatter down hard against the timber.

Three times he did this. 'Come on! For Christ's sake, come on!' Jacob Hunter was not known to be a patient man.

During the short periods when he was not banging on the door, he used the time to admire the building. Of sturdy design with stone mullions and stained-glass windows, the building housed several offices, all reached through this one handsome entrance. At the top of a flight of stone steps, the door was solid oak, panelled and figured, with an extravagant lion-head knocker – which he now thumped once more against the timber.

'Goodness me!' The young woman who opened it was slim and plain, with an expression of horror on her pasty face. 'You're very determined, sir.'

'And *you*, young woman, have kept me waiting!'

Without waiting for a response he pushed past her, ignoring her apologies. 'I'm sorry, sir. The usual receptionist is ill, and I was called into Mr Martin's office . . . sir! You can't go through there without an appointment . . . SIR!'

She was relieved when the office door opened and Alan Martin himself came out. 'It's all right, Jean.' His smile belied the anger he felt at Jacob Hunter pushing his way through like that. 'You'd best come inside.'

Stepping away, he waited until Jacob was inside before rounding on him. 'What the hell do you think you're doing, man? How dare you make a spectacle of yourself! I thought you wanted to keep our little business transaction quiet.'

As he said this, he lowered his voice and spoke through gritted teeth. 'I'm beginning to wonder if I should refuse to have anything more to do with you!' Throwing himself into the chair behind the desk, he stared at Jacob. '*I will not have you drawing attention to me like that.* Do you understand?'

Jacob ignored him. 'I had to see you.' Without

waiting for an invitation, he sat himself in the chair at the front of the desk. 'Time's running out. I want them off my farm, and if *you* won't help me, I'll find somebody else who will.'

The older man, large-bellied and whiskered, went red in the face. 'You forget, Hunter . . . apart from you, I'm the only one who knows that your father paid back every penny on that loan. If you were to approach anybody else, I'd stand up in court and tell the truth. So, unless you want to go to jail, you'll do business with me, or you'll do it with no one!'

'It's taking too long.'

'On the contrary, I believe we've made good progress. I've spent these past three nights doctoring my records, in order to show how your father still owed a tidy sum on that loan. And, as such, I can foreclose any time.'

Jacob liked the sound of that. 'So – are we ready now?'

'Have you the receipts intact?'

Jacob smiled. 'I certainly do – and they're safely hidden away.'

There was no answering smile on Alan Martin's face. 'I thought I told you to burn them.'

'Now, why would I do that?' Jacob was quick. 'While I have them, you won't think about doing me out of my share. Because if we haven't split the proceeds from the sale of that farm within twenty-eight days from receipt of the auction, the "missing" receipts will suddenly reappear, and I'll deny all knowledge of any underhand deal. If anybody takes the blame for it, I'll make damned sure it's not *me*!'

The older man considered that for a moment. 'Very well,' he said. 'But *you* understand this: I hand no money over, unless I get the original receipts.'

'Of course.' Jacob sniggered. 'Once I've got my hands on my share of the money, I'll have no use for them anyway.'

Suddenly the older man lapsed into deep thought. 'Something occurred to me the other night,' he murmured. 'Something that could easily trip us up.'

'I don't see how it could. We've thought of everything.' But seeing his accomplice so thoughtful, made the doubt creep in. 'We have, haven't we?'

'We've removed all the receipts, isn't that so?'

'Yes. I just said so, didn't I?'

'Well now, put yourself in the place of the bailiff. My ledger will show that Mr Ronald Hunter paid the first twelve months off that debt, and nothing after that.'

'So?'

'So . . . I would have issued him with receipts for those twelve payments, but where are they?'

'Are you going deaf or what. I've already told

you . . . *I've* got 'em!' Jacob was growing impatient. What the devil was the fellow getting at?

'Don't you see, Hunter? Those twelve receipts would have been kept by your father. You and I both know he was not the kind of man to lose something that important.'

'You're saying I should have taken just the ones we don't want them to find?'

'And left the others right where he'd hidden them, yes!' In an instant Martin was out of his chair and walking Jacob to the door. 'Put them back.' Leaning forward he whispered harshly in Jacob's ear. 'Put that first year's receipts back *as quickly as you can*!'

'Consider it done.'

'And stay out of my way. It has to be a clear case of bad debt. Your father owed me money – two years of repayments on a three-year loan – and I have to recover it. I foreclose on the farm and put it to auction. That's the black and white of it.'

'And I'm the fortunate purchaser.' Jacob sneered. 'Ironic, isn't it? We swindle Father out of two years' repayments on the loan, and when the farm goes up for sale to recover the debt, I buy the farm with half the money you steal back from him.' He shook his head in admiration of the scheme. 'That's what I call justice.'

'We'll have to put a higher guide price on the farm, to discourage any other would-be buyers.'

'Suits me.' He grinned. 'It's not my money paying for it.'

'Stay low.'

'When do you make the first move?'

'Next week.'

Jacob rubbed his hands. 'The sooner the better.'

'First, I have to apply to the courts, but that shouldn't take too long. I believe I can pull a few strings there.'

'Good.'

'As from today, you *must* stay away from me. Your visits to date can be explained away if needs be. In fact, as your father's friend and adviser, I would be surprised if his eldest son did not pay me the occasional visit. However, we must now be careful not to arouse anyone's interest.'

'You won't see hide nor hair of me, until I come for my money.'

'Even then you will not come here. I'll contact you.' Martin consulted his pocket notebook. 'I take it you'll be staying at this same lodging-house for the foreseeable future?'

'Until I get what's mine, then I'll be off to pastures new.' Jacob frowned darkly. 'Once the farm's been sold from under them, I dare say Miss High and Mighty Louise will be more agreeable to coming away with me.'

Alan Martin had long since been aware of Jacob's obsession with his brother's wife. 'You're a bloody fool!' he snapped. 'Now go on . . . leave me.'

Jacob did not take kindly to being dismissed. 'Think on,' he blustered. 'I'll be watching your every move.'

But in Alan Martin, Jacob had more than met his match. 'Don't threaten me!' he warned, and, seeing the look in his eyes, Jacob quailed.

'Are you sure we've talked it through?' he said sulkily. 'I mean, we haven't left any stone unturned, have we?'

'Not now you're about to put the receipts back. Stop worrying, man. Now that we've set out the ground rules, you can safely leave the rest to me. Our business can be concluded after the sale of the farm.'

'How will I know when I'm to make my move?'

'You do nothing, till I tell you.'

'When will the farm be offered for sale?'

'Watch for the notice going up in the Town Hall.'

'When will that be?'

'Two weeks, no more.'

On leaving, Jacob shook him by the hand. 'I won't come here again.'

'No, you won't. I'm glad I've got that through to you at long last.'

As he was shown out, Jacob thanked him again. *It was all going his way. He'd waited long enough already. Two more weeks would soon pass.*

Chapter Five

S ALLY'S LAUGHTER ECHOED across the land. 'You brazen hussy, Louise Hunter! Since when did yer start showing your knickers to all and sundry!' Shading her eyes with the flat of her hand she peered upwards, the sun half dazzling her. 'If I'm struck blind it won't be the sun as does it,' she chuckled. 'It'll be the sight o' your bare backside smiling down on me.'

Hanging on for grim life, Louise inched herself along the bough, trying desperately to get back to the main trunk of the tree, but then had to abandon the idea when the bough began creaking dangerously. 'I'm glad you're enjoying yourself, Sally,' she remarked light-heartedly, 'only it's not so funny from where I am.'

She didn't dare look down at Sally, who somehow seemed not to realise the seriousness of the situation. 'If you don't get that ladder back a bit quick, I'll likely fall to the ground and break me neck.'

'It's your own fault. I told you to leave it to Ben,' Sally chided. 'I *said* you'd lose your footing.'

'Yes. You were right and I were wrong, and now I'm stuck here and can't get back. So stop laughing and help me, will you?'

'Don't know as I can.' Sally was still chortling. 'Besides, you got yerself there, so you should be able to get yerself back again.'

Wrapping her arms tighter round the bough, Louise yelled down, 'I'm really stuck, Sally! For God's sake, put the bloody ladder back, will you?'

At last Sally seemed to realise that here was a delicate situation. 'Stay there,' she ordered. 'Don't you move now.'

This time it was the younger woman's turn to smile. 'I'm hardly going anywhere, Sal.' She rolled her eyes to heaven. 'Except flat on my face if you don't get a move on.'

'I'm sorry, lass. It seems to be stuck.' Tugging at the ladder, which had slipped sideways and got tangled in a mass of branches, Sally pulled it this way and that, and still couldn't free it.

'Hurry!' Louise was desperate now.

'I'm doing me best.' As the old woman panicked and tried to shake the ladder free, she shook the branches too; the consequence being that the half-filled basket which Louise had wedged in the fork of the tree crashed to the ground.

The sight of the split wicker basket, and the apples rolling and bouncing on the ground, had a curious effect on Sally. 'I can't do it, lass!' she screamed. 'I'll get Ben. Hang on. Don't you fall now!' And off she went, running and hopping, and calling out for her son. 'Ben! Come quick. Our Louise is stuck up the apple tree!'

Ben was in the shed, searching for his father's receipts; a thankless task that seemed neverending. 'What's wrong, Mam?' Coming outside, he wiped the sweat from his face. 'Is there a fire or what?'

The smile on his face was quickly wiped away when his mother told him about Louise. 'She were weeding out the worm-eaten apples y'see, an' she asked me to hold the ladder at the bottom, only it slipped and Louise were left hanging in the tree and now she can't get down . . . an' I can't seem to shift the ladder . . . an' oh, Ben. She's stuck good an' proper!' After a tirade of words, she paused for breath.

'It's all right, Mam. Don't worry.' Taking her by the shoulders, he sat her on the workbench by the door. 'You stay there and catch your breath.'

'I were laughing, silly old bugger that I am. I thought it were funny, an' now she can't get down.'

He smiled. 'What goes up, must come down – ain't that right?'

Sally gave a sigh. 'Go on, lad. Hurry up.'

Losing no time he went at a run to the orchard, where he found Louise sprawled across the farthest and highest branch. 'Your mam couldn't help it,' she groaned, looking down with sorry eyes. 'I should never have asked her to hold the ladder.'

With hands on hips and legs astride, he stood there, the smile on his face growing by the minute, and a naughty twinkle in his eye. 'By! This is a lovely sight . . . petticoats and bare thighs. It's enough to drive a man wild.'

Clinging to the bough with both arms, Louise couldn't even shake her fist. 'Get me down, Ben, and stop tomfooling about.'

He deliberately made no move. 'I'd rather stay here a while longer, and enjoy the view.'

'Ben, you bugger, GET ME DOWN!'

Having got her breath back, Sally made her way to the orchard, still tut-tutting. 'I told the lass not to go that far out on the branch. I said she'd lose her footing, but oh no, she knew best. By! She's a hothead that one, an' no mistake.' All the same, her daughter-in-law meant the world to her. 'I hope the lass ain't hurt.'

With that in mind, she quickened her footsteps.

F ROM HIS HIDING place, Jacob had seen it all.

He saw Ben rummaging about in the shed and he saw Sally come and fetch him. He gave a sigh of relief when the old woman went away, and now he was creeping towards the shed, hoping and praying they wouldn't come back before he had a chance to plant the receipts in the place where he'd found them.

Arriving at the mouth of the shed, he saw how his brother had turned the place upside down. 'Hmh! He's determined, I'll say that for him.' His shifty gaze went to the box in the corner. It appeared untouched; left exactly as he himself had found it. 'So, he hasn't got as far as the old man's newspaper box then?' His eyes lit up. 'Best be quick. The last thing I need is for them buggers to catch me at it.'

Like a thief in the night he took out the old papers and, removing the envelope containing a smaller number of receipts from his pocket, he wedged it in the bottom of the box. Then he replaced the old papers on top, and slunk out of the shed as fast as he could.

In a whisper, he was gone; away through the spinney, across the fields and back to the lane where he'd left his car. Falling against the vehicle, he gave himself time to catch his breath; with the hot sun beating mercilessly down, the running had sapped his strength.

Before getting into the car he took a hankie from his pocket and wiped the sweat from his face and neck. That done he climbed into the car and drove like the very devil, away from there.

'A good job well done,' he congratulated himself. 'It's only a matter of time before he finds them receipts. *Then* he's in for a shock an' no mistake!'

A vicious smirk lifted the corners of his mouth. 'Hah! I'd give anything to see our Ben's face when he finds them receipts!'

<hr />

THE THREE OF them came back laughing. 'I reckon you'd have left me up that tree till a month o' Sundays, you blighter!' Yet Louise was none the worse for her experience.

'I'm glad it were *me* as got yer down, and not some other bloke.' Putting his arm round her, Ben kissed her soundly on the mouth. 'Or he might have run off with yer.'

Louise laughed up at him. 'Then what would you have done, eh?'

'I'd have searched high and low till I found yer again.' A look of passion lit his eyes. 'No man takes *my* woman!'

And so fierce were his words that Louise was struck silent for a time. She knew he was thinking of Jacob, and her heart turned over. It was not an easy thing for a woman, when she seemed to come between two brothers through no fault of her own.

Sensing the sudden atmosphere, Sally intervened. 'So, yer no worse for yer little adventure then.' she asked slyly.

''Course not.' Louise took hold of the old lady's hand. 'I don't blame you for laughing,' she admitted. 'I must have looked a comical sight.' Holding up the hem of her skirt she groaned. 'I've spoilt my dress though.' She revealed a jagged tear from waist to hem.

Ben kissed her again. 'I'll buy you another,' he promised, 'but first I'd best get on an' find them receipts. Mr Bryce is getting impatient. I've to see him tomorrow, with or without them. It seems Alan Martin's contacted him, and he needs to talk something through with me.'

Sally looked up. 'It could have been him as lent your dad that money. Your dad knew him since we were all at school together.'

Ben nodded. 'Could be,' he agreed. 'In fact, I've been of a mind to pay him a visit. It'll be interesting to hear what he has to say. But I can't just ask him straight out if he were the one as loaned our dad that money.'

'Happen that's why Mr Bryce has called you in so soon.'

Having listened to the conversation, Louise had something to say. 'If he *is* the one who lent the money, he'd have records and such, wouldn't he?'

Ben nodded. 'I hope so. But I've heard some troubling things about his business over the years.'

'So we'll know soon enough, one way or the other, I expect.'

'Aye, lass, I'm sure we will.' But would they hear something to their advantage, or would it raise more problems than it might solve? That was the question going through Ben's mind just then.

He took a moment to assess his thoughts. 'I've searched the house from top to bottom, and there's no sign of any receipts, not even in the box where he kept the birth certificates and marriage licence. The only place left to search is this old shed.'

'You carry on then,' Louise told him. 'I'll make the tea and happen a plate o' sandwiches. I reckon we all deserve a break.'

'I'll help you,' Sally offered. 'I'll do the tea while you make the sandwiches.' And off they went, quietly chatting.

'Alan Martin's long been a friend of Ronnie's, though I never really trusted him,' Sally said. 'Some people say he wasn't always honest in his dealings, but I'm sure he wouldn't let down an old mate.'

Somehow, the shadows were beginning to lift. 'Once this business of the loan is cleared up, the farm can go into Ben's name, and everything will be all right,' she declared.

Louise looked up at the skies; filled with sunshine. That was how their lives had been before. Now, unlike Sally, she couldn't help but feel a twinge of anxiety.

'How can you be so sure Ronnie kept those receipts?' she asked. 'I mean, you said he never even told you about the loan.'

'That's the way he was,' Sally answered fondly. 'He would never tell me anything that might worry me. But he would have kept them receipts safe.' She was sure of it. 'My Ronnie was a meticulous man in matters of business.'

Sensing the old lady's regrets, Louise linked arms with her. 'None of this has been easy, has it, Sal?'

Her mother-in-law shook her head. 'No, lass,' she replied softly. 'I've lost a good man, and my very best friend.'

Now, when she turned to smile at Louise, the teardrops trembled on her droopy eyelids. 'But I'm still luckier than most,' she said. 'I've got you and I've got Ben. Moreover, once our lad finds them receipts, we'll all be assured of a roof over us heads.' Squeezing the girl's arm, she beamed at her. 'What else can an old woman ask for?'

As they went into the cottage to prepare the refreshments, both women seemed quieter of heart.

———»•«———

WHILE LOUISE AND her mother-in-law busied themselves in the kitchen, Ben was delving into every nook and cranny in the shed. 'They've *got* to be here!' The more he searched, the more disillusioned he became.

Pausing a moment, he sat back on his haunches and ran his hands through his hair. He closed his eyes in anguish. 'Where've you put them, Dad? You must have known how important they were. Why in God's name didn't yer confide in me?'

Opening his eyes he saw the box in the corner. 'I wonder . . .'

He knew his father kept old newspapers in that box; they were kept for wrapping the spring carrots and keeper apples and, occasionally in the chilly, autumn evenings, he might use a few papers to light the kindling in the brazier. But on the whole, the majority of papers were rarely disturbed.

'There's nowhere else to look.' He had searched this property upside down and inside out.

As though afraid to search in the box, he remained where he was, reluctant to look and be disappointed, yet knowing he must, for he had exhausted all other possibilities. If the receipts were not hidden in that box, then they were nowhere on this property that he could tell.

Hesitantly, he got to his feet. Walking to the box, he picked it up and carried it to the workbench. Here, he began the task of removing and examining every piece of paper that came out; some were so old they had welded together in the damp of the shed; and others, stiff and brittle, fell apart in his grasp.

At last, with the discarded newspapers piled up on the bench beside him, he spied the envelope, lying squashed up against the side of the box.

His heart skipped a beat. 'Please . . . let this be it!'

Eagerly now, he opened the envelope, immensely relieved when he saw that they were indeed the receipts he'd been looking for. 'Now at last we can get things underway.'

He counted the receipts once; he looked at the document alongside, then he counted the receipts again, his eyes widening in disbelief.

The truth hit him like a ton weight. *Dear God! According to this . . . only a third of the loan was ever paid back!*

For a time, his mind would not accept it. 'I don't understand any of this. Dad led me to understand . . .' He stopped himself. 'No.' He shook his head slowly from side to side, trying to remember every word his father had told him about that loan.

Like a bad dream, it all came back to him. 'When I think about it, he never once told me it was paid off. When I asked him why he was working himself into the ground, all he said was that he didn't like owing anybody anything.

'I just assumed the debt was paid, the way he slogged every hour of the day and night. I just *assumed* he wouldn't stop until it was paid. Now I know . . . when he *did* stop, it was the illness that made him rest, not because he had honoured his debt.'

Tears of anger filled his eyes. 'What killed him was the strain of owing that bloody money! Because of Jacob! Because that lazy bastard was too bone-idle to go out and earn himself a living. What kind of man is he, to stand back while his own father gets into debt, to set him up in a business that went the same rotten way as he did!'

If Jacob had been there in that moment he would have given him the sound thrashing he deserved. But Jacob wasn't there. And *he* was the one being punished, like his father before him.

His thoughts were bitter. 'So! The laugh is on me, eh, Jacob? It seems I don't have first call on this farm after all.' It was a hard pill to swallow. So engrossed was he in the awfulness of the situation, he didn't hear the two women at the door.

When he turned, it was to see Sally, white-faced, her voice little more than a whisper. 'Are you saying Ronnie never lived long enough to pay off his debts?'

Ben held the papers up. 'I'm sorry, Mam, but you'll know the truth soon enough.' Going over to take her in his arms, he held the envelope out. 'There's a charge in here for the sum of two thousand pounds,' he told her gently. 'The receipts amount to less than a third of that figure.'

Her heart in her boots, Louise stepped forward. 'What happens now?' she asked.

He had no suitable answer to that. 'I don't know, lass.' He thought of his father and his heart broke. 'Happen *this* is why Alan Martin approached Mr Bryce.' Drawing her attention to an official slip of paper in his hand, he explained, 'Mam was right. It was him who made the loan.'

'So why did he go and see Mr Bryce?'

'As executor, Mr Bryce was duty bound to give public notice that he was acting on behalf of Dad's estate. He explained all that to me. O' course we didn't think there'd be any money owed on this property, but it seems there is. Because he wants his money back, Alan Martin had every right to make himself known to Mr Bryce.'

'Can anything be done – about the loan, I mean?'

Lost for ideas, Ben shrugged his shoulders. 'It has to be paid, that's all I know.'

Sally had a suggestion. 'Mr Martin always said he were your dad's friend. Happen he'll let *you* pay the debt off, instead o' your father.' She was grasping at straws. She tugged at his sleeve like a child. 'What d'you think, Ben?'

'We'll know tomorrow,' he said, 'when I've been to see Mr Bryce. All we can do is ask.'

Other than wait for the outcome of that meeting, there was nothing else they could do.

MR BRYCE GAVE them no comfort. 'Unless you have the money to pay off what's owed, I'm afraid my hands are tied.' Shaking his head despondently, he reminded Ben, 'The farm was put up against the loan. That makes it a serious matter.'

'Yes, but according to what you said before, it was never put down on paper.'

'But it *was* discussed and agreed by both parties . . . what is called in legal terms a "gentlemen's agreement".'

'You've only got Alan Martin's word for that.'

'That's true, of course, but—'

'Oh, I see! Being as Alan Martin is a member of the business community, and richer than my father ever was, they're bound to accept his word as gospel.'

When Mr Bryce put out his hands in a gesture of helplessness, Ben had his answer, and it was not good.

'Tell me, young man, do you have any money put away at all?'

'Hmh! I only wish I had.'

In the face of it, Ben was fighting a losing battle so, for what it was worth, he set out his offer. 'You know I don't have that kind of money,' he said. 'What farmer has?' He had been thinking half the night, trying to see a way out. 'Look, Mr Bryce, I'm ready to put in long hours to earn it. I'll even take on extra work at the neighbouring farms if I have to. I can pay the debt off bit by bit, if only he'll let me.'

'I've already suggested something along those lines.' In truth, Mr Bryce had pleaded long and hard with Martin, but to no avail. 'I can tell you now. He won't agree to that.'

'Why not? Why should he care as long as he gets his money back?'

'Apparently he's considering making a rather heavy business commitment, so he needs the money, and he needs it now.'

'Surely to God he can't be that hard up?'

Mr Bryce sympathised with Ben, but the law was the law. 'Whether he's hard up or not doesn't even come into it. The facts are these; he loaned your father money when no one else would. He entered into an agreement with your father, that the money should be paid back within a certain period of time. It wasn't. In his defence, he has all the necessary documents, signed by your father and duly witnessed.'

'Did you tell him my dad made every effort to repay that money on time? I was with him. I saw how he shackled himself to the land. I worked alongside him and my heart bled for the way he pushed himself . . . even when he was ill. For Christ's sake, he killed himself because of that bloody loan!'

'I understand how you feel, but we have to follow the rules, I'm afraid.'

Like the other good folks hereabouts, Mr Bryce had known and respected Ronnie Hunter and he knew what kind of man he was. He too had been surprised that the loan was never fully paid. 'Listen to me, son. Because your father had already missed a considerable number of payments before he died, the terms of the agreement are clearly breached. The debt is still outstanding, and what's more, Alan Martin is now claiming interest on the balance owing, which of course he is quite at liberty to do.'

Ben was outraged. 'The man's a bloody monster!'

'We don't know his circumstances, so we're not in a position to judge. But there is no denying, he was a good friend to your father.'

'I'll talk to him.'

'I doubt if that would do any good. In fact, it might have the opposite effect. He has already explained to me how deeply he regrets the situation, but because of his own commitments, he has no alternative but to lodge a claim against the estate.'

'And what does that mean exactly?'

Leaning back in his chair, Mr Bryce took a moment to answer. He hoped he could word it kindly, for it was bad news.

When he next spoke, it was to deliver a shattering blow to Ben's hopes. 'What it means is this . . . The farm, the surrounding land, and even the furniture inside the farmhouse, is considered to be the estate. As a creditor, Alan Martin has a legal right to be paid from the estate.'

'I've a feeling you're trying to tell me summat I won't much like. What is it?'

Mr Bryce took a deep breath before going on in a quieter voice, 'Unless the money can be repaid in some other way, the farm – the "estate" – will be called in as collateral, and put up for sale.'

'He can't do *that*!'

'Yes, he can. The property will be sold to the highest bidder. Martin will be paid his money from the proceeds, and the residue of any remaining monies from the sale will be paid to your father's benefactor, which of course, is *you*.'

Ben was beside himself. Clambering out of his chair, he lunged forward, his fist coming down on the desk with the force of a sledge-hammer. 'Like hell it will! That farm was my father's, and his father's and grandfather's before him. I'm damned if I'll stand by and see it sold from under us.'

Mr Bryce was not intimidated. He had seen it all before. 'I'm truly sorry, but we may have no choice.'

'We'll see about that!'

'Please. Sit down?' Seeing the despair in that young man's eyes, Bryce wished he had taken up any profession other than that of a solicitor. 'Let's see what alternatives there are.'

Deaf to everything but the questions in his own mind, Ben walked the floor for a while, constantly running his hands through his hair and groaning about the injustice of it all. 'I won't let it happen,' he muttered. 'Mam's only just beginning to come to terms with one great loss. If she loses her home on top of everything else, it'll be the end of her.'

'Mr Hunter – sit down. Please!'

Clenching his fists one into the other, Ben leaned over the desk. 'Will *you* talk to him? Ask him if he'll let me pay the loan back so much a month?'

'Have you no capital at all?'

Ben tried to explain. 'We don't go short, and we

don't waste anything. We pay our bills and do a bit of bartering with the neighbours. But there's never any spare cash as such.'

'Very well. Is there anyone who can lend you the sum of money you need to repay the debt?'

'No.' Hanging his head, Ben knew in his heart there was no one with a small fortune like that going spare. 'Even if there was, I don't know if I could bring myself to ask. We're not a borrowing family, y'see. There were pressing reasons why Dad got himself into this kind of debt. He's never done it before that I know of.'

The older man was perfectly aware of the reason for the loan. 'You've nothing to reproach yourself with,' he assured Ben. 'You're here trying to do the best you can for your family, but sometimes a man can only do so much.'

He saw the desolation in Ben's eyes and was saddened by it. 'Your father would have been proud of you.'

'Not if I lose the farm he wouldn't.'

'Did he ever tell you he was putting the farm up against the loan?'

'No.'

'I see.'

'Please! Ask Alan Martin if he will change his mind. I'll work my fingers to the bone to pay back the loan. Tell him that.'

Mr Bryce could not promise anything. 'I can but try.'

'That's all I ask.'

The two men shook hands.

Mr Bryce stood at the office window, watching Ben stride away down the street. 'You're a good man, Ben Hunter – much like your father. But Alan Martin is another kettle of fish. He said no when I asked him before: I can't see any reason why he should change his mind.'

Walking back to his desk, he sat there for what seemed an age, tapping his pencil against the wood, and going over everything he and Ben had discussed. 'I'm sorry,' he murmured, 'but I don't think there is anything I can do to stop the farm being sold.'

It was a daunting prospect, and he was not looking forward to the day when the Hunters' property went under the hammer.

As it surely must!

Chapter Six

'GEROFF! YOU'RE TICKLING me.' Patsy Holsden collapsed in a fit of the giggles as her husband frantically filed at her toe. 'Aah! Geroff, you daft bugger. I can't bear it.'

Steve took no notice; in fact, now that he had the corn on the run, he worked even more vigorously. 'I'm sorry, gal, but this corn's got to come out, unless you want your foot to turn septic.'

'Stop tickling me then, will you?' Stretched on the sofa with her foot elevated to his knee, she felt horribly at his mercy.

Steve tweaked her toe. 'If you sat still instead o' jiggling about, I'd have the job done in no time.'

'All right. But be quick.' Fearing murder, she gritted her teeth and closed her eyes. 'Don't go digging too deep,' she pleaded. 'The first drop o' blood an' you'll have to stop.'

'I never knew you were such a coward,' he teased.

'I'm not,' she argued. 'It's you. You're too heavy-handed, that's the trouble.'

'Come on now, love.' Knowing her from old, he realised she would have to be cajoled rather than bullied. 'Keep your foot still and let me do my job.'

They were a close couple, these two. Married these thirty-eight years with two daughters, they were as much in love as ever. They knew each other's moods and habits, and when there was a conversation going strong, they often answered the other's question even before it was put.

Steve was the quiet, reliable one.

Patsy was the mother figure. With her caring nature and homely manner, she radiated warmth and confidence.

Their daughters, different as chalk from cheese, were the light of their lives, though while Louise was dependable and content, Susan was something of a heartache.

Lying there, trying not to think of what her husband was doing to her toe, Patsy wondered about Susan. 'She's such a worry, that one.'

'Who, our Susan?' Steve guessed. He daren't look up, in case he sliced her toe clean off.

'Who else?' Patsy sighed.

'Now don't go getting yourself all riled up about

our lass,' her husband counselled. 'She's big and ugly enough to take care of herself.'

'What a thing to say. Our Susan's not ugly!' Like any mother, Patsy imagined her children were beautiful, whatever their failings.

'It's just a saying. I never meant she were really ugly, you daft 'aporth!' Agitated, he looked up; Patsy moved her foot and the edge of the razor jabbed her toe. 'Jesus, woman!'

'You clumsy devil!' With an almighty shriek she was off the sofa and hopping round the room. 'I knew you'd do that. I told you to be careful!'

'Give over, woman. Come and sit down. I'm almost done.'

'Oh no! You are not touching my foot again, not now, not ever.'

With that she swung her leg up and resting her foot on the arm of the chair examined the wound, though it was only a small, pink puncture, hardly noticeable to the naked eye. 'Look what you've done.'

He peered at her foot. 'It's nothing.'

'Says *you*!'

'It were your own fault, going on about our Susan and fidgeting like a two year old after I asked you to keep still. She's a grown woman, for Gawd's sake.'

'Men!'

'Look, love, our Susan's in her twenties. It don't matter what *we* say, she'll do whatever she pleases, you know that. Time and again we've tried reasoning with her, but does she pay any attention? Does she 'eck!'

'She's hot-headed, that's why.'

'All I know is this; she makes the two of us fall out among ourselves. Every argument we have is because of her, and you're partly to blame, for not letting her get on with it. When she comes a-cropper, she'll realise her mistake soon enough.'

'I know, but I do worry about the lass.'

Steve watched her hobble to the kitchen. 'Let me see to that toe, love,' he tried one more time. 'It'll only take a minute.'

'NO!'

'Hmh! It's easy to see where our Susan gets her stubbornness from.'

'Pity she didn't get an ounce o' common sense from me an' all. It might help her to stop and think what she's doing.' Limping across the kitchen, Patsy washed her toe under the tap then dabbed it with Germolene ointment. 'I fancy a mug o' cocoa. Do you want one?'

He thought a moment. 'Aye, go on then, love.'

A moment later Patsy returned from the kitchen with a tray containing two mugs of steaming hot cocoa and a plate of ginger biscuits. 'Lovely.' Her husband's face lit up at the sight. 'I've always been partial to a gingernut.'

Plonking a mug of cocoa into his hand, she sat herself down, groaning as she leaned back to enjoy her cocoa. 'Bloody hell, Steve, you've not done my toe any good, I can tell you that. It hurts like merry hell.'

'I'm sorry.' He took a long sip of his cocoa and leaning back on the sofa, told her firmly, 'All the same, I were only trying to help. So will you stop making such a fuss about it, please?'

'But it *hurts*.'

'Aye, well, I've said I'm sorry, so let that be an end to it.'

There followed a moment of contentment while they each drank their cocoa. The mood changed when Patsy brought up the subject on both their minds at that moment. 'I am worried about our Susan though.'

'Oh, why's that?' He hoped ignorance might be the best policy.

'You know very well why.' They had talked about it often enough these past few days. 'I don't like her hanging round with that fella.'

'We don't even know who he is, or even if there *is* a fella.'

'*I* know who it is, even if you don't.' Her instincts had always served her well. 'She's seeing Jacob Hunter, I'm sure of it.'

'You don't know any such thing. I should think

our Susan's got more sense than to mix with *that* bad lot. As for you, you'll not get no peace till you let her live her own life. She'll find out her own mistakes soon enough.'

'Whatever will we do with her?' she asked despondently. 'Susan won't listen to anything I say, and now, God help us, if she *has* picked up with Ben's brother, he'll find a way to break her heart, you'll see.'

As was his way, Steve let her remark play on his mind before giving a response. 'Are you certain about all this?'

'I'm never wrong, you know that. I wish to God I were.'

'But . . . Jacob Hunter of all people.' Leaning forward in his chair, he regarded her with concern. 'It doesn't make sense. Why would she want somebody like him, when she can have anybody she sets her cap at?'

'I reckon it has to do with our Louise.'

'Now you've lost me altogether.' A woman's mind was a mystery to him.

'Well . . .' Though it stuck in her throat she had to say it. 'All her life she's wanted what our Louise has got; her little red bicycle instead of her own blue one; if the pair of them had a new coat she'd throw hers aside and demand Louise's, and what about that nice lad on Montague Street? Him and Lou were the best of friends at school, until our Susan stirred trouble between them, and won him away from her.'

'That were a long time ago, love.' Although Steve remembered it like it was yesterday. At the time it caused a lot of rows and upset, leaving young Louise in tears. 'Look, it were just kids' stuff,' he finished lamely. 'It didn't mean nothing. Louise got over it, didn't she?'

'Yes, after a fashion, but she cried for days. It was a nasty business, and it were Susan who caused it.'

'I don't see what all that has to do with her going about with Jacob.'

'Because she hasn't changed, not really. It's just the same now. Louise buys a new frock and Susan has to go one better, even if she can't afford it. It's like a competition to see how she can get one over on her sister.' Patsy sighed.

'If that's the case, why hasn't Louise said summat?'

'Because she won't, will she? In spite of Susan's nasty little ways, she thinks the world of her. She wouldn't have anything said against her sister when they were children, and she'll not have anything said against her now . . . though for the life of me I don't know why!'

He smiled at that. 'Because for all her faults, you're both fond of Susan.'

'That may be. After all, she's our own flesh and blood, but I don't mind admitting I'm worried she might come between Ben and Louise.' It was more than a feeling, for she had seen the way Susan looked at Ben, though thankfully he wasn't yet aware of it. 'It's just like the lad on Montague Street all over again,' she murmured. 'Susan resents Louise having a man like Ben for her husband. If she could cause an upset I'm sure she would, and to hell with the consequences.'

Shocked, Steve looked up. 'You're not making sense, love. How could our Susan come between Louise and Ben? An' how would Susan going out with Jacob cause trouble for Louise?'

'Because Jacob Hunter would walk over hot coals for our Louise. Susan might think there's a relationship starting there and so she means to get in first.' Throwing her arms out in a gesture of helplessness, she confessed, 'I don't pretend to know what goes on in that devious little mind of hers. All I know is she's out to make trouble for Louise, and there's not a thing I can do about it.'

'Look, lass, like you, I can't imagine what our Susan might be thinking, but Louise wants no part of Jacob, surely? You told me yourself how he asked her to go away with him when he found out the farm was to be sold – and what did she do? She told him in no uncertain terms to bugger off and keep away!'

He lowered his voice. 'By hell! It's a damned

good job Ben never found out about it, or he'd have had Jacob's head clean off his shoulders.'

'Happen that wouldn't be such a bad idea.' Patsy looked her husband in the eye. She had not been surprised when Louise had told her that Jacob had visited the cottage while Ben was out in the fields. As it turned out, Louise had seen him off with the shotgun, but it had played on Patsy's mind ever since. 'I wouldn't have minded if she'd shot him clean through the head with that shotgun!' she said.

'By! That's a bit vicious for you, ain't it, love?'

'I'm frightened, Steve . . . frightened that he'll cause trouble in this family. He's up to something, and whatever it is, Susan's playing right into his hands.'

She paused, her mind racing ahead. 'I'll tell you something else an' all . . .'

Steve anticipated her thoughts. 'I know what you're thinking, and I feel the same way. You reckon he had something to do with the notice being served on the farm, don't you?'

She nodded. 'I know it seems unlikely, but I can't help the way I feel. Susan should keep well away from him. I still wouldn't put it past that silly girl to think that by going out with Jacob, she were somehow getting one over on our Louise.'

'Get it out of your head,' Steve advised gently.

'It's a known fact that Jacob is besotted with Louise. Jacob can't do Ben and her any harm; they're too much in love, and you know it.'

'Yes, but *Susan* may not know it. She's up to something, I'm sure of it.'

'I see.' Although he didn't. Puzzled, he took a sip of his cocoa.

'No, you don't,' Patsy smiled. 'Only a woman can understand another woman's thinking.'

But Steve wasn't listening any more. His thoughts had already taken another direction. 'Do you really think Alan Martin will put them out on the street?'

'Well, according to what's been said, he's already served notice. The farm is due to go up for auction next week, unless it gets bought beforehand.'

'Has Ben been able to raise any money yet?'

'No, but if I had that kind of money he'd be welcome to it and no mistake,' Patsy said fiercely.

'Huh! We should be so lucky.' Her husband gave a wry little laugh. 'If we worked till we were a hundred, we'd never see the like of that kind of cash. Folks round here are all the same. They work for a wage and come Tuesday the money's gone, and they're already waiting for the next pay-packet.'

'You're right love. To tell the truth, I never really thought he'd be able to raise the money to buy back the farm.' She smiled, a sad smile. 'I'll tell you something for nothing though. It'll break his heart to see that place go.'

'Aye, but go it will.' Steve was ever the realist. 'Unless a miracle happens, and in case you haven't noticed, miracles are few and far between round these parts.'

'I always thought Alan Martin was a friend of Ronnie's.'

'Aye, and so he was. He lent Ronnie the money when nobody else would.'

'So it's true then?'

'What's that, love?'

'That there are no friends in business.'

'Look, Pat. It's simple enough. Alan Martin lent his money to Ronnie; Ronnie popped his clogs before he could repay the debt. Now Martin wants his money back. Ben can't pay him, so he's taken on a solicitor to recover his money from the estate, and if that means selling the farm and land with it, there's nothing can be done.'

'Well, I think it's wicked.'

'Mebbe. But it's the *law*.' He gave a long shuddering sigh. 'The pity is, that Ronnie gave his word to put up the farm against the loan.'

'What if the farm sells for more than Ronnie owed?'

'Well, having been left the farm by his dad, Ben should be entitled to what's left over after the debt is paid. If the auction goes well, there should be more than enough to set him up, in a smaller way o' course.'

'What if it goes badly? What if there aren't many folks with money enough to buy it?'

'I wouldn't like to say.'

'And what about old Sally, eh?' Patsy wanted to know. 'What must all this be doing to her?'

Her husband slowly shook his head. 'Gawd only knows.'

'I've already told Louise they can all come here if need be.'

'Well o' course, that goes without saying.' All the same, at the risk of sounding insensitive, he had to remind her, 'We've only the one spare room, mind . . . and the front room downstairs. But no matter, if the worst comes to the worst, we'll put the three of them up the best way we can.'

Pausing a moment, he went on quietly, 'It's not a permanent solution though, is it? And what's going to happen to their belongings and such? We've no room to store anything.'

Patsy had already spoken to her daughter on that very issue. 'It won't come to that,' she explained. 'According to Louise, the house, land and all the furniture is down as belonging to Ronnie's estate. Everything will be sold, except for Sally's personal belongings, and Louise and Ben's bedroom furniture, which they bought with their own money so they did.'

Deeply disturbed, Steve turned the whole thing over in his mind. 'It never rains but it pours.' Taking a long, slow breath, he let it out in a sigh. 'Poor devils. I shouldn't think any of them have slept a wink this past week or so.'

A simple man with simple ambitions, Steve Holsden had never experienced such shocking things as were going on with Ronald Hunter's farm. 'Thank God I've never been in a position where I might lose our home, so happen I'm not the one to judge. All the same, love, I reckon there should have been a way out of all this, without turning good folks out of house and home . . . especially when one of 'em's an old lady, just lost her husband an' all!'

Having exhausted his emotions, he leaned back in the chair to regard Patsy with a pained expression. 'If Ronnie knew what a mess he'd left behind, he'd be turning in his grave.'

When at that moment the door was suddenly flung open, they almost leapt out of their skins. 'It's only me!' Bouncing into the room, Susan flung her arms round her mother. 'Missed me, have you?' From the smell on her person it was obvious she had been on the booze.

Releasing herself from Susan's hold, Patsy rounded on her. 'Have you been drinking again?'

'No, I haven't!' Indignant as ever, Susan scowled at her parents in turn. 'Why should you think that?'

If there was one thing Patsy hated, it was being lied to. 'Don't take me for a fool,' she chided. 'I can smell the booze on you.'

Susan laughed it off. 'All right then, I might be a bit tipsy, but look!' She flung out her arms. 'I haven't come to any harm.' Giggling, she ran to the door and reaching out, caught hold of Jacob's arm. 'See?' Drawing him in from the passage where he'd been skulking, she announced proudly, 'This here's my fella, and he's brought me home, safe and sound.'

Patsy and Steve could hardly believe their eyes; the sight of Jacob Hunter in their living room momentarily stunned them into silence.

'What's the matter with you both?' Looking accusingly from one to the other, Susan threw a sulk. 'You're acting as if you've never seen him before.'

It was Steve who answered, and it was to Jacob he addressed himself. 'It might be best if you leave now, young man.'

'No!' Defiant, Susan turned to Jacob. 'Go on, tell them how you looked after me all night.'

'That's right, Mr Holsden.' The idea that he had them riled was a pleasure to Jacob, but he didn't show it; he was a man who played his cards close to his chest. 'Susan's all right with me,' he said. 'She had a good time tonight ... we both did.' In a defiant gesture, he put a possessive arm round the girl's waist. 'Only she had too much to drink and got a bit merry, so I thought I'd best fetch her home.'

Grabbing him to her, Susan smiled at Patsy. 'Don't you think he looks handsome?'

Patsy pretended not to have heard, but on discreetly glancing at Jacob, she could see how he might turn a young girl's head. Immaculately dressed, in expensive green-cord jacket and grey trousers, with a white silk cravat at his neck, there was no denying he presented a dashing picture.

Susan was full of it. 'We went to the club in Manchester. I was the proudest girl in the room.' After kissing him on the mouth she crossed the room to drape her arms round her father. 'Don't be angry with Jacob, Dad,' she pleaded. 'It was my idea to go there.'

'Then you should have had more bloody sense.' Getting out of the chair, Steve took a step towards Jacob. 'I think I asked you to leave, young man.'

Jacob's smile was for Susan. 'See you tomorrow then?'

Before she could answer, Steve came between them. 'Close the door on your way out, will you?' He made no pretence of his dislike for Jacob. 'You never know what bad thing might be lurking out there in the dark.'

Disappointed, Susan insisted on walking him to the door. 'They'll get used to you,' she told Jacob. 'Give it time.'

Closing his arms round her he drew her close. 'I don't give a sod if they do or if they don't.'

Giggling, she kissed him on the mouth. 'Neither do I.'

Drawing her down the steps and into the cellar doorway, he held her close. 'So, you'd defy your own parents on my account, would you?' He liked the feeling of power he had over her.

'You know I would.'

Sliding his hand up her skirt, he stroked her thigh; at the same time kissing her with a passion that shook her. When he broke from the kiss, he whispered softly, 'What d'you think your sister would say if she could see us now?'

Taken aback at the mention of Louise, Susan looked away in a sulk. 'What's *she* got to do with us?'

'Nothing.'

'That's all right then.'

Having fooled her, he kissed her hard on the mouth. 'You've got me all worked up now.' He was a man after all, with a man's feelings, and if he couldn't have Louise yet, her sister would do in the meantime. 'What say we go for a walk . . . away from here?'

Realising he wanted her again, she wagged a finger and giggled. 'You randy devil! We've already done it once tonight. You'll have to wait until tomorrow.'

'Oh? Gone off me already, have you?' He could play her silly little game if he had to. In the end all he wanted was her sister.

'You know I haven't, only me Mam and Dad will be waiting for me now. I'm already in their bad books.'

He thrust her aside. 'You'd best get indoors then, hadn't you?'

When he strode away she was left staring after him, feeling bad and wishing she hadn't turned him down. 'I'll see you tomorrow,' she called, but he had already turned the corner.

Climbing the three steps to the front door, she looked longingly down the street. 'I'll not turn you down again,' she muttered. 'I don't want you looking to Louise instead of me. Besides, she's had her chance. Now it's mine!'

❧

HAVING LEFT HER behind, Jacob leaned against a wall and lit a cigarette. Taking a deep drag, he sneered, 'Silly bitch! She thinks I fancy her. I'm using her, that's all. It's Louise I want, and it's Louise I'll have.'

His obsessive thoughts were rudely interrupted when a woman of the streets strolled up. 'You shouldn't be on your own.' Stroking his trouser leg, she sidled up. 'A good-looking fella like you should be tucked up warm in bed.'

Tempted, he looked her over. Tall and slim with a thick mass of hair, she wasn't too badly used. 'You're right,' he said. 'So what d'you reckon then?'

Leaning forward she licked his mouth. 'I reckon you and me should go to my house. It's cosy there.'

'Go on then.'

'It'll cost you.'

Pushing her off, he asked cagily, 'How much?'

'No more than you can afford.'

'Right then. What are we waiting for?' Dropping his cigarette to the ground he stamped it out. 'Lead on.'

Doing as she was bid, the woman walked in front. Keeping a discreet distance, Jacob followed. 'See what you're making me do, Louise?' he whispered. 'It's not what I want!'

The woman paused. 'What was that you said?'

'None of your business!'

'All right, all right. No need to shout.' With that

she went on at a faster pace, in case he should lose interest.

Arriving at the door of her house in Bent Street, she turned to invite him inside, but he was gone. 'Why, the sly bastard!' Disgruntled, she gave the door a kick. Then she shrugged her shoulders, and went off in search of some other lonely soul.

'I didn't think much to him anyway.' She often talked to herself. 'He were a miserable bastard, if ever I saw one!'

HIS ARDOUR TEMPORARILY subdued, Jacob found a pub and a game of cards underway. 'Mind if I join you?'

There were five men, all experienced in the art of card-playing. 'Know how to play, d'you?' The speaker was a big gruff man with a long, straggly moustache.

'I know enough.'

'Got your stake, have you?'

Taking out the roll of notes he'd won on the horses the previous day, Jacob threw it on the table.

The big man grinned. 'I see you're a bit of a gambler.'

Jacob didn't like being put to scrutiny. 'Gambler or not, it's good money,' he snarled. 'So – am I playing or what?'

'Hmh!' The big man nodded. 'Yer a man after my own heart.'

Seating himself, Jacob picked up the hand he was dealt. It was a good one.

He smiled to himself. Tonight hadn't been wasted after all.

Chapter Seven

LOUISE WAS LIKE a cat on hot bricks. 'Where is he, Sally? I woke up at six o'clock and he were gone. I've been down as far as the meadow and I've walked to the top of the lane, and there's no sign of him anywhere.'

Tucked up in her armchair, Sally laid down her newspaper. 'Don't worry, lass,' she said. 'You know what he's like. He'll have gone off somewhere to think things through.' Peering at the girl over her spectacles, she asked, 'Has he said much to you, about the farm going?'

Louise shook her head. 'He's hardly said a word these past few days.' Falling into the other armchair, she looked at Sally with troubled eyes. 'Oh Sal, he's taking it real bad,' she said. 'I've told him we'll be all right, but he can't get used to the idea that he won't be working his father's land any more.'

Sally laid down her spectacles. 'I never thought it would come to this.'

'I know.' Louise saw the desolation in the old woman's eyes. 'It's a terrible thing, Sal, and nobody knows that better than you, but we can't change it. We've no money to speak of, and Alan Martin won't even discuss Ben's idea, so we've no choice but to make a new life for ourselves.' She smiled reassuringly at the old woman. 'We can't do that if we don't pull together.'

Sal regarded her daughter-in-law with renewed respect. She knew the young woman felt every bit as bad as Ben and herself, yet here she was, being rational and sensible while she and Ben were falling apart at the seams. 'By! Yer a grand lass, Louise. An example to us all, that's what you are.' She paused for a moment, trying to come to terms with what lay ahead. 'There's Ben walking the hills first light of a morning, 'cause he can't sleep; and then there's me – I'm so deep in thought about it all that yer can be talking to me and I don't hear a single word. I've gone right off me food, and when I do manage to eat, I'm so taken with indigestion I feel like summat they've dragged up from the quarry.'

Laughing at herself, she said fondly, 'I'm sorry, lass. We're neither of us much use to you, are we?'

Louise's answer was to come and give her a hug. 'I won't have you talking like that. You and Ben are *everything* to me.' Holding onto Sal's hand, she told her, 'It's only right that you should both be upset. I mean, this farm has been in your family for generations, and now, because of Alan Martin's refusal to let Ben repay the debt in his own good time, the farm has to go. It's no use hoping for a miracle, 'cause it won't happen, an' we all know it.'

Sally let out a great withering sigh. 'D'you know, love, I can't imagine anybody else living in this cottage ... in this here room, where I've spent many a happy hour alongside my Ronnie.' Her eyes grew moist and her voice shook. 'We made our lives here when we were first wed. We raised our two sons and worked the land and loved every minute of it.' Her voice breaking, she dabbed away the tears. 'Where did it all go wrong?'

Louise didn't need to answer, because both women knew who was to blame, and now, Sally spoke it out loud. 'I've raised a bad 'un,' she said bitterly. 'I should have drowned him at birth!'

Taken aback by the vehemence in the old woman's words, Louise gently reproached her. 'No, Sally, you don't really mean that. Do you?'

Sally smiled, though her eyes remained sad. 'No, lass. You're right. However bad he is, he's still my flesh and blood, more's the pity!' Her voice hardened. 'Though to tell the truth, I don't ever want to set eyes on him again. If he hadn't been the lazy no-good bugger he is, my Ronnie would never have had to take out that loan in the first place. But you see, much as Ronnie could never respect Jacob, he couldn't turn him away neither. We never gave up hope that he'd come right in the end. But he never did. And he never will.'

'It doesn't matter whose fault it is. It's too late to worry about all that now. The plain truth is, we've got to move. It won't be easy, but we'll survive. We'll have to!'

Frowning, the old woman turned away. 'I can't understand why he didn't tell me. He *always* told me everything – but not about that loan. I recall the day Jacob came up and the two of them were talking in the shed. I heard Jacob shouting and then he went away, and Ronnie came in, all upset he were. But he never told me what they'd been talking about. All he said was how it were time Jacob stood on his own two feet, and that he were ashamed of him.' She looked up. 'I've been thinking about it a lot, and I expect he never told me, because he didn't want me to worry about money and that.'

'I imagine you're right, Sal.'

'I should have known though. I can't see how I missed it.'

'What d'you mean?'

'Most o' the money we took were *cash*, d'you see? It came from the market-stall, and from the folks who came to the farm and paid for their vegetables and eggs – all in cash.'

'I don't understand.' Louise hadn't discussed it too much with Sal, because the old lady had been too upset. 'What's that got to do with the loan?'

Like a conspirator, Sally moved to the edge of her seat. 'Every Sunday night, Ronnie would get all the cash together, ready for the bank on the Monday morning.' She pointed to the table. 'He'd sit there and he'd count it all into one big pile, entering it into the book as he went. Then one day, everything changed. It were the Saturday after Jacob had been to see him. He put on his best shirt and tie, and he went out – "on business", he said. By! He hadn't worn that suit since the boys were christened.'

'Where did he go?' Louise was intrigued.

Sally shook her head. 'He never told me that neither, but I've been thinking, and I reckon it must have been Alan Martin he went to see . . . about that loan for Jacob. Well anyway, soon after that, Jacob came to see him again, and this time they went into the front room. They weren't in there long afore Jacob were on his way, and Ronnie came back and sat here with me.'

'And did he say anything then?'

'No. We had us cocoa and went to bed, same as usual, but he didn't sleep. He were agitated, like. I asked him what were wrong, but he told me to go to sleep, that he needed a breath of air. He went out, and I lay awake till he came back. After that, he would count his takings in the front room.'

Her old face wrinkled as though it was an effort to remember. 'One night I took him in a cup of tea, and I couldn't understand why he were counting in a different way . . . one pile to the left, which was entered in the book, and another pile to the right . . . which was *not* entered. Y' see, lass, that pile must have been the repayment off the loan.'

Louise understood now, but, 'It's all water under the bridge,' she said sadly, and Sal had to agree.

'When do we go and look at this house in Derwent Street?'

Viewing what might have to be their new home was something that both Sal and her son had been putting off, but now, after her long conversation with Louise, the old woman could see how it might be wise to at least have a look at the place.

'Whenever you're ready.' Louise was delighted. For days now, Sal had been refusing to come and see the house. 'We can go tomorrow if you like. I've got the key until five o'clock.'

'Aye, go on then, lass. We'll take our Ben an' all, eh?'

'Good idea. If you like it, me and Ben will make it nice for you, I promise.' However painful it was, they had to be realistic. 'The auction is next week. We've a lot to do and a short time to do it in.'

Leaning back in her chair, Sal seemed easier for having talked everything through. 'Happen it might not be so bad,' she said, and when she smiled, it was a meaningful smile. 'Look, lass, being as you cooked the breakfast, I'll do the washing up. Meanwhile, you'd best get off an' find that man o' yours. I expect he'll be ready for your company about now.'

Relieved that she was getting through to Sal at long last, Louise gave her a hug. 'I'll not be gone long,' she promised. 'I've an idea he might be in with Eric, so I'll make my way there now.'

Firstly, because it always struck cold in these old cottages early on a morning, she piled a few more logs on the fire, then, satisfied that the old woman was all right, she put on her coat and beret and set off at a run, across the fields and down towards Eric Forester's cottage. 'He must be there,' she told herself. 'I've looked everywhere else.'

———❧———

E RIC'S COTTAGE WAS of the picture-postcard variety; painted white, with a thatched roof and tiny lead-light windows, it had stood proud near the spinney for many ancient years. Inside, with the fire crackling cheerily in the hearth and the smell of freshly brewed coffee permeating the air, Eric stood at the window, absent-mindedly listening to Ben's outpouring.

Yet, even while he listened, his mind was wandering.

These past few days, since it became clear that the Hunter family were bound to lose the farm, he couldn't stop himself from wondering how it would be without Louise near. Only now, when he really thought about it, did he realise her going would leave a gaping hole in his life that no one else could ever fill.

He had tried hard not to think about her, because when he did, he was filled with shame and guilt; his feelings towards Louise were a shocking betrayal to his best friend, and right now Ben had more than enough to cope with.

As, ironically, did Eric himself!

Engrossed in his thoughts, he almost leapt out of his skin when Ben's anxious voice sounded in his ear. 'You didn't hear a word I said, did you?'

Concerned about Eric's lack of attention and the worried look on his face, Ben had come across the room to speak with him. 'What's wrong, mate? You seem miles away . . . staring out the window with a look on your face that says you've got the weight of the world on yer shoulders.'

Eric mentally shook himself. 'Sorry, I was just

thinking.' He thanked the Good Lord Ben wasn't able to hear his treacherous thoughts.

Putting his broad hand on Eric's shoulder, Ben asked, 'You're not worried about me and the family, are yer? Because if you are, there's no need. I know I've been half out of my mind, but Louise gave me a good talking to, and it made me think. She said I mustn't break myself up over all this business. She said we'd be all right, that we've got each other and we can face whatever comes up. I reckon she's right. Oh, it'll take time, it's bound to. But it's not like we're totally penniless, is it? We've got a few quid put by, and when the farm's sold, there should be a reasonable sum coming in, so when it comes right down to it, I'm better off than most. Besides, once I get used to it, I might even *like* living in Blackburn town.'

Eric turned to look at him. It was the kind of look that said, 'You're lying.' And it drew a truthful response from Ben.

'All right!' Ben thumped Eric playfully on the shoulder. 'Happen I *won't* like it. But that's between you and me.'

His longing gaze went to the fields beyond the cottage. 'It won't be easy, that's for sure.' His words faded to a whisper, his memories like a hard fist in his chest. 'I've been a part o' them fields all my life,' he murmured. 'I know every bump and dip, every inch of every acre. I've climbed every tree and swum the river more times than I can remember. And once, before Jacob showed his true colours, we raced from the old quarry all the way up to the cottage.'

He smiled at the memory. 'When we started out we didn't think it was that far. By! It very nearly crippled us, I'm telling yer. But neither of us would give way to the other. Me legs were buckling under me, and me lungs felt as if they'd burst wide open. I desperately wanted to stop, but I forced myself to keep going.'

He laughed aloud for the first time in days. 'I'd have run my heart out, rather than let my big brother get the better of me. But my God, it were hard. By the time we got to the cottage we were so hot and out o' breath, we were just about ready to faint. Our mam had to swill our faces with cold water afore we recovered proper.'

'Young and foolish, eh?' Eric smiled. 'Precious times.'

For a long nostalgic moment, both men were steeped in their own quiet thoughts, when suddenly Eric imparted his own shocking news. '*I've been given notice to quit.*'

Ben was astounded. 'What?' With mouth wide open and eyes big with shock, he stared at Eric, unable to believe his own ears.

His friend explained. 'The estate's been sold and

the new owner doesn't want my services – he's fetching in his own people. So, I've been given my marching orders. I'm to be out of here within the month.'

'My God! I can't believe it. I never thought old Jonesey would sell Salmesbury Manor, not in a million years.' Ben let out a deep sigh, then looked Eric in the eye. 'And here's me, so swamped in my own troubles I didn't even know. I'm really sorry, mate.'

'So am I.' Like Ben, Eric had pleasant memories of his life here. 'I were only seventeen when I took the job of gamekeeper to the gaffer in the big house. Then some years later, soon after you brought Louise to live in the valley, I moved into this cottage, and d'you know, Ben, I've never been happier.' That was mainly because in one way or another, he had caught sight of Louise every day since.

Unaware of Eric's deep feelings towards his wife, Ben told him, 'You've been a good friend to me over the years. If I can help, you know I will.'

Eric acknowledged these words with a thoughtful nod of the head. 'There's nothing you can do to help, but thanks all the same.'

Ben was still shocked by the news. 'I'll tell you what, though, the new folks can look far and wide, but they'll not find any man o' *your* calibre, an' that's a fact.'

The two men talked a while longer, until Louise came to the door and Ben went away with her.

From the front doorstep, Eric watched them leave. When Louise turned at the brow of the hill, he waved to her and she waved back. 'You'll be all right, Ben,' he murmured. 'With a fine woman like your Louise, you won't go far wrong.'

Long after they had gone from sight, he stayed on the doorstep, Louise's image strong in his mind. 'I'm sorry, Ben,' he said, almost in despair. 'I'm about to do something that will test our friendship to the limits. I hope to God you can forgive me.'

Head down and thoughtful, he returned to the kitchen, where he sat for an age, searching his heart for a way out, and finding none.

For too long he had agonised over what to do. Now, he must press ahead with his decision.

Later, he would have to face the consequences, whatever they might be.

Chapter Eight

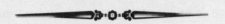

Having thought it through, Eric put the plan to his employer. 'What do you think?' he asked. 'If I went ahead, would I be asking for trouble?'

Arnold Jones was a big, hairy walrus of a man. Patient by nature, he had listened to Eric's bold plan and been amazed that this quiet man could even consider such a daring proposition. 'I can't advise you one way or the other,' he answered sombrely, 'but if you really intend to go ahead with it, and are ready for any eventuality, then I don't think that I, or anyone else, could dissuade you.'

Having said that, he peered at Eric through probing eyes. 'Are you sure you know what you're doing?'

Eric had no doubts. 'I've thought about it long and hard, and yes, sir. I'm very sure.'

'I see.'

'I haven't made the decision lightly, but now that it's made, I won't change my mind.'

'I can see that.' The older man did not altogether agree with Eric's intention, but he admired his resolve. 'Perhaps you'd care to join me in a brandy? I'd like to know more about this plan of yours.'

'Yes, sir, that's very kind of you. Thank you.'

With so many worries playing on his mind, Eric had not been sleeping well. It was good to talk things over with someone else. If it had been any other matter than the one he had in mind, he would have turned to Ben. But because of the nature of his plan, that idea was most definitely out of the question.

'Right then.' Handing Eric a glass of brandy, Arnold Jones sat himself behind his desk. 'Start at the beginning,' he suggested. 'That's always the best way.'

And, with his heart in his mouth, Eric began.

While he outlined what was on his mind, the estate clerk from the outer office had her ear to the door.

Once she got the gist of what Eric Forester was planning, she could hardly wait to spread the word.

———◆◆◆———

TWO DAYS AFTER he had been to see Arnold Jones, Eric was walking back from the river where he'd been fishing. The daylight was closing in fast, but he didn't mind. In fact, this was the time he loved best of all. And besides, he was almost unaware of the fading light, because his mind was alive with thoughts of Louise.

Nearing the cottage, he began whistling. Behind him the leaves on the trees were stirring in the heightening breeze. 'Brr!' Suddenly the evening seemed to have taken on an eerie chill. 'Feels like a storm on the way,' he said aloud, quickening his steps.

He was almost home when he heard another sound . . . like the soft tread of a creature in his wake. He turned, but it was too late. Leaping out of the darkness, the two men gave him no chance to defend himself. Grabbing him from behind, they threw him to the ground and beat him senseless. Using fists and wooden poles and the hard edge of their boots, they showed not an ounce of mercy.

When they were satisfied, they melted silently into the woods; leaving Eric face down on the ground, seemingly lifeless and covered in his own blood.

The night thickened and still he lay there, unmoving.

He would lie there until morning, by which time Ben would find him, and raise the alarm.

T HAT SAME NIGHT, Jacob paid a visit to a neighbouring farmer by the name of Barry Jackson.
'What d'you want with me?' The man was in his
forties, a dedicated and hard working farmer who,
like Ronnie Hunter, had contentedly worked the land
all his life. 'You're Jacob Hunter, ain't yer?' he asked.
'Ronnie's eldest.'

Jacob stood silent.

Sensing trouble, the other man peered at him
through narrowed eyes. 'Get away from 'ere! I don't
want your sort on my land,' he told him. 'We all
know how you treated your father and you should
be ashamed. Go on – be off with you!'

When Jacob made no move the older man shook
his fist. 'Are you deaf or what? Get off my land afore
I throw you off!'

Jacob took a step forward. 'I'll go,' he answered
menacingly, 'when you tell me what I want to know.'

'Oh aye, an' what's that then?'

'I've heard you're thinking of going after my
father's farm when it comes up for sale the day after
tomorrow.'

'Well you 'eard right, then. It's good land an' it's
up for the taking, so why shouldn't I go for i—'

The words caught in his throat as Jacob took
hold of him by the shirt collar. 'You listen to me,'

he snarled. 'Go anywhere near that sale, an' you'll rue the day.'

Shaking himself free, the older man was defiant. 'You don't frighten me, you no-good bugger you! You can say what you like, but I'll be at that sale. I've me money ready, an' the men to work the land. Besides, if I get the farm it'll be a damned good thing. At least it'll be kept in fine fettle, just like it were when your poor dad were alive. Your brother ain't got the means to buy it, but I have. So! Threats or no threats I'll be there when the bidding starts, an' if all goes well, I'll have the deeds to that place afore you know it.'

Closing the door in Jacob's face, he issued a threat of his own. 'Go on! Clear off an' be quick about it, afore I set the dogs on you!'

In the same instant the door banged shut, Jacob clicked his fingers and out of the darkness came two shadowy figures. 'See to him!' Jacob whispered harshly.

Then he turned away and left them to it.

◆◇◆

J ACOB HAD TAKEN a reluctant liking to Maggie, the prostitute who had accosted him that night he'd seen Susan home. Although he'd given her the slip that time – had gone to a pub instead – he remembered the number of the house in Bent Street and was now a regular visitor there.

Tonight was no different.

'You're late.' Dressed in a short black slip and wearing pink furry mules, Maggie had loosened her long hair and taken extra care over her make-up; the end result being curiously pleasing to the eye.

Surly as ever, Jacob pushed past her. 'I had business to attend to,' he snapped. 'Besides, I've told you before . . . no woman keeps a watch on me. You'd do well to remember that.'

Used to his moods, she dared not rise to his comments. Instead she closed the door and followed him inside.

Without turning to look at her, he asked, 'Where's the brats?'

With a mother's instinct, she walked towards the back bedroom and stood in front of the door. 'They're asleep,' she said, lowering her voice. 'They've been asleep these past two hours.'

'Lock them inside,' he ordered. 'I don't want them coming out when I'm here. You know I can't stand kids round me.'

With her children's safety uppermost in her mind, Maggie opened the bedroom door and peeped inside. Hannah, four, was lying half out of her bed, one arm turned up towards the pillow and her long chestnut-coloured hair spilling like autumn across the pillow.

The boy, Adam, aged six next birthday, was sleeping on his side in the bed by the wall; his thick, dark hair tumbled over his closed eyes, and a dog-eared *Beano* comic lay open beside him.

'I thought I told you to lock them in!' Having drunk from the whisky bottle got from the cupboard, Jacob was lolling against the wall, his avaricious eyes ravaging the woman's long, bare legs.

Quickly, she turned the key in the lock, and slipped it under the clock on the nearby dresser. She didn't want the children coming out while Jacob was here. Not because he had dictated it, but because she didn't trust him not to harm them.

Coming to where he stood, she offered, 'I can make you a cheese sandwich, or some chips, if you're hungry? It won't take long.'

Snatching her by the waist, he growled deep in his throat. 'Stupid cow! It's *you* I want,' he said, 'and I won't take long neither.' His searching hands began roaming her lower regions.

She laughed. 'Feeling randy, are you?'

Kissing her hard on the mouth, he pulled down the straps of her slip, laughing out loud when he discovered she had nothing on underneath. 'You brazen little bitch. You're half-naked.'

Sidling up to him, she undid his shirt and fondled

his bare chest. 'I must have known you were on your way,' she teased.

As always he had no time or inclination for the niceties of courtship. 'Come on then.' Taking her by the hand he propelled her into the front bedroom, where he threw her onto the bed. 'It's strange how a tot o' whisky can make any woman seem attractive.'

It was an insult that cut deep. But she had to humour him, or lose the few shillings he paid her.

Removing his clothes, he climbed on top of her. 'You'd best not have had another fella here today,' he warned. 'You know what I told you.'

A rush of fear showed in her eyes. 'I haven't forgotten your instructions,' she said. 'I'm to see other men at weekends, and keep myself for you in the week.'

Running his hands through her hair he yanked her towards him. 'You'd do well to keep that in mind. Otherwise I might have to get nasty, and we don't want that, do we, eh?'

Her answer was to reach up and wind her arms round his neck. It was an invite, but Jacob didn't need her permission. His women's needs and feelings were of no concern to him. He took them when and how it suited him.

And that was what he did now.

When afterwards he climbed away without a

fond word, she felt saddened and degraded. But she made no comment. She was used to men who treated her like the dirt under their shoes.

Later, when they sat round the table enjoying a sandwich with Maggie chattering and Jacob silent, she told him, 'There's a lot of talk going about.'

'What kinda talk?' Stretching out his legs he put his arms up behind his head and stared at her through tired eyes. Feeling like a fat cat who had been at the cream, all he wanted now was to sleep it off.

'According to gossip in the shop today, somebody's putting the frighteners on any man who has a mind to bid for your dad's farm.'

'You don't say?' Reaching for the whisky bottle he took a long, hard swig, afterwards smacking his lips before asking slyly, 'What else did you hear?'

'Nothing.' She began to think she'd said more than enough already.

'What the devil are you doing anyway, listening to idle gossip. Keep your nose out of it if you know what's good for you.'

'I'm not one to gossip, you know that. I went in for a loaf and a pound o' spuds for the kids' teas. The women were talking, and I couldn't help but overhear, that's all.'

Fearing he might let slip the truth, he changed the subject. 'Them brats o' yours . . .' Turning his head he glanced towards the bedroom door.

Instinct made her sit up, ready to protect them if she had to. 'What about them?'

'Do you reckon your old man would take them off your hands?'

'He might, if I was to let him, which I won't.'

'Why's that? He's their dad, ain't he?'

'He's not having 'em. The kids are better off with me.'

He laughed at her. 'You're a prostitute, for God's sake. You lie between the sheets with all kinds of men. What sort of a mother does that make you, eh?'

Bristling with anger, she forgot to be meek. 'I'm a *good* mother! All right, I have to earn a living the only way I know how, but it feeds and clothes them, and I love them as much as any other woman loves her kids. As far as I'm concerned, that's all as matters.'

She stole a glance at him and was disgusted with herself. Slouched in front of the fire, with the whisky bottle in his hand, his face flushed from the heat and booze, she began to question the wisdom of letting him into her life. He was right. To her shame she had been bedded by many men, yet none were so cruel or insulting as this one.

When suddenly he turned unexpectedly to stare at her, her heart almost stopped. 'What the hell are you looking at, woman!'

Quick as a flash she came back with the answer. 'I was just thinking what a handsome man you are.'

He liked that. 'Too good for the likes of *you*, that's for sure.'

'Are you staying the night?' If he stayed it would be extra money, and that was always welcome. Whether he was welcome or not, was a different matter altogether.

He looked away. 'I might. I might not. I'll let you know when I decide.'

There was a moment when she felt his hostility and was afraid. At times like these she thought it best not to antagonise him. 'Whatever suits you is all right by me,' she said, and left it at that.

'What if I wanted you to be rid of the brats. What would you say to that, eh?'

Taken aback, Maggie thought it best to hedge. 'Why would you want rid of them?' she asked nervously. 'They never get in the way.'

'Send them to your old man. Let him pay for their upkeep.'

'I've already said . . . I won't do that.'

His face stiffened. 'You might *have* to!'

'He's not fit to have 'em.'

'Is that so?'

'He's a spiteful bastard.'

'A bit like *me*, is that what you mean?' The look he gave her was a warning, which she wisely took to heart.

'No, I didn't mean that,' she lied. 'But he's a

nasty piece of work. He's got a temper like a mad bull. Two years ago, on Hannah's second birthday, I gave her a little party – nothing grand, we couldn't afford that. Just a few toddlers and a cake I made myself. Only she dropped her piece o' cake on the rug and he went crazy.'

'Hmh! Can't say as I blame him.'

'I didn't know until afterwards when Adam told me. I'd gone down the street to walk the other kids home. When I got back, Hannah was under her bed screaming, an' Adam was fighting his daddy off. The poor little bugger were black and blue where he'd belted him. I reckon if I hadn't come back he'd have killed the pair of 'em.'

'Aye, well, kids can make you do things like that.'

'Not *my* kids! The next morning, I waited till he'd gone to work, then I packed our bags and I've not looked back since.'

'If you were *my* wife I'd have tracked you down and given you the hiding you deserve!'

Getting out of her chair, she collected his empty plate and took it together with her own, into the scullery, muttering under her breath, 'It's just as well I'm *not* your wife then, ain't it?'

'WHAT DID YOU SAY?'

Maggie poked her head round the door. 'I were just thinking, it'll be nice to have somebody to cuddle up to in bed tonight.'

'Well, it won't be me, 'cause I'm off to my *own* bed.' Without waiting to say goodnight, he tipped a handful of coins onto the table, threw on his coat and went.

'Can't say I'm sorry to see the back of you, neither!' Maggie told him through the front window.

As always she went into the children's rooms and kissed them goodnight. 'Your mam loves you,' she whispered as she tucked them both in one after the other.

'Love you too, Mam.' That was Adam.

She gazed down at his dark uplifted eyes and her heart sang. 'Goodnight, sweetheart,' she said, and softly departed the room.

Not yet tired, she sat by the dwindling fire for a long time, cradling a hot cup of tea until it went cold. 'Why would he ask me to get rid of my kids?' she wondered aloud. 'Happen he intends us setting up house together, eh?'

She chuckled at that. 'I can see us, squashed in those tiny lodgings he's got above the chippie. Heaven help us, no thank you very much, and anyway, there's no man nor woman alive as'll make me get rid o' my kids.'

She thought about Jacob, and imagined herself on a more permanent footing with him. 'It might not be so bad if only I could persuade him to accept the children. But, oh, wouldn't it be grand not to have all kinds of men coming here at all hours. And how long will it be afore the children know what's going on?' The thought gave her nightmares.

'That Jacob's a nasty bugger, but he never goes without paying for my services.' She rattled the coins in her pocket. 'That's 'cause he knows the door would be locked against him next time if he didn't fork up.'

For a moment or two, she allowed herself to imagine life with a man like Jacob. 'Happen I could tame him in good time,' she mused. 'If I learned to keep my trap shut, it might not be so bad.'

She thought on it a while longer, before getting out of the chair. 'We'll see,' she murmured. 'I dare say time will tell what's in store.'

Now, with the tiredness creeping up on her, she put the guard in front of the dying fire, then went into the kitchen and shut the flap on the Formica dresser. With everything secure, she turned out all the lights and made her way upstairs. 'Could I trust him though?' she asked herself. 'Or would I be letting myself in for more trouble than I could handle?'

Like she had already said. Time would tell. Though, if only she could have seen where he was headed at this moment, she wouldn't have given him another moment's thought.

A FTER STOPPING OFF to swap tales with his cronies in the pub, it was 2 a.m. before Jacob arrived in Derwent Street.

There was not a sound to be heard, except for the wailing of mating cats and the occasional clatter of a dustbin lid as it fell beneath some scampering tom's paws. Everywhere was in darkness; every household had gone to bed, all but the house where Louise's mam and dad lived. Here the front-room light was blazing and inside, Susan was pacing the floor, growing more agitated by the minute.

She heard the tapping on the window and when she lifted the curtain, there he was, grinning at her through the glass. 'I'm sorry,' he mouthed. 'Didn't mean to keep you waiting.' In fact, he'd forgotten all about her.

Putting her fingers to her lips, she bade him be quiet; smiling when he made a face. 'I'm going to the door,' she gestured for him to do the same. 'And for God's sake, be quiet!'

Softly she let him in, making him tiptoe to the back room. 'Mam's a light sleeper,' she warned, and because he didn't want his carefully laid plans spoiled, he didn't need telling twice. He had to keep Susan dangling for his affections. That way he believed he would persuade Louise away from

Ben. It was only a matter of time, he was certain.

Once inside the back room she closed the door and opened her arms to him. 'I thought you'd never get here,' she complained. 'I were just about to go to bed.'

Pressing his body to hers, he whispered in her ear, 'Not without me, I hope?'

'Where've you been?' She didn't like being taken for granted.

As always he was ready with an answer. 'I've been talking things over with Alan Martin. Dad's farm is going under the hammer the day after tomorrow. There are things to be talked through.'

'Liar! You stink of beer, and whisky and God knows what else.' Something, in fact, that smelled much like a woman's perfume. 'You've been with some woman, haven't you?' Anger surged up in her. 'I won't be two-timed. Either we're a couple, or we're not. So which is it to be? You'd best tell me now!'

The awful truth was, Susan had fallen under his spell. She hadn't meant to become infatuated with Jacob, but he was different and exciting, and she was all alone.

Jacob, on the other hand, knew his plan was working well. He felt he had Louise's kid sister in the palm of his hand.

And now, as he calmed her fears, he felt her

submitting to him. It gave him a wonderful sense of his own power. 'You're right,' he murmured, caressing her body from breast to thigh. 'I *have* been drinking, but not with a woman. I've spent the evening with Alan Martin. If you don't believe me, ask the landlord at the Swan. He'll tell you the very same.'

Stroking her hair, he drew her to the floor. 'Why would I want any other woman, when I've got you?' Kneeling before her he began to undress her. First her shoes, then her cardigan, and now he was unbuttoning her blouse buttons, one by one. 'I love you, Susan. You know that.' His voice was sweet and soothing, and like a fool, she drowned in his every word. Closing her eyes she let him touch her.

'*Susan?*' Out of the darkness, her mother's voice sailed down from the upper reaches. 'Is there some-body down there with you?'

Scrambling up, she hurried to the bottom of the stairs. 'No, Mam,' she called softly, trying to sound unflurried. 'I were listening to the wireless. I've turned it off now. Night night.'

To Susan's great relief, Patsy could be heard padding back to her bedroom. 'It's all right,' she whispered to Jacob. 'She's gone back to bed.'

Half-naked and still kneeling on the floor, Jacob groaned. 'Oh hell, I've lost it now. I'll never get it up again . . . not tonight anyroad.' He'd had one too many beers, and more than enough lovemaking with the rapacious Maggie.

Seeing him there, his trousers round his ankles and his sad member sagging down his leg, Susan couldn't help but giggle. 'You look a right sketch,' she chuckled.

Suddenly, at the sound of someone coming down the stairs, the two of them panicked. Rushing across the room, Susan stood with her back to the door, arms out wide as if to keep the intruder at bay. Jacob threw his clothes on and holding his trousers up, gasped, 'Which way? For God's sake, woman . . . which way do I get out?'

Pointing to the scullery, Susan gestured for him to go that way. 'Through the cellar. QUICK!' And as he went, hobbling and stumbling, she put her hand over her mouth to stem the laughter.

Patsy was almost at the door. 'What's going on down here?'

Going swiftly across the room, Susan satisfied herself that Jacob was clear. She then threw herself into a chair and waited for her mam to enter. 'Oh, Mam! I were just dozing,' she lied. 'I'm that tired. I'd best get off to bed.'

Patsy was no fool. Regarding her daughter with suspicious eyes, she saw how her blouse was hanging out and her skirt was partway undone. Her shoes were flung haphazardly on the rug, and her face was flushed, even though the fire had long since gone out.

'You're going nowhere, young lady, till you tell me what you've been up to down here.' Taking a step forward, she stopped when a noise caught her attention. 'What's that?'

Susan sat bolt upright. 'What? I never heard nothing.'

Turning quickly, Patsy hurried to the front room. There she went straight to the window and on looking out, saw Jacob making good his escape, frantically dressing himself as he went.

Having followed her mam to the front room, Susan knew the game was up, though she was not prepared for the slap across the face her mother gave her. 'You lied to me!' Patsy was mortified. 'I *knew* you had somebody here and you lied to me!'

Susan retaliated. 'I'm no longer a kid, Mam! I'm old enough to have whoever I want, at any time of the night or day, and you can't stop me!'

'Not in my house you're not.' A look of utter disgust shaped her kindly features. 'Look at yourself.' Patsy's contemptuous gaze went from Susan's dishevelled hair to her unkempt clothes and bare feet. 'How could you? Jacob Hunter of all people! My God, you could do better than him without even trying.'

Whether it hurt Susan or not, she had to voice her suspicions. 'It's our Louise, isn't it? You've got a warped idea that by going out with Ben's brother, you can get your claws into Ben?'

'No, Mam, you're wrong.' The tears ran down Susan's face as she tried to explain. 'All right, I did think like that at first, but not now. I love Jacob, Mam. I really love him.'

'Oh, lass.' Patsy had always known when Susan was lying, and she knew the girl was telling the truth now. 'What kind of a mess have you got yerself into, eh?' Putting a strong arm round her daughter, she said, 'You mustn't see him again, lass. Promise me you'll send him packing for good an' all.'

'I can't, Mam.' Susan broke away. 'I *won't*!' With that she ran up the stairs and into her room.

Alone, Patsy contemplated the future. 'My God, can't she see the danger? If she gets tangled up with that one, there's no telling where it might end.'

But, knowing Susan, there was little she could do, except tie her to her bed and lock her in, but that would be like trying to cage a wild animal.

'No, lass. You've got yerself into this mess,' she sighed. 'There's nobody can get you out of it, only you.'

Chapter Nine

INSPECTOR LAWSON STOOD up to leave. 'So, as far as you can tell, Mr Jackson had no enemies to speak of?'

Ben could think of none. 'Barry were a man who spoke his mind and nobody's ever been known to win an argument over him, but no, I can't think of anybody who might want to *murder* him.' He gave a wry little smile. 'They might not have agreed with everything he said, but folks round 'ere respected him for his straightforward manner.'

'What about Eric Forester? Did he have any enemies that you know of?'

Ben didn't have to think twice about his answer. 'Never! All the farmers he worked for hereabouts, and his old employer Arnold Jones will tell you the same. Eric Forester is a gentleman . . . minds his own business and works hard from morning to night. As far as I can tell, he shouldn't have an enemy in the world.'

'So you've no idea who could have attacked him?'

Ben shook his head. 'None at all.' He'd had the shock of his life when he'd found Eric lying there battered and hurt. 'Thank God he's all right. Apart from a deep gash on his neck, and a few sprains and bruises, he's come through in one piece. At least he's alive.'

The whole business had been playing on Ben's mind. 'Why anybody would want to do such a thing is beyond me.' Turning away, he stood at the firegrate; his two arms stretched outwards and his fists closed round the mantelpiece. 'By! If I could get my hands on the bugger who did it, I'd swing for 'im an' no mistake!'

Having sat quietly, listening to the two men, Louise had a question for the Inspector. 'Do you think Eric was attacked by the same man who killed poor Barry?'

The policeman considered her question for a minute, before admitting, 'At this stage we can't be certain, but I can tell you one thing; we believe it was more than *one* person who attacked them. From what we know, there were at least two, if not more.'

'Have Mr Jackson's family been informed?' Louise asked quietly. Her heart went out to them. 'From what he told me once, they live somewhere in Ireland.'

The Inspector nodded. 'We've already notified them,' he revealed. 'We discovered their whereabouts from documents found at his house.'

Having thanked them for their help, he followed Ben to the front door, where he spoke to him in a whisper so his wife couldn't hear. 'Best keep vigilant, Mr Hunter,' he warned. 'What with one man hurt and another dead, you might want to watch your back, if you know what I mean?'

Ben understood. 'Thanks, I'll bear that in mind.' After seeing the Inspector off, he returned to the living room, where he told Louise, 'I don't want you wandering about the fields on your own at the moment, pet. It's not safe any more.'

She promised. 'What's going on, Ben?' she asked worriedly. 'Why would anybody want to kill Barry, of all people? And why would they attack Eric like that? Were they robbers, d'you think?'

'No, lass. I asked the Inspector the same question afore you came down. He said there was nothing taken, and no sign of intruders. Eric was attacked out in the fields, and he still had his wallet in his inside pocket. Barry was found on his doorstep by the milkman. Neither properties had been rifled.'

'So *why* were they attacked?'

Ben, too, had been puzzled by events – and

like his wife, he could find no sensible answer. He shrugged. 'Your guess is as good as mine, lass.'

'There were gypsies on the top common last week.'

'It weren't them. According to the Inspector, the police checked them out. It seems they were miles away when the attacks took place.'

Louise still found it hard to believe that men like Barry and Eric had been the victims of such brutal attacks. 'So who would want to hurt two good men like that?'

A voice from the passage put a stop to the conversation. 'Can't smell no breakfast cooking!' The door opened and in came Sally, still yawning and looking like something the cat dragged in. 'Why didn't you wake me?' Glancing at the mantelpiece clock she gave a groan. 'Good God. It's half-past nine.' Rubbing her eyes she slumped down in the armchair by the empty grate. 'I'm that tired, I could have slept till suppertime.'

Ben strode across the room. 'Morning, Mam.'

She lifted her face for a kiss. 'Morning, son. I heard you talking. You and some man.'

'The police.'

She lowered her gaze. 'Oh.'

Knowing how low Sally had been of late, and how hard she was trying not to let things get her down, Louise came up behind her and, putting her arms round her, she said fondly, 'I heard you in the night, wandering up and down. Couldn't you sleep?'

Sally patted the girl's hands, drawing them tighter round her neck. 'Oh lass, I'm sorry. I didn't mean to wake you. Only, it's one thing after another lately. First my Ronnie, then the farm being sold tomorrow, and now some madman going round attacking folks. What next, I wonder?'

Ben intervened, sounding cheerful and optimistic. 'What's next, Mam, is that we move to that nice little house on Derwent Street. We've all seen it and it's not that bad at all . . . needs a bit o' decorating and suchlike, but after the debts are settled, there'll be some money coming in from the farm, so we'll soon have the place shipshape and homely, you'll see.'

'And it's just down the street from our mam,' Louise reminded her. 'You and her get on well, don't you?'

Sally nodded. 'Patsy's a dear, kind soul.' She smiled up at Louise. 'Like mother, like daughter.'

Embarrassed, the girl rolled her eyes. 'See? You'll be able to go on shopping trips and catch the bus into Blackpool if you've a mind. You won't be isolated, not like you are here.'

Sally knew they were trying to soften the blow, and she was grateful for that. But her heart was in this farm and always would be. Still, she wouldn't be so cruel as to dash their hopes for her. 'It all sounds nice,' she answered. 'And besides, we've no choice, have we? Not once this farm goes.'

'Look, Mam.' Concerned, Ben knelt before her, his hands on the arm of the chair and his eyes entreating her. 'I know it won't be easy. This farm has been your life, just like it's been ours. But we can't change the way things are . . . I only wish to God we could! It won't be so bad. We'll do the house up, and any money left can go into the bank, for a rainy day. I'll find a job – happen I'll get meself a little van and do a bit o' farm delivering or summat. We'll not go short, I can promise you that.'

Sally cupped his face in the palms of her hands. 'I know you'll do your best,' she acknowledged. 'And I know you'll take care of us.' Her eyes grew moist. 'Your dad knew it an' all, God bless him,' she said brokenly. 'If only he'd managed to pay back what he borrowed, none of this would have happened. But he couldn't, and we can't blame him for that. So, for *his* sake, we'll make it work, won't we, eh?'

'You bet we will.' The tears burned deep in his throat, but he kept them at bay. He was a man, and men didn't cry; not even when faced with a mother's heartache and the loss of their home.

All the same, he had to walk away from that sad little face and look out the window, or he might well have shown the emotions he was working so hard to suppress.

Louise saw how his shoulders bowed and she knew the pain he was going through. These days emotions were running high. 'I'll get the breakfast on,' she suggested, though Sally's question kept her there for another minute.

'What did the police want?'

'They just wondered if we knew of anybody who might bear a grudge against Eric and Barry.'

'Shocking business. I've known both men for longer than I care to remember . . . Ronnie spent a lot of time working with Barry, and Eric was always on hand when needed.' Coming on top of everything else, the latest news had been a severe blow.

Seeing how upset Sal was, Louise wisely changed the subject. 'Right then, Sal. What d'you fancy – eggs, bacon . . . tomatoes?'

'Have you and Ben had your breakfast?' Sal wanted to know.

'Not yet. I was about to get it ready, when the Inspector knocked on the door.'

'Good. We can have us breakfast together.'

'So, what's it to be?'

'What are you having?' Sal wasn't all that hungry.

'I fancy bacon and egg, smothered in tomato

sauce, with two slices o' toast alongside.' Louise smacked her lips. It wasn't often she had breakfast, but this morning for whatever reason, she was starving.

'I'll just have a slice o' toast and a few fried tomatoes,' Sal volunteered, 'with a mug o' tea to wash it down.'

'That's not much.' Louise worried about her.

'It's enough, lass.' Getting out of the chair, she told Louise, 'I'll make the tea and toast, and no arguments mind!'

While Sal pottered about, Louise got the breakfast going, and soon the whole house smelled of fresh, hot toast and sizzling bacon.

'Go on then.' Seeing the bacon curling and cooking in the frying-pan, Sal's tummy started to grumble. 'You can put a slice o' that bacon on me plate if you want.'

In a short time they were all seated round the table, content in each other's company, but each with their own, worrying thoughts. 'D'you think the farm will bring a high price?' Though she hated raising the subject, Louise was anxious to plan ahead.

'Your guess is as good as mine.' Ben toyed with his food, eventually pushing his plate away. He never stopped hoping. 'Happen we can still come to some agreement with Alan Martin.'

Louise was more realistic. 'It won't happen,

love. You've been all through it with the solicitor. The farm's been taken for the loan, and it's to be sold on the open market.' She knew the anguish he was going through, and had to be strong for him. 'You'll have to face it, Ben. Tomorrow, the farm will be sold. If there's money left after the debt's been repaid, then it'll be yours. But unless a miracle happens and we find the money to repay Alan Martin today, this farm will belong to somebody else.'

Sal had been silent, but now she reached out and took hold of her son's hand. It broke her heart to say it, but it had to be said. 'I'm sorry, love, but Louise is right, and hard though it is, we all have to face up to it.'

Ben raised his eyes and there was so much torment there that both women were deeply moved. 'I know,' he murmured. 'I know, and there's nowt I can do about it.' He had tried every which way to save the farm, but it was no good. He knew what the outcome would be, and he could hardly bring himself to think about it. 'I can't believe some stranger will be taking over here. It's not right!'

Scraping back his chair he stood for a moment looking from one woman to the other; his pretty wife Louise who had stood by him for ever, and his frail old mother, quietly breaking her heart yet not showing it. And here he was, a grown man who should know better, yet still unable to cope with what was happening.

A deep sense of shame took hold of him. 'I don't deserve you,' he murmured. 'Either of you.' Squeezing his mother's hand he smiled on her, then kissing the top of Louise's head, he strode away. 'I'm going for a walk,' he said. 'I might just drop in and see how Eric is.'

'That's a good idea,' Louise said. 'Tell him, if he's finding it difficult to make his meals, he's welcome to join us anytime, even if it's only on the spur of the minute.'

Sal was in agreement. 'There's allus enough for friends,' she added. 'We've not gone by the wayside yet.'

Ben gave a nod and went on his way.

'He's put his heart and soul into this place,' Sal remarked. 'He'll find it hard, living in a street of back-to-backs. He's used to space round him, d'yer see? And endless green fields as far as the eye can see.'

Louise was well aware of it, but, 'It'll be hard for *all* of us, Sal,' she answered. 'All the same, I hope he does go and see Eric. He'll know what to say and Ben is bound to listen.' She smiled at the thought of Eric, his lopsided grin and that canny way of putting you at ease. 'Eric's a good friend.'

ERIC SAW HIM coming from afar. 'Dammit! It's Ben.'

Swinging round, he addressed the other man in pleading tones. 'I hope you don't mind, sir, but I think it might be best if you leave now,' he said. 'If Ben sees you here, he'll know there's summat up, and I can't lie to him. If he asks, I'll have to tell him the truth.'

'Why not tell him now and get it over with?' Arnold Jones had come to the cottage to discuss final arrangements with Eric about the loan. 'My God, man! It's not a crime. You're borrowing money from me to buy the farm. Where's the harm in that? The farm *is* going up for sale, isn't it?'

'Well, yes, but—'

'And you have as much right to bid for it as any other man, isn't that so?'

'Yes, it's true what you say. But I'd rather tell him in my own good time, sir, if you don't mind.'

He had thought long and hard about making a clean breast of things to Ben, but had come to the conclusion that there was no point causing friction between them until he was sure of his position. 'The bidding might go way above my head, so if I told him I was going after the farm, and then couldn't afford to bid for it, I'd be losing a friend for nothing.'

'Look, Eric, I've already told you, I can lend you as much as you need. I know you're capable of working the Hunters' farm and I have no doubt but that you will return an excellent profit. Bear it in mind, at least. I'll place no limit on what you borrow tomorrow. It's an open cheque, good for whatever you want to pay.' He walked to the back door. 'I'll leave it to you.'

Eric was adamant. 'I've set myself a limit, sir, and it's what we already discussed. I'll not go a penny over it.'

'As you will.' Passing through the door, Jonesey paused; turning to Eric he apologised, and not for the first time. 'I'm truly sorry about this,' he said. 'You've been the backbone of the estate for many years and now I've put you in a bad situation. If I hadn't sold up, you wouldn't be having to move at all. So, whatever you want to pay at the auction is all right by me. I know I'll get it back, sooner or later. The papers are already drawn up to our mutual satisfaction. As you know, I've made sure that, in view of the sad situation regarding the Hunter family, you've been well safeguarded in the agreement.'

Eric thanked him. 'I appreciate that.' Then a movement outside caught his attention. 'Quickly, sir. He's coming up the path.'

By the time the knock came on the front door, followed by Ben peering into the room, Eric's visitor had already left via the back door and was making his way across the fields. Jonesey looked the proper squire in his knee-boots and tweeds, but he was a good man, and Eric was grateful for his offer of help.

'It's good to see you, Ben.' Eric hobbled across the room, his gaze going beyond Ben to the outside. 'On your own, are you?' He had hoped Louise might be following.

'I needed to be on me own,' Ben confessed. 'I've been out a while. I walked a mile or two up by the river then made my way here across the long field.' He gave a shuddering sigh. 'By! It's so peaceful. There can't be no place like it in the whole world.'

Seeing how the sweat poured down Ben's temples, and hearing his laboured breathing, Eric imagined he must have been deeply troubled to walk himself into such a state. Anxious for this honest man whom he was about to betray, he put a friendly hand on Ben's broad shoulder. 'You look done in, mate.'

'I'm all right now,' the other man replied. 'I had some thinking to do. I needed to clear me head and get some air into me lungs.' He smiled, a sad, weary smile. 'I tell you what though, I'm that parched, I'd kill for a pint glass o' something cool. Does Mrs Jones still bring you a jug of her home-made sarsaparilla from time to time?'

Eric was mortified. 'Good God! What am I

thinking of. Come in, Ben, come in! Make yourself comfortable an' I'll see what I've got.'

Instead of seating himself, Ben followed him through to the kitchen. 'I'm glad to see you're walking easier.' He knew Eric had suffered a severe blow to the knee in the attack. 'How are yer feeling . . . in yerself, I mean?' A closer look at Eric's face revealed the many cuts and bruises; the angriest of all being the deep red gash from temple to jaw, extending to his neck.

'I'm doing all right.' His wounds causing him to stoop awkwardly, Eric rummaged in one cupboard after the other. 'For the life of me, I can't think who might have wanted to give me a hiding like that.' It crossed his mind that Ben himself might want to do the very same, come tomorrow.

'Bloody cowards, whoever they are.' Ben's disgust was obvious. 'If somebody's got a grudge against yer, why in God's name couldn't they come right out and face you with it in daylight, 'stead o' creeping about in the dark like wild animals.'

'Well, I've puzzled my brains ever since, and I can't think of anybody who'd go for me like that.' Eric straightened from his task for a moment. 'And what about poor Barry, eh? The gaffer told me about it. Jesus, Mary and Joseph! Barry was always a straight talker and sometimes he said more than he should have, but I can't believe anybody would murder a man for speaking his mind. So *why* was he killed? What's it all about?'

Ben shook his head, his mind going over all that had happened. 'Beats me,' he answered thoughtfully, 'but one thing's for sure . . . there's a bloody madman on the loose. The sooner they catch him an' lock him up where he belongs, the better for us all.'

Groaning from the sustained stooping, Eric resumed his task of searching the cupboards. 'I were sure I had a jug o' sarsaparilla here somewhere.'

'Give us a look, matey.' Easing Eric aside, Ben searched the cupboards again, his fist soon closing on the object right at the back. 'Is this it?' He drew out a large earthenware jug.

'That's it.' Eric got out the glasses, and Ben pulled the cork. Eric explained as they went back into the living room, 'The boss's wife still sends me lots o' things – plump rhubarb pies, baskets o' veg and mountains of apples in the season.' He paused. 'I'll miss all that when they're gone.'

'I'm sure yer will.' Ben was sorry for his friend's predicament, but if truth were told, he was even more sorry for his own; after all, he had a family to take care of, while Eric had no responsibility, except to himself. 'Have yer found anywhere yet?'

Eric almost choked on his drink. 'Er, no, not yet.' Giving a little cough, he took a deep breath. 'Look, Ben, there's something I should—'.

He was on the verge of confessing his intention to bid for the farm, when a knock came on the door; it opened immediately to admit Louise. 'Hello, you two. Can I come in, or is it fellas only?'

'You're welcome any time, you know that.' Eric scrambled out of his chair, wincing. 'Would you like a glass o' sarsaparilla?'

Assuming she would be thirsty after her long walk, he hobbled into the kitchen. 'Or I'll make some tea if you prefer.' Blushing to his roots, he stumbled over his words. Every time she looked at him, he felt like some lovesick schoolboy.

Following him to the kitchen, Louise leaned on the door-jamb. 'It's all right, thanks.' She absentmindedly brushed her hair back, from where the summer breeze had blown it over her face. 'I'm not staying. I just got worried when Ben was gone for so long. Then I remembered he said he might drop in and see how you are.' She shrugged. 'So I thought I'd take a walk in the sunshine.'

Steadying himself with one hand on the wall as he went, Eric crossed the room to her. 'If you're certain?'

'I am.' Louise accompanied him to the living room, where Ben had drained his drink and was ready to leave. 'Are you sure you're all right?' he asked, and Eric assured him he was.

'Come to supper with us tomorrow night,' Louise

offered. She had it in mind that once the sale was over, Ben might need a friend to talk to.

Knowing what he knew, and feeling ashamed about it, Eric muttered a thank you. 'We'll see.' He couldn't help but wonder if he and Ben would be at each other's throats by tomorrow night.

'Oh, go on. It'll be nice, the four of us.' Taking him by the lapels, Louise smiled up at him, her eyes sparkling with mischief. 'I'm baking steak and kidney pie,' she tempted, '. . . with new potatoes and baby carrots pulled out of the ground this very morning.'

'Sounds wonderful.' When she smiled up at him like that, he found it hard to draw his gaze away.

Chuckling, Ben hurried across the room. 'Come away, yer little devil.' Taking his wife by the waist, he swung her round, and to her surprise, not too gently. 'Yer embarrassing the poor fella.'

The truth was, just now when she smiled up at Eric, he felt a surge of jealousy; even though he knew she meant it in all innocence.

Louise persisted, only this time more gently. 'I'm sorry,' she told Eric, 'I didn't mean to bully you. But you look as if you need friends about you right now.'

Before Eric could answer, Ben intervened again. 'Leave him be, Louise. The poor sod's been through enough without you going on at him.' Addressing Eric he said, 'All the same, matey, the invitation's there if you want it.'

'Thanks, both of you.' Eric had sensed Ben's animosity and had, like Louise, been taken aback by it.

'Right then, come on, you.' Propelling his wife through the door, Ben told Eric, 'It's good to see you on yer feet an' in good fettle. All the same, yer know where we are should yer need us.'

Softly, Eric closed the door behind them. Making his way to the window, he watched them go along the path; Ben with his arm round Louise, and she hurrying along beside him. They made a perfect couple, he thought.

'Farm or no farm, you're a lucky man, Ben Hunter,' Eric murmured. 'You might lose one cherished possession tomorrow, but you'll be keeping the best one of all.' Guilt washed over him again. 'I nearly told you,' he whispered. 'If yon Louise hadn't come in when she did, you'd have known what a bastard I really am!'

But his mind was made up. The situation was not of his making, and if he missed the opportunity to stay here where he was content, someone else would buy Maple Farm. It would make no difference to Ben who bought the place. Surely Ben himself would see that?

Seating himself in the chair he agonised over his decision. 'If that lass were mine, I wouldn't care *where* I lived. I'd be happy on a canal barge if she were with me. But she's your woman, Ben . . . not mine. So, if I'm to be lonely, I'd rather be lonely here, in this place among familiar things, than in the hustle and bustle of town, in a street full of strangers.'

His thoughts dwelt on the morrow.

'I'm not looking forward to being at that sale, but if the farm comes within my reach I'd be a bloody fool not to take it. So, I'm hoping, Ben, that if I find myself bidding for your house and home, you can find it in your heart to forgive me. After all, we're grown men and reasonable.'

But it wasn't just Ben's reaction that was worrying him. 'And what about Louise?' he asked himself.

His heart lurched. 'I don't think I could live with it if she turned against me.'

A T THE TOP of the hill, Louise paused to catch her breath. She had seen the look on Ben's face when she and Eric were talking, and ever since they had left the cottage, her husband had said not a single word. Instead he was brooding and silent.

Now, as he strode ahead, Louise called him to a halt. 'Just now, in Eric's house, why did you grab me like that?' she demanded angrily. 'What were you thinking of?'

Turning his back to her, Ben grumbled an

answer. 'Fancy him, do yer? Feel sorry 'cause he's taken a battering, is that it?'

Louise couldn't believe what he was saying. 'Don't talk rubbish!' Running to catch him up as he strode on, she tugged at his sleeve. 'Eric's a friend. I thought he was *your* friend, too?'

'Hmh! The way you were looking up at him, he must'a thought he were *more* than a friend.'

Clutching his arm, she brought him to a halt. 'Is that what you really think?' she asked incredulously. 'For God's sake, Ben! This is *Eric* we're talking about. I could no more think of him like that than I could a brother.'

Her words rang so true he was filled with shame. Turning his face to look down on her, he saw those puzzled eyes and the bright truth in her face, and he loved her so much it hurt. Taking her in his arms, he apologised. 'I'm sorry, lass,' he said. 'I don't know what I'm saying half the time. It's this business about the sale tomorrow. I'm all churned up at the thought of it.'

Louise pressed him close to her. 'I know,' she murmured, 'but I won't have you thinking things like that.' She smiled up at him, her smile easy and inviting. 'You know there's only one man for me.'

His heart racing, he drew her to the ground. 'Prove it,' he whispered.

And there, beneath the summer skies with the

sun warm on her face and the grass cool beneath her back, she gave herself to him.

Afterwards, content together, they ambled on, talking about tomorrow and how, in Louise's words, 'We'll cope, whatever happens.'

In her heart though, she feared the outcome.

These past few days had taught her things about Ben that she had never known before. Things that had taken her by surprise; like the way he had seemed to distance himself from the family when they needed to pull together, and that awful suspicion, when he imagined he had seen something happening between her and Eric.

Now, because of what Ben had thought, and in spite of herself, Louise was astonished to find she was beginning to see Eric in a different light.

Of all the surprises she had endured lately, none was more riveting than that.

Chapter Ten

SUSAN COULDN'T KEEP her eyes off him. 'I'm glad we've made up,' she whispered. 'I couldn't bear it if we were to fall out for good.' Lately Jacob had come to mean more to her than she could ever have imagined. When he was out of her sight she drove herself mad with images of him in some other woman's arms.

She had become hopelessly besotted with the very man she had lured in order to make Ben and Louise jealous. The irony of it did not escape her.

Sliding her arm through his, she sighed, 'I love you, Jacob. I don't want us to argue any more.'

'For God's sake, shut up!' Jacob hissed. He gave her a sharp nudge with his elbow. 'I'm trying to watch the bloody picture!' She irritated him more every time he clapped eyes on her. Even when he hoped it would bring him closer to Louise, he found it hard to bear Susan's company.

'It's too hot in here.' In the past, Susan had been used to getting her own way. She still hadn't grown accustomed to the idea that Jacob called the tune these days. 'Please, Jacob,' she whined. 'I'd much rather go dancing.' Blind to his growing anger, she closed her arms round him. 'Let's go to the Palais in town. They've got a new band on.'

Pushing her away, he told her harshly, 'I'm not in the mood for company. Why d'you think I brought you to the flicks? I thought we could sit quiet and enjoy the picture.' He glared at her. 'I should have known better. You can't sit still for five soddin' minutes at a time!'

Thinking he was weakening, she gently shook him. 'Oh, come on, lover. Let's get out of here.'

'Oi, you!' From behind them came various angry comments. 'Can't yer keep quiet down there? We can't hear a damned thing with you two ranting on. If you don't want to watch the picture, why don't you bugger off out of it.'

'That's it, you tell 'em!' another voice joined in. 'Hey – you down there! Sod off and argue outside, why don't you?'

Angry with Susan for spoiling his enjoyment of the film, and enraged by the abuse behind him, Jacob stood up. 'Who the hell d'you think you're talking to?' he bawled, shaking his fists. 'I've paid my money same as you, and if you don't like it then it's you who can bugger off 'cause I'm not moving.' He squared his shoulders in a show of defiance. 'If you reckon you can throw me out, you're welcome to try.'

When back came another torrent of abuse, he leapt onto the seat, fists held in a boxing stance and a look of madness on his face. 'Who's for it then, eh? Come on, let's 'ave yer!'

Just then, having been alerted by a rankled customer and now hearing the uproar for himself, the manager marched down the aisle towards Row C. Like two little soldiers, the usherettes followed behind.

'Now then, young man, we can't have this behaviour.' Shining his torch on Jacob, he told him, 'You'd best leave, sir . . . you and your friend.' Focusing the torch on Susan's face he warned sternly, 'I don't want no trouble, miss. But if he doesn't listen to reason, I'll have no option but to call the police.' In his experience it was always wiser to caution the woman. They seemed to have a greater fear of authority than did the men.

'Come on, Jacob,' Susan pleaded. 'It won't do you any good if you're arrested, will it?'

'Bloody fools!' Jacob was still boiling, ready for a fight.

'You're the fool, mate.' The voice was thick and

threatening. 'Best do as your woman says and sling yer hook, eh, before some of us lads decide to teach you a lesson.'

'Let it go, Jacob. Don't take any notice.' Susan wanted to get him outside and away, before they got caught up in something bigger than they could handle. 'They're just goading you, that's all.'

'I should take your friend's advice, sir,' the manager said. 'We don't really want to bring the police in, now do we?'

But the manager's words fell on deaf ears. 'Nobody talks to me like that.' Climbing down off the seat, Jacob prepared to seek out the hecklers; the last one in particular, as he had threatened him personally. 'Stand up, you coward!' he yelled. 'Let's see if yer fists are as big as yer mouth!'

When a tall, well-built fellow stood up some two rows away, Jacob thought twice. The sight of that man, built like a tank and slowly thumping one great fist into the other, was enough to put the fear of God into him. 'You'd best watch out,' he warned the big man limply. 'I know your face now.'

When his cowardly comment brought a roar of laughter from everyone there, he knew he'd lost. Pushing his way through the row of arms and legs, he went down the aisle, scowling at everyone as he passed.

Outside in the twilight he ranted and raved at

Susan. 'It's your fault!' he cried. 'You couldn't keep your bloody mouth shut, could you?' Raising his arm he brought his fist crashing down on the side of her face. When she reeled back with a cry he grabbed her by the shoulders and shook her like a rag doll. 'I'll think twice about fetching you again.'

Pressing the flat of her hand against her face she looked up with tearful eyes. 'I'm sorry.'

He thrust her away. 'I should bloody well think so an' all.' Striding ahead he knew she would follow. It was exactly what he wanted.

By the time they reached Penny Street and the canal, his anger had subsided. With Susan some safe way behind, he waited in the alcove between two buildings. It was perfect; dark and shadowy, where a man could see out, but no one could see in.

Smoking his cigarette he waited; slyly smiling when he heard the heels of her shoes tap-tapping on the cobbles. 'Silly cow!' he chuckled. 'If I threw meself into that canal, I'm sure she'd throw herself in behind me.'

As Susan neared the alcove, she began to wonder if he'd deserted her again. 'Jacob?' Barely a whisper, her voice echoed through the air.

Desolate and scared, she looked round with big eyes; this area was not somewhere she would come on her own of a night-time. 'Jacob, where are you?' The fear trembled in her voice.

When suddenly he reached out and took hold of her from behind, she screamed out; the scream was cut short by the flat of his hand over her mouth. 'Ssh!'

Spinning her round he saw the terror in her eyes turn to relief and then to anger. 'Why didn't you answer?' she demanded. 'You scared the life out of me.'

He sniggered. 'It'll do you good to be scared.' Flicking the stub of his cigarette into the water, he drew her towards him. 'Happen if you're scared, you might not be so bloody cocky.'

'What? Like you, you mean?' There were times when she felt she could handle him and times when he made her tremble. But his dark mood had lifted and now he seemed much more amiable.

'Come here!'

Twisting a hank of her hair in his fist he drew her deeper into the dark alcove, where he quickly opened her blouse. Reaching round the back of her shoulders he undid the brassière and let it slide down. Running his hand over the taut curve of her breast, he took immense delight in the touch of her bare skin. 'You're trembling,' he murmured. 'Is that because I'm exciting you?'

'No, it's 'cause I'm bloody shivering.' Though the day had been warm, the evening was chilly, and besides, her confidence had returned enough to tease him. 'But I'm always ready for some excitement.' To prove it she dropped her hands to the fly-buttons on his trousers; one by one she undid them, until she could slide her hand inside. '*He* must be frozen,' she giggled, ''cause he's hard as iron!'

'Like it, do you?' If he knew one thing above all others, it was how to please the women.

'You know I do.'

Jacob needed no encouragement. Right there, in that dark alcove with only the occasional passer-by to hear their grunts and groans, they enjoyed each other to the full.

Shameless to the last, their modesty and their clothes lay about them like so much discarded paraphernalia; until at last they scrambled them back on and walked, arm-in-arm, back to Derwent Street.

As they passed number twelve, Jacob paused, his curious gaze scrutinising the rundown house; from the rotting window-sills to the rusty iron railings that separated the pavement from the cellar steps. 'Is this the one you told me about?' he asked. 'The one where your sister and my brother intend living?'

This was the reason he stayed close to Susan; to find out everything he could about what was going on in his sister-in-law's life. So far, apart from the occasional fiery exchanges between him and Susan, his little ruse had paid off. Through her, he knew everything that went on in his brother's house. He knew the police were nowhere nearer finding the culprits who beat up Eric Forester and murdered his neighbour; not to mention the others who had been warned off, in fear for their lives.

More than that, he knew how Louise was coping. Susan had told him she had paid them a visit the other evening, to tell her mam how she was having a bad time with Ben because he was taking it all so badly. It seemed Ben was trying every which way to save the farm, and only now had he come to realise there was no way out.

Every time Jacob took Susan out, he heard another useful snippet of information. It was worth enduring her company, just to hear about Louise. And the more he heard, the more he believed she would come to him, once he had the deeds to the farm. In his arrogance, Jacob had no doubt at all that Louise would rather live with him at the farm, than in a rundown house in Derwent Street with his younger brother.

Disgruntled, Susan gave him a prod. 'I'm talking to you.'

Momentarily thrusting Louise to the back of his mind, he answered lovingly, 'Oh, I'm sorry, sweetheart. What were you saying?'

Susan suspected he'd been thinking of some other woman. 'You were miles away. What were you thinking of?'

He resented being questioned. 'None of your business.'

'I were only asking. There's no need to talk to me like that, is there?' Disgruntled, she walked on. 'Are you coming in for a minute or two?' she asked sullenly. 'Mam and Dad'll be in bed by now.' It was already gone eleven.

He winked suggestively. 'Don't tell me you're after *more*?' he joked. 'I don't know if I could manage it again, so soon.'

'We could try.' She didn't want him going away to satisfy himself somewhere else.

'Oh no, not tonight, I can't. I'm away to a game o' cards down at the Swan. There's a private party going on, and there's a chair reserved for me. Besides, I've a good feeling about tonight, and I've won a tidy sum lately.' In fact, he'd become something of a dab hand at cards. 'I'll see you tomorrow, eh?'

Disappointed, she watched him go. 'You'll not let me down, will you?' she called, but he wasn't listening. Already his thoughts had returned to Louise. Everything he did, was for her.

When she turned to go inside, Susan came face to face with her mother. 'Where've you been till this time of night?' Patsy wanted to know.

'I've been to the pictures, not that it's any of your business.'

'With Jacob Hunter, I've no doubt.' She thought it wiser to ignore Susan's nasty little comment.

'I'm a grown woman,' Susan protested. 'I can go with whoever I please.' With that she pushed by her mam and, hurrying to the kitchen, went to the sink. 'I'll not be long before I'm up, Mam,' she called out. 'Go back to bed.' She had to clean her face and comb her hair over the mark, before her mam saw how she'd been bruised by Jacob's fist.

It was too late. Patsy had already seen it as Susan passed under the passage light. '*He* did that, didn't he, lass?' She was at the kitchen door, her sorry eyes appraising her wayward daughter.

'He did what?' Keeping her face right-side to her mam, Susan continued filling the kettle.

Coming across the room, Patsy raised her hand and, holding Susan's chin, gently turned her head until the bruise was plain to see. She shook her head in despair. 'What is it about that man, that makes you let him do that to you?'

Snatching herself away, Susan retorted angrily, 'It was an accident!'

Patsy knew she would get nowhere with her tonight. 'If you mean to defend him, then there's nothing me or your dad can do,' she said wearily. 'You're a defiant little bugger, you always have been, but you're not so bad that you have to put up with *that*.'

Taking the kettle to the stove, Susan lit the gas ring and, keeping her back to Patsy, impatiently suggested, 'Go to bed, Mam.'

Instead, Patsy lingered. 'Think what you're doing, lass.' Crossing the kitchen, she put a caring hand on her daughter's shoulder. 'I know you think I'm interfering,' she said quietly, 'but it's only 'cause I'm afraid for you.'

'Well, you've no need. I can look after myself.' In fact, there were times when in Jacob's company, *Susan* was afraid for herself. But she would never admit it, not to anyone.

'Goodnight, love.' She would talk to her again tomorrow.

When her mam was gone and the house was quiet once more, Susan leaned forward on the wall, and sobbed till she thought her heart would break. 'Serves you right, Susan Holsden,' she choked out in a half laugh. 'You thought you could use him, and now he's turned the tables on you, 'cause now, you can't do without him.' It was a sorry state of affairs. *And one which would cost her dear.*

S OME WAY DOWN the street, Jacob lingered outside number twelve. He looked up at the windows and he tried the door handle and stood there for an age; mesmerised by this house, where Louise would soon be living. He imagined her warm, bright soul bringing that house alive, and he bitterly regretted that it would be his brother Ben who would share it with her, when he himself would have given his right arm to be her husband.

But he lived in hopes. Right now it seemed an impossible thing, but he had no intention of giving up. Tomorrow would bring him the farm. After that, it wouldn't be too long before he had Louise as well. He went off whistling. It was all worth waiting for.

Quickening his steps, he made his way to the Swan public house; and that all-important game of cards.

They were waiting for him – four rough-looking men with bulging wallets and a lifetime's experience of gambling.

The weasel-faced man on the far side smiled as Jacob walked in. 'We've been waiting for you,' he said in a thin voice. Indicating the chair on the other side of the table, he invited, 'Sit yourself down, Jacob, and let's see the colour of your money.'

Taking out a wad of notes, Jacob waved it under their noses. 'That do, will it?' He felt confident, a match for any one of them.

All four men smiled back at him, their eyes dark with greed. In Jacob they saw an easy touch and, unlike him, they were well-prepared.

———◆———

I T WAS WELL past midnight when Jacob emerged from the pub. The night had not gone as well as he had hoped. 'You win some, you lose some.' In his heart he wanted revenge, but he did not have the means.

Taking the remaining banknotes from his pocket he held them in his fist. 'Just as well I stopped when I did,' he told himself, 'or I'd have been cleaned out good and proper.'

Having been disappointed in one way, he felt another need. 'I could do with a woman's company,' he grumbled, 'but not Susan. I've had enough of *her* for one night.'

There was only one other woman who gave him what he wanted and asked for little in return, and that was Maggie. Besides, he had another reason for wanting to see her.

'Maggie!' He rolled his eyes to heaven. 'Not the brightest nor the best-looking woman on God's earth, but she'll do when needs must.' And right now, his needs were demanding.

———◆———

M AGGIE WAS IN her bed fast asleep, when the sound of stone chips rattling on her bedroom window woke her up. Rubbing her eyes she glanced at the bedside clock, astonished to see it was almost one in the morning. 'Who the devil's that?' Yawning, she climbed out of bed, gasping with shock when the lino struck cold beneath her feet.

Gingerly lifting the net curtain and opening a window, she peeped out, none too pleased to see Jacob Hunter standing down in the street. 'Let me in,' he pleaded. 'I need to talk.'

'It's too late.' Shaking her head, she called softly, 'Come back tomorrow.'

Taking a pace forward, Jacob would have none of it. 'Please, Maggie, let me in. I really need to talk.'

After making a sign that she would come down, Maggie dropped the curtain and closed the window, shivering. 'Hmh! Needs to talk indeed, the liar. I daresay what he really "needs" is a warm body to curl up against.'

Frozen, she scuttled across the floor to put on her slippers and robe – a flowing pink affair given her by one of her grateful clients. Ned was a young merchant seaman whom she brought home from the pub. They didn't go to bed as had been her intention. Instead, he spent a couple of hours talking to her about his family, and how he missed being at home with them.

Feeling sorry for him, Maggie cooked him a generous supper, took him to her bosom and afterwards, sent him on his way with a lighter heart.

A week later, the robe arrived by post, all wrapped in pretty bows, with a letter attached saying he would never forget her.

'For God's sake, woman, you took yer time, didn't yer?' Jacob was up in arms at being kept waiting in the street.

Just as annoyed at having been woken from a warm bed, Maggie opened the door and stepped aside to let him in. 'What d'you want?'

Unused to having a woman speak to him like that, Jacob found it amusing. 'You're a surly bugger when yer want, aren't yer?' Looking her up and down he liked what he saw. 'Snapping at me when I come to visit. Is that any way to treat a friend who's brought you a present?'

'What present?' She could see nothing in his hands.

From out the depths of his jumper, he lifted a bottle of gin. 'For you,' he said. 'Let's you and me have a drink together, eh?'

Maggie closed the door. 'You smell like you've had enough already.' Pushing her way past him, she hurried to the living room. 'You'd best come in. And don't make a noise!'

'You needn't worry. I'll not wake the kids . . . I'll be as quiet as a mouse.'

'I weren't meaning the kids,' she corrected him. 'They've gone to their grandma's, at top o' Montague

Street. Every now and then, they stay with her overnight, when their daddy's in the area, which isn't often, the useless bugger.'

'Aren't you worried yer old man might run off with 'em?'

'Nah!' Maggie made a face. 'He'd never do that – he's far too selfish to take responsibility for them. Anyway, he ain't my old man, just somebody I shacked up with when I were young and stupid. But you needn't worry. He knows better than to show his face round 'ere.'

'So, if the kids aren't here, why am I expected to be quiet?'

'I were thinking o' the neighbours. I don't want 'em rounding on me in the morning for having got them out their beds.'

'I've already said I'll be as quiet as a mouse. Now, will you join me in a drink?' If his plan was going to work, he needed her tipsy. Tonight he had suffered a disappointment, because he had lost money and the card games hadn't gone his way. She didn't know it yet, but Maggie could be his saviour.

Eyeing him suspiciously, she asked, 'What are you up to?'

'What's that supposed to mean?' he bridled. 'Why should I be up to anything?'

'I don't know, but it seems odd, that's all, you turning up at this hour. You never have before, let alone with a bottle o' gin and a need to talk.' She cocked her head to look at him from another angle, as if trying to catch him out. 'Normally, it's open the door, straight up the stairs and off with the clothes. There's never any time for chit-chat.'

'Look, darlin', I'll go if you want,' he said insincerely, hoping she would feel sorry at not having made him welcome. 'I didn't mean to turn up on your doorstep at this late hour, but tomorrow is a big day for me. And I really *do* need someone to talk to.'

He could see she was beginning to listen. 'Say the word and I'll be gone,' he wheedled. 'I'm not a man to stay where I'm not wanted.'

Maggie had to laugh at that. 'Liar!'

'Well, I'm buggered!' He laughed with her. 'You know me better than I thought.'

'Right. What's it to be?' Standing brazenly before him, she opened the front of her robe. 'D'you want me dressed or undressed?'

'My God, Maggie, you're a goer – I'll say that for you.' His eyes devoured her. 'No wonder the men like you, and as far as I can tell, you never turn them away.'

He let her believe he was admiring her, when in truth he thought her a slut of the worst kind – even though he had been glad to use her whenever it suited him.

'I wish I *could* turn 'em away, but I need the money,' she said quietly. 'You forget, I've got two kids who need their mam. I won't always be entertaining for a living. I want my own house, and furniture that's not been bought at a second-hand shop. Afterwards, when I'm set up, I wouldn't mind a job in a cake shop or a factory, when I can be one of the girls, and hold my head up high.'

Her eyes glazed over as if the tears were never far away. 'I want the kids to go to a good school, in a good district, and I want it *before* they know what their mam does for a living.'

She took a deep breath, which evolved into a smile of pride. 'I'm not far off my dream,' she confided. 'I've saved half of everything I've earned these past few years. It's for my kids, y'see? To give 'em a better life, with a mammy who's got time to walk 'em to school and listen to their tales when they come home.'

Excited by what he was hearing, Jacob knew he would have to be careful how he went about his little plan.

Maggie smiled at herself. 'I want a bicycle too. I'd cycle to work on it, and keep it polished and shiny as a new pin.'

Jacob threw himself into a chair. 'Bloody hell, woman. You want a lot, don't yer?'

Maggie fastened her robe. 'I'll get it too,' she

retorted. 'Another year maybe, an' I'll be away from these parts.'

Jacob's mind was working overtime. 'Well, I never! So, in one year from now, you reckon you'll have enough money to set yourself up?'

'That's right. But I've worked bloody hard for it. Sometimes, when I've hated what I'm doing, I've kept my dream alive in the back o' my mind, and it's easier to bear. Yes, it's true, I'll soon have enough money, but nobody can say it's been handed to me on a plate.'

'I thought I heard you mention all this once before, but I weren't listening proper.' He had remembered it, though. That was the main reason he was here tonight. 'So, it's all true, eh? And where is it, your little nest egg? Under the mattress, I dare say.'

Maggie wagged a finger at him. 'That's for *me* to know.' She gave him a warning glance. 'I might be easy and cheap, but I'm not stupid.'

Realising he was raising her suspicions by taking too much interest, Jacob decided to play it crafty. 'Yer right. It's nobody's business but yours. Still, I reckon we should celebrate the fact that you'll soon be outta this life altogether.'

Maggie wasn't too sure about his motives. 'I've a better idea,' she said. 'What if we celebrate with a mug o' cocoa, or happen a cup o' tea with just a trickle o' gin to warm the cockles? After that, I can send you on your way and take meself back to my nice warm bed.' She winked suggestively. 'Unless, o' course, you've a couple of half-crowns burning a hole in your pocket? Like you said yourself, I've never been known to turn anybody away.'

'Fair enough.' He jangled the change in his pocket. 'But there's no rush, is there, not with the kids at their grandma's? Besides, what's worth having is worth waiting for.' He chuckled, confident that he'd got her where he wanted her. 'First we'll celebrate,' he decided, 'then we'll be off up them stairs together – what d'you say to that?'

'Show me your half-crowns first.' Jacob wouldn't be the first man who'd taken advantage of her, then run off without paying.

He feigned indignation. 'Have I ever left without paying my way?'

The slightest flush of guilt crossed her features. 'No, you haven't,' she conceded. 'But there have been them as *has!*'

To make amends for her unfortunate remark, she went quickly into the kitchen and returned just as quickly with two glasses. 'Let's forget the tea shall we?' she suggested. 'I don't suppose a drop or two o' gin will do us any harm.'

Jacob bade her sit down, and when she was relaxed in the armchair, he filled her glass, deliberately deaf to her half-hearted protests. 'Here's to you,' he said, and clinked glasses. When she had the glass to her lips he took a long swig of his own gin and smacking his lips declared with a satisfied sigh, 'By! That's just what I needed.'

Following his example, Maggie swilled it down and coughing and giggling told him, 'You bugger, Jacob Hunter. You'll have me sozzled, so you will.'

'Rubbish!' But she was right. Getting her sozzled was exactly what he wanted. 'Here.' Topping up her glass, he said with a wink, 'One more, then I'll be after me money's worth, if you know what I mean.'

But it wasn't her body he was after. It was the years of savings she had stashed away. He could have used violence to make her tell him where it was, and taken it anyway. But if he could get her to join forces with him, so much the better.

In no time at all, he had her laughing at nothing, and when the first bottle of gin was finished, he produced another from his pocket. 'Well, will yer look here,' he beamed. 'Where on earth did *that* come from?'

Maggie was past caring. 'You're a devil,' she said, but he was the only real company she had, and right now, Maggie was feeling less alone than she had done in a long, long time.

'You know what?' By this time, he thought her drunk enough to broach what was on his mind. 'You and me could make ourselves a bit o' money – if you're interested, that is?'

Appearing not to have heard, Maggie knocked back the dregs of her glass and, holding it out for a refill, gave him a cheeky wink. 'That's funny.' Peering at him through bleary eyes she laughed out loud. 'You've never been what I'd call a looker, but I'll tell you what . . .'

Humouring her, he leaned forward. 'What?'

'I don't mean to insult you, but . . .' Breaking into a fit of helpless laughter, she moved about so much that the drink he'd just poured into her glass began to slop over the sides. 'You look a damned sight more handsome to me now I've had a drop o' gin,' she cried. 'It's true! The more I drink, the prettier you get!' Rocking backwards and forwards she could hardly contain herself.

Angry though he was, Jacob could see she was in the mood to hear him out. 'I thought you weren't going to insult me again?' he said, pretending to be heartily wounded. 'I always thought I were more a friend than a client.'

'Happen you are.' Though his words had sobered her a little, the tears of laughter ran unheeded down her face. 'Aw look, it's only a bit o' fun. Don't go getting all upset now.' Wiping away the tears, she suddenly remembered. 'Hey! What did you mean just now . . . when you said we could make ourselves a bit o' money?'

'Aw, we'd best forget it.' Jacob was a master at

cunning. 'It was just an idea. I don't suppose you'd be interested anyway.'

Sitting forward on her seat, she stared him in the face. 'We won't know till you tell me what it is, will we?'

Having drunk enough himself to feel less in control than usual, he searched his brain to think of a way in which he might get her hooked on his plan; at least enough to part with her hard-earned cash. He knew she was no fool. If he was to have her in on his little scheme, she would have to know all of it. Otherwise she'd guess he was holding back and want no more to do with it.

'I'm waiting, Jacob. If there's money to be made, you can count me in.'

'What if it's a bit dodgy, like?'

She laughed at that. 'Dodgy's my second name.'

'Huh! You'd best know straight off, Maggie, that I'm not talking about stealing a few bob from a man's trousers when he's not looking.'

'I've never done that in my life!'

'I'm not saying you have. All I'm saying is, well . . . what I have in mind will take some commitment on your part.'

'If we get caught, will we go to jail?'

'No.' He daren't frighten her off altogether. 'There are them as would move heaven and earth to make sure we don't, 'cause if they incriminate us, they incriminate theirselves. In fact, it would be *them* as took any punishment that was about, 'cause it's them as is in a position of authority an' should have known better.'

'Go on then. Spit it out.' Intrigued, she put her glass down in the hearth. 'Let's hear what you've to say. Then I'll decide if I'm in or out.' She suddenly gave an almighty burp. 'Whoops!' Clapping her hands to her knees, she gave a chuckle. 'You'd best blurt it out, Jacob, whatever it is you've got in mind, 'cause I'm feeling a bit worse for wear, an' once I get to that stage, I'll be past making any decisions.'

'Not a word of what I'm about to tell you must pass your lips, not now, not ever.'

'Don't you worry about that, love. I know how to keep my mouth shut.' She winked knowingly. 'I could tell you things about my clients that would make your hair stand on end, but I'm not in the market for gossip, if you know what I mean.'

'Okay.' He believed her. So, starting at the beginning, but leaving out any mention of Louise, he told her everything.

While Maggie listened, wide-eyed and shocked, he described how he and this businessman he knew had cooked the books to show false figures with regard to his father's loan. Instead of showing how the debt was paid off in full, the records showed a substantial amount, over two-thirds, still owing, and the farm taken as collateral.

'What's that?'

'It means the farm is put up as security against the loan, and if the loan remains unpaid, the farm is taken instead.' He went on to explain how, because neither Ben nor his mother could find the money to settle the debt, the farm was being offered for sale to the highest bidder. 'The debt will be paid out of the proceeds, and the remaining money, if any, will be returned to the estate. That means Ben will get it, because my father in his great wisdom . . .' his dark expression betrayed the depth of his hatred '. . . left the farm to my younger brother, God rot them both.'

With the drink burning away his inhibitions and making him reckless, he confessed how he had stolen most of the receipts from his father's secret hiding-place. 'Only me and Alan Martin know the score,' he told her.

'And now *me*.' Maggie was amazed and a little worried that he should have imparted such information to her.

Jacob put his finger to her lips. 'Ah yes, but *you* know how to keep your mouth shut, remember?' Though his smile was open enough, there was just the inkling of a threat in his voice.

'I don't see what you're really after.' Maggie

was usually quick-minded, but like Jacob, she had consumed too much alcohol. 'If you're saying we can make money out of all this, I don't see how. Somebody else will buy the farm and so Ben will never own it, and neither will you. Happen it's enough for you to cheat your brother out of it, eh? Is that what you planned? You resent the fact that your daddy left it to him and not to you, so you set about making him lose it?'

'Something like that, yes. But I hope to make a mint o' money as well.'

'Like I said, I don't see *how*!'

'Listen to me, Maggie. There isn't really *any money* owing on the farm. It were all paid up by me father. For God's sake, woman, haven't you been listening to a word I've been telling you?'

Now she finally began to understand. 'So when the farm sells, this Martin bloke will take what's claimed to be owed, and split it with you?'

'There you go!' Jacob clapped his hands. 'I knew you had a brain in that head o' yourn.'

Maggie was still puzzled. 'Suppose the farm doesn't bring enough to pay the money he claims is owed?'

'Oh, but it will.'

'You can't know for sure how the bidding will go.'

'It'll go my way.'

'What d'yer mean?'

'I intend buying the farm. And I intend buying it for just a little more than what it's worth; that way, Ben will get next to nothing.'

'You're a hard bastard, Jacob Hunter.'

He smiled at that. 'So! Not only will I have the farm, I'll have half the share of what it sells for as well, when it's turned over to repay the supposed debt.'

He liked the idea so much, he leapt out of his chair and cried out loud, 'It'll be *justice* done! Like it should have been from the start.' In one fell stroke, he would have paid back his father and Ben, too. On top of his revenge, he would be left with the farm, and in time, he'd have Louise by his side where she belonged.

It seemed so easy, it took his breath away.

Maggie had just one question. 'What if somebody's prepared to pay more than you?'

'They won't.'

'How d'you know that?'

'Because . . .' Too excited to be cautious, he explained how he had eliminated anybody who'd openly expressed an interest in bidding for the farm. 'The fewer people there, the better for me.'

Maggie had a terrible thought. 'It weren't you as killed that poor farmer, were it?'

Jacob saw the horror in her face and sobered up very quickly; he realised he would have to tread carefully. 'I never killed nobody,' he assured her. 'Come on, Maggie – do I *look* like a murderer?'

The woman visibly relaxed. 'No, 'course you don't,' she answered readily enough. 'You're a bad bugger, an' there's times when you deserve to be taught how to behave, but no, I don't reckon you'd kill anybody.'

'So there it is, love. The farm goes on sale tomorrow, an' I mean to buy it.'

'Sounds like your gambling's paid off then, being as you're allus saying you've no money to speak of.'

'Well no, Maggie, because this evening the gambling took a little turn for the worst. So that's where *you* come in . . . as a partner.'

She was adamant. 'Oh no. I want no part of it.'

''Course you do! You can see there's money to be made. Besides, once I've got the deeds to the farm, I can sell it to the highest bidder. I'll look after you, darlin', you know that. You'll get your money back, and as much again on top. Think of that!'

Despite her initial reaction, Maggie's brain was working fast. By! If she could double her money at one stroke, she and the kids would never look back.

Jacob was desperate. 'D'you hear what I'm saying, Maggie? You'll double your money. You can't afford *not* to come in with me.'

'Aye, an' mebbe I can't afford to risk losing what I've already got.'

He decided to play it softly. 'It's up to you, love. There are others who'd jump at the chance, but I thought I'd come and see you first. So, there's the proposition, an' you can see for yourself, you've nothing to lose and everything to gain.'

Maggie gave it some considerable thought, before replying with a proposition of her own. 'You say you mean to sell the farm, once you've got the deeds?'

'That was the plan, yes.'

'If I lent you the money, I'd have to have it done all proper like. I'd find a solicitor of me own.'

'That's fine by me, lass. As far as I'm concerned, it'd be a straightforward loan.'

'If I'm to part with all my savings, I've a few conditions of my own.'

'I'm listening.'

'I'd want you to *keep* the farm.'

'What!' Jacob looked dumbfounded. 'Why the devil would I do that?'

'Because it's one of my conditions. If you can't agree, then I won't lend you the money. It's as simple as that.'

'Huh!' For once, though, Jacob did not fly off the handle. He was curious; he was also in a corner. 'I think I'd best hear the rest o' your conditions.'

'You and me and the kids should live at the farm. Oh, I'm not asking you to wed me. Even I would have to think twice about *that* sort of commitment, but at least we'd be a family.'

Jacob laughed out loud. 'Have you gone mad or what?'

Maggie shook her head. 'I mean it, Jacob. You need my money, and I need a stable family life for my kids. Besides, you'll still be able to come and go as a single man. I'm not asking you to tie yourself to us. But, being as the farm will have been bought with some o' my money, I'll want a small claim on it. You'll have all the money that's coming to you, and I'll not ask you to pay me back.'

'What! Even if I agreed to your demands, you surely don't expect to entertain your menfriends there?'

'No, you've got it all wrong. All that will be in the past. That's the reason I'm making these conditions, so the kids can have a proper life.'

Growing anxious, he took a long swig from the gin bottle. 'How the hell d'you expect to make a living, you silly cow. You needn't think *I'd* be keeping you.'

'I'd work on the farm.'

'Now you *are* talking bloody stupid! What would you know about farming?'

Maggie smiled, a slow, contented smile. 'I were brought up on a farm,' she revealed.

'Were you now?'

'High up in the Yorkshire hills, it were. My dad kept sheep and pigs, and we even had two hundred chickens. My mam grew vegetables and I helped her. Every Saturday we'd go to market with a wagon loaded up wi' stuff. It weren't much, but we made a living. Then Dad got arthritis and Mam couldn't cope. They sold up and moved out.'

She paused, the memories flooding back. 'They're gone now,' she said, 'but the thing is, I could earn a living with chickens and such, and you could do whatever you liked. The money's yours if you want it, Jacob. But only if we can live on the farm as a family.'

'It's a lot to ask,' Jacob replied. 'Mebbe too much.'

When Maggie didn't answer, he got out of the chair and took to pacing the floor, up and down, round the room and back again.

Maggie sat, head down, eyes closed, praying he would agree. If he didn't, she would have to endure this awful life for years to come, and meanwhile her kids were growing up and becoming more aware, and she dared not think about the future.

Jacob, too, had some thinking to do. He wanted the money and he wanted the farm. What he *didn't* want was Maggie and her snotty-nosed brats. But she was shrewd. He knew she wouldn't change her mind, damn her to hell!

Suddenly he stopped in his tracks, his thinking going in a different direction. What if he went along with everything she said? What if he took her money and bought the farm – and afterwards refused to let her move in? *What if he strangled her in her bed?* Who was to say it wasn't one of her many clients?

He began pacing the floor again, thinking and scheming, convinced he would find a way out. After all, when it came right down to it, she was only a woman. He could outwit her if he had to.

While he continued to pace the floor, Maggie daren't speak, nor move. She had images of the farm in mind; of her feeding the chickens and harvesting the vegetables, and the children running freely about the field and climbing the trees. 'Oh, please, Jacob,' she silently prayed. 'Please say you agree.'

For what seemed a lifetime, the silence in that little room was unbearable.

Until suddenly Jacob plucked her out of the chair. 'It's a deal,' he said. What he didn't say was how he meant to get out of it at the first opportunity.

Maggie cried with joy, and they drank another tot of gin to celebrate. 'I'll want the agreement signed and sealed,' she reminded him.

'Tomorrow,' he promised. 'Right now, I think we should take ourselves and what's left of this gin upstairs.' He'd had enough of talk. Suddenly he had need of her.

They went upstairs, laughing, excited. But when he tried to make love, he couldn't. 'The little bugger won't stand up,' he complained. 'It's the drink.'

Maggie snorted. 'Brewer's droop!' she gurgled, and they fell about laughing.

They drank some more, and climbed into bed. As they did so, the gin bottle tipped over on the lino, its meagre contents trickling across the floor.

They were not aware. Naked and drunk, with the blanket loosely covering them, they lay in bed, arms round each other and out to the world.

Each dreaming their own little dream.

Chapter Eleven

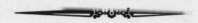

BEN WATCHED FROM the window as the auctioneer put up his stand. 'Vultures,' he groaned.
'They're nothing but bloody vultures.'

Sally drew him back. 'Come away, son,' she said
compassionately. 'It won't do you any good, watching
every move they make.'

Turning, he put his hand on his mother's shoulder.
'You're right, Mam.' He looked around. 'Where's
Louise?'

'Across the top field, walking the dog. That's
what she said, anyway, but I've a feeling she's sitting in some corner, as far away as she can get
from here.'

'I should have known.' Shame engulfed him. 'I'm
not the only one to feel bad.' Drawing Sally to him, he
held her tight for a moment. 'Oh Mam, I'm sorry. I
can't imagine what *you* must be feeling.'

She smiled up at him. 'I'll tell you a little secret, shall I, son?'

When he held her at arm's length and looked her in the eye, she amazed him with her confession. 'I won't miss the farm. I miss your dad, and I'll miss the open fields, but not the farm. I've been happy here, but only because I've had my family round me.' Her eyes grew moist. 'Wherever we go, I'll be content, because I know I'll have you and Louise.'

Emotion flooded through him. 'You're a remarkable woman, Mam.'

'Look to your wife now,' she entreated. 'Go and fetch her back.'

'I'll not be long.' Kissing her on the cheek, he strode out of the cottage and down the lane.

Feeling wretched for her son and the predicament he was in, Sally watched him go, and for a while, she looked out the window at the one or two locals already gathered. 'He's right,' she muttered. 'They *are* like vultures.'

EAGER TO FIND Louise, Ben pressed on. At the back of his mind, he wondered if she had gone to see Eric. He didn't like the idea, nor did he like the churned-up feelings it aroused in him.

Along the lane, he met up with a straggling of

folk, all heading in the direction of Maple Farm. 'How do, Ben?' That was old Johnny. What he didn't know about tractors wasn't worth knowing.

'Well enough,' Ben answered. 'But I dare say I could be better.'

'Aye, I can see that.' Johnny was sympathetic. 'It's a sorry day for you an' the family.' Passing on his commiserations to Sal and Louise, he went quietly on his way.

A mile down the lane, Ben passed the time of day with the couple from the old village pub, closed these past ten years. 'Hope you don't mind,' they said. 'We thought we'd see who ends up with the farm.'

'Well, one thing's for sure, it won't be *me*!' Ben could never understand folk's mentality. 'They think it's a damned picnic,' he muttered as he went on his way. 'Happen it is to *them*.'

He found Louise just as Sal had predicted; like a dot in the distance he spotted her, sitting on the tree stump where they often sat when they let Boris the mongrel loose to run about. Lost in thought, she didn't see him coming up the hill; though the dog saw him and scampered down to greet him.

Realising his wife hadn't seen him approach, Ben greeted the dog, then as Boris bounded away he followed him back to where Louise was still sitting deep in thought. For a minute, Ben wondered if she might have Eric on her mind. Then he told himself off. 'What would she be thinking of *him* for, you silly bugger! You're making a rod for your own back, entertaining ideas like that.'

At the last minute, when the dog jumped up and licked her face, Louise turned and saw him. 'Ben! What are you doing here? I thought you'd be waiting for the sale to start.'

Sitting beside her, he shrugged, suddenly inexplicably nervous in her presence. 'Mam said I'd find you here.'

'I needed to get away, just for a while. I would have started back soon.'

'Why didn't yer say you were going off like that?' he queried. 'I were worried about you.'

'You needn't have been.'

'What's wrong, love?' Lately she had been hard to fathom.

Louise shook her head. 'Nothing . . . at least, nothing apart from the business with the farm.' She was lying. She still loved him, but something precious had gone from their relationship . . . a kind of trust. He had not only cut her deep with his remark about her and Eric, but he had started her thinking things, and now she was assailed with all kinds of emotions; some of which she had never encountered before, and didn't know how to deal with.

'Lou?' Unsure of himself, he took hold of her hand.

'Yes?' She smiled on him, but it was a quiet kind of smile. 'What is it, Ben?'

'Are you happy . . . with *me*, I mean?'

Sensing his anxiety, her smile deepened. 'You *know* I am.' In spite of everything, it wasn't a lie.

'I do love you, sweetheart.'

'I love you, too.'

Scrambling off the boulder, he took to pacing, running his hands through his hair as he always did when agitated. 'I know the future is uncertain, and I can't promise it'll all come right in the end, 'cause I don't even know that myself.'

'I know you don't love, but none of this is your making, you have to remember that.' Apart from his nasty suspicions about her and Eric.

Seeming to read her mind, he couldn't bring himself to look at her. 'What with losing our home and . . . everything . . . any other woman would have buggered off by now.'

Suddenly she was at his side, her arm linked with his and a mischievous grin on her face to warm his heart. 'Well, I'm not any other woman, am I?' she asked cheekily.

'Thank God.' Catching her full in his arms he swung her round. 'For there's no other woman on this earth I'd rather have than the one I've got.' And his long, searching kiss told her so.

When the dog started running round and barking

at them, Ben laughed. 'I'd best put yer down, afore he bites me arse!'

With her feet well and truly on the ground, Louise straightened her clothes. 'Is Sal all right?' she asked with concern. 'Only she were a bit quiet this morning . . . not in the mood for conversation. I thought if I went for a walk, it would give her some time to herself.' Though that wasn't the only reason, she thought.

'She's okay.' He put her mind at rest. 'But I'd best get back all the same. It's my place to be there, but *you* don't have to come with me, not if you don't want to. You can stay up here till it's all over, if you've a mind.'

'No, Ben.' There he went again, she thought bitterly, talking as if she had already turned her back on him. Her place was with her family. He knew that. 'I want to be there,' she said.

'Come on, then. We'd best make tracks.'

With the dog running ahead, they lost no time in making their way back.

———◦◦◦———

A s THEY ROUNDED the bend into the farmyard, they noticed Alan Martin, plus the auctioneer and another man, whom Ben assumed to be the enforcing officer – all of them deep in conversation.

'Look!' Louise pointed to the half dozen or so people who were gathered before the auctioneer's stand. 'There aren't many people here,' she observed. 'I would have thought there'd be a lot more than that.'

'You're right.' Ben had also imagined there would be quite a crowd, all eager to bid for what was a decent, small farm. 'Go back to the cottage,' he told Louise. 'Make sure Mam's all right. I'll be along, soon ever I find out what's going on.'

While Louise went one way, Ben went the other.

As he neared the men, all eyes turned in his direction. 'Is there summat wrong?' He glanced at his pocket watch. 'I was of the understanding that the sale would be starting any minute now.' He would have given his right arm for it not to be so, but as Louise had pointed out more than once, he must learn to accept it, or go out of his mind.

'No, there's nothing wrong, Mr Hunter.' It was the auctioneer who spoke. Ben had met him before, when he came to tag all items being offered for sale. 'We've been going through the usual rigmarole. But we're about to start now.'

He didn't reveal how he and the other two men had had a difference of opinion. While he himself was all for postponing the sale, or at least waiting another half hour or so, in order to see if there would be more likely bidders, the other two were insisting the sale must take place now, at the time agreed.

Ben glanced at the people already assembled for the sale. 'Don't you think you should wait another hour or so?' he remarked. 'I know for a fact that at least half of this little lot won't be bidding. Some are here out of morbid curiosity, and the others are here because they've got nowt better to do.' The ones who really cared what happened to Maple Farm and its occupants, had considerately stayed away.

'We'll not get a decent price out o' this lot, I can tell you that now.' Ben was beginning to panic. He had counted on getting a fair amount back once the debt was settled, but now he could see his cash payment dwindling before his eyes.

'I'm sorry, sir. There are no rules to say there should be a bigger crowd before we start,' the enforcing officer pointed out. 'Moreover, I'm straight on to another sale in Bolton after this, so I don't have time to stand about waiting. No, sir, I'm afraid the sale must go ahead as planned.'

'But it's not right! You can see that for yourself.'

Alan Martin spoke up at that point. 'Who's to say if we waited another four hours, that more people would turn up? I'm in full agreement with the officer here. The sale must go on as advertised.'

'And what if you don't get all of the money owed you?' Ben was agitated now, and deeply concerned.

'If it falls short you needn't come after me, 'cause I've got nowt. *You've* seen to that, you bastard!'

Sensing a confrontation, the officer came between them. 'There will be no question of *that*,' he told Ben. 'Your father offered the farm as collateral, and if it doesn't reach a figure to settle the debt, then the debt is wiped out. It won't fall on your shoulders, sir, I can assure you of that.'

Ben still wasn't satisfied. 'What about my chances then? What if *I* end up with nothing?'

'I'm afraid none of us have control over that, sir. If Mr Martin loses out, then so do you.'

'Look, I think we'd best get on with it,' Martin urged, 'before the people who *are* here start moving off.' His conscience was pricking him and he wanted it all over and done with as soon as possible.

In addition he was shaking in his shoes at the knowledge that he had tied himself up with Jacob Hunter, especially now, when he suspected that Hunter had murdered that poor farmer. He only had to see the small turnout here, and the whole thing began to make sense. Hunter had frightened away anyone who might have shown an interest in Maple Farm. It was plain enough: he meant to buy the farm himself, *and* take half of what it brought. But devil take it, where *was* the fellow?

'I demand you start *now*!' Addressing the auctioneer, his voice shook.

If the authorities ever found out he had shaped an underhand deal to defraud Ben Hunter of his rightful inheritance, they would put two and two together and come up with five. The whole truth would out. Jacob would be hanged as a murderer, and he himself as accomplice!

The very idea sent him into a state of panic. So much so, that he didn't care if the farm sold for tuppence. But sold it must be, and Hunter paid off for good and all.

Beaten, Ben retaliated. 'Yer all the bloody same! Look after them as can afford to give the orders, and grind the others into the ground. Bastards, all of yer!' With that, he swung away. He had his wife and his mam to take care of. The way things were going, he didn't want them to see the farm fall under the hammer.

As he strode angrily towards the farmhouse, he heard the auctioneer start the bidding. By the time he had reached the front door, the bidding had risen to six hundred pounds. 'A long way to go yet,' he muttered. 'God help us!'

Inside the cottage, the two women sat quietly beside the empty fireplace. 'Oh Sal, I wish it were over.' Now that she knew there was no chance of them staying here, Louise couldn't wait to get away.

Sal understood, for didn't she feel the very same. When Ben came through the door, the mood

changed instantly. 'The filthy swine!' Throwing himself into a chair, he groaned like a man in pain. 'They
don't give a sod, none of 'em!'

For a while they sat quiet; each unable to convey
their own feelings to the other, for fear of causing
distress.

The silence was ominous. The clock ticked loudly
on the mantelpiece and from the kitchen could be
heard the dripping of a tap. Sensing something very
wrong, the dog began mooching round and round
their legs. They took no notice and soon he laid
himself at their feet, looking up with hangdog eyes.

After a while Louise suggested she make them
all a brew, 'to calm our nerves'.

But nobody wanted any, so she stayed where she
was, and the silence thickened in that little room.
In the background, the low, rhythmic tones of the
auctioneer could be heard, though it was impossible
to know the actual figure reached so far.

Another moment and Ben could bear it no
longer. 'I'm going out,' he announced, and before
they could react, he had gone out the door and was
on his way.

As he came down the path to the field, he heard
the auctioneer's voice clearly. 'I'm selling to the man
on my right – going, going . . . gone. Sold for the sum
of one thousand and two hundred pounds.'

The sound of the hammer clattering against the

wooden bench was like a death knell to Ben. His heart sank. 'Not enough. Dear God, it's not nearly enough.'

Desolate, he rounded the corner – and he couldn't believe his eyes. For reaching up to the auctioneer with his numbered card was none other than *Eric Forester*!

The sight of his old friend signing the papers brought Ben to a halt. 'No, it can't be!' But it was. And Ben wanted blood.

Lunging forward, he grabbed Eric by the throat. 'I thought you were a friend! Yer a traitor, that's what you are, a bloody traitor!' His hands were so quick and tight round Eric's throat, it took three men to prise him away.

'It's over, Mr Hunter.' That was the enforcing officer. 'The sale was conducted fair and square and this gentleman bid the highest figure.'

He turned to see Eric being helped up from the ground. 'In fact, I have to say, if it hadn't been for this man coming in at the last minute, I'd have had to let the farm go for under the thousand. It was Mr Forester's determination that drove the price up.'

Even though he saw the sense of that, Ben could not be consoled. 'What do I care if it brought a thousand or two thousand?' he snarled. 'It only means *he* . . .' he pointed to Alan Martin, who had kept well in the background, '. . . *he* gets summat towards what he's owed, and I get nowt!'

Eric's quiet voice gentled through the air. 'Think about this, then, Ben. Me buying the farm made no difference to the outcome. I know how much you love this place and I'm sorry for the way things turned out.'

Eric had been giving the whole matter some serious thought. 'I had a mind for us to form some kind of partnership . . . you and me, working the land together. That way, you'd be earning your living, and still have the good earth beneath your feet. So, all that will have changed is you living somewhere else.'

'What!' Ben laughed in his face. 'You must be mad if yer think I'd ever agree to summat like that.'

'It's the best I can do, Ben – a partnership. At least think about it.'

'You conniving bastard, this is *my* land. And I want you off it . . . NOW!'

Surging forward, Ben was again held back by a number of men; some of them friends of his father. 'Leave it, son,' they counselled. 'You can't blame Eric for what's happened to you.'

From a distance, and with a number of men between them, Eric and Ben faced each other; Eric white-faced and sorry, Ben a picture of hatred, the veins on his neck standing out like tram-lines. 'I'll not forget this,' he murmured. 'I'll not forget what you did here today.'

If truth were told, it was little to do with Eric buying the farm, and more to do with Louise. In his heart he knew there was nothing between those two, but the seeds of jealousy were sown, and rightly or wrongly, he could never again look on Eric as a friend.

At that moment, alerted by the shouting and uproar, Louise came running. Quickly taking in the situation, she went to Ben's side, her eyes drawn to where Eric stood. 'Eric?' She didn't want to believe what her eyes were telling her. 'Was it *you*?' Even now, when she saw his face and realised the truth, she still could not believe it. 'Eric? Was it you who bought the farm?'

'I'm sorry, Louise. I wanted to tell you, but there was never the right moment.' Torn by the look on her face, he took a step forward. 'I'm still a friend to you and Ben, whatever you might think. I'd been given notice to quit. I needed a place to live. The farm was being sold and it seemed the natural thing to do. What does it matter whether it was me, or somebody else who bought it?' His eyes beseeched her. 'You do understand, don't you, lass?'

'*Leave her out of it!*' Whether it was the way Eric looked at Louise, or the fact that he felt betrayed by someone he considered to be a friend, Ben suddenly went berserk.

With an earsplitting scream he broke away and, throwing himself at Eric, sent him backwards at astonishing speed into the trunk of a tree; slamming him so hard against it, the impact shook him to the heart, making him cry out. In a burst of crimson, the blood spurted from his nose like a fountain, covering Ben's shirt from neck to waist.

'STOP IT!' Not for the first time Louise found herself trying to stop her husband from fighting like a madman. She held onto Ben's jacket and wouldn't let go, but she was like a match in a gale against his manic strength.

Enraged and humiliated, Eric gave as good as he got. Each man was convinced he was in the right, and each man was determined to defend that right. The blows hit home and the blood flowed, and try as they might, no one there could separate them.

In the midst of chaos, Sal's clear angry voice cut the air. '*That's enough!*'

So unexpected was the intrusion that each man backed off to turn and look at this frail old woman; a woman with astonishing strength of character, her calm, quiet manner commanding respect from everyone there.

'Mam!' Ben straightened himself to wipe the

sweat from his face. 'Go back to the cottage, Mam. *Please!*'

Sal came forward, her face white and hard-set. 'I'll do no such thing,' she answered. 'I'm ashamed of you!'

Glancing at Eric through eyes brilliant with tears, she chided, 'As for you, Eric Forester, have you altogether lost your dignity?'

Mortified, he lowered his gaze.

Turning away, Sal addressed her son. 'How could you?' Her voice broke with emotion. 'Your father only recently laid to his rest, and now the farm going from over our heads. And all you can think to do is fight the man who bought it.'

'He deceived us, Mam,' Ben panted the argument still alive in him. 'Pretending to be a friend, when all the while he were planning to buy us out of house and home!'

'No, son.' Sal gave a small, weary smile. 'It wasn't Eric who did that to us. It was your father, God rest his soul. He did what any father would have done in the same circumstances. He put himself in jeopardy, in order to help his son. He made a mistake. But we can't blame him for that.'

She raised her gaze to Eric. 'Any more than you can blame Eric for wanting a roof over his head, in this place where he has lived and worked for so many years.'

Seemingly antagonised by his mother's defence of Eric, Ben swung round to say something vicious. But, head bowed and shoulders hunched, Eric was already walking away, a look of shame and regret etched on his sad face.

A moment later, everyone had left, all except Ben, with Louise and Sal; and standing some way apart, the enforcing officer, waiting to finalise things.

With the rage still bubbling inside him, Ben wiped his face once more, tucked his shirt in where it had fallen out, and, walking to Louise, asked her, 'Take Mam inside, lass. I'll be there in a minute.' He looked at Sal, and his heart broke. 'I trusted him,' he said brokenly. 'An' all the time, he *weren't* to be trusted.'

Saddened by what she had witnessed, Sal let Louise lead her away. 'It's as well his father isn't here to see this.' She wiped away a tear, and the young woman loved her all the more.

'He'll make it up with Eric, I'm sure,' she told Sal. Then she found herself beginning to wonder if he ever would. Today had told her something she had already suspected. Since his father's death, Ben had changed. And not for the best neither!

With the women gone, the enforcing officer approached Ben with the warning, 'You'll be getting notice any time now as to when you'll be required to vacate these premises.'

He would have gone on to discuss more official matters, but Ben walked away, leaving him standing there. 'No matter!' the officer mumbled angrily. He had seen it all before. In the end they had to buckle under. Raising his voice, he called after Ben, 'Mr Forester's got the law on his side. It's all over bar the signing. MR HUNTER . . . !'

Frustrated, he ran after him, coming to an abrupt stop when Ben turned to glare at him. 'I'm sorry, Mr Hunter,' he said nervously, 'but there's no use you turning a deaf ear.'

'Now you listen to me.' His voice low and grating, Ben stood head high, feet apart, and a look of terrible defiance in his eyes. 'If you think I'll hand this farm over without a fight, you'd best think again!'

Faced with such a threat, the officer warned, 'Try anything, and you'll end up in jail. Don't be foolish, man. Think of the womenfolk.'

Ben's answer was to take up a pitchfork and chase him all the way to the lane, where the little man ran off without a backward glance. 'Good shuts!' Ben gave a sigh of relief to see the back of him. But he knew it was not the end. Sooner or later, they'd be back.

'Do yer worst!' he challenged. 'I'll be ready for yer!'

Mumbling and sweating, he made his way to the

cottage. 'You'll not make me turn this farm over to no man. I'll burn it to the ground first.'

>>◦<<

IN THE COTTAGE, Louise and Sal were discussing the awful events. 'I can't believe it was Eric who bought the farm,' Louise told Sal, 'I honestly thought Jacob would find a way to get his hands on it.'

'Oh, I'm sure he meant to be here, and no doubt he'll have turned up with his pockets bulging with money, got by some bad deed or another.'

'So why wasn't he here, then?' Not that she wasn't pleased at his absence, because she most certainly was.

Sal smiled a quiet, knowing smile. 'It'll be a game o' cards, or a fight down some dark alley,' she mused regretfully. 'Or it could even be a woman.'

She sipped at her tea, then cradled the cup and saucer in her lap like she might a child. 'That'll be it,' she said wryly. 'It's well known that Jacob Hunter never could resist a good-looking woman.'

When Louise leaned back in the chair, closing her eyes to let the weariness wash over her, Sal gave her a worried glance. If anyone should know about Jacob's weakness for the women, Louise should – for hadn't he already got his evil eye on his brother's wife? 'You're a good lass,' she murmured now.

'You've more sense than to be swayed by his loose words and promises.'

Disturbed, Louise sat up. 'Sorry, Sal, I were nearly asleep. I don't know what's wrong with me.'

'It's the strain. It's been a tiring time for all of us,' Sal reminded her. 'Sleep if you want to, I'll not wake you.'

Louise thanked her, but said, 'I'd best go and see where Ben is. He's been in such a funny mood lately, he worries me.'

'He'll be fine,' Sal promised. 'Once we move out of here to Derwent Steet, we'll all buckle down to a new life soon enough, I expect.'

'Right, well, I'll not be long.' Louise yawned; she still felt exhausted. 'If he can be persuaded, we'd best sit down and talk things over,' she said tiredly. 'Whether he likes it or not, Ben has to start thinking about moving out of here.'

Recalling how she had been shaken out of her malaise, she asked, 'What were you saying, just now when I nearly nodded off?'

Sal shook her head. 'It must have been summat and nothing, lass,' she lied, ''cause I can't remember.'

When Louise was out the door and away, Sal got out of her chair and went to the window. Here she watched Louise swinging down the path, her hair blowing in the breeze like that of a young girl. 'You don't know how pretty you are, love,' she muttered, 'but Jacob does, God help us. If he could break you and Ben up, he'd do it tomorrow.'

There was something else too. 'I saw the way Eric looked at you, and so did Ben. As good and decent as he is, Eric Forester is no different from any other man when it comes to a pretty woman.'

All kinds of fearful emotions beset her. 'My Ben is like a sleeping tiger, content with his lot until he's threatened. Then he's like a thing demented.'

A short time later she saw Louise return, Ben by her side. 'Watch out, lass,' she murmured. 'Three men . . . all with an eye for you.'

That was not Louise's fault, but it was so, all the same – and it filled her with terror. She hardly dared think about it, but right now, any kind of contentment was just out of reach for all of them.

'I fear for you, my darlin' girl,' she whispered. 'I fear for all of us.'

Now, the sight of Ben and Louise coming along the path together was instantly pleasing to her old heart. Ben had his arm round his wife and Louise was looking up at him with the light of love in her eyes.

Yet, looking deeper, Sal noticed something that chased the smile from her face.

She couldn't help but recall how before, whenever they were walking together, Louise would have her arm round Ben's waist, and be chatting merrily away. Not today though. Today she had nothing to say, and as she walked alongside him, her arm swung loosely by her side. Even in the merry twinkle of her eye there seemed just the slightest shadow of doubt.

Sal saw it and her heart dropped inside her.

'Three men, all wanting the same woman,' she whispered fearfully. 'Heaven help us if there ever comes a day when you're made to choose.'

———————➤•◄———————

I T WAS MIDDAY when Jacob was startled out of his sleep. Still groggy from the drinking last night, he clapped his two hands round his head. 'Will somebody answer that bloody door, before I go crazy!' The persistent banging on the front door was like the sound of great hammers clattering inside his head.

Waking beside him, Maggie clambered out of the bed. 'I'll go,' she yawned. 'You'd best get dressed.'

'What time is it?'

She squinted at the clock out of bleary eyes; though feeling as she did, she couldn't recognise one number from the next. 'It's still early,' she guessed. 'I'll see who's at the door, then I'll fetch us a hair of the dog.' Laughing, she threw herself at him. 'Fancy a bit o' fun, do you, eh?'

'Get off, woman.' He pushed her away when the

banging started again; this time loud enough to cave the door in. 'Who the hell's that?'

Groaning, he eased himself to the edge of the bed. 'Get an' answer the bloody door, will you?' He sent Maggie sprawling with a hefty shove. 'Move yer fat arse before the whole damned house comes down round us ears!'

Scrabbling on his trousers, he heard her open the door; he then heard her greet the children. Almost immediately, a series of volatile, angry exchanges rang out. Then the door slammed shut, followed by what sounded like a fist against the timber. He heard a man's voice yelling out, and then silence.

And now Maggie's voice could be heard above the pattering of smaller feet going towards the living room.

'What the devil's going on?' Doing up his flies, Jacob then belted his trousers and tucked in his shirt. As he leaned down to fasten his shoelaces he caught sight of the clock on Maggie's bedside cabinet. *It was gone midday.*

Panic-stricken, he rushed out of the room and down the stairs. 'Bitch!' Taking Maggie aside he instructed, 'Get the money. If I'm quick, I'll just be in time.' When she hesitated, he shook her by the shoulders, then thrusting her aside, he went to the place where he thought he had seen her hide something. There was nothing there.

'All right, you. Where is it?' he snarled.

From behind them came the voice of a child. 'Leave our mam alone!'

Fearful for her children, Maggie broke away and, shoving them in the front parlour, she told them sternly, 'Stay here. I'll come for you in a minute.'

As she closed the door, Jacob grabbed her by the hair. 'Where've you put the money?'

Maggie was adamant. 'Beat me up if you like. Kill me if you've a mind, but you'll not get that money. Not till you set your signature on legal paper.' All her life she had been used by men, in one way or another. If she let him take what she had saved over the years, there would be nothing left, not for her or the kids. 'I mean it, Jacob.'

For a long, harrowing moment he held her to him, his unshaven face close to hers, his breath still smelling of spirits, his hands slowly tightening the collar of her night-robe. Suddenly he thrust her aside. 'I ain't got time to fight with you right now,' he snapped. 'I need to be at the auction.'

His mind worked quickly. 'I don't expect I'll need the money straight off. Besides, I've a few quid deposit in my jacket pocket if needed.'

Maggie was relieved. 'I said I'd lend you the money and I will,' she confirmed. 'But the deal's got to be done proper.'

Slinging her aside, he went into the living room

to fetch his jacket and shrug it on, at the same time feeling in his pockets to make sure his own meagre amount of money was still safe; it was.

'Who was that at the door?' He almost knocked her over as he rushed into the passage.

'The kids' daddy.' She looked away. 'Nobody for you to be concerned about.'

'Hmh!' Grunting like the pig he was, he shoved his way past her and in a minute was gone, running full pelt down the street. Unwashed and unkempt, he looked like a tramp on the run.

Behind him, Maggie let the children out of the other room. 'Your daddy didn't hurt you, did he?' There had been a nasty confrontation at the door when he brought them home.

Little Hannah looked up with big, frightened eyes. 'He was angry and shouting,' she said.

'Why?' Maggie hated it when the children saw their father. A born wanderer with an unpredictable nature, she never knew how he would behave with them.

Adam put a protective arm round his sister. 'Daddy was in a bad mood.'

'He didn't hurt you though, did he?' Maggie persisted.

'No.'

She ruffled his thick dark hair. 'Did your grandma feed you both this morning?'

The boy nodded. 'She and Daddy had a row. Grandma said he was "neither use nor ornament".'

Maggie laughed at that; then seeing how the children were still worried, she smiled fondly on them. 'Aye well, yer poor Granny has to put up with a lot.' She took them, one into each arm. 'Anyway, never mind. You're back home now,' she declared with a grin. 'What say I get myself ready and we'll make our way up to Corporation Park and feed the ducks?'

Her suggestion was greeted with leaps and shouts of delight, and soon they were on their way. 'That Jacob had better get used to the idea that my kids come first!' she muttered when closing the door behind her. 'They've got enough to worry about with that crazy father o' theirs!'

<hr />

S AL WAS IN the kitchen when Jacob came bursting through the door. 'It's not over, is it?' Breathless and red in the face, he straddled the doorway.

Moving away from the sink where she had been washing the breakfast dishes, Sal wiped her hands on the tea-towel. She looked at him for a moment, wondering how she had come to give birth to this man who was more like a stranger than a son. 'If you mean the auction, it was over hours ago.'

'Yer lying!'

'Don't you call me a liar. The auction was over long since. The farm's been sold. It didn't bring enough money to repay the debt, so there's nowt left over for Ben.' She looked at him steadily. 'But then, thank God, you'll not get your hands on anything neither, will you?' It was a small measure of compensation.

Jacob was beside himself. Howling with rage, he loped across the room. 'You'd best tell me!' He stared Sally in the eye, his voice unnervingly threatening. 'Who bought it?'

'Eric Forester.' At the look of incredulity on his face, the corners of her mouth lifted in the whisper of a smile. 'Surprise you, does it? Thought he was out of action, is that it? And what—'

He didn't answer. Instead he dashed out of the door, leaving her standing there, mouth half open and her sentence not yet finished. '. . . what will yer do now, you nasty piece o' work?'

Finishing the sentence gave her a degree of satisfaction, but it was tempered with anxiety, because she suspected he had gone to see Eric Forester; though judging by today's performance, that young man would not take kindly to being put under pressure by Jacob, or anyone else come to that.

With the incident over she returned to her washing-up. 'It's a good job Louise and Ben are in the orchard,' she muttered thankfully. 'If Ben knew Jacob was here demanding to know the ins and outs of a cat's backside, he'd have shown him the door, and there might have been another set-to.'

Dropping a plate, she almost leapt out of her skin when it shattered into fragments at her feet. 'By! Me nerves are allus on edge when he's about, an' that's a fact.' Taking a dustpan and brush she collected the fragments one by one. It helped to calm her.

———◆◆◆———

ERIC WAS NO more pleased to see Jacob than Sally had been. 'What d'*you* want?' Opening the door he stood on the threshold, making no move to invite his unwanted visitor inside.

Jacob sidled up to him. 'I should have been at the auction, but I got held up, y' see.'

'So? What's that got to do with me?'

'I understand you bought the farm, is that right?'

Eric nodded. 'It's right enough, yes.'

Taking note of Eric's fresh crop of cuts and bruises, Jacob smiled cunningly. 'I see someone gave you another hiding. Our Ben, was it? Snatched the farm from under his nose, did you?'

'Look, why don't you tell me what you're after, or clear off, eh? I've better things to do than stand at the door passing the time of day with you.'

'I want to buy the farm.'

'It's not for sale.'

'I'll pay you a handsome sum . . . enough for you to make a profit on the deal.'

'Like I said, it's not for sale . . . not at *any* price!'

'You'd be foolish to turn me down.'

'Shame. Because that's exactly what I'm doing.' With the flat of his hand he pushed Jacob aside. 'I'm turning you down, and turning you away, so don't come bothering me again, because it'll do you no good.'

Jacob glared at him, his hands itching to reach up and grab Eric by the throat, but his brain telling him this wasn't the way to do it. 'I'll be back,' he warned. 'You see if I'm not.'

Eric was no fool. 'If you mean you'll send in the heavies again, I wouldn't if I were you. You see, I might just tell the police about two men I saw hanging about Barry's place, just afore he were murdered.' He had in fact seen no one but Jacob wasn't to know that.

'And it's a funny thing, Jacob, but I'm sure I've seen *you* with the very same men. Well, that's what I'd tell the police . . . friends of Jacob Hunter, that's who they were.'

'You're getting in over your head, Forester!'

'Is that so?' Eric smiled at Jacob with the same

cunning smile that Jacob had used on him. 'That's not the way *I* see it,' he taunted. 'The way I see it is this: the police haven't yet found the men who murdered poor Barry Jackson. What I tell them might just send them in your direction. So, if you've any sense, you'll keep well clear of me.'

He scratched his chin. 'In fact, it might be a good idea if I write a note and give it to a trusted friend to hold. Yes, I might do that this very day . . . or I might *already* have done it.'

Even though he knew he was beaten, Jacob had to act the big man. 'You'll regret this.'

'Oh, I don't think so.' Moving fast out of the doorway, Eric took hold of Jacob by the scruff of his neck and sent him hurrying down the garden path. 'Now bugger off and leave a man in peace!'

He stayed at the door until Jacob was well out of sight. Then he went back inside, lit up his pipe and sat in his armchair, thinking of Louise.

Day or night, she was never very far from his mind.

Chapter Twelve

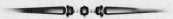

Louise could see no sense in making an enemy of Eric. 'Why won't you go and see him?' she demanded of Ben. 'The pair of you have had time enough to lick your wounds and think again. You've known each other too long for it to end like this.'

Sal looked up from her sewing. 'The lass is right.' Having listened and tried hard to stay out of the argument, she now felt obliged to speak her mind. 'As far as I'm concerned, Eric did nothing wrong. Like he said, he had need of a home and this was up for sale. If he hadn't bought it, some other fella, happen less likeable, might have got his hands on it – and then how would you have felt?'

But Ben was not in a forgiving mood. 'It's not what I'd have expected a mate to do, and don't give me the argument about him needing a place to live. To tell you the truth, I'd rather it *had* gone to somebody else. Happen that might have been more acceptable. We'll never know now, will we?'

Louise got out of her chair, her angry eyes regarding Ben, and her heart unbelievably heavy, though she didn't quite know why. One thing was certain; she felt strongly that her husband was being unnecessarily peevish. 'For goodness sakes, Ben, why can't you see reason?' Exasperated at his attitude, she wanted to make him see the situation from Eric's side. 'Eric is probably at home right now, feeling just as bad as you do,' she pointed out. 'Go and see him. Please?'

'Leave it, Lou.' Ben remained sullen. 'There's been enough said.'

She put up her hands in a gesture of resignation. 'I'll say no more,' she promised, though she had a lot to think about, and none of it good.

Sal hadn't finished though. 'It's a bad thing to leave this place, having made an enemy of a friend.' Looking her son in the eye, she put her sewing down. 'I know how you must feel, lad,' she conceded, 'but this isn't the right way to go about things.' Leaning forward she spoke with a mother's soft tongue. 'He's been more of a brother to you than Jacob ever was.' She smiled wryly. 'You've said that yourself, many a time.'

Ben thought on her words, but what Eric had

done in buying the farm, was still raw in him. 'They're two of a kind.'

'You're just pigheaded, that's what you are.' Louise was at the end of her patience with him.

Making an upward gesture with the palm of her hand, Sal managed to warn her that it might be a good idea if she held her tongue.

The subtle warning was enough for Louise to take herself into the kitchen. 'I'll put the kettle on.'

With Louise out of the room, Sal appealed once more to Ben's common sense. 'I don't understand you,' she told him. 'Eric even offered you a partnership on the land, working together, just like you worked with your da. Instead of being shut up in some dark noisy factory where you can't see daylight except through a window, you'll be here, on the land you love, with the valleys and hills all about you.'

It was small compensation, she knew, but better than the alternative. 'At least think about it, love. Working here every day, just like you've allus done. Surely that counts for summat?'

'It's not the same, and it never can be!' He was adamant. 'Partner or not, I'd be answering to Eric at every turn. By! I'd feel like a beggar on my own land.'

It was his last word on the subject. 'I'm off to the pub.' Taking his cap and coat from where it hung behind the door, he caught his wife's worried glance as she came into the room. 'Don't wait up for me,' he snapped. 'Like as not I won't be back till late.'

Sorry that she and Ben had exchanged harsh words, Louise went to the window, her troubled gaze following his long, angry stride as he went down the lane. 'What's happening to us?' Her innermost thoughts spilled over.

Sal took it on herself to answer. 'Ben's normally a reasonable man, but he can be a stubborn bugger when he's a mind,' she said. 'Yer can talk till yer blue in the face, but he'll not listen to either of us. If you ask me, it's best we leave him alone. I dare say he'll sort himself out sooner or later.'

'I don't like the idea that he and Eric have made enemies.'

'Neither do I, but there's nowt we can do, lass. The more we go on about it, the more Ben will dig in his heels.'

Louise had to agree. 'You're right. I'll not say anything else to him.'

'That's the way, lass.' She went back to her sewing. 'I need more wool.' Biting off the stray end with her small, sharp teeth, she remarked, 'When next you go into Blackburn town, pop into Nan Draper's and get me a ball o' grey, and a ball o' black, will you? There's no point buying more socks while there's plenty o' life in these.' Stretching the sock over her fist, she dug the needle in and skilfully picked up the threads.

Louise smiled. 'You must be the only woman in the world who still darns men's socks.'

Sal chuckled. 'Oh, you'd be surprised, lass,' she said. 'Us women are known for being thrifty. Besides, the old ones never forget how to stretch a loaf to three.'

Past listening, Louise had other things on her mind. 'What time do you think he'll be back?'

Pursing her lips as she always did when considering something, Sal answered thoughtfully, 'You know what they're like. Once they get gabbing and card-playing, they don't know when to stop. I wouldn't be at all surprised if he didn't show his face till midnight.'

For the next hour or so, the two women sat and talked of the future. At nine o'clock, Sal laid down her sewing. 'I'm tired, lass.' The strain of these past weeks showed on her old face. 'I'm off to me bed.' Easing herself out of the chair, she groaned and winced. 'Me poor ol' bones ain't what they once were,' she chuckled. 'I'm like Ronnie's red tractor . . . in need of an oil change.'

Louise laughed at that. 'Go on with you!' she chided. 'You'll outlive the lot of us, so you will.'

'Lock up afore yer come up, won't yer, lass?' Sal was always wary of intruders, though in all the years they had lived here, there had never been a moment when she had been frightened. 'Ben's got his key, so he'll not be locked out.'

Louise promised she would make sure the house was secure. 'Goodnight, God bless,' she said, and gave the old woman a fond kiss.

'G'night lass.' Ambling across the room, Sal was soon on her way up the stairs. 'Don't forget to lock up now!' she called, and once again, Louise promised she would.

With Sal gone to bed, Louise felt very lonely. 'Dammit, Ben, I were only trying to make you see sense.' Even though she loved him dearly, there were times when her husband tried her to the limit. 'Ben and his pride,' she sighed. 'It'll be the undoing of him.'

Getting out of the chair she began pacing the room, her thoughts turning more and more to Eric. Suddenly she knew what she must do. 'Right then, you stubborn bugger. If *you* can't put things right between the two of youse, then I'll have to do it for you!'

Listening at the foot of the stairs, she heard Sal get into her creaking old bed. 'Sleep tight, sweetheart,' she whispered. 'I've an errand to do before Ben comes back. I'll not be gone above an hour.'

A few minutes later, satisfied that the old woman was fast and hard asleep, she put on her coat and beret, and going to the back door, made certain it was securely locked. In case Sal woke and needed to go out for whatever reason, she took the key out and hung it within reach.

Sneaking softly out the front door, she pulled the door up behind her; there was no need of a key should Sal wish to leave by this way, because the door could be opened from the inside by the turn of the sneck. 'Anybody would think I were going away for days,' Louise chided herself, 'when I should be back in no time at all.'

A word with Eric was all she needed, and if she didn't do it now, while Ben was out drowning his sorrows, there might never be another opportunity.

Louise went like a shadow across the fields, running one minute, pausing the next, gazing with wonder at the beauty of the world about her; the magnificent silhouette of trees and church spire against the night skies; here the sound of a night creature on the prowl, and just above her the unmistakable 'whoosh' of a barn owl on the wing.

She loved it all. Like Ben, she would badly miss this place. But, unlike Ben, she had learned to be realistic. Her dearest wish in life was to have a child, but it seemed that was not to be. These past years she had come to realise that craving for something that was out of reach only made the pain sharper. Ben was not able to think like that, so he was suffering badly, and there was little she could do. Even so, she could try. That was her sole reason for visiting Eric now.

Suddenly, the heightening breeze struck chilly. Shivering, she set off again, wanting to get it over with and get back to Sal. She didn't like leaving her alone of an evening, though the old lady would quickly tell her not to be so silly if she were to hear of her daughter-in-law's concern for her. Independent to the last, that was Sal.

Eric's cottage was not far now. Just over the brow of the hill and down towards the valley and she would be there. 'I hope he's in,' she mused. 'Serve me right if he's down in the pub along with the rest of 'em.'

But maybe he was still smarting from the attack, and now, like as not, he would travel miles before he'd sup in the same pub as Ben Hunter.

At the top of the hill she hesitated. 'What if Ben finds out I'm asking favours from Eric?' she wondered aloud. 'By! He'd never forgive me, and I can't say as I'd blame him neither.'

From here she could see Eric's cottage; such a pretty little place, with its quaint thatched roof and tiny lead-light windows, and masses of roses climbing over the porch. It had been home and hearth to Eric for so long, Louise had never known it any other way.

'Right then, I'd best get on.' Now that she was

so close, her courage was beginning to desert her. 'If he's not in, it's a wasted journey. I'll not come here again. I dare say I'll not get the chance without Ben knowing.' In fact, in her deepest heart she was hoping Eric would not be in.

But he *was* in, because the light was blazing from the front kitchen window, and even from here, she could see his shadow as he walked backwards and forwards past the window, as though agitated in some way.

Before she could change her mind and flee, back to Sal and the comfort of home, she took to her heels and ran like the wind, down the hill and along by the spinney. In minutes she was knocking on his door, her heart beating fifteen to the dozen.

Opening the door, Eric took a minute to realise who it was; in the twilight he couldn't be certain, until he opened the door wider. When the soft light from the passage fell on her face, he gave a cry of pleasure. 'Louise!' Only a moment ago he had been thinking about her and now, here she was.

Knowing the reason she was here, Louise was acutely embarrassed. 'I hope you don't mind me calling on you at this time of night,' she said lamely. 'Only, there's summat I need to ask you.'

Eric's smile warmed her heart. 'It's a real pleasure to see you, lass.' Standing aside, he waited for her to enter, his soft loving eyes watching as she went by him into the tiny sitting room. 'You shouldn't have come across the fields in the dark.' He closed the door and followed her inside. 'I don't suppose for one minute that Ben knows yer here?'

She shook her head decisively. 'No, and he wouldn't be too pleased if he knew I were here to ask a favour.'

Gesturing to the chair, he suggested, 'You'd best sit yerself down.' When she did so, he asked, 'D'you want a drink – tea, is it?' He smiled and she was at ease. 'Or is it to be summat that'll send the night-chill from your bones?'

'I don't need a drink,' she answered gratefully. 'I need to talk.'

Seeing the determined look in her eye, Eric sat in the chair opposite, where he could see the colour of her eyes and the attractive curve of her full-lipped mouth. 'I'm listening.'

Louise observed him discreetly. She saw the bruises still vivid on his face and neck, and the slash of red down his arm where his shirt-sleeve was rolled to the elbow. 'I'm sorry you got beat up,' she said. 'It was a cowardly thing.'

Having been unaware that she had noticed the bruises so closely, he rolled down his sleeves. 'Water under the bridge.' Leaning back in the chair, he hoped his injuries were not so prominent. 'Now

then, lass, what is it you've come to see me about?
A favour, you said.'

'It's Ben . . .'

'I gathered as much.' A frown crossed his handsome face. 'What about him?'

She gulped. The resentment was still on him, just
like it was on Ben. 'Must you two be at each other's
throats?' She had not meant to ask that question,
but with his intense gaze focused on her, it seemed
a natural thing to say.

'It's what he wants.'

'No, Eric, it's not.'

'You could've fooled me.'

'About the farm?' There was no use hedging
about it.

'Yes?' His voice betrayed a certain wariness.

'Do you mean to live there?'

'Aye, lass, that's why I bought it.'

She nodded, needing to ask the question that
burned in her mind, yet afraid to. 'I'm sorry you've
been given notice to quit.'

'So am I.' He leaned forward, his eyes burning
into hers. 'In a short time, I'll be homeless. I didn't
make the circumstances that forced the sale of the
farm, but I needed a home, so, when the opportunity
came I took it. I had the chance to stay here, where
I'm alive. Not stuck in some back alley where I
can't breathe.' He looked at her desperately. 'You

do understand, don't you, lass? I never meant for any o' this to happen.'

'Yes, I know.'

'I'm not happy about the situation between me and Ben.'

'He's much like you, Eric. The idea of living in town in a row of houses fills him with dread.'

'Aye.' Getting out of the chair he looked down on her. 'Why did you come here tonight?'

Louise took a deep breath. 'I wanted to ask if you'd consider letting me and Ben . . . and Sal, stay where we are. In the farmhouse, I mean.'

He looked at her incredulously. 'Haven't I just finished telling you how I'm soon to be homeless?'

She nodded. 'Happen if you and Ben could talk it through, and you let him think it were *your* suggestion, we could all live under the same roof . . . for a time anyway, until Ben could find work on a farm, and mebbe a house to go with it.'

He smiled at her innocent suggestion. 'No, it would never work.'

Dejected, Louise could only apologise. 'I should never have asked, I'm sorry.' She walked to the door. 'I'd best get back before he's home.'

Turning quickly, she bumped into him as he walked forward; the touch of his warm hands on her shoulders as he steadied her sent a wonderful shock right to her soul. 'You won't tell him I came to see you?' Her voice trembled. 'He'd hit the roof if he knew I'd gone behind his back.'

Eric shook his head. 'It would never have worked. You know that, don't you, lass?'

The truth hit her like a fist in the stomach. 'What . . . you and me under the same roof, you mean?' He loved her, she could see it in his eyes. 'I'd best go.'

But he wouldn't let her leave, not now. How could he? 'I love you, lass . . . I allus have.'

Somehow, Louise was not shocked or surprised. Since the day when Ben had suspected something out of nothing, she had seen Eric in a different light, but this was wrong, so amazingly, wonderfully wrong. The thought of her husband haunted her. 'I have to go.'

There was no conviction in her voice, and in her eyes he could see the mirror of his own feelings. 'Don't go yet. Please don't go.'

When Louise hesitated, he raised his hands and taking her gently by the shoulders, drew her to him. He didn't speak, neither did she, because in that moment as they looked into each other's eyes, something inexplicable happened between them; a certain need, a meeting of lonely souls – or maybe it was some deeper attraction that Ben had sensed, and they had not.

Whatever the emotions between them in that

moment, both Louise and Eric were stunned into silence. Softly, he took her by the hand and, leading her to the stairway, collected her into his arms and carried her up to the bedroom.

It wasn't planned, and later they would both come to regret it, but just then, nothing else seemed to matter; there was no one else in the world but the two of them.

When they were both naked, they lay together for a while; he kissing her over and over on her neck and face, then his open lips following the curve of her breast. He had never needed a woman more than he needed Louise. The want was like a searing heat inside him.

While he touched her, with the tenderness of love, Louise held him to her. When a moment later, he entered her, nervously at first and then with desperation, she clung to him, giving herself freely, her body and her love.

When it was over and he lay exhausted beside her, she reached out to touch him, stroking the long slender hairs on his chest, and now softly kissing him on the mouth.

He turned towards her, his eyes coveting her beauty. 'Don't hate me,' he whispered. 'I never meant . . .'

'Ssh!' Holding his face between her hands, she told him, 'I could never hate you.' When he went to touch her cheek, she slowly shook her head. 'I have to go now. I can never come back.'

While Louise got dressed, he sat on the edge of the bed, his head bent into the palms of his hands. When suddenly he felt the gossamer touch of her lips on his neck, he turned hopefully, only to see her hurrying out of the door; out of his life, for ever.

Going to the window he looked out into the dark, and there she was, like part of the shadows, fleeing across the grass and into the wilderness beyond. 'I'll always love you,' he murmured, but he could not get her words out of his tortured mind. 'I can never come back,' she had said. And he knew it was so.

He was a man devastated. He had touched heaven, then all in a moment, it was snatched away from him.

But for all that, his love for Louise was stronger than ever.

———◆◦◆———

S AL HAD HEARD Louise go out, and now she heard her come back in. As the young woman trod slowly up the stairs and into her room, Sal knew in her heart that all was not well. 'Talk to me, child,' she murmured. 'A trouble shared is a trouble halved.'

Like Louise, she had seen the change come over Ben, and like Louise, she found it difficult to deal with.

She heard Louise pacing the floor and her heart went out to her. Over the years, she had come to know and love the girl like her own daughter. 'You'll cope, lass,' she whispered. 'You'll find a way.'

Herself weary and tired, she turned over and went to sleep.

Louise, however, could find no solace in sleep. Instead, filled with a terrible guilt at what she and Eric had done, she stood by the window, still dressed, watching for Ben to come home, wanting to make amends, and hating herself for having betrayed him.

Several times she glanced at the clock on her bedside table. 'Where is he?' She grew increasingly anxious. The minutes ticked away, then the hours, and now it was two in the morning, and still he was not home.

She paced a while longer, then lay down on their bed, and before she knew it, her eyes were closed and her troubled mind overwhelmed by much-needed sleep.

⇒·◦·⇐

IT WAS ALMOST four in the morning when Ben finally let himself into the house.

Treading carefully on every step he went up the stairs and into the bedroom. He was not surprised to see the bedside light still burning, but his heart broke to see his wife lying on top of the bed, fast asleep.

Standing over her, he gazed down on this good and lovely woman, who had seen him through the worst crisis of his life. Uncomplaining and always supportive, she had stood by him through thick and thin, when a lesser woman might have gone her own way.

With the tears streaming down his face, he could not take his eyes off her. 'I'm sorry, lass.' Falling to his knees, he marvelled at her quiet loveliness, and the kind, strong nature beneath. She looked so incredibly young and vulnerable. With her long brown hair, one arm reaching over the pillow, the other across her face, as though hiding from the cares of her world, she looked innocent as a child.

As quickly and quietly as he could, he slipped out of his clothes and into bed, at the same time covering her over.

When she stirred, he laid his arm across her. 'I'll make it up to you,' he promised, 'you see if I don't.' With his arm round her, he drifted into a restless sleep.

Night was setting and day beginning to creep in, when he woke. But it wasn't the early light coming into the room that shook him from his sleep. It was the unmistakable sound of someone sobbing.

Alarmed, he sat up in bed, his bleary eyes slowly

becoming accustomed to the mixed morning light. When his gaze alighted on Louise, hunched by the window, breaking her heart, he leapt out of bed and snatched her into his arms. 'I'm sorry,' he whispered, over and over. 'Oh sweetheart, I'm so sorry. Can yer forgive me?'

While she rested against his broad shoulder, he poured out the guilt he felt at having hurt her. 'I didn't mean to make you worry. I got talking to the landlord, y'see? He made me realise it isn't the end of the world. I've still got you and Mam, and I've got me health and strength. Leaving here won't be so bad, and happen I'll find work on the land . . .' his voice hardened '. . . without kowtowing to that bastard, Forester.'

Sensing her stiffen in his arms, he regretted having said that to her. 'Look, sweetheart, even if I have to buckle down and work in a factory, it won't matter so long as I've got you.'

Reaching down, he crooked his finger under her chin, his love for her overwhelming. 'You'll never know how much I love you,' he whispered. Raising her face to his, he kissed her softly on the mouth. 'In spite of everything, we've got a future, you and me. Just give me a chance, and you'll see. I'll do everything in my power to make it all up to you. Derwent Street isn't so bad. Once we're settled there, I'll soon forget this way o' life.'

In his heart though, he knew he would never settle anywhere but here.

Quiet in her own thoughts, Louise clung to him. She heard his promises and his declaration of love for her, and she knew he meant it all.

'We'll go and see this little house on Derwent Street again tomorrow, take some measurements,' he went on, trying to please her, wanting to make it all right for her. 'It's nearer town. You'll not have to wait for the tram every time you want to go shopping, and it'll be easy enough for me to find work, I dare say. What's more, you'll have yer mam close by.'

Louise could hear him, urging her that everything would work out. He had found her crying and thought she was upset because he was making life difficult for her. 'I wouldn't hurt you for the world,' he was saying now. 'Come on, lass. Get back into bed . . . let me give yer a proper cuddle.'

When he tugged at her hand, she went with him, under the covers and into his arms, where he gently held her before falling asleep again. Riddled with guilt, Louise was far from being sleepy. Her thoughts were tormented; something had changed and her relationship with her husband would never be the same again.

Because even when he held her as close as any man could hold his woman, her mind was filled with thoughts of another man.

The truth was like a hammer blow to her. She did not love Ben in that way any more. It was Eric she wanted.

But it was too late . . . all too late.

Chapter Thirteen

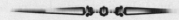

IT HAD BEEN a busy week, but now the packing was done, and they were ready to leave.

'By! I never want to do that again in a hurry, lass.' Sal was perched on top of a packing case, her feet barely touching the ground. 'I never knew we'd collected so many things.'

'It's horse's work.' Louise folded the last of the curtains and came to sit beside her. 'I could do with a brew. What do you say?'

For a moment Sal gave no answer. Then she lifted her head and looked at her daughter-in-law, and the heartache was written all over her face. Her small, homely features crumpled. 'I can't believe we're leaving this place,' she said brokenly, and then the tears came and wouldn't stop.

'It's all right, Sal. You cry if you want to, sweetheart.'

And while she sobbed uncontrollably, Louise cuddled the little woman, amazed that Sal had been able to hold in her grief for so long.

Emerging from the kitchen where she had been helping to box the last of the crockery, Patsy Holsden looked at Louise, and Louise shook her head.

On that, Patsy returned to the kitchen. 'It's a bad day for all of 'em,' she declared, shaking her head. 'Let's hope to God the old woman can be happy on Derwent Street.'

After all, she herself had lived there for enough years. It wasn't the worst place in the world. But then again, it wasn't the best neither – especially when you were saddled with a daughter like their Susan!

In the other room, Louise let the old woman cry the bitterness out.

From where they were seated on the packing box, she could see out the window and down towards the orchard, and there was Ben, leaning against a tree and gazing out over the hills and valleys of Salmesbury. He made a sorry sight, that lonely, bitter man.

And because of what she had done, her heart went out to him. Not with love of the kind she had once felt, but with fondness and pity, and a determination to make him as content in his new life as she could.

After all they had been through together, she owed him that much.

<hr />

AT HALF-PAST THREE, Mike Ellis the milkman arrived with his horse and cart. 'All ready for off, arc wc?' Puffing his old pipe, he waddled up to the front door where the entire family had been waiting for him. 'Sorry I'm late,' he apologised. 'Only I've had a few problems.' Looking sheepish, he told Ben, 'I've had to alter me plans to a certain extent . . . as yer can see.'

Ben had already noticed and was none too pleased. 'I thought you promised to move us in a lorry,' he accused sharply, 'and here you are, turning up with that scruffy old horse and cart, after I med it clear enough. The last thing I wanted was to arrive in Derwent Street looking like some horde o' gypsies fresh outta the woods.'

'Now then, young Hunter!' Mikey was deeply insulted. 'First of all, that horse might be old, but he ain't scruffy, not by a long chalk. What! I'm allus washing and brushing his coat, and I even 'ad his feet trimmed special for today.' Giving the animal the once-over, he declared, 'I'm right proud o' that old nag, an' I'd not be ashamed of him no matter where I took him.'

'That's as may be. But what the devil d'yer think the new neighbours'll make of us turning up on the back end of a horse and cart, eh? Most folk get a wagon to move 'em. An' that were what I asked you to do. So, what's gone wrong?'

'I tried me best, lad, honest to God I did. But the wagon were already spoke for. I even went to see Sam Benton as works for the Coal Board. I had every intention of borrowing his wagon and giving it the best clean of its life. But it seems everybody's stocking up wi' coal, ready for winter. Sam's been asked to work overtime, so the wagon's not available.'

Taking a deep puff of his pipe he then knocked it out on the porch wall. 'So there y'are, son. That's the way of it, and yer must tek it or leave it, I can't do no better.' He addressed himself to Sal who, like Louise, was thoroughly enjoying the banter between her son and this likeable old fella. 'I really am very sorry, missus.'

'It's all right,' she answered. 'We're not too proud to be seen following your horse and cart into Derwent Street.' Turning to Louise she asked, 'What d'you say, love?'

Louise was all for it. 'What they see is what they get,' she chuckled. 'It'll give 'em summat to talk about, I dare say.'

Realising he was outnumbered, Ben conceded.

'Go on then,' he told the old fella irritably. 'You and me can load up the furniture, while the women take the light stuff. We'd best get on with it if we're to be settled in afore dark.' There had been enough time wasted already, he thought.

There wasn't all that much to load, since much of the farmhouse contents was included in the sale: two beds with matching dressers and wardrobes; a sofa and two armchairs; one small sideboard and table, and a few odds and ends including the cooker, and all the small stuff like linen and personal belongings.

With everyone helping, it wasn't long before they were ready to leave.

'Now, yer sure yer ain't forgot nothing?' Mike prided himself on being thorough. 'It's a fair old lick back here from Blackburn town,' he reminded them. 'What's more, the old horse has been standing too long already.'

'Will you stop worrying,' Louise chided. 'Once we leave here, we won't be coming back.' She thought of Eric and her heart turned over. 'There'll be nothing to come back for,' she added regretfully.

Loading up the last of his tools, Ben caught the sadness in her voice and once again, he misunderstood the reason. Going to her, he put his arm about her shoulders. 'Don't be sad, sweetheart,' he murmured fondly. 'Happen we'll be happier in Derwent Street than ever we were here.'

Louise looked at him, at the feigned, reassuring smile on his face and she knew the heartache inside him. 'Happen we will,' she answered, and for a long, poignant moment they held onto each other.

At that moment, Louise raised her gaze and there, some way off, standing against the fence surrounding what was now his own land, stood the proud, lonely figure of Eric. His gaze met hers and each read the other's mind.

Quickly, she looked away. 'We'd best be off,' she said smartly. 'Me and Sal mean to put up the new curtains before it gets dark.'

From the doorway, Sal had seen Louise and her son embrace each other. *She had also witnessed the silent, brooding exchange between Louise and Eric, and was deeply shaken.*

'Come on then, Mam. Don't keep us waiting.' Ben had already started the car.

A few moments later and it was time to go.

Following the milkman's horse and cart, Ben manoeuvred his little black car along the rutted driveway leading from the cottage. He didn't look back and, for different reasons, neither did Louise.

But Sal did. And she saw Eric, his soulful gaze following them as they left. A discreet glance at her daughter-in-law's downcast face raised all manner of suspicions in the old woman's mind. But she would not cast aspersions. Instead, she would quietly watch, and wait for Louise to turn to her; as she surely would.

In all the years she had known her, Louise had been a good wife and a wonderful daughter-in-law; Sal could not have wished for better. Whenever the girl had been unsure or troubled, she had found a friend in Sal. That had not changed, and never would.

This time though, it seemed that Louise had been drawn into something deep; something which, in the end, would touch on them all!

'All right, are you, Sal?' Louise was concerned for the old woman.

'Aye, lass, don't you worry yerself about me.'

From the front, Ben glanced at the two women in his rearview mirror. He wanted to reassure them, but couldn't bring himself to utter comforting words. Not when in his heart, he felt like a man going to the gallows.

Louise settled back in her seat. Closing her eyes she held the mental picture of Eric. Seeing him there like that, catching his sorrowful gaze, had upset her. If she had doubted her newfound love for him, she didn't doubt it now. A woman knew. *She* knew. It was a strange, disturbing thing. She still loved Ben, and yet there was no joy or magic any more.

She asked herself the same question that she had asked many times these past twenty-four hours; what did she *really* feel for Ben? And yes, the answer was 'love'. But what *kind* of love? All she knew was that it had never been the kind she felt for Eric – that all-consuming, overwhelming need that turned her heart and soul inside out.

There was a sadness in her now, a feeling of emptiness that she must learn to endure. Because, love him or not, she could not put Ben through any more pain. What had happened to her was not his fault, any more than it was hers. Ironically though, had it not been for him thinking wrong things about her and Eric, this might never have happened. But it had, and there was no going back.

The more she thought about it, the more her heart ached.

Suddenly jolted out of her thoughts by the gentle touch of Sal's small hand, Louise sat up, the guilt bright on her face.

Sal leaned towards her, her voice low and soft. 'D'yer want to talk about it, lass?'

Louise caught her breath. 'Talk about what?'

'About what's ailing yer.'

'Nothing's ailing me.' How could she lie like that, and to Sal of all people. The shame engulfed her.

Sal patted her hand. 'All right, love,' she said. 'But you know I'm here if yer need me?'

Louise squeezed her hand. 'I know.' She looked into the old woman's quiet eyes and realised that

Sal had seen her turmoil. It was clear she suspected something – but not the awful truth, Louise hoped.

'Thank you, Sal,' she murmured. 'I am a bit unsettled, but I expect it's just the move and everything.'

'We're almost there!' Having chatted to Ben for most of the journey, Patsy was blissfully unaware of the quiet conversation between the other two. 'Another five minutes and we'll be in Derwent Street.'

Sal smiled at Louise. 'Everything will turn out for the best,' she whispered. 'You'll see.'

The girl returned her smile. 'I'll make sure it does,' she replied, and meant it.

———◦———

S USAN WAS WAITING at the door. 'Quick, Dad, they're here!' Excited as a two year old she ran down the street to meet them. 'We thought you'd never get here,' she cried, running alongside the car. 'What took you so long?'

'Stop moithering.' Her dad Steve wasn't far behind. 'I expect they've been too busy to worry about the time.' Like Susan he was glad to have them here in Derwent Street. He and Patsy hoped Louise being close by would be a good influence on their wayward lass.

Preferring animals to people, Mike Ellis confided in his old horse. 'Such a fuss!' he complained with a little grin. 'Anybody'd think I were fetching royalty, so they would.'

Bringing the whole ensemble to a halt, he quickly settled his four-legged friend. 'Shan't be long afore we're on us way home, old fella,' he promised. 'We'll have the cart emptied in no time at all.'

As good as his word, Mike lost no time in throwing back the tarpaulin cover put over the furniture and such in case of an unexpected downpour.

'Right then, my friend, which way do we go about offloading this little lot?' Knowing how temperamental the old man could be, Ben thought it best to ask before barging in, hamfisted.

The little milkman tutted. 'It's plain to see *you've* not done much furniture moving,' he said, with some slight disgust.

'Yer right there,' Ben admitted. 'I've never had reason to, seeing as I've lived at the farm all me life.'

Mike was mortified. ''Course not, lad.' He cursed his big mouth. 'Look, there's a knack to it,' he imparted with pride. 'Start with the largest first. Climb up to the front an' edge that dresser towards the back,' he suggested. 'Then get yersel' down an' we'll have it away into the house.'

While the two men unloaded the furniture, with

Steve Holsden's assistance, Louise and her mam, together with Susan, carried the lighter articles into the house.

Susan was delighted with her own efforts. 'I've done what you asked,' she told her mam. 'I've put bread and milk in the pantry, and I've laid a fire in case the house is damp.'

Louise was grateful. 'Thanks, sis,' she said. 'That was really thoughtful of you.'

'And look there.' She pointed to a vase of fresh flowers in the window. 'I got them off the market. I thought they'd cheer you up.'

Her sister looked across to the window-ledge and there, lovingly arranged in a small jug, was a pretty bouquet of different coloured roses. 'They're lovely.' Deeply touched, Louise put her arms round her sister. 'They *have* cheered me up.'

'I knew they would.' Like a puppy dog with two tails, Susan beamed at her sister's gratitude. 'I'm glad you're here,' she told her.

'So am I.' In a way that was true, even though part of her was still back there, with Eric.

While Susan and her mam went back outside to collect more items, Louise stood looking round the little room. It wasn't filled with sunshine the way the cottage had always been. The walls were drab and the ceiling a dirty grey colour. There was an old brown carpet on the floor, but it was clean and had a lot of wear in it yet. And the house seemed to have a warm, welcoming atmosphere.

It wasn't what Louise had envisaged, but it was all they could afford just now. 'We'll make it a home,' she vowed softly. 'Later, when the money starts coming in, we'll paint the walls and have a new carpet, and . . .' She smiled at her growing excitement. 'All in good time,' she told herself. 'Rome wasn't built in a day.'

Inevitably she thought of Eric, and the excitement dimmed.

It would take more than a new carpet and a wash of paint to drive him from her heart.

PART TWO

AUGUST, 1952
NEW BEGINNINGS

Chapter Fourteen

Patsy and Steve Holsden rarely went out in the evening, but tonight was a special event. 'It's not often we get invited out,' Patsy remarked as she put on her best hat and coat; the coat being ten years old and the hat a delightful thing got from the market for half a crown. 'Your dad hasn't seen Leo Woolward for that many years he didn't even recognise him when he came across him on the tram the other day.'

'Well, he looked different. He were fatter, and he had a beard when I knew him.' Steve gave a cheeky wink. 'By! Me and 'im had some wild old times when we were young. It's a wonder we weren't thrown in prison! I recall a time when we were coming out the Roxy on King Street . . . There were these two lasses – long legs an' big, "come-on" eyes as I remember.' Rolling his own eyes, he giggled. 'Well, me an' Leo—'

'That's quite enough o' that.' Patsy dug him in the ribs. 'I'm sure our Susan doesn't want to hear about your randy goings-on.'

Putting her magazine aside, Susan laughed. 'Yes, I do,' she declared. 'It's *you* who doesn't want to hear, in case it makes you jealous.'

Patsy gave her daughter a look of horror. 'What me? I've never been jealous in my life.'

'Sorry, Mam.' Susan realised she had gone too far. 'I were only saying.'

'Well, *don't*.' Turning to Steve, Patsy propelled him into the passage. 'One word from you,' she threatened, 'an' you'll meet this old mate o' yours on your own.'

Steve took umbrage at having the blame thrust on him like that. 'Whatever are yer talking about, woman?' he demanded sulkily. 'I never said a word about your bloody old hat.'

'Oh! So you think it's old, do yer? An' I suppose you don't like me coat neither, is that it?'

Susan heard the banter all the way down the passage, until the front door slammed shut and it was peaceful once again. 'Thank God for that.' Sighing, she gave a little chuckle. 'Happen I can read me magazine in peace now.'

But the peace didn't last long.

No sooner had she settled down with the magazine open on her lap, than there came a determined knock on the front door. 'Who on earth's that?'

Trudging resentfully down the passage, she flung open the door, amazed to see Jacob standing there.

'Can I come in?' he asked.

'No, you can't.' Last Saturday night, not having heard a peep out of him for several days, she'd gone into town with a friend and spotted Jacob and Maggie arm in arm coming out of the Palais. She couldn't forgive him. 'You'd best clear off,' she said coldly. 'Our mam doesn't want you anywhere near this house. If you'll take my advice, you'll bugger off before she hears you.'

'Is that right?' Leaning on the door-jamb he smiled, that irresistible boyish smile that made her go weak at the knees. 'Your mam's not likely to hear me,' he said. 'I've just seen her and your dad get on the tram.'

'Well, it doesn't make any difference,' she protested, 'because *I* don't want you here either.'

When at that minute she went to close the door in his face he stopped it by jamming his foot there. 'You don't mean that.'

'I saw you,' she revealed angrily, 'you and that dark-haired tart, coming out of the Palais the other night. Go on, get back to your fancy piece, why don't you? I've had enough of your two-timing.'

'You're a fool, darlin'.' He was the world's best liar. 'I don't give a sod for her. She's got a house an' I need somewhere to live. I'm keeping her sweet, that's all. It's *you* I want and always have.'

'I don't believe you.' Already she was weakening.

'Why don't yer let me in and I'll explain.'

'No.'

'We've a lot to talk about, you an' me. Plans to make.'

Visibly relaxing she sighed and then smiled. 'What kind o' plans?'

'Any kind yer like.' He slid his arm round her waist. 'You an' me,' he whispered dangerously in her ear. 'We can do whatever we like . . . once I've sorted meself out.'

Melting into his arms, she kicked the door shut with the heel of her foot. 'You're a bastard.'

'Mebbe. But yer still want me, don't yer?' His hungry eyes looked her over. 'How long will yer mam be out?'

She looked at him steadily. 'Long enough.' Taking him by the hand she led him along the passage and up the stairs.

'I knew you'd see sense,' he said slyly. 'That other woman means nowt to me, and never will.'

'You're a liar an' a cheat,' she said, regarding him with suspicious eyes. 'But you're right – I *do* love you.' She paused, staring at him a moment longer, until he began to feel oddly uncomfortable.

When she next spoke, he wondered at the darker

side of her nature that she had never shown him before; that secretive, brooding side that only a woman could hide. 'Remember this,' she warned. 'If ever I find out you're lying to me, I won't be responsible for my actions.'

A thrill of fear ran through him. 'What's that supposed to mean?'

'Never you mind,' she answered, stroking his face with the tenderness of a woman besotted. 'Let's just say the sooner you're rid of *her*, and have got a place of your own, the better I'll like it.'

They were so frantic to be with each other, they couldn't wait to get into bed. Instead they rolled about on the floor, stripping each other's clothes away, until fired with the passion of lust, he took her to him like a man starved.

Susan would have preferred to be fussed and pampered and the loving to be tender. But it was never like that with Jacob. It wasn't like it now. But, in their own way, each was satisfied.

Less than an hour after he'd arrived, he was wanting to leave. 'I'd best go,' he told her. 'I've things to do . . . business to tend.'

The dark anger rising, she questioned him. 'What kind of business is it, that can't wait till morning,'

He wagged a finger. 'Hey! One thing yer should know. I don't discuss my business with *anybody*.'

Susan's eyes narrowed. 'Not even with *her*?'

Sensing her hostility, he took her into his arms and soothed her. 'No,' he lied, 'not even with her. Besides, haven't I just got through telling you she's only my landlady? She's never been any more than that and never will be.'

'You'd better not be lying to me.'

The fear trembled fleetingly inside him, but his smile was teasing. 'There yer go again, threatening me!'

They parted at the door with a kiss. 'Will I see you tomorrow?' Susan hated to see him leave.

'I dare say.'

'Where?'

'I'll let you know.'

Afraid she might lose him because of her temper, she apologised. 'I'm sorry if I've angered you, but you know how I feel, Jacob. I so much want us to set up home together, and all you've done so far is make excuses to put me off.'

'You're wrong.'

'I hope so.'

'Have you got enough money for me an' you to find a place of our own?' He was cunning to the end.

'You know I haven't.'

'Right. So don't make life any more difficult for me than it already is.'

'What do you mean?'

'I mean that it takes money to set up in a house from scratch; not to mention a month's rent in advance. So, if yer really want it to happen, you'll just have to trust me.'

'And if I can't trust you, it's nobody's fault but yours. You've lied and cheated, until I don't know where I am with you.'

'Look, sweetheart.' Taking her by the shoulders, he gave a long, weary-sounding groan. 'I'm doing the best I can, so for Christ's sake, will yer stop harping on before I start to wonder if you an' me moving in together is a good idea.'

'Oh Jacob, I'm sorry.' Grabbing him by the lapels she reached up and kissed him on the mouth. 'It's just that I want to be with you, all the time.' Her eyes filled with tears. 'It gets to me when I don't see you.'

Thrusting her off, he argued, 'I can't be everywhere at once. And right now, I'd best be on me way. I've a business deal going, an' it needs to be gentled along. If it goes sour, God only knows when we'll be able to set up in our own little place.'

Reassured yet again, she smiled up at him with big cow eyes. 'I love you, Jacob.'

'I know you do.' When she clung to him like that, it turned his stomach over. 'I love you too,' he lied. 'Now let me go, you bitch.' He laughed. 'Or I'll have to take you back upstairs and show you who's boss.'

Susan quite liked the idea of that. 'I wouldn't complain,' she said coyly, 'but I expect you'd best get off. Like you say, the sooner you clinch the deal, the sooner we'll be together.'

'Right.' Wrapping his hands over hers, he eased her away. 'Isn't that what I've just been saying?'

She stood at the door, watching him walk down Derwent Street and wishing with all her heart she could go with him. 'I mean it,' she whispered harshly. 'I won't let *her* take you away from me.'

Whenever she thought of him going back to another woman's house, *she felt the urge to kill.*

Aware that she was watching, Jacob quickened his steps. 'I'd best watch my step with that one,' he muttered. 'I only went after her because I hoped it would get me to Louise. And so far it's done nowt o' the sort.'

He had a strange feeling there was more to Susan Holsden than met the eye. 'I sometimes wonder if she ain't as mad as a bloody hatter!' Still, she'd do for a good time yet. The thought of Susan's voracious sexual appetite put a spring in his step.

The feeling of elation didn't last long though. Sobered by a pressing matter not yet resolved, he hurried along. 'I'd best get back to Maggie, or I'll have her on me back, too.'

For some reason which completely escaped him, his life was getting more and more involved. 'Bugger

Susan,' he decided. 'There's things me an' Maggie need to settle. And soon.'

⇒●⇐

WITH BEN LISTENING to the wireless and his mam gone to bed early, Louise was in the front room trying the new curtains up at the windows. She had just partly opened them for the third time after checking length against width, when she saw Jacob come out of her parents' house and walk by on the other side of the street.

It was an unpleasant shock to see him there. Her first thought went to Susan. She had tried so hard to dissuade her sister from having anything to do with Jacob Hunter, but it seemed her words had gone unheeded. She had recently been given to understand from Susan that Jacob was well and truly out of her life, but he was obviously back in it now.

She found herself talking aloud, and not for the first time, either. She found it comforting, if only because the sound of her own voice was better than none at all. These days, Ben seemed to have little to say and Sal, God bless her, was often lost in her own thoughts.

All in all, life had become very lonely since moving here to Derwent Street, though it was good to have her mam and dad nearby, and Susan too, if only she would listen to sense where that man was concerned.

Suddenly, Jacob paused and looked towards the window where Louise was standing. His gaze was intense, brooding. Her heart lurching, Louise quickly drew back. Pressing herself against the wall, she held her breath and hoped he hadn't seen her.

After a moment or two she heard the clunk of his shoes as he hurried along the cobbles. 'Good riddance!' Gingerly taking a peep from the side of the curtains, she satisfied herself that he was gone. 'That's enough for tonight,' she decided, closing the curtains. 'They'll do till morning.' She had the awful fear that he might return.

Closing the front-room door, she thought of Susan and how weak she was where Jacob was concerned. 'You're all kinds of a fool, Susan.' She would have a word with her tomorrow. 'You just couldn't wait for Mam and Dad to turn their backs before you had him in the house, could you, eh?!'

Swinging round she almost leapt out of her shoes when Ben caught hold of her. 'Talking to yerself, is it?' He smiled down on her. 'They take you away for less than that.'

'Happen I should be taken away.' Pushing past him she went into the living room. 'I might have somebody else to talk to then, instead o' talking to meself most of the time.'

'I'm neglecting yer, is that what yer saying?' He was quick to flare up these days.

She went straight to the kitchen, where she put the kettle on. 'You said it,' she turned to accuse him. 'Not me.'

'I'm sorry, Louise, but what with this driving job and being cooped up all day in a lorry cab, I sometimes feel like I'm going out of me mind.'

Louise was ashamed. 'Oh look, I didn't mean to be miserable,' she apologised 'I know it's hard for you, love, but it's hard for me as well. I'm having to adjust the same as you, and so is your mam, but we don't go silent with each other. We talk about it, and sometimes it helps.'

'I don't want to talk about it.' Frowning, he threw himself into a chair. 'What bloody good would that do?'

Coming back into the living room, Louise pursued the matter. 'We're all of us finding it hard, Ben. Don't you think me and Sal miss the farm – the fresh air and the fields all round us? I often stand at that front window and look down Derwent Street, and me heart sinks to me boots.'

'You never told me that.' He was shaken. 'I thought you'd settled in here really well.'

Louise shook her head. 'Sometimes, when I see the folks coming and going about their business, I feel trapped. Then I wish to God I was up at the farm, working in the orchard with the sun on my face, and your mam some way off in the garden, hanging out the sheets.' Her face glowed with pleasure at the memory, then grew sad again. 'It's another world, my love, and we've lost it.'

'Huh! Don't yer think I know it?'

'I'm sure you do, like the two of us. But it's no use craving over what we can't have. We've all to settle in here whether we like it or not, 'cause there's no alternative.'

'And you blame *me* for that, don't yer?' Suddenly he was on his feet, and she knew it was the start of yet another row.

'No, Ben, of course I don't blame you. It's nobody's fault. All I'm saying is we've to knuckle down.'

'Easier said than done!'

'I've been thinking . . .' Coming to sit on the arm of his chair, she put a proposal to him. 'What if you looked for work on one of the farms hereabouts? You're well experienced, and mebbe you might even find us a house that goes with the job.' Leaning over she put her arm round his shoulder. 'What d'you say?'

Thrusting her off, he got out of the chair and grabbing his coat from the back of the door, he threw it on. Scowling, he told her, 'It's come to summat, when a man's wife thinks she knows best.'

Louise was mortified. 'I didn't mean it like that, Ben, and well you know it. I was only trying to help. It hurts me to see how miserable you are.'

'Oh, I see.' Feigning surprise, he mocked her. 'So yer think I'll be content breaking me back on somebody else's farm, do yer? Slogging day and night seven days a week, helping some other lucky devil to keep his farm going, when I should be working for meself?'

He had not wanted to quarrel with his wife, but when she made suggestions like that it was like a stab in the back to him. 'Look, I don't want to talk about it. I'm off out.'

'Where are you going?' It seemed he was never in these days. He was either working late or down the pub.

Ignoring her question he told her, 'I'll happen be late home, so it's no use yer waiting up for me.'

'No, Ben, please.' She needed him here with her. 'Stay and talk to me.'

For a long moment it seemed he might agree, but then he looked at her with empty eyes. 'Like I said, don't wait up.' In two strides he was gone; down the passage and out the front door, and she was all alone once again.

Feeling dejected, Louise remained on the arm of the chair for what seemed an age, her mind filled with all manner of regrets. As always when she felt sad, her thoughts came right back to Eric, and that wonderful, unforgettable night.

'Are yer all right, lass?' Sal's voice cut through her reverie.

Startled by her mother-in-law's sudden appearance, Louise stood up. 'I thought you'd be fast asleep by now.'

'Aye, well, these days I don't seem to need much sleep.' Sal's face crinkled into an odd, wonky smile. 'Happen it's right what they say.'

'And what's that?'

'"Every sleep is a little death", and to tell the truth, I don't feel ready for me Maker just yet.'

Louise returned her smile. 'I should think not.'

When Sal came to sit beside the fireplace, Louise commented, 'I'm making a brew. D'you want one?'

'Aye, lass. Go on.'

While Louise bustled about in the kitchen, Sal discreetly watched her through the open door; she noticed how pale the girl was, and how drawn her pretty features were.

When a few moments later Louise returned with two cups of tea and a packet of ginger snaps, Sal waited until she was sat down before in the tenderest voice she told her, 'He doesn't mean it, you know.'

Louise was not surprised at her comment. 'I wondered if you had heard.'

'I'm sorry, lass, only I weren't asleep. It takes

me a long time to get off these days. It's the noise, you see – all the coming and going outside. And the street-lamps . . . even with the curtains closed, they seem to light up the room.'

Louise understood. 'I know what you mean.'

Sal nodded. 'I suppose it's only to be expected.' Like Louise she was realistic enough to know they would have to get used to it. 'Ben's finding it harder than either of us,' she said at length.

Louise remained silent. She and Ben seemed to be drifting apart, and it worried her.

Sal read her thoughts. 'That son o' mine has been giving you a hard time since we moved here. Nobody could blame yer, least of all me . . .' she paused, the words momentarily stuck in her throat, 'if you left him to it – though I hope to God it never comes to that.'

Louise shook her head. 'It won't,' she promised.

The two women talked awhile, and when Sal felt the need for sleep, she bade Louise goodnight. 'Don't wait up for him, pet,' she told her. 'Happen he'll have had a pint or two, an' there's no talking to a man when his brain's addled with the drink.'

Louise hadn't realised Sal had been watching him that closely. 'You don't miss much, do you?' she said with a grin.

Sal laughed. 'Not if I can help it,' she answered.

'Goodnight, Sal.'

'Goodnight, love, an' don't worry. He'll see sense soon enough.'

'I know he will.'

In her heart, Louise had no doubt it was only a matter of time before Ben found contentment.

Unfortunately, she was wrong.

Chapter Fifteen

MAGGIE COULDN'T BELIEVE her luck. 'A corner house, you say?'

The big balding man behind the desk nodded at her. 'Yes, missus. The poor fella passed on all of a sudden last month. I've been trying to shift it since then.'

'Why, what's wrong with it?'

'There's nowt wrong with it. I'll admit the place is not in too good a condition, but there's nowt a lick o' paint an' a scrubbing brush can't put right.' He looked at her high-heeled shoes, the cloud of dark hair and bright pink paint on her nails and put two and two together. 'Still, I'm sure you'll soon have the place spick and span,' he commented slyly. 'You seem like the sort who could turn her hand to *anything*.'

Maggie prickled. 'And what d'you mean by that?'

'I mean no insult,' he assured her. 'It's just that,

well, some of us have to do what we can to earn a living and there's nowt wrong with that. Then there's them as might turn their nose up at a woman like you moving in next door, if you know what I mean.'

'You mind your mouth!'

'Hey, there's no need to get on your high horse. I mean no harm. You seem like a good enough sort to me, but I've a reputation to mind, so there'll be none o' *that* going on in my premises, you understand? The place is to be kept respectable and clean and not used as a knocking-shop. The first inkling of any goings-on, and I'll be round there myself, to put you and them . . .' he pointed to the children standing beside her '. . . on the street. Do I make myself clear?'

'You cheeky bugger! If I weren't desperate for a place, I'd tell you where to shove your bloody corner house, an' no mistake.'

'Right – well, enough said. Now, do you want the place or not?'

'Haven't I just said so?'

Wagging a finger, he chided, 'Now, now. I'll not have you showing your temper in here.'

Maggie laughed. 'If you think *that's* a show of temper, you've not seen nothing yet.'

Ignoring her remark, he asked abruptly, 'Have you got the deposit?'

Maggie showed him the five pound note she was

clutching. 'It's all I've got,' she warned, 'so you'd best not try any funny stuff.'

'Like what?'

'Like saying there's extras to be paid for.'

'There are no extras,' he said haughtily. 'I already told you, I've a reputation to mind.' He was not too pleased with Maggie's attitude, but admired her pluck all the same. 'I'll have you know, I'm not one of your back-street dodgers. I've been in the property business man and boy, and my father before me. We're well known for our honest dealing.'

Maggie was in a hurry. 'That's all well and good,' she answered, 'but I'm not here for a history lesson. I'm here for the key to that corner house, and I'd appreciate it if you'd get a move on, before me feet fall off.' Shifting from one foot to the other she gave a moan. 'I've been out all morning. Me back aches, I'm fed up, and the kids are tired. So get on with it, would you?'

Placing the key on the desk, he held his hand over it when she reached out to take it. 'Not so quick, missus. Show me the colour of your money first.'

Maggie laughed out loud. 'You're right – you *do* know your business. You sound just like me – money first, service after.' It tickled her to see him blush to the roots of the few hairs left on his head.

'Five pounds,' he reminded her.

Ever cautious, she held onto her money for

a minute or two longer. 'You say it's got three bedrooms?'

'And another little boxroom in the attic, yes.'

'With a backyard and a lavvy?'

'Of course.'

'Right.' Maggie gave over the meagre remains of her savings; the few pounds she had hidden in a place where Jacob couldn't get his hands on it. He had long since discovered the loose brick beneath the kitchen window-sill, behind which she had kept her secret fund. 'Where do I sign?'

'Sign here,' he said, pointing to the dotted line on the form.

Taking up the pen she was offered, Maggie put her signature on the paper. 'It ain't often I put my name to a paper,' she told him. 'There had better be no tricks. My man can be a nasty devil when the mood takes him.'

Frowning, he told her sternly, 'There's no need for that kind of talk, Mrs Pringle.'

Maggie shrugged her shoulders. Reputation or not, it didn't hurt to let the buggers know they were being watched. 'Being as I've not even seen this place, would you mind telling me exactly where it is?' she wanted to know.

He pointed to the address. 'Fourteen, Craig Street,' he told her. 'Right on the corner of Derwent Street.'

'Thanks, mister.'

She paid her money and took the key, and as she left he said slyly, 'I might come round and see you now and then . . . when your man isn't home, if you know what I mean?'

She saw the twinkle in his eye and knew exactly what he meant. 'Why, you dirty old sod!' Bustling the children out of the door, she glanced back at him. 'You're welcome to come and see me,' she told him, 'but you'll not leave on your own two feet, I can tell you that. Not when I tell my man what you're up to.'

He gulped. 'You've got me all wrong,' he argued. 'I didn't mean . . .' His voice trailed away as she slammed shut the door.

Maggie smiled all the way down the street. 'We'll not see hide nor hair of *him* in a hurry,' she chuckled. Clutching the key in her hand, she went down that street like a dog with two tails. 'You'll have a backyard to play in,' she told the kids. 'And you'll not have to share a lavvy neither.'

'Where's Craig Street?' Adam wanted to know.

'I've no idea,' Maggie admitted. 'All I know is, it's on the corner of Derwent Street.'

Now all she had to do was convince Jacob he had no choice in the matter. 'Leave it to me,' she told the kids. 'We've paid our deposit and we've got the key, and for now, that's enough.'

Then there was no more time for talk, because in the next minute, they were off and running for the tram.

———✦———

'WHAT!' JACOB DID not take the news well. 'If yer think I'm taking on the responsibility of a house, yer can bloody well think again.'

'It's too late,' Maggie reminded him. 'I've paid five pounds cash. And besides, you've no choice in the matter.'

'Oh yes, I have! An' I'm buggered if I'll go rushing off to live in some strange house, all that upheaval an' paying more rent just so's yer can have a backyard, when we're perfectly settled where we are.'

'I'm not settled,' she argued. 'I never have liked it here, and you know that.'

'Well, we're not shifting, an' that's an end to it.'

'Right then.' Marching angrily to the back door, Maggie got her hat and coat. 'If that's the way you want it, then it's fine by me.' Squashing the beret on her head, she put on the coat and fastened it against the cool evening chill. Pushing past him, she made her way to the front passage. 'I'll not be long.'

'Where are yer off to now?'

'It's all right,' she snapped. 'The children are fast and hard asleep, so they'll not be bothering you, if that's what you're worried about.'

'I asked where you were off to.'

'I've an errand to run.'

'Where?'

'I'm away to have a word with your brother, Ben, if you must know. I'm sure he'd be pleased to learn how you and that friend o' yours cheated him out of his inheritance, falsifying receipts when all the time your dad had finished paying off the loan.'

At her words, Jacob leapt out of the chair. Grabbing her so roughly her beret fell off, he pushed her down into the chair. 'Who told you about that?'

'You did – but you won't remember, 'cause you were drunk to the world.'

'It's a lie. Whatever I said, it were a lie, spoken out of the drink. It doesn't mean owt.' His eyes stuck out like beacons.

'In that case I'll not be doing no harm if I tell Ben what you said.' She had learned to play him at his own game.

White with rage he stood before her, his eyes boring down into hers, and his voice shaking. 'You set one foot outside that door, an' I swear I'll do for yer!'

'Oh, aye?' Maggie wasn't afraid of him any more. 'And what would you say if I told you that I've written a letter to an old friend – somebody I can trust. It's all about your goings-on with the receipts. If anything happens to me, they'll know what's to be done.'

In the face of ruin, and possibly prison, he quickly changed his tack. 'Oh, darlin', what did you go an' do a thing like that for?'

Knowing she had won, the woman could hardly conceal her delight. 'Because you're a liar and a thief. Once you found my hiding-place, you took all my money and gambled it away, like you gambled away all the money you had left from when your business went bust, and your share of the money from Martin.' Her voice rose. 'You promised to look after me and the children. You said you'd buy the farm with me, and then when that went wrong, you said you'd find us a house and you never did. And now that *I've* found us one, you're doing all you can to back out of your promise.'

'So, if I go with you to this house, you'll have the letter destroyed?'

'Not straight off I won't, no.'

'What then?'

'I don't trust you, Jacob.' She had to be brutally honest, or lose the ground she had gained. 'First I need to see you keep your promise . . . *all* of it. You're to get a job and bring in the wages, so's I can stop doing what I've had to do, in order to keep body and soul together and provide for the children.'

'Hmh! Yer don't want much, d'yer?'

'Only what I deserve, and what you promised.' Her voice softened. 'Look, love, I don't want to see you put in prison, or have the lights beaten out of you by your brother if he should ever find out what a terrible thing you did to him.'

'He must *never* find out.' Jacob shook at the idea. 'I can't let that happen. I *won't*.' His heart sank at the thought of Louise finding out the truth.

'I know that, and like I say, I don't want to be the one to shop you, but as God's my judge, I'll do it if I have to.'

'Spiteful cow!'

'I'm sorry, Jacob, but all I want is for us to be a proper family. I want the children to have a daddy who takes care of them, and a mammy who stays home to see to their needs.'

'You've trapped me, you bitch!' Turning away, he paced the floor, head down and heart racing. After a time he returned to stand before her. 'This house you've found . . . where is it?'

'Craig Street – off Derwent Street, the man said.'

His eyes took on a mad kind of gleam. 'Off Derwent Street, you say?'

'I've got the key here. I thought we might go and take a look tomorrow.' Getting out of the chair, she went to the mantelpiece and taking down the key, held it out to him. 'Here, Jacob. Take it . . . you keep it safe.'

Without thinking, he took the key. Absent-mindedly turning it over and over in the palm of his hand, he felt torn three ways.

Firstly he was concerned about having to find a proper job. He was used to letting others do the work while he sat back and collected the money – one reason why his own business, funded by the loan which had destroyed his family, had failed so resoundingly. Then he was worried about Susan. If she found out he was moving into Craig Street with Maggie, like as not she'd throw a blue fit. But then she was like putty in his hands, so happen he was worrying about nothing where that silly bitch was concerned.

Thirdly, and by far the most important issue, was Louise.

The idea of being just a heartbeat away was almost unbearable. It was what he had been after – the chance to stay close; the opportunity to coax her away from Ben. And here it was, dropped right into his hands by Maggie herself. It was ironic to say the least.

'Well?' The woman was growing impatient. 'Are we moving or what?'

'Well, o' course we are!' Swinging her round, he laughed out loud. 'I'm already warming to the idea. In fact, I can't thank you enough.'

'Well, I never.' Maggie was astonished. 'You've changed your tune. You sound as if you're really pleased at the idea.'

'Oh, I am!' he assured her. *More than you know.*

Chapter Sixteen

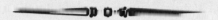

LOUISE COULDN'T SLEEP. 'Whatever's wrong with yer, sweetheart?' Lately, Ben had tried hard not to upset the family, but though he was easier to live with these days, the discontentment had not gone from him. Instead, it lay deep inside him, like a ticking time-bomb.

Having paced the floor these past two hours, his wife told him to go back to sleep. 'I'll go downstairs for a while,' she said, wishing she'd done that straight away and then she might not have woken him. 'Happen a cup o' cocoa might help me to sleep.'

Bleary-eyed he stared at the clock. 'God Almighty! It's only half-past three.'

'Yes, and you've to be at work in three hours, so go back to sleep. I'll try not to wake you when I come back up.'

'Are yer sure?'

'Go back to sleep, love. Please.'

'All right then, pet.' He gave a groan, then a yawn, and seemed to settle again.

On tiptoe, so as not to wake Sal, Louise made her way downstairs.

She boiled up the cocoa and, sitting at the table with it, bent her head in torment. 'You *can't* be!' she muttered aloud. 'You just *can't* be!' But the more she thought about it, the more afraid she was. 'If I *am* pregnant, it can't be Ben's, not after nine years and more of trying. And all these past weeks, ever since the auction, he's not been near me. So there's no hiding the fact: the child cannot be his.'

She took a sip of her cocoa and started pacing the floor again. 'What will I do?' she kept asking the walls. '*What in God's name will I do?*'

She almost leapt out of her skin when Ben's arm slid round her shoulders and drew her close. 'You can go back to bed, that's what you can do,' he gently chided.

Flushed with guilt, she jerked away. 'Ben! You scared me.'

He gave a deep yawn. 'Get off to bed, lass,' he told her. 'I'm up now and wide awake, so there's no point both of us losing sleep.'

She shook her head. 'It's no use me going back to bed. I'll only lie there awake.'

For a long minute he regarded her anxiously. 'I

know what's wrong with you,' he said in a serious voice. 'I've been watching you.'

Horrified by his curious remark, Louise didn't know what to say. Instead, she sat down and, looking up at him, waited for him to explain.

'Look, sweetheart, yer mustn't worry.' Sitting beside her, he took hold of her hand. 'We'll work it out, you and me.'

She hardly dared look at him. 'What do you mean?' she whispered.

'It's my fault,' he began. 'I've been a pig to live with . . . drinking and arguing, and putting a heavy load on you. That's why yer can't sleep. It's why the two of us have been drifting apart, an' it's why we never make love like we used to. It's all my fault. An' now yer can't settle no way, 'cause you've got me on yer mind all the time, an' no bloody wonder, the way I've been behaving.'

He cradled her to him. 'Can yer forgive me, sweetheart?'

Deeply relieved, she clung to him. 'It's all right,' she assured him. But it wasn't all right. It was a nightmare. If she was pregnant – and she would know one way or the other later this morning – then God help her, because it had to be Eric's child.

She tried to think what she would do if it was all confirmed. How could she tell Ben? He'd be bound to know it wasn't his. So, what could she do? How would she cope with it?

His voice brought her back. 'Go on, sweetheart,' he urged. 'Go back to bed and get some rest.'

So she went back to bed and lay there thinking and worrying until the clock struck eight, when she clambered out, anxious to be away on the early tram, and find out what the doctor had to tell her.

By the time Louise got washed and dressed, Sal was already up and cooking breakfast. 'Want some bacon?' She turned it over in the pan. 'I've put enough in for two.'

'No, thanks.' The very idea of bacon turned her stomach over. 'I'm off to market this morning,' she fibbed. 'Is there anything you want?'

Sal dug in her purse. 'I need some dark blue darning wool,' she said, laying a shilling coin on the table. 'Ben goes through his socks like nobody's business.'

'Oh Sal, I've told you before – it's nearly as cheap to buy a new pair o' socks.'

'Aye, I suppose it is, but I do enjoy the darning. It keeps me mind an' fingers wick.'

Louise collected the coin and gave it back. 'Go on then,' she said kindly, 'I'll get the wool. But only if you let me treat you to it, being as it's my husband's holey socks you're mending.'

Sal put the coin back in her purse. 'Your Susan said she were going to the market this morning.'

'Oh? When did you see her?' Louise suspected that Susan was deliberately avoiding her, probably because she was still going around with Jacob Hunter and letting him take her for a fool.

Sal flicked the bacon over, prodding it and shifting it until it sizzled and rose like something alive. 'She called round yesterday while you were down town . . . said summat about wanting to see you.'

'Did she say why?'

'Not a word.' Taking a plate out of the cupboard, Sal held it over the frying pan. 'Just that there were summat she wanted to talk over with yer.' Shovelling the bacon out of the pan, she slid it onto the plate. Bending down to sniff it, she licked her lips and sighed. 'By! There's nowt like freshly cooked bacon to give you an appetite.'

By the time Louise had got her jacket on, Sal was seated at the table, her breakfast laid out before her; two slices of bread and butter, a mug of tea, and a plate heaped with bacon.

Louise smiled at her. 'You don't mean to go hungry, that's for sure.'

'Not if I can help it, no.' And to prove a point, she shoved a huge forkful of bacon into her mouth, afterwards washing it down with a swill of tea.

Louise was pleased to see her eating so well. There had been a time soon after they moved to Derwent Street, when she worried about the old dear. Now though, it seemed Sal had begun to settle down better than any of them.

Cheered, Louise gave her a brief peck on the cheek. 'I'll be off then.'

'Ta ra, lass. Oh, an' don't forget my wool.'

'I won't.' In fact, she had already forgotten it, but now that Sal had reminded her, she wouldn't forget again. She'd buy it on her way to the doctor's. That way, it wouldn't be playing on her mind.

Going at a fair pace to the tram stop at the bottom of the street, Louise was relieved to note she had another five minutes before it was due. 'Seems like we're in for another nice day.' Small and round, with bright beady eyes and a turban over her greying hair, the woman was a neighbour.

'You could be right, yes.' Normally chatty, Louise had too much on her mind to get engaged in a lengthy conversation about the weather.

'I've seen you and your family coming and going,' the woman persisted, 'only you've never stood still long enough for me to get to know you.' Holding out her plump little paw, she said, 'I'm Mavis Darnley from number eighteen.'

Louise took the gesture of friendship. 'Nice to meet you, Mavis,' she answered. 'I'm Louise Hunter.'

There followed a relentless series of questions, about where had Louise come from, and what had made them move into Derwent Street. Were there any children, the woman asked, because, 'I've seen your husband . . . well I *think* he's your husband, and I wondered if there might be children.' She gave a dreamy sigh. 'Oh, I do so love little 'uns.'

'No. There are no children,' Louise answered, and couldn't help but think about the one that might be forming in her body right at that moment.

'Oh look, it's early!' Excited by the approach of the tram, the woman stepped forward and, putting out her arm, almost got run over by the slowing vehicle; in fact, if Louise hadn't pulled her back, she might well have got mangled.

'Oh, dear!' Mavis held her hand to her heart. 'My husband's always telling me how clumsy I am, and he's right,' she apologised. 'I've always been clumsy, ever since a girl. I just can't seem to help it.'

'At least you're not hurt.' Taking her by the elbow, the young woman helped her on board. 'Is it all right if I sit with you?' the woman asked, but before Louise could reply, the two of them were roughly separated; Louise being unceremoniously shoved into the seat by the window, and the woman sent flying against a passenger comfortably seated and about to close his eyes for a nap, instead of which he yelped like a startled animal and gave the woman a stare that sent a chill right through her.

As Louise might have expected, the culprit was her sister Susan, causing havoc as usual.

'I'm sorry I'm late,' she told Louise, who was more surprised to see her than was the poor woman.

It seemed Susan had taken it on herself to save her sister from what she had assumed was 'an interfering old biddy'. 'You'll be all right if I sit here with my sister, won't you?' she asked Mavis Darnley, after easing her somewhat forcefully into a nearby seat.

'Oh, dear!' The old woman had not properly recovered from the shock.

Then Susan went in for the kill. 'If you like, we can sit on the row of three, and I'll go between you, but I do tend to fidget a lot, so you might feel uncomfortable, if you know what I mean.'

'Oh, no!' The woman was still badly shaken by the suddenness of everything. 'I'll be fine, thank you.' To tell the truth, she had taken an instant dislike to Susan and would not have sat beside her, even if she was paid for the privilege.

'You hard-faced little bugger!' Louise was none too pleased. 'You could have given that poor dear a heart attack.'

Susan glanced over her shoulder at Mrs Darnley, who was already engaged in hearty conversation with the man she had fallen on. 'Not her,' she chuckled. 'She's tough as old boots.'

'Where are you off to then?'

The girl shrugged. 'Nowhere in particular.'

'So, what are you doing on the tram?'

'Following you.'

'Whatever for?'

'I need to talk.'

'Well, you can't. Not now.' Louise needed to deal with her problem alone. 'And you can't come with me neither. Go home. I'll see you later.'

Susan was adamant. 'Just let me tag along, eh?' she pleaded. 'I really need to talk to you. Please?'

Her sister sighed. 'You're a pain, d'you know that?'

'But you will let me tag along?' She leaned closer. 'I could do with some advice.'

'I can't understand why you should come to me for advice.' Louise had lost count of the number of times she had tried talking to her sister, and not once had she taken any notice. 'You've never listened to me before.'

'This time it's serious.'

'How serious?' Now she had Louise worried.

'I'll tell you when there aren't so many ears wagging.'

And Louise had to be content with that.

'Anyway, where are *you* off to, so early in the morning?' the girl asked.

Louise realised she would have to share her troubles; in fact, she was relieved. 'Being as you intend following me, you'll find out soon enough,' she answered quietly, and for once Susan knew better than to take it any further.

For the remainder of the journey into Blackburn town, they each silently brooded about their problems; Louise about whether she was pregnant or not, and Susan wondering what her sister would say when she found out that she intended moving in with Jacob.

After alighting from the tram, they hurried through Ainsworth Street and along Penny Street. Being as the mills were already filled and working, and the shoppers not yet out in force, the streets were still relatively quiet.

Impatient from restraining herself all the way here, Susan could not hold out any longer. 'If I tell you what I'm thinking o' doing, you won't go screaming and shouting, will you?'

Louise took offence at that. 'Do I ever?' she retorted.

'Oh, all right, but I don't need you telling me what a fool I am an' all that. I want you to listen and then help me make the right decision.'

'Go on then. Out with it.'

'I went out with Jacob last night.'

'Tell me summat I don't already know.'

'He's asked me to go away with him. He says we can be wed soonever I say the word.'

'*What?*' This news was so startling it brought Louise to a halt. 'And what did you say?'

'I said I might.'

'Huh! Only "might".' Louise was relieved.

'I said I'd give him an answer tonight.'

'And you want my blessing, is that it?' Marching off again, Louise replied smartly, 'You'll never get my blessing, our lass. Jacob Hunter is a bad lot, and always will be.'

Suddenly something occurred to her, causing her to stop again. 'That's not all, is it?' she asked suspiciously. 'You knew all along I wouldn't give my blessing, yet you followed me here this morning. There's summat else, isn't there? Summat you're so worried about, you needed to talk.'

'Mebbe, but now I've changed my mind, 'cause you're hell-bent on splitting us up.'

'Has he made you pregnant, is that it?' That would be a cruel coincidence, she thought.

Her sister looked astonished. 'D'you think I'm that stupid?'

The remark was like a slap in the face, if only because Louise herself had been stupid. But no, she chided herself. Whatever had happened between Eric and her had not been a stupid thing. It had been natural and wonderful, but now it seemed she was the one to pay the price.

Suddenly afraid, she shook it from her mind, and

returned her attention to Susan. 'You have to tell me what it is you're worried about,' she pleaded. 'If you're in some kind of trouble, you know I'll help if I can.'

'I don't want your help, thanks very much,' the younger woman said sulkily. 'I'm not telling you now. You'll only have another go at me.'

Knowing how stubborn her sister could be when she put her mind to it, Louise shrugged her shoulders, feigning indifference. 'Okay. If that's how you feel, there's no use you hanging about, is there? I'll see you later.' With that she started walking on again, fingers crossed and hoping Susan would relent.

'All right! All right!' Breathless and irritated, the girl caught her up. 'I'm not really worried,' she lied. 'I know I can trust him, even if you don't think so.'

'That's good. I'm glad.' She played her along.

'He really does want to marry me. And he wants us to move right away, where nobody can find us . . . in our own little hideaway, he said.' She smiled. 'People think he's hard but he's not. He's real romantic, is Jacob.'

'Yes, I can see that.' What she really wanted to say was: 'Don't be taken in so easily. That toe-rag is up to summat and he's using you to do it!' But she wisely kept quiet.

'We can't do it without money, that's the trouble. Even you can see that.'

'O' course.'

'He tried to get a loan but nobody will trust him.'

'Really?' Bit by bit Susan was opening out. Cautious, Louise just went on walking and pretending to be interested, but not condemning.

'I'm getting on really well in my job now. There's talk of a rise in the pipeline.'

Louise paused to hug her sister. 'Oh, lass, that's wonderful!'

They turned the corner and slowed down; they were almost at the doctor's surgery. Susan had only just realised where they were headed. 'You're not ill, are you?'

'No, love, I'm not ill.' Louise didn't want to go into all that now. 'You were saying . . . about you and Jacob?'

'He wants me to sign summat.'

'What kind of summat?' Suspicions were already rising in the back of her mind.

'A form – for a loan.'

'What!' Louise was seriously alarmed now. She couldn't believe Susan would even give something like that a second thought.

'It's only so's we can get away from these parts, he said. When we're settled, he'll get a job and pay it all back.' She began to gabble. 'Jacob says I don't even need to go out to work if I don't want to. Oh look, I know it'll be all right, sis, I just know it.' Yet her voice shook and there was doubt in her eyes.

Realising how close Susan was to tears, Louise knew she would have to tread carefully. 'Look, love, I'm not saying you shouldn't do it,' she assured her. 'That's for you to decide.' She stayed calm and collected. 'All I'm saying is, you should never put pen to paper unless you've thought about it long and hard. It's only common-sense.'

'There y'are!' the girl accused her. 'You're giving me a lecture, just like you allus do.'

'No, I'm not. I just told you – sign the paper if you want to, I'll not say anything. But think on this, love. Once you've signed it and Jacob's got the money, there'll be no going back. It'll be *your* name that's on the agreement, not his. It's *you* who'll be responsible for paying it back, not him. You might even go away with him and find you're not happy. You could split up, with him going one way and you the other. But the loan will still be there, and it'll still be *you* they'll ask for the money. Not Jacob.'

'I won't be unhappy, and we won't split up. I love him too much.'

'But you have thought it all through, haven't you?'

''Course I have. I'm not daft!'

'And aren't you even a little bit worried about being responsible for the loan?'

'No. Jacob will pay it all back. He said so.'

'How much is the loan?'

Susan paused, reluctant to say.

'Come on – how much?'

She took a deep breath. 'One thousand pounds.'

'My God!' Her sister was shocked to her roots. '*One thousand pounds!* By! That's more than four times your yearly wage,' It took her breath away. 'Don't sign it!' She couldn't believe that Susan would even contemplate doing such a thing. 'Please, love,' she begged, 'whatever else you might do, you must not sign that paper. You'll never pay it back, never in a million years.'

Susan looked to be deep in thought, and for a moment, Louise thought she was going to tell her to mind her own business. Instead, she said quietly, 'I so much want us to go away and make a new life . . .'

Louise was hopeful. 'But . . . ?'

'But I hope we might be able to do it without the loan. I mean, it's so much money it frightens me. But I'm fit and well, and so is Jacob. We can do without the loan. We're both capable of working for a living and I'm sure we could rent a place wherever we go.'

Louise's hopes faded. 'So you're still fixed on going away with him?'

The girl smiled dreamily. ''Course I am. I'm seeing him tonight, to name the day for when we get wed. After that happens we'll be leaving Blackburn, only I won't know where we're going till I get there. Jacob says it will be a wonderful surprise, and that I'm sure to love the place.'

The excitement trembled in her voice. 'So you see, we've already made plans.'

'Be careful, sis.' Louise led the way up the steps to the surgery. 'Promise me you won't do anything unless you talk it over with me first.'

'Only if you promise not to tell Mam.'

'Don't tell me you'd get wed and go away without even telling our mam? Even you wouldn't be that cruel.'

'No. I just want to tell her myself, in my own good time.'

'We've a lot more to talk about, you and me,' Louise said grimly, pushing open the door to the surgery, 'but right now, I've got other things on my mind.'

'Is it to do with you coming to see the doctor?' Susan had momentarily forgotten about their destination.

'Yes.'

'Good morning, ladies. Can I help?' The auburn-haired assistant behind the desk smiled up at them, her teeth as white and gleaming as the newly-starched overall she was wearing.

'Yes, thank you,' Louise answered. 'I'm here

to see Dr Thomas. I've made a special appointment.'

'Name?'

'Mrs Hunter.' Realising there were others in the waiting room, she instinctively lowered her voice. 'Mrs Louise Hunter.'

The clerk thumbed through the file. 'Ah, yes. Look, I'm sorry, Mrs Hunter, but the doctor was called out on an urgent case earlier. He's back now, but it's put him half an hour behind schedule. I'm afraid you'll have a wait before he gets to see you.' She began flicking through the appointments book. 'I can fit you in some time next week if you'd rather not wait?'

'No, that's all right,' Louise answered. 'I'll wait and see him now. I don't want a new appointment.' She couldn't put herself through the same agony for one more day, let alone a week.

While the assistant sorted out her file, they went and sat down, uneasy when all eyes turned in their direction.

A tiny little man with a nervous wink leaned forward to speak to Louise. 'Doctor's late. Half an hour, the girl said.'

'I don't mind waiting,' she told him with a ready smile.

'There's five of us afore you.' Raising a bony finger he counted them one at a time. There were two women sitting huddled together across from them, a middle-aged fella with a sour expression and a young girl, who at that minute blew a bubble with her chewing gum, then took out her compact and began making up her face.

'An' I'm next in,' he finished.

Louise liked to know where she was in the order of things. 'Who was last in before me?' she enquired.

'I were in after him, lass.' That was one of the older ladies. 'Me an' my friend came in together. It's easy enough to remember. This old fella's in next. Then it's me, followed by my friend. The girl came after us, and, last of all, it'll be him . . .' she pointed discreetly to the scowling gentleman, 'then the girl. It's my friend after the girl, and last of all, it'll be me.'

She gave a toothless grin. 'So watch for him going in. After he comes out, it's your turn. Mind there aren't more folks in 'ere by that time, or like as not, they'll shove afront of yer.'

Louise had taken a liking to the woman. While Susan remained unsociable, they chatted on for a while longer, before the woman asked her and Susan both, 'Live round 'ere, d'yer? Only I've not seen neither o' yer afore, an' what with my back an' all, I'm often at the doctor's.'

'We're from the other side of town,' Louise informed her.

'Whereabouts?'

'Derwent Street.'

The old woman's eyes lit with recognition. 'Well, I never! I'm up that way once a week to see my cousin . . . she lives on her own now, poor soul. I'm the only visitor she gets these days. She has two sons, but they're more than bloody useless to her. One's gone off to God only knows where, and the other lives on Whalley Banks.' She tutted. 'For what she sees of him he might as well have gone off with his brother. Bloody kids! Drown 'em at birth, that's what I say.'

When Louise looked saddened by her remark, the old woman gave a little cry. 'Oh lass, I am sorry. What a thing to say! An' you like you are an' all. 'Course they're not all alike, are they. I mean, my own brood are round my place all the time.'

She eyed Louise's stomach with a knowing grin. 'What d'you want – a lass or a lad? If you ask me, lasses are best. They understand what a woman has to go through, if you know what I mean.'

While she babbled on, Susan was trying not to giggle. 'The daft old bat thinks you're pregnant,' she whispered. 'She must have bad eyesight.'

The look on Louise's face told another tale. 'My God! You're *not*, are you?'

When Louise didn't answer, she leaned closer, grateful that the old woman had now struck up a conversation with her friend. 'You are! Why, you crafty bugger an' you never said.' She wouldn't let it be. 'What does Ben say? Oh, I bet he's over the moon.'

Louise was relieved that Susan knew, but worried in case she said something to Ben. 'He doesn't know yet,' she admitted. She had to delay the moment when she might have to confide in her sister. Susan was not the best person in the world with whom to share a secret.

'What? You mean you haven't told him yet?' She groaned. 'Oh, Lou, that's cruel. You know how desperate he is to have a family.'

'I don't even know myself whether I'm pregnant or not. That's why I'm here.'

'You should still have told him.'

Louise got more and more nervous. 'Mind your own business!'

Taken aback by her sharp rebuke, Susan regarded her for a minute; noting how nervous she had become and how her fingers twisted round and round the hankie in her hands. Suddenly it all became clear. 'God Almighty!' Her suspicions spilled out in a harsh whisper. 'It's not Ben's, is it? That's why you haven't told him. You're hoping you're not pregnant . . . *because it's not Ben's!*'

Shifting over to her, Louise hissed, 'Let it go, will you? I've enough on my mind as it is, without you bothering me.'

But the girl was wickedly persistent. 'Whose is it?'

'I said, leave it!'

And for the minute, that was what Susan did, because now the old woman was addressing Louise again. 'You might know my cousin,' she was saying. 'She lives round the corner from you, in Craig Street. She's lived in that same house for nigh on forty years. A little woman, she is, grey hair and spectacles . . . walks with a stick. Ever seen her about?'

Grateful for the timely intervention, Louise shook her head. 'Can't say as I have, no.'

The old woman sighed. 'Craig Street isn't what it used to be,' she imparted sadly. 'It's got noisy . . . with unsavoury folk moving in an' all that. I mean, take that family as have rented the corner house there.' She scratched her head. 'Hobson, Hilton . . . ?' She smiled. 'By! Me old memory's not what it was.'

Louise prompted her. 'Noisy, are they?'

'You could say that, aye. There's a rumour goin' around that the woman was a prostitute at one time, not that I'm one to listen to gossip, o' course. Nice-looking creature though, and pleasant enough, so my cousin claims. They exchanged a few words yesterday afternoon, while they were moving the furniture in. By! They'll have their work cut out, I can tell you that. But they'll not get any joy from the landlord. He's not one to splash out on repairs, is that one.'

'Most landlords are mean like that.' Louise had heard some real horror stories at one time or another. 'But to be fair, they're not all the same.'

Seeming not to have heard, the old woman had been racking her brains. 'For the life of me, I can't recall their names,' she fretted. 'There are two childer . . . a lass and a lad; the lass is a quiet little bairn, and the lad seems to take care of her. He's a lovely little fella, so my cousin says. D'you know, he helped carry all the things in from the removal van? Most lads would have been off down the rec on the swings, or kicking a ball about in the street, but this one apparently kept an eye on the bairn *and* helped shift the stuff in an' all.' She smiled serenely. 'Bonny lad, he is, too . . . real dark eyes, long-limbed and handsome too.'

She gave a sudden gasp. 'Now I remember the name! It's *Hunter*. The father's a real rough devil – turned up drunk as a lord and started throwing his weight about. Jacob – that's his name. That's what the woman, Maggie, called him. Jacob Hunter.'

Unaware of the chaos she had caused, she went on gabbling. 'Men, eh?' She gave a sigh. 'How that poor woman puts up with him I don't know. But she obviously thinks the world of him, 'cause they ended up kissing and cuddling, right there on the front doorstep for all and sundry to see.'

Shocked by what she had heard, Louise turned

to look at her sister and her heart sank. White as a sheet, Susan, too, had heard every word. When she went to rush out of the waiting room, Louise held on to her. 'Wait till I come out,' she urged. 'We'll get to the bottom of it, I promise you. Happen the old woman is wrong. It's a common enough name.'

Susan turned to her, eyes swimming with tears. 'It's him, and you know it,' she said shakily. 'How could he do that to me?'

Having witnessed the frantic scene between the two young women, their informant started to get curious. 'I hope I haven't spoken out of turn,' she said. 'If he's a relative o' yourn, I'm very sorry, I'm sure.'

To Louise's consternation, it seemed she might have dug a bit deeper, but just then the doctor's receptionist called out, 'Mrs Fraser. The doctor's ready to see you now.'

As quickly as she could, the old woman struggled out of her chair and went into the surgery at the double.

'Sit down, love.' Louise was afraid to wait her turn now, in case Susan took to her heels. 'We can go if you really want to,' she offered. 'I'll make another appointment.'

Calmer now, Susan sat down again. 'No, sis, it's not fair on you,' she answered dully. 'There's nothing I can do right now anyway. I need to think about it.

If I go barging in, he'll only lie through his teeth like he allus does. Besides, I'm meeting him tonight, so I'll just wait and see if he tells me what's been going on.'

'And if he doesn't?'

It took a moment for Susan to answer; and there was an anxious minute when she glanced at the door and Louise thought she might make a run for it.

When she did answer, her words made Louise's blood run cold. '*I'll do for him.*' As she spoke she looked up and her eyes were like hardened glass, glittering with hatred. 'I mean it, sis. If he's been lying to me all along . . . about her, and the loan and everything, I swear, I'll do for the bastard.'

'Now don't talk like that. He's not worth it.' Louise had never seen her sister in such a black mood; tormenting and aggravating, yes – that was always her nature. But not hard as nails, and filled with such a terrible hatred. That wasn't like Susan. It was what *he* had done to her, and Louise loathed him for it.

'I know it's not easy, but you must try not to brood on it,' she warned. 'We'll sort it out, one way or another.'

'You're right,' Susan said reluctantly. 'But if he's made a fool of me, I'll make the bastard pay.'

'Did you not have any inkling of what was going on?'

'I knew he was with a woman,' she confessed, 'but he said it were nothing, that she was his land-lady and he was "keeping her sweet", till he found somewhere else to live.'

'If the old biddy's right, it would seem he *has* found somewhere else to live.' She had to keep Susan calm. 'Mind you, I'm surprised he'd have the gall to move right into the very next street.'

At Louise's remarks, Susan gasped with delight. 'That's it!' she exclaimed. 'Happen he *has* split from her, just like he said. Happen it's just the woman and her kids who are living in Craig Street.' Looking for every excuse, there was no stopping her now. 'You heard what the old woman said — that he wasn't there when they offloaded the furniture; she said the lad did most of it with his mam, and that Jacob turned up afterwards. So, it looks like it's *her* that's renting the house, and not Jacob at all.'

'It's possible, but I wouldn't count on it.' For the moment Louise thought it safer to let her think whatever pleased her.

Excited by her own deductions regarding Jacob, Susan soon forgot how he had lied to her in the past. For now, she could only believe what her heart told her; that he loved her after all, and that the loan really was to pay for the wedding and a new start right away from Blackburn.

While she chatted on about her plans, Louise quietly listened, her mind filled with thoughts of Eric, and the child she might be carrying.

Thankful that Susan seemed to have forgotten about the reason for them being here, she let her prattle on, hoping and praying that Jacob would not let her sister down, like the two-timing no-good excuse for a man he was.

'I wish the doctor would get a move on.' She had grown so nervous about the ordeal ahead, that she was the one wanting to escape now.

Fortunately, she didn't have to wait too long. In no time at all, the patients went in quickly one after the other. 'By! He's going through us like a dose o' salts.' That was the sour-faced man. 'I thought I'd have to sit here for hours.'

Soon, it was her turn. 'Are you frightened?' All of a sudden it seemed Susan had woken up to why they were here.

'A little,' Louise confessed.

'D'you want me to come in with yer?'

Her sister couldn't help but smile. 'No, thanks. You just be here when I get out.' And Susan promised she would.

Nervously, Louise made her way into the doctor's surgery. 'Now then, Mrs Hunter, what's the problem?' A tall skinny being with a sallow face and kind eyes, Dr Thomas stood up respectfully as she entered. 'Close the door and sit yourself down,' he invited. And she did.

Outside, Susan grew impatient. 'What the devil's taking so long?' She began pacing the floor. 'By! I'd not like to be in Louise's shoes if she's having some other bloke's kid.' She paused at the enormity of what she was saying. 'She must have been mad! But if she *is* expecting, and it's not Ben's . . . whose could it be?'

At first, she could think of no man with whom her sister might have been involved, then after further consideration, she thought she might know who the father was. 'I can't understand it. Our sis is not the kind to carry on. Whatever possessed her?'

When the door opened and Louise came out, the truth was written all over her troubled face, though Susan was considerate enough not to say anything in front of the receptionist.

Outside though, she came straight to the point. 'You're pregnant, aren't you?'

Louise nodded.

'It's not Ben's, is it?'

Looking away, Louise shook her head.

'I think I know whose it is.' When Louise didn't respond, she went on. 'It's *Eric*'s isn't it?'

Louise was astounded. 'What on earth makes you say that?'

'Because I've seen the way he looks at you.'

Needing someone to confide in, Louise told her

everything. 'Ben was being unbearable. Me and Sal tried everything to help him, but he just wouldn't be helped.' Remembering how he was, Louise felt a pang of resentment. 'For no reason I could see, he began to get suspicious of me and Eric.'

'Why?'

'He seemed to think I had my eye on Eric, but I had never even thought about him in that way, until Ben started accusing me of things.' She leaned against the wall, wearied and concerned. 'When Eric bought the farm and everything, he offered Ben work on the land. He tried his best to heal the rift between them, but Ben would have none of it.'

'So, how did you and Eric come to . . . well, you know?' Susan glanced at her sister's midriff.

'It was my fault,' Louise confessed. 'If I hadn't gone over that night, it would never have happened. Only Ben had been bad-tempered all day, and I so much wanted them to be friends again. I knew Ben would need a friend somewhere along the way.'

Susan began to understand. 'So, you thought you'd go and see Eric and try to put things right between them?'

Louise nodded. 'He's such a good man,' she said softly, 'and I was in need of someone to talk to. The way things were, I couldn't talk to Ben, and Sal was doing so well coping with it all, it wasn't fair to unload my worries on to her. But Eric . . . well, he was just there. We talked and then, when I was leaving, he took hold of me, and . . .' Filled with shame at the recounting of it, she had not been able to look at her sister. 'I swear, I never meant for it to happen.'

'Do you love him?'

Louise couldn't deny it. 'Though I wouldn't hurt Ben for the world, I don't feel the same way about him any more,' she confessed. 'He's changed too much.'

'What will you do now, sis?'

Astonishingly, after years of Louise worrying about Susan, the tide had turned. Now it was Susan's turn to wonder about her sister's future.

Louise looked up, her pretty eyes betraying a deep heartache. 'I don't know,' she answered. 'It's all such a mess, I can't seem to think straight any more.'

Suddenly she began sobbing, deep, wrenching sobs that poured out all the pain and worry of the past few weeks. 'You mustn't say anything,' she pleaded. 'You mustn't tell *anybody*!' She began to regret ever having told Susan; especially when experience had shown how the younger girl could be unthinkingly callous about other people's feelings.

'It's all right, sis.' In a rare moment of compassion, Susan put her arm round her sister. 'Don't worry. Your secret's safe with me.'

As they walked on, they fell silent, each absorbed in their own worries.

So much had happened recently. In all the upheaval, only one thing was certain. Their lives would never be the same again.

Chapter Seventeen

SAL COULDN'T UNDERSTAND it. 'What's wrong with yer, lass?'

Setting the table for when Ben came in, Louise was stopped in her tracks. 'Nothing, why?' Her heart skipped a beat. If the woman in the surgery had guessed she was pregnant, happen Sal had done the same.

From the armchair, her mother-in-law regarded her thoughtfully. 'You don't seem to have your mind on what yer doing.' She pointed to the knives and forks being laid the wrong way. 'Yer setting the table all wrong. And just now, when you got back from town, you didn't have a word to say.' She wagged a finger. '*And* yer forgot me darning wool.'

'Oh no! I'm sorry, Sal. I were rushing about, and it completely slipped my mind.'

In a well-meaning way, Sal was relentless. 'For

all yer rushing about, I can't see what yer brought home.'

On the way back, Louise had called in at the corner shop for a loaf and a packet of cornflour for the gravy. 'It was so busy,' she said lamely. 'You know how it is.'

Sal went quiet for a minute, watching while Louise finished laying the table, then, in a soft, understanding voice, she asked, 'Why were yer crying, lass?'

Louise was visibly startled. 'When?'

'Just now, when yer came back from town. Yer eyes were all red. And don't tell me yer weren't crying, 'cause I'm not so old and stupid I can't see it for meself.'

Louise was lost for words.

'Don't punish yerself, lass.'

'What do you mean, Sal?' Fear struck at her heart. 'Why should I punish myself?'

'Look, yer a lovely, kind-hearted woman, an' I'm terrible fond of yer, but yer can't be all things to all people. It's not your fault, what's happened to this family, any more than it's mine. But our Ben has led yer a merry dance and I'm sorry for that. You've been the best wife a man could have, and he should go down on his knees to yer for the way he's been behaving. It's no wonder yer go off to some quiet corner for a cry. By! When the going gets rough, the men get going, that's what my old mam used to say, and she were right. They do things and don't stop to think o' the consequences. I mean, just look how my poor Ronnie changed all us lives, and all for that no-good Jacob!'

Louise gave a secret sigh of relief. 'All water under the bridge,' she said.

'Not when yer crying, it's not. I've a good mind to give that Ben a piece o' my mind!'

Louise couldn't allow that. 'No, Sal,' she said firmly. 'Please don't do that.'

'All right, lass, I'll leave it to you,' Sal agreed. 'But it's just as well he came to his senses when he did, or I'd not have been able to sit back no longer while he made your life a misery.'

'Thanks, Sal.'

Sal had wondered of late. 'Everything's all right between you two, isn't it?'

'Right as rain,' she lied. 'Why do you ask?'

'No reason – except it would serve him right if yer went looking for some other man.'

It was so close to the truth that Louise held her breath.

'If it had been anybody but you, they'd have been gone long since.' Sal smiled knowingly. 'But then, that's not your way is it, lass?'

'No, Sal, it's not my way at all.' Louise sensed that the old woman had an inkling of something untoward, though as far as she knew, there was no way Sal could have found out about her and Eric. 'Besides,' she chuckled, 'I'd never leave *you* behind, not in a million years. I mean, who'd make your Yorkshire pudding of a Sunday?'

Sal had a weakness for her daughter-in-law's Yorkshire puddings; they rose to the top of the oven like nothing she had ever seen before, and though she was herself an accomplished cook, she couldn't hold a candle to those light and fluffy Yorkshire puds. 'In that case you'd best stay right where yer are,' she ordered. 'What! Sundays wouldn't be the same without your lovely Yorkshires. Light as a feather, they are.'

Taking the tray, Louise returned to the kitchen for another pile of crockery. When she returned, Sal was humming a tune.

On seeing Louise she stopped. 'Then there's that sister o' yourn. By! If you weren't around, she'd be up to more mischief than a sackful o' monkeys. She listens to you, where she'll not listen to anybody else.'

'She doesn't always listen to me.'

'Aye well, happen that's 'cause she's a mardy little bugger. Wants it all her own way or she plays nasty tricks. She's another who'll never change her ways. Her and our Jacob are a matching pair an' no mistake.'

Discreetly, without involving Susan, Louise asked, 'Do you think he's the marrying kind?'

'Never! He's far too bloody selfish.'

'They say he's got a woman.'

'Huh! When has he *not* got a woman?'

'They say he's moved in with her, and that she's got a couple of kids.'

'*Who* says?'

'Nobody in particular. It's just gossip. You know what folks are like.'

'Now listen here, my girl.' Sal moved to the edge of her seat. 'If your Susan's expecting him to put a ring on her finger, she'd best think again, 'cause if I know my own son, he'd just as soon put a ring through her *nose!*'

Sal often wondered how she could have given life to a heartless creature such as Jacob. 'If it's true, an' he *is* with some poor woman who's got two kids in tow, you can bet he wouldn't be within a mile of her unless there was summat in it for him. An' I *don't* mean bedding her neither, 'cause he can get that anywhere he chooses.'

'So, what are you saying, Sal?'

'I'm saying that either she's got a heap o' money tucked away, an' he's hoping to get his mucky paws on it,' she tapped the side of her nose in the way of a confidante, 'or she's got summat on him, an' he daren't mek a move in case she shops him to the police.'

'That's a harsh way of thinking about your own son, isn't it?'

'I'm only saying what I know – an' I know our Jacob's a liar an' a cheat. An' there's no way on God's earth he'd stay cooped up with one woman, and abide two kids round his arse – not unless he stood to gain by it.'

Louise knew the old woman was speaking the truth. 'I'm just glad Ben didn't turn out like his brother,' she said. 'All right, he went off the rails after losing the farm and everything. But he's a good man. He would never deliberately do anything to hurt anybody.'

Sal considered that for a minute, before leaning back in her chair. 'Yer right, lass,' she uttered softly. 'It's strange though, when you think how the same blood runs through Ben as runs through Jacob.'

Made curious by Sal's comment, Louise cast her mind back to when Ben was behaving out of character. Some of the spiteful things he did and said, could almost have come from Jacob himself.

She instantly shook the deceitful thought from her mind. Ben was far and away a better man than his brother, and she told Sal as much now.

When Sal bent her head to her darning once more, Louise went about her work; but her mind was wick with torment.

There was no doubt she was carrying Eric's child. She could not ignore the fact that, before too long, it would begin to show to all and sundry.

To her mind, she had three alternatives. She could tell Eric and make him face up to his responsibilities – whatever that might mean. She could consider terminating the pregnancy, may God forgive her.

Or she could tell Ben, and take her punishment. The more she thought about all three, the more she realised that, for different reasons, none of them were feasible.

There was one more alternative, which Susan had unwittingly placed in her mind today. She could pack her bags, cut all ties with her family, and have the bairn somewhere far away from here.

One thing was certain. She would have to make up her mind, and soon.

◆

PATSY WAS NOT surprised to see Susan enter the room all done up to the nines and looking pleased with herself. 'One of these nights you'll stay in and keep me and your dad company,' she complained. 'You're forever off out.'

'Hmh! Why should I stay in with you old fogies, when I can be out on the town?' Susan could be cutting when she had a mind to.

'Cheeky young devil!' Her father glanced up from his newspaper. 'I'll have you know, me and your mam could show you a thing or two when we were your age,' he said with a sly little grin at Patsy. 'We could be as naughty as anybody else when the mood took us. I might tell you, young lady, we've spent many a pleasant hour round the back o' the Palais, when we should have been home in us beds.'

Mortified, his wife tutted. 'Give over, Steve! You're making me blush.' Then, addressing Susan, who couldn't help but giggle at the idea of her mam and dad 'round the back o' the Palais', she remarked in a serious voice, 'I hope you're not still chasing that layabout, Jacob Hunter?'

Susan slung on her coat, a tight-fitting green affair with swirly hem and large buttons. 'That's for me to know, and you to find out, Mam,' she taunted. 'Who knows . . . I might even spend a pleasant hour round the back o' the Palais.'

'Hey! That's enough o' that.' Her father was already cursing himself for having mentioned it.

'G'night.' Without another word Susan was up the passage and out the door.

Once outside she lingered awhile, her anxious gaze going to the far corner where Derwent Street ended and Craig Street began.

It was in her mind to go and see if Jacob was really living on Craig Street, as the woman had told them. Then she decided not to. 'Whether it's true or not,' she told herself, 'it's best if you meet him at the boulevard, like you planned. He'll tell you then what's going on. Besides, if you intend signing that paper, you'll *need* to trust him.'

She went on, down the street and towards the tram stop. But it seemed funny her going one way while he might be just round the corner. If she caught him coming out of the house, they could go into town together. It made sense. But then, if he'd wanted that, he would have told her, wouldn't he?

Suddenly, she paused, looked round, and in a minute was running back up the street.

At the corner she stopped, torn two ways. 'Go on!' she whispered. 'You've got this far.' But what was she doing? Did she intend knocking on the door? Did she think she might see them through the window? And if she did, what would she do then?

'You're a silly cow!' she told herself. 'And Jacob wouldn't thank you for spying on him like this, would he?' All the same, she had a burning need to see the woman who had taken Jacob into her household.

Like Derwent Street, Craig Street was a long meander of terraced houses, built for the cotton mill and foundry workers and tight together as peas in a pod. Susan walked from one end to the other, staring in windows and watching for any sign that Jacob was about. 'I knew it!' she muttered. 'That woman in the surgery was talking out the back of her head, silly old biddy.'

'I'd best go before I miss the tram,' she said, and glanced at her watch – a present from Jacob on a good gambling day. 'Quarter-past eight.' She had arranged to meet him by nine. 'I'm all right for time,' she realised, but decided to hurry her steps all the same.

She was just turning to head in the direction of the tram stop when she caught sight of him through the windowpane next to her; he was in the front room of the corner house. 'Jacob!' Tapping on the window, she waved at him when he looked up. Delighted, she waved again, gesturing to the front door, asking him to come out.

When the door was flung back, she opened her mouth to greet him, but he was on her before she could utter a word. 'What the blazes are you doing 'ere?' Wild-eyed, he grabbed her by the throat and shoved her into a passageway next to the house. 'Are yer mad or what?'

Gulping for breath, she explained, 'I heard you were living here, and I've come to see you. What's wrong with that?' Even now, she could not bring herself to believe he was doing anything underhand.

'Jacob!' Maggie's voice rang out. 'Jacob! What are you doing out there?'

Panic-stricken, he clamped his hand over Susan's

mouth and, pressing her backwards against the wall, hid them both from sight. It seemed an age before Maggie went back inside.

Releasing Susan, he told her, 'I don't want you coming round here. I already told you . . . I've to keep her sweet, or I'm out on my ear. Look, it's only a matter of time before we're away, so until then, do as I say and don't show yer face round 'ere no more, all right?'

Susan was riddled with doubt. 'What does she *really* mean to you? I want the truth.'

'I've told you. She's my landlady. She means *nothing* to me.'

'So, why was she calling after you just now? And why are we hiding like this?'

'What's this – the bloody Spanish Inquisition?'

'If I thought you were lying to me . . .'

'You'd do *what*?'

In the lamplight, her face darkened, together with her mood. 'I'd swing for you, an' that's the truth.'

Like before, he was unnerved. Something in her voice – maybe the light in her eyes or the way she looked at him with that weird stare – whatever it was, it sent him crazy. 'Are you threatening me?' With one mighty swipe of his hand he smacked her hard round the mouth. 'Nobody threatens Jacob Hunter!'

Reeling back, she mopped the blood from her

face with the sleeve of her coat. She didn't say anything. Instead she just looked at him, hating him, knowing how everything she had heard about him was true.

Just as suddenly as he had lost his temper, he was sweet and light again. 'Oh, darlin', I'm sorry. I didn't mean to hurt you like that.' Taking her in his arms, he raised her face to his and with the flat of his hand he wiped away the trickling blood. 'Go home,' he said. 'Get washed up and meet me in half an hour at the other end of Derwent Street. And mek sure you bring the paper. It has to be signed tonight if I'm to get the loan. If I *don't* get it . . . you and me are finished.' He planted a sloppy kiss on her forehead. 'And you wouldn't want that now, would you, eh?'

'Jacob! Are you out there?' It was Maggie at the door.

Thrusting Susan away from him he ordered, 'Go on – do as I said. I'll see you in half an hour.' With that he hurried back inside the house, and she was left out there, in the chill of an autumn evening, hurt and broken, and her beautiful coat all stained with blood.

With tears rolling down her face she walked to the window where she had first seen him, and there they were; him and the woman, she with her back against the wall and he pressed close to her. They were kissing like two teenagers, laughing and giggling together.

The sight of it was torture to the girl.

Finally facing the truth, she rolled away from the window and stood for an age with her face to the wall, her forehead cold against the brick. 'It's true,' she murmured brokenly. 'All of it . . . all true.'

Then through her tears she began to laugh – harsh, terrible laughter. 'What a fool I've been. He must have been having a good laugh on me the whole time.'

With something akin to morbid curiosity, she peered into the window again. The woman was still up against the wall, but now she had her skirt above her waist and Jacob was up tight to her; what they were doing was painfully obvious.

Sickened and humiliated, Susan ran down the street, demented by what she had witnessed here tonight. But he would pay for what he'd done to her.

Oh yes, he would pay all right.

———◗ ◊ ◖———

'BY! IT'S BLOWING up a real storm out there.'
The night-watchman was just clocking on. Normally all the drivers had gone home by the time he arrived, but Ben was only just now finishing. 'Landed you with another late delivery, did they?'

Ben was in no mood for talking, but he liked the

old fella a damned sight more than some of the men he worked with on the road. 'I've just got back from the other side of Birmingham,' he explained. 'They threatened to cancel the order if the load wasn't delivered tonight.'

'Aye, well, I'm sorry it were you as got the short straw again.' There wasn't much the old fella didn't see. 'Some of them buggers don't want to work. They're in late and off early, and nowt's ever said. An' here's you . . . kept back time and again.'

Ben nodded. 'Still, it's extra money for the pot, eh?' He sounded calm, but inside he was boiling at the way he'd been treated.

'Straight off home, are you?'

'That was the idea.'

The old fella took out a hip flask. 'Want a drop, do you?' He offered it to Ben. 'Warm the cockles of your heart it will.'

Taking the flask, Ben took a swig. 'You're right.' Licking his lips he handed it back. 'That were just what I needed.' For Louise's sake, he'd been away from the drink these past few weeks, but now, with the taste of it on his tongue and the weariness smothering him, he began to weaken. 'Happen I'll stop off for one on the way home.'

'I don't blame you.' The old fella was partial to a drink himself. 'I reckon you've earned it.'

By the time he got to the Swan public house, the

storm had gained momentum; with the rain lashing down and the wind howling like a banshee, Ben was glad to get inside.

''Ere, get that down you.' The landlord was sharp in fetching Ben's pint of ale. 'You look like summat the wind blew in.' Laughing at his own pathetic joke he walked away to serve someone else.

Ben downed the beer and ordered another. By this time he was beginning to feel relaxed.

The big clock over the bar loudly ticked the minutes away; the minutes turned into hours and soon it was half-past ten. From the time Ben came in, he never moved from the bar. He was content just to lean on the bar, face front and eyes down to his pint, and let the day's work wash away from him.

When he ordered his fourth pint, the landlord got worried. 'Just finished work, have you, son?'

By this time, Ben was not so amiable. 'What's it to do with you?'

'I were just wondering, ain't it time you got home to your wife and kids?'

'Hmh!' Snatching up his glass, Ben drained the last of his beer. 'Me wife's used to me coming home late, and I ain't got no kids.' He banged down the pint pot. 'Nor likely to, neither.'

The landlord quipped, 'What? You mean you ain't got no lead in your pencil?'

Thinking he had made another joke he began

laughing, until Ben caught him by the collar of his shirt. 'Happen you'd best explain what you mean by that.'

'I didn't mean nothing.' The man could see he'd gone too far this time. 'Can't you take a joke, eh? It's a poor thing when a man can't take a joke.' He began gabbling, afraid for his life.

Ben thrust him away. 'Give us another pint and be quick about it.'

Seated at a table close by, two men had been doing business; one making an order, the other arranging delivery of the same order. For some time, they had been observing Ben's erratic behaviour and now, when he became violent, one of the men, tall and slim with staring eyes and a bright yellow tie, stepped forward. 'It's time you got off home,' he instructed Ben, 'before this good landlord sends for the police and has you thrown out.'

Bleary-eyed, Ben stared at him. 'Well now, if it isn't my considerate boss. Come to tell me I've been a naughty boy, is that it . . . *sir*?' Smartly saluting, he gave the man a shove. 'You've nowt to say that I'm interested in,' he snarled. 'I've done your lousy deliveries, and now I'm relaxing in my own time, so push off, an' leave me be!'

The man stood his ground. 'Didn't you hear what I just said?' he persisted. 'I told you to *go home!*'

Ben gave him another shove. 'And I told *you* to *piss off*!'

'HEY!' The landlord feared more for his furniture than he did for his life. 'There'll be no fighting in my bar.'

'Then get this worm off my back, will yer?' Ben pushed the man hard.

This time, his boss retaliated. Raising both hands, he smacked them hard against Ben's chest, sending him off balance. 'You're a drunken slob, Hunter! A man like you is no use to me. You're finished, d'you understand? Sacked! Collect your cards when you've got your head together. After that I don't want you anywhere near my factory.'

Ben laughed in his face. 'You think that worries me, d'you?' He punched him lightly on the arm. 'Ever since I've been on your payroll, you've treated me like I'm worth nothing. You've found me every dirty job and every late delivery that you could muster. I'm *glad* I'm finished, d'you hear? I'm glad. But I'll tell you this: now that I've got nowt to lose, happen I can give you the hiding you bloody well deserve, eh?' With a cry of rage, he grabbed the man and holding him against the bar with one hand, he drew back his fist.

But the blow never landed, because now the landlord and his barman had Ben by the shoulders, arms back and pinned against the wall. 'You're out of here, matey!' The barman manhandled Ben across the room, and was about to throw him out in the rain, when the door opened to admit a woman. Ben could hardly believe his eyes. 'Susan!'

The barman too was surprised. Addressing the lass, he asked, 'D'you know this drunken bugger?'

Susan nodded. 'He's my brother-in-law.' Taking Ben by the arm, she asked, 'Is it all right if I take him in the back room?'

The barman shrugged. 'It's okay by me. You'd best ask the boss.'

The landlord reluctantly agreed. 'If you hadn't rescued me many a time when I were short of help behind this bar, I'd say no straight away,' he told her, eyeing Ben with contempt. 'But go on, Susan. See if you can dry the bugger out. Then I want him off my premises.'

Susan nodded. 'Thanks,' she said. 'I won't forget.'

He laughed. 'You can pay me back at Christmas when the staff forget to turn up, eh?' He thumbed her towards the inner door. 'That way. You'll not be bothered by anybody out 'ere.'

The room was small but cosy. 'You stay here,' she told him, 'while I go and make some black coffee.'

'No. I'll be right in a minute.' Ben sat on the sofa, head in hands and too ashamed to look at her. 'Whatever possessed me?' he groaned. 'I've drunk so much I can't think straight, and now I've lost me job. Christ! What a bloody mess.'

It only took a minute for Susan to make him a cup of Camp coffee in the tiny kitchen out in the passageway. 'Here.' She placed it in his hand. 'This'll help clear your head.'

He took the coffee and sipped at it, then he put it down in the hearth and stood up, his hands thrust deep into his pockets, and a look of despair on his face. 'I'm finished,' he said. 'I've got no job, no proper home, and now Louise seems to be losing all respect for me – though I can't blame her for that. In fact, I wouldn't blame her if she went off with some other fella, the way I've been behaving lately.' Though the prospect was unthinkable. 'By! If she ever did that, I don't know what I'd do. Top meself, I shouldn't wonder.

'I'd best get sobered up and get off home,' he muttered, 'though I don't know how she'll tek it when I tell her I've lost me job an' all.' Agitated, he began pacing the floor, stumbled, then almost fell over. 'See that?' he whined. 'I can't even stand on me own two feet.'

Susan had spent a wretched week recovering from Jacob's betrayal. She was struck by a deep depression. Nothing seemed to matter. She had listened to Ben harping on and bemoaning his lot and she couldn't stand it any longer. 'For Christ's sake shut up, Ben! You're not the only one with problems,' she snapped, 'so don't feel so bloody sorry for yerself.'

'Hey! There's no call for you to have a go at me.' Swaying, he came over to stand before her, his eyes boring down into her face. 'Look, I'm grateful you stepped in when you did, or I might have got thrown in jail, and then what would Louise think of me?'

'"What would Louise think?"' she mimicked him. 'It's allus bloody Louise, isn't it!' Giving him a push, she burst out crying. 'Just go! Go on . . . get out of here!' Rushing into the little scullery, she closed the door on him.

Sobered by her outburst, he followed, albeit unsteady on his feet. 'What's wrong, lass?' Gingerly opening the door he poked his head round. 'What have I said to upset yer?'

Quietly sobbing, Susan was bent over the sink. 'You're a fool,' she accused him, her mind going to Louise and Eric, and the baby that was already in the making.

'I know *that*.'

Turning, she studied his face and knew straight off that the feelings she had once had for him were not really dead. Because of her obsession with Jacob she had lost sight of what she really wanted, but now she was beginning to see clearly again. 'There are things you don't know, though.'

'Oh? And what are they?'

With Louise's strained face in her mind, she turned away. 'Please, Ben. Just go.' But even now she couldn't resist a snide swipe at her sister. 'Go home to your precious Louise.'

Suddenly he was directly behind her, his hand on her shoulder. Tenderly he turned her round. 'Yer jealous of her, aren't yer,' he murmured, stroking her hair. 'You've allus been jealous of her.'

Excited by the knowing look she gave him, he bent to kiss her; surprised and delighted when she offered no resistance.

Each of them had found someone who would listen, and now, warm in each other's embrace, one thing led to another. In a minute they were on the floor, half-naked, making love with a frenzy, and no thought for anyone but themselves.

There was no love in the sense of what she felt for Jacob, or what he felt for his wife, but it was a powerful giving of themselves to each other, all the same.

When they were calm and drained of passion, she felt no regret, while he was beside himself, riddled with a terrible guilt and mortally ashamed to walk out of the room past all those eyes that were bound to be watching. 'I'm so sorry, Susan,' he almost wept, running his hands through his hair. 'I don't know how I'll look your sister in the face. How could I do that to her . . . to *you.*' He looked for excuses. 'I were drunk, y'see? I can't think straight when I'm drunk.'

Uncaring about his guilt, or the fact that she had taken her own sister's husband, and he while under the influence of drink, Susan calmly dressed herself. 'Oh, stop your whimpering!' she told him off-handedly. 'Louise will never know anything about it.' She sniggered. 'Not unless *you* tell her.'

'I'm finished,' he kept saying, his voice breaking. 'I've got nowt. Nowt to be proud of, and nowt to look forward to.'

For as long as possible, Susan ignored him. But when he kept on and on, she could contain herself no longer. 'How could I ever have thought I were in love with you!' she snarled. 'You're bloody hopeless. First time anything goes wrong, you're no good to man nor beast. No bloody use at all. You can't find your own wife and mother a home . . . Our Louise had to do it for you. You can't hold down a job for two minutes, and you can't face things head on. Instead you turn to the booze, and you bed your wife's sister. By! No bloody won- der our Louise turned to some other m—' She tried to stop the outpouring. But the damage was already done.

In two strides he had her by the shoulders, shaking her so hard she couldn't breathe. 'What were that yer said?' Dark with rage, his face was close to hers, eyes bulbous like a madman's. '"No wonder she turned to some other . . ." *man* – that's what you meant to say, isn't it?' He drew her to him, until she could see the whites of his eyes.

'No!' Shaking with terror, Susan brazened it out. 'You've got it all wrong.'

'You as much as said it, Susan, that my wife went with some other man. Now I want the bugger's name.'

'Go away, Ben. You're drunk. You're imagining things. Go home.'

With the back of his hand he smacked her across the mouth, so hard he made her nose bleed; the blood ran like a tap down her face.

'Who was he?'

Knowing he was in the mood to beat her to a pulp, she began yelling, '*Bob!* Bob, for God's sake, help me!'

The door burst open and the landlord rushed in, the barman at his side. He saw straight off what was happening, and before Ben could resist, he and the barman had him, arms pinned behind his back, and were wrestling him across the room to the door. 'You ungrateful bastard!' Bob gave him a jab in the ribs. 'I'd have had you off these premises quick as a wink, only she wanted to help you.' He gave him another jab. 'And that's how you treat her, you bloody pervert! If it weren't for losing my licence, I'd send you home in pieces.'

Fighting them hard, Ben turned to Susan, his face distorted by a sly smile, and his tactics cleverly changed. 'Slag! Wait till I tell Jacob what we've been doing – and I will, you mark my words! He'll want nowt to do with you then, will he, eh? He'll see you for what you really are. A cheap and nasty little bitch!'

'Piss off!' With the men taking him away, Susan felt safe. But then a thought struck her. What if Jacob still wanted her? What if the plans they had made were still good? Mebbe he really was playing that woman along, and what did it matter if he'd bedded her, 'cause hadn't she just bedded Ben? All manner of doubts and hopes began to flood into her mind.

As the men began dragging him out of the door, Ben kept on shouting, 'What man wants a whore for his wife, eh? Your chances of Jacob ever putting a ring on your finger will be gone for good. SLAG!'

Suddenly she could stand it no longer. Thinking of herself and with no care for Louise, she ran over to the three men. She saw them pause. Defeated, Ben turned, his face wreathed in tears. 'His name, Susan,' he begged. 'Give me his name and Jacob will never know what went on here tonight.'

Desperate, she took a minute, wringing her hands and pushing the image of her desperate sister out of her mind. '*It were Eric,*' she whispered. There! It was said. There was no going back now. 'The man was ERIC!' The words were bitter on her tongue.

When his face fell with horror, she ran back inside. Sitting at a table, with her head in her hands, she sobbed as though her life was ended. 'I'm sorry, Louise,' she wept, 'but Jacob means more to me than anybody.'

After they'd thrown him out on the streets, the landlord gave Ben a stern warning. 'Show your face round here again, and you'll be sorry,' he said. 'I don't want your kind in my bar.'

The barman laughed in Ben's face. 'Sounds to me like you've got real trouble, matey.' He gave him a shove which sent him sprawling across the pavement. 'Wife gone off with somebody else, has she? Well now, who can blame her? This Eric has got to be a better bet than a loser like *you*.' He kept on with his cruel gibes. 'If I were you, I'd throw meself in the canal. That's where the rats usually end up.'

'Hey!' The landlord caught hold of him. 'That's enough. Inside with you.'

Half out of his mind, Ben wandered aimlessly along the street. He couldn't believe what Susan had just told him. He couldn't imagine how his wife could go with *any* man, let alone his worst enemy.

When he came onto Penny Street he had no idea where he was going. 'Happen he were right,' he muttered. 'Happen I'd be best off in the bloody canal. There's nowt here for me any more.'

Without even thinking, he headed towards the canal. He gazed into the dark, murky waters and felt afraid. 'You're a coward, Ben Hunter,' he told himself. 'Susan's right. No wonder your wife's gone after some other man.' He was quiet for a time, the tears rolling down his face and his whole body trembling. 'How could you shame me like that Louise? With *Forester* of all people!' His humiliation was tenfold.

He climbed onto the bridge. It would be so easy to jump, he thought. But he was afraid. Happen Susan was lying. But no. She wasn't lying, he knew that now.

Calm at last, he stood up straight, fearless and committed. Like the man he yearned to be. Then with his arms wide and eyes closed, he leapt. It wasn't long before the waters swallowed him up. *And the silence was awesome.*

PART THREE

WINTER, 1952
CONSEQUENCES

Chapter Eighteen

T HE KNOCK ON the door came at eight o'clock the next morning. 'I'm sorry to have to bring you this bad news.' The officer was a kindly individual, well suited to the task he'd been given.

While he imparted the shocking details, of how a man had been walking along the canalside when he saw Ben leap from the bridge, his female colleague went to the back of the room and stood beside Sal, who had fallen back in the chair, the blood draining from her face. When she began shaking uncontrollably, the WPC knelt beside her and took her in her arms. She didn't say anything. She merely held the old woman and gave her some measure of comfort.

Louise was inconsolable. 'It's my fault,' she sobbed. Eric was strong in her guilty thinking. 'God forgive me. It's all *my* fault!' Mercifully, no one there knew why she should think that.

When the officer enquired if there was anyone he could bring to the house, Louise shook her head.

By the time the officers left, the old woman had composed herself to a degree. Louise was seated by the empty firegrate, manically rocking back and forth in the chair, her eyes staring into the distance, unseeing.

For a long, soul-searching time, the quietness in that little room was unbearable.

With her old heart aching, Sal got out of her chair and, walking across the room, took hold of the young woman by the shoulders. 'Come on, lass, you mustn't keep the grief in,' she said shakily. 'Let the tears fall.'

Shocked out of her deep reverie, Louise was mortified. 'Oh Sal, I'm so sorry!' Seeing the old woman's white face and hollow eyes, she was devastated. 'I'm sorry . . . I'm so sorry.' Now the tears fell and wouldn't stop, and her heart was broken.

These two women were never so close as they were in that tender moment. Holding each other, they sobbed and opened their hearts to talk of Ben. 'We'll miss him,' his mother said in her wisdom, 'but he's made his choice, lass. And now there's nowt we can do to fetch him back.'

It took a long time, and there was much to be said, but gradually the pain grew bearable; though, for Louise, the guilt she felt was crippling.

A t the inquest, the landlord of the Swan was called as a witness to say that Ben had drunk so much he couldn't possibly have known what he was doing. No one mentioned his argument with Susan. A verdict of accidental death was duly recorded. It was a huge relief to Susan; her sense of guilt was overwhelming enough without the shame of Ben being denied a Christian burial.

Exactly one week later, Ben Hunter was laid to rest in St Peter's churchyard.

The church was packed and the sense of disbelief filtering through the aisles was like a physical presence.

After the service when they were all preparing to leave, Susan waited on a bench with Sal, while Louise lingered at the place where her husband lay; safe from the cares and worries of this cruel world.

Louise told him how sorry she was at losing him. 'You have to believe I never stopped loving you. Oh, not like it was before, because when we left the farm, everything seemed to go with it. But I did still love you, and I always will.'

She held her breath, thinking of how he had taken his own life. 'Why didn't you talk things over with me?' she asked angrily. 'I might have been able to help.' But in her heart she knew she had helped all she could with Ben's desperate unhappiness. Nothing she had said or done had made any difference.

The anger melted and the awful pain returned. Sadly, she walked away.

Susan and Sal saw her approach. She was walking slowly, seeming even older at that moment than her mother-in-law. 'She's punishing herself too much,' Sal said. 'She weren't to blame for what he did, but she can't be told. It's like she means to take herself with him.'

Susan said nothing. In her heart she knew she had more to do with Ben's state of mind than Louise, because he hadn't known about Eric until she had told him. Worse still was what she and Ben had done to Louise . . . and Susan would never forgive herself for that.

From the far corner, Eric stood hidden from view, feeling as guilty about Ben's fate as any one of them. When Louise walked past, so close he could have reached out and touched her, he could not stop himself from stepping forward. Taking off his cap in respect of the circumstances, he nodded to the old woman, his face crumpled with compassion; Sal nodded back in acknowledgment. There was no need of words.

Turning to Louise, he told her awkwardly, 'I'm sorry, lass.' Just that and no more. And while old Mrs Hunter thought he was referring to her loss with Ben dying, the two sisters knew the shocking truth.

For a fleeting second, Louise glanced up, her eyes red from the weeping. She looked deep into those quiet eyes and held Eric's gaze for the space of a single heartbeat. Then she turned away, and walked on without a word.

Behind her, Eric let out a long, shuddering sigh. Then he stood a while longer, before he too, turned away. He wanted to hold her and keep her safe, but he knew he couldn't. He had seen it in her eyes just now, and he knew her love was still there, as was his . . . a forbidden, powerful thing.

For now it was too painful for her to contemplate. His heart sank. Maybe it would *always* be too painful to contemplate.

There was someone else watching. Some way off, where the lawn of the churchyard ran up to the stone wall, Jacob wisely kept his distance. 'You've all done your fair share,' he muttered, 'but it were me as put him where he is now.' With a surge of rage, he kicked the ground until the turf curled up beneath the toe of his shoe. Then he thrust his hands into his pockets and strode away.

A COUPLE OF weeks afterwards, late at night, Jacob called on Louise. 'I'm sorry to knock so late,' he stood at the door as if it was the most natural thing in the world, 'only I needed to give you my condolences, like, about the way things turned out.' He still wanted her, now more than ever, and because of the twist of circumstances, he saw his chance improving.

Sal's voice sailed down from the bedroom. 'Who's that?'

'It's all right, Sal.' Keeping Jacob at the door, she told him, 'It's a pity you didn't talk more to your brother when he needed you, then things might not have turned out the way they did.'

Climbing to the top step he stood close . . . too close for her peace of mind. 'Is there owt I can do?' His voice was sugar-sweet.

'Yes, there is.'

'I'll do anything, you know that.' He came even closer, his eyes devouring her. 'All you have to do is say the word.'

Louise loathed his nearness and it showed now in her voice and in the way she stared back at him with cold emotion. 'The word is "MOTHER!".' Glancing towards the stairway, she reprimanded him. 'Sally could do with a word or two of comfort. Or is that too far out of your capabilities?'

'I'll drop in and see her tomorrow.' He had no intention of doing any such thing; unless of course it was to impress Louise. 'Right now, it's you I need to talk to.'

'I've got nothing to say, Jacob, except clear off.'

'I'm here if you want me, you do know that, don't yer?'

'But I *don't* want you, Jacob. I thought I'd made that clear?'

'Aye well, it's only right that you don't want me at this minute. Later though, mebbe you'll be in need of me.'

'Never!' When she reached out to push him away, he caught hold of her and drawing her close, tried to kiss her on the mouth.

'Yer don't fool me,' he leered at her like a madman. 'You want me as much as I want you. Don't deny it.'

When she hit out at him, he was too strong for her. They fought fiercely, with Louise struggling with all her might, but making no impact. She was both relieved and startled when Sal appeared, carrying the yard broom like a javelin in her hands. 'GET OFF HER!' the old lady squawked. Running at him with the brush-end she caught him off-guard; he went to steady himself, lost his balance and sprawled backwards down the steps.

'You're not welcome here,' she told him. 'My only son is gone. You're a stranger to me now. So be off with yer, afore I call the police.'

As he went scurrying down the street swearing and cursing, she saw how he had hurt Louise; her left arm was bleeding where he'd scraped her against the wall, and there was a sore place on her face, got from when she struggled with him on the steps. 'Come on, lass.' Sal took her by the arms. 'Let's get you inside, eh?'

But there was no time to get her inside, because just then Louise gave a cry; falling to the ground she clutched at her stomach. 'It's the baby!' she cried. 'Get help, Sal. Get Susan!'

Sal was flabbergasted. 'Baby?' She had suspected, but wasn't really certain, and now it seemed it might be too late. 'Lie still, child.' Taking a coat from the back of the door, she threw it over Louise. Taking a second one, she swung it over her own shoulders and went out of the house, going down the street as fast as her old legs would take her. 'A baby?'

She offered up a prayer. 'Oh dear God, let it live,' she pleaded. 'Let them both be all right.'

It was a wonderful thing, but, 'If Jacob has killed his brother's child, I'll kill *him* with me own hands, so I will!'

Chapter Nineteen

STEVE HOLSDEN WAS like any other man. When it came to things of a deep, emotional nature, he could not find the right words to express how he really felt.

When he brought his lass home from the Infirmary, he just held her for a while, and when he smiled on her it was not the kind of smile that said, 'Everything will be all right.' Instead, it was a quiet, understanding smile that said, 'I can't imagine what you must be going through, but I'm here for you, lass.' And Louise knew he was feeling every bit as broken as she was herself.

The journey home in the taxi seemed never-ending. Patsy and Sal were waiting at the door. 'How are you feeling, pet?' Sal had seen what the girl had gone through and her heart went out to her.

'Come here.' Patsy gave her daughter a hug, and

told her she was glad to see her home again. But the baby was lost and that was something she could not bring herself to mention.

Life must go on, Louise thought. There was no use trying to fathom the way of things. The child had been Eric's, and maybe this was her punishment for what she had done to Ben.

When Patsy had gone home and Sal was having her afternoon nap, Susan popped in to see her sister. 'Happen it's for the best,' she said, but Louise didn't see it that way. With Ben gone and now the child, she felt incredibly alone.

'Would you have let folks believe it was Ben's?' Susan had a way of persisting with things that created even more pain.

Louise had thought a lot about that. 'I couldn't have told Sal the truth,' she confessed. 'She's been through too much already, bless her old heart. It would have made her so happy to think the baby was her grandchild.'

'Whatever possessed Jacob to come round here like that?'

'Conscience, mebbe.' Louise had not told anyone of his real reason for searching her out.

'Will you go to Eric now?'

Louise gave a wistful little smile. 'There's nothing I'd like to do more in all the world,' she admitted. 'But no . . . that's all over and done with now.'

After a time, Susan left and the house was quiet. Louise went to the window and looked out. It was a beautiful, sunny day; children playing in the street and women chatting on the doorsteps. There was the coalman on his rounds and down the street a man cleaning his precious car. 'Everything's just the same.' She smiled. It was oddly comforting to see all the people, especially the children.

From the corner of her eye she saw Susan come out of the house and walk across to the coalman. They chatted for a time; Susan paid him for the two sacks of coal he put aside ready for delivering, then she went away laughing at some crude joke he'd made.

Louise shook her head, unable to resist a little chuckle. 'You randy little bugger, you'll never learn, will you?' Though Susan had been a thorn in her side for some long time, she loved her all the same.

Her mood grew serious. 'One of these days you'll bite off more than you can chew.'

It was just as well she didn't know the truth.

<hr>

THE BEAUTIFUL AUTUMN had long since waned and the dark winter nights had set in.

'You're getting overweight, my girl. You want to get out and do a bit o' walking, instead o' sitting on yer backside in front of the fire all day.' Although the neighbours were beginning to gossip about Susan, Patsy refused to see what was in front of her. 'What's wrong with you?'

Susan folded her arms and refused to budge, even when her mam tried to shift the chair in order to hoover underneath. 'Leave me alone, Mam. You're forever nagging. Nag, nag, nag all bloody day long.'

Pausing in her work, Patsy dropped herself into the nearby chair. 'I'm worried about you, lass,' she confessed. 'Since you lost your job, you don't go out the door if you can help it. And look at you! Half the time you can't be bothered to comb your hair and you've a temper on you like a raging bull. If there's summat wrong, you can tell me about it can't you? Or if you won't talk to *me*, at least have a word with our Louise. She's bound to help.'

'I don't need no sodding help!' Scrambling out of the chair, Susan flounced heavily across the room and stomped upstairs, where she sat on her bed, brooding and wondering what to do. 'Hmh! I can just see me going to our Louise and telling her I'm carrying Ben's child. The truth would come out about how it were me as got him thrown out of the pub and it were me as told him about her and Eric.' She saw it all in her mind like a moving picture. 'That was when he threw himself off the bridge. It were me as killed him. I can't let her find out. I can't!'

The thought of her sister learning the truth made her shudder in her shoes. 'No, this is summat I've to deal with myself, and I will. One way or another.'

She sat there for a long time, thinking and planning and deciding what to do.

'I should go away,' she told herself. 'I've no choice now but to have the baby, seeing as I've let it carry on this long without going to see a doctor. So, happen I might leave and have the baby, then I'll get it adopted, and nobody'll be any the wiser.' She shook her head. 'No, I'm too much of a coward. I want to be near Mam when it happens. Besides, nobody knows whose baby it is. I can tell the buggers what I like!'

She felt better for having thought it through. 'I'll not be the first to have a baby out of wedlock and I'll definitely not be the last. It's not the end of the world. I'll get a new job and have money in me pocket.' She cheered up. 'There's still time enough for me to enjoy meself.'

<hr />

ONE EVENING LATE in the year, Maggie travelled home to Craig Street with the children. 'Have you enjoyed staying with your daddy and grandma?' she asked as they boarded the tram.

Little Hannah promptly fell asleep on her lap, but not Adam; he was all talk and chatter as they rumbled along. 'When will you and Daddy get married again?' he asked.

'Never!' Maggie was not one to hedge about.

'Oh.' Puzzled but not concerned, he focused his attention on the street-lamps outside.

'What makes you ask that?' She was curious.

''Cause Daddy said so.'

Maggie laughed. 'Oh, I'm sure he'd *like* for us to get together again,' she admitted, 'but we won't.'

'Why not?'

She took a moment to study his face; such a handsome little face with those intense dark eyes and strong, square chin. 'Because it won't work, that's why.'

'Oh.'

'Does that answer your question?'

He nodded. 'Grandma bought us fish and chips.'

Maggie chuckled. Only an innocent could switch from one thing to another like that.

While Adam counted the street-lamps through the window, Maggie overheard a conversation taking place two rows in front. 'Oh, aye! She's nigh on five months gone, so they say.' The fat woman in the turban was imparting the news to her friend, a slight creature with a nervous twitch.

'Well, I think it's shocking!'

The fat woman leaned over. 'There's talk it might be Jacob Hunter's child.'

'But he's got another woman, hasn't he? I heard they live down Craig Street . . . him and this fancy piece.'

'Oh aye, it's true right enough, but you know what men are. They want one at home and one between the sheets. I shouldn't think he's any different from the rest, would you?'

Her friend shook her head. 'Not in *my* experience,' she answered slyly.

'What d'you mean, "in *your* experience"?' the fat woman demanded. Her friend gave a cheeky chuckle. 'Dora Armstrong! What naughty secrets are you hiding from me?'

The skinny woman blushed. 'I'll have you know, I've not been without my fair share of men,' she answered. Having said as much, she would not say another word on the subject, no matter how hard she was tested.

As a rule, Maggie paid no attention to idle gossip, but the conversation played on her mind all the way home.

Once they were inside the house, she lost no time in getting Hannah to bed. 'Come on, son, it's time you were off to bed an' all.' Ushering Adam into the kitchen, she gave him a hands and face wash. 'It's gone half-past ten already.' She looked at the clock, wondering where Jacob was until now. The questions were already burning in her troubled mind.

A FTER HANGING ABOUT on the corner for an hour, Susan was relieved when she saw him coming down the street. 'Jacob!' Going towards him, she smiled into his surprised face, her delight obvious beneath the halo of light from the street-lamp. 'I thought you'd never come home.'

Amazed to see her there, Jacob did not share her enthusiasm. As far as he was concerned, they had been finished for ever. 'What the 'ell do *you* want?'

'I need to talk,' she replied sweetly. 'A few minutes of your time. Please, Jacob?'

Bleary-eyed with the booze, he stared at her as though she were a stranger. 'We've done all our talking.'

Susan was determined. 'We could still have a future, you and me.'

He laughed in her face. 'What – with you big as a ship from some other fella? What d'you tek me for . . . a bloody fool?' He poked her in the stomach. 'Whose is it, eh? The milkman's? The coalman's? Who's been poking about where he shouldn't?'

'It might be yours – have you thought of that?'

'It bloody well ain't mine, an' well you know it, you little slag.'

'All right, it's not yours.'

'So what d'you want with me then?'

'I want us to go away, just like we planned. I'll have the baby adopted. I'll get a job. I'll work my fingers to the bone for you, Jacob. You see if I don't.'

'Piss off!'

'Please, Jacob. I mean it. I still love you. If you turn your back on me now, I'll have nobody, nothing.'

He was getting impatient. 'You'd best get off to whoever put that bun in your oven.' He dug her in the stomach, this time hard enough to hurt her. 'I don't want you, you little idiot. I only went with you to draw your sister out, but she weren't having none of it, and now I'm bloody well lumbered with somebody I hate a little bit more with every passing day! And all because you let me down. You should have signed that form and I'd have had the money to do what I liked, and none of this would have happened.'

'I'll get money, Jacob. I can do it. I'll sign anything you want. Please, don't desert me, not now when I need you the most.'

'Y'mean like when I needed you to sign that form and you never did?' Pushing past her, he strode away. 'Keep out of my sight, it makes me sick to look at yer!' For good measure he turned and spat on the ground. 'You mean nothing to me. I don't give a bugger *what* happens to you. What's more, I don't want you whimpering round me any more. Got that, have yer?'

Devastated, she stood there, listening to the echoing of his shoes as he went on his way. 'I hate you!' she muttered. 'I could kill you.' A murderous rage rose up in her. *'You and her both!'*

When his footsteps died away, she took a deep breath, calmed herself and went away in the opposite direction.

Chapter Twenty

'Looking for work, are you, lass?' The Post Office clerk took out her hankie and blew her nose, making a loud raspberry noise that sent a nearby child scurrying behind its mammy's skirts.

'There's nothing here.' Louise moved away from the noticeboard. 'Not that I can do anyway. There's vacancies for drivers and navvies, and there's one advert for a dustman, but that's all.'

Taking a sheet of paper from beneath the counter, the clerk told her, 'I've a couple more to be put in today. There's one here might suit you, being as you've worked on the land an' all.' She began to read, '"Wanted, to start right away, an able-bodied man or woman, with experience of chicken-minding and egg-collecting. Also, to include seasonal orchard maintenance. Good wages for the right person, and a possibility of accommodation".'

Louise was thrilled. 'Sounds exactly what I'm looking for, except I'll not want the accommodation. Where is it?'

The clerk smiled knowingly. 'It's your old place,' she confided. 'Eric Forester brought this in yesterday. I haven't had a chance to put it on the noticeboard yet. By! You'd know that job inside out and back to front. If you went to see him, I'm sure he'd give it you straight off.' She paused, looking uncomfortable. 'Only, would you want to work there? I mean, being as it were your place an' all?'

Louise evaded the question. 'What I really want is work in a factory,' she lied. 'Our Susan had a good job at Marshall's Mill, before she left. It's better money and you don't have the same responsibility.'

'How *is* your Susan? . . . Due any day now, isn't it?'

'Just under a month to go, and she's fine, thank you.'

'No news of the father then?'

'I don't press her on that,' Louise answered smartly. 'It's not really my business.'

Handing Louise her stamps and writing material in a paper bag, the clerk held out her hand. 'That'll be one and ninepence, please.'

After paying over the money and passing the time of day with the other customer, Louise was glad to leave. 'Nosy buggers – why can't they mind their own business!' she grumbled all the way down the street. Although she too had often wondered about the father of Susan's baby. She thought her sister might at least have confided in *her*. But then, who else's baby could it be but Jacob's?

———————⟫•⟪———————

S AL WAS NOT surprised when told of Eric's advert. 'I wondered how he'd manage that place all on his own,' she remarked. 'Are you sure you wouldn't want to work there, lass? It'd be out in the fresh air, and I'm sure he'd give you a free hand on the place.'

'No, I'd not be happy, Sal. Besides, when the weather's bad, as you know yourself, it's a worry. No, I'd rather be in the factory. I'll go out in the morning, and see if there's anything going. I've lived off you for too long already. I need to earn a wage and pay you back every penny it's cost since we've been here.'

'There's no rush.' Sal didn't like the idea of being left alone all day. 'Besides, it's not all been on my shoulders, lass. You've been paying the rent out of the bit of money you had put by, and look, I've still got a few shillings left in my box upstairs. So don't worry too much about rushing out for work.'

'I *have* to, Sal,' Louise answered kindly. For my own peace of mind, she thought.

<hr />

T HAT NIGHT, LONG after Sal was fast asleep, Louise paced the floor. Seeing that advert had disturbed her. She couldn't get Eric out of her mind. 'He put the advert in that Post Office for me to see.' She was convinced of it. 'Otherwise, why didn't he put it in the Post Office nearer to the farm, or in the centre of Blackburn where more folks would see it?'

It was 2 a.m. when she heard the noises – like somebody fighting a long way off. Going to the window, she looked out into the crisp winter night, but there was no one there. 'Cats, I shouldn't wonder,' she mused. 'Or drunks coming out of a private party.'

Weary now, she got into bed and closed her eyes. Sleep crept up on her, and soon she was dreaming, of Eric and that night, and Ben standing there watching. Restless, she tossed and turned and found no peace.

When the knock came on the front door, she was already awake. 'It's all right, Sal.' Frightened, the old woman had come to her bedroom door. 'Stay where you are. I'll go.'

Stepping nervously down the stairs, she was

relieved when her father's voice called through the letter-box. 'You'd best come quick,' he shouted. 'It's Susan. She's having the bairn.'

'I'll be right there, Dad,' she replied. While he ran back home, Louise quickly threw a robe over her nightie.

A few minutes later, when Louise came rushing into her parents' house, there was Susan, laid out on a sheet on the floor. 'She wouldn't go upstairs.' Patsy was beside her. 'There, there lass.' Soothing the girl, who was in a state of panic, she told her, 'Your dad's been down and phoned the ambulance. It'll be here in no time.'

'It won't wait, Mam!' Susan caught sight of Louise and cried out. 'Tell her, sis! There's no time for an ambulance. The baby's coming *now*!' She began sobbing. 'Help me, I'm frightened.'

Kneeling beside her, Louise gave her a telling-off. 'It won't help if you keep screaming and shouting,' she said sternly. 'If the baby's coming now, we'll have to help it, won't we, eh?' Looking up at her mam, she was surprised to see how she, too, was beginning to panic. 'Come on, Mam. You know more about this than any of us. What do we do now?'

Taking comfort from Louise's calm manner, Patsy soon got a grip on herself. 'Father, it's best if you go back to bed,' she told her husband, who was nervously pacing the floor, 'but first, get back down the street and phone to see if the ambulance is on its way. Tell them she's already having the bairn, and that they should be quick about it, if they're to get here on time.'

While he went away, the two women set about removing some of Susan's clothing, so they could see what was happening down below. 'By! Look at that!' Patsy couldn't believe her eyes. 'It's the top of the baby's head! You were right, love,' she told Susan. 'It won't wait for no ambulance. Eeh, it's an impatient little bugger an' no mistake.'

Louise was thrilled. In the next few, dramatic minutes, assisted by the two women, easing out of Susan was this tiny, dark-haired miracle, perfect in every way, with little hands and feet, and big blue eyes that looked up, straight into Louise's face, turning her heart upside down. For a while, she couldn't speak, then when her mother told her to hold the baby while she made Susan comfortable, it was all too much. Holding that beautiful innocent in her arms caught at her heart like nothing before; she was made to think of the child she had lost, and the love she had lost; and of the husband who lay in the churchyard not far away. The tears rolled down her face thick and fast, while she gazed on that tiny being. 'It's a girl,' she said tearfully. 'A bonny baby girl.'

———▸•◄———

WHEN THE AMBULANCE arrived, the cord had been cut, the afterbirth delivered and disposed of, and the baby was washed and wrapped up warm. Susan herself, although sleepy, was already recovering. 'I'm not going to hospital,' she told them. 'I'm all right where I am.' She was expertly examined and, seeing that all was well, she was then carried upstairs by her father and put to bed, with the child beside her. 'The midwife will call round tomorrow,' she was told. It was normal procedure.

'I'm off to my bed.' Steve felt he had done his fair share. 'I'm shattered.'

Louise gave him a kiss. 'You did really well, Dad,' she said, and he went to bed proud of himself.

Afterwards, Louise and her mam enjoyed a well-earned cup of tea. 'I can't understand it.' Patsy was puzzled. 'She came in late, all in a fluster, gabbling on about how it were all "his" fault. She had a graze on her arm, and when I asked her about it, she said she'd fallen against the wall when the pains started. Soonever she got in the door she was buckled up. I had to get the sheets down and lie her right there on the floor.' She gulped at her tea. 'By! It were all a bit fast. It took me by surprise.'

She looked up at Louise. 'You don't know who the father is, do you, lass?'

Louise shook her head.

'You'd tell me if you did, wouldn't you?'

'Only if Susan wanted me to.'

Patsy smiled. 'By! She has treated you summat terrible over the years, but you still look out for her, don't you, eh?'

'Did she say where she'd been?'

'No. I couldn't get a word out of her, except that the baby were coming, an' I had to do summat. I'm glad you were here, love,' she admitted. 'I think I were panicking afore.'

'Did you hear a noise – down the street some-where, about half an hour before Dad came knocking on the door?'

When her mam said she'd heard nothing, Louise put it down to her imagination. Though she won-dered where Susan had been.

———◦———

'WHAT TIME IS it?' Peering out of her bed-room door, Sal looked like she'd been pulled through a hedge backwards.

Louise apologised. 'I'm sorry, it's only five o'clock,' she yawned. 'Go back to sleep, sweetheart.'

'Is everything all right?'

'Everything's fine,' Louise smiled. 'Susan's had her baby . . . a lovely little girl.'

Sal was amazed. 'But I thought she had another month to go?'

'She had, but it seems the baby couldn't wait.'

'Are they both well?'

'They're both marvellous. The ambulanceman made sure everything was in order before he left; he said the baby was one of the strongest little things he'd ever seen, and he's seen a few. The midwife will be calling round first thing.'

'You look exhausted, lass. Try and get some sleep.'

'You, too. Goodnight, Sal.'

'Goodnight, love.'

———⋙◦⋘———

LOUISE HAD BEEN deeply asleep when she was woken by some sound or another, though she couldn't quite make it out. She glanced at the clock. 'Ten past seven.' She'd been asleep about two hours.

Padding over the icy lino to the window, she looked out. The street was fairly quiet yet. From the corner of her eye, she saw someone walking across the bottom end of the street, a woman carrying a suitcase. Though she walked slowly, as though in some discomfort, Louise recognised the woman at once. It was her sister. 'Susan?' She shook her head in disbelief. 'It can't be!'

Running down the stairs, she grabbed a coat from behind the front door. As she went to unlock the door she saw the envelope lying there. Recognising her sister's handwriting, she tore it open and quickly read what was written there:

Dear Louise,

Please forgive me for what I'm about to tell you, but I can't look at the baby or you, and live with such a bad, bad secret.

The baby is Ben's. It was only the one time, when I was upset because of Jacob. Ben comforted me, and that was when it happened. I'm so sorry. Please don't hate me. I'm going away, and I'm never coming back. Don't any of you come after me, or I swear I'll go the same way as Ben.

Keep the baby. Say it's yours, if you like. Or say you're minding the baby because I've gone away for a time. Better still, you can adopt it. I'll gladly give my consent. I don't care what you do, but I don't want to see it ever again. Besides, you'll make a much better mother than I ever could.

Forgive me, for everything. Now that you know what I did, I don't suppose you'll ever want to set eyes on me again. But it won't matter, because I'm never coming back.

*Please, sis, tell Mam and Dad I do love them,
even though I never acted like it.*

*The baby is my gift to you. She might even make
up for the one you lost.*

*Be good. Take care of everybody, just like you
always have,*

Your selfish, ungrateful sister, Susan.

Louise read the letter and still could not believe
that Susan could have done such a terrible thing
– but then it took two to make a baby, so her late
husband was not entirely innocent. '*Ben's baby!*' She
could hardly believe it.

It seemed so unreal, and yet here it was, down
in black and white. 'I don't understand . . .' She felt
faint. It was all too much to take in at once.

Instinctively, she opened the door, and there she
was; swathed in warm blankets and tucked into a
carrying basket, that beautiful baby girl was left on
the doorstep like a bottle of milk or a parcel from the
postman.

Louise was deeply moved. 'You don't deserve to
be treated like that.' Collecting the basket from the
ground, she turned back the covers and looking up
at her were those deep, innocent eyes. 'Let's get you
inside,' she said, tickling the tiny face under the chin.
'Then we have to think about what to do.'

Sal was already awake and making her slow way

down the stairs. 'Whatever's going on?' It seemed to be one thing after another. 'Has the world gone mad?'

Louise led the way into the sitting room. 'You might think so when I tell you what's happened.' She laid the carrying bag on the table. 'Look here, Sal.' Turning back the covers, she revealed its contents, and when the old lady saw what was there, she gasped, 'My God! Whose is it?'

Louise handed her the note, and while she read it, Sal had to sit down. 'Oh, lass, I'm so sorry.' Her eyes were big with astonishment, and wet with tears. 'As if you haven't been through enough.'

'I'm not concerned for myself.' Louise had other priorities now. 'I'm worried about the baby, and Susan too. She shouldn't be up and outside walking the streets, not so soon after giving birth.' She glanced at the door. 'She'll be long gone by now.'

Sal's thoughts were for Patsy and Steve. 'There's a lot to be thought through,' she said, 'but for now, I reckon you'd best find out if your parents know what's happened.'

'You're right, but I'll not take the baby. She can stay here with us for the time being. After all, if what Susan says is true, and I'm sure it is, then we've as much right to this baby as anybody. She's your granddaughter, Sal, and the daughter I should have had with Ben.'

Sal agreed with her wholeheartedly. 'A blessing in disguise.'

———————※◦※———————

Louise's parents were terribly shocked. 'We've got to find her.' Patsy was beside herself with worry. 'Who knows what damage she might have done to herself, getting up from her bed so soon after giving birth . . . and carrying a suitcase.' Because of what Louise claimed to have seen, Patsy had gone to check the cupboard under the stairs where she kept the suitcases. One of them was gone. 'We should tell the police,' she said. 'They'll find her.'

Steve did not agree. 'The lass felt strongly enough to take off and leave the bairn behind,' he reminded her. 'Who are we to get the police on her trail and drag her back here, and what good would it do if they did, eh? Tell me that.'

Louise had to agree. 'He's right, Mam. She would only go off again at the first opportunity. What's more, she threatened to harm herself if we went after her.'

'So what can we do about the bairn?' With eyes hollow from crying, Patsy looked from one to the other. 'However much our Susan wants Louise to have the bairn, there are laws. You can't just give a baby away, whatever the circumstances.'

Louise had thought about that. 'Look, Mam, our Susan has abandoned the baby and if Ben *is* the father, and I'm certain he must be, that makes me responsible for her. I'll fight tooth and nail if anybody tries to take her away, you can count on that.'

Again, Steve came in with his quiet words of wisdom. 'There'll be no need of that,' he said. 'Our Susan has entrusted that baby girl to you, and as Ben's wife, I reckon you're more her mam than anyone else. I can't see the authorities taking her away and letting some other woman raise her, can you?'

Patsy shook her head. 'No,' she answered. 'It wouldn't make any sense at all. You could say nowt, love, and keep the bairn all the same,' she suggested. 'Tell them as wants to know that our Susan's gone away for convalescence, and that you're minding the bairn till she gets back.'

Louise was adamant. 'Whichever way it goes,' she decided, 'that little girl is *my* responsibility, and I'll not let her down.'

While they were still talking, a knock came on the door. 'That'll be Sal.' Louise went through to the front door.

But it wasn't Sal.

It was a police officer, come to ask them a few questions. Horrified that somehow, someone had reported Susan abandoning her baby, Louise had no choice but to invite him inside.

To her immense relief, his mission had nothing to do with Susan, but it was a shocking and awful thing he had come to tell them, all the same. 'Did you see or hear anything at all out of the ordinary, in the early hours of this morning?' he asked.

They answered that, no, they had heard nothing, though Louise was reminded of the sounds she thought she had heard. Yet, thinking about Susan and of how she had gone off like that, she kept quiet.

As they talked, the policeman wrote everything down in his notebook. When it was clear to him that there was no information to be got here, he prepared to leave. 'Wait a minute, officer.' Like the others, Steve was curious. 'What's all this about?'

The officer tucked the notebook into his top pocket. 'I'm afraid it's a murder enquiry, sir.'

'Murder!' Steve fell back in his chair. 'What? Here on Derwent Street?'

'No, sir.' When he gave the address, Louise cried out in shock. 'Oh my God – NO!' White-faced, she stared at him. 'Was it Jacob . . . Jacob Hunter?'

'I believe so, miss, but we can't be certain just yet. There were two victims, a man and a woman. The children were found hiding in the cellar.' His voice fell. 'I'm a family man myself,' he said. 'I've got two kids of my own, and I feel for them young 'uns.'

Patsy wanted to know. 'Are they . . . ?' Her voice shook.

'No, they'll be fine,' he told her. 'The ambulance is on its way. The girl was hurt, but not too badly. The boy – Adam she called him – is a brave little fella by all accounts. It seems he saved her life.' He shook his head in despair. 'Poor little devils, they're both in shock. They're not able to tell us exactly what happened.'

'Officer.' Louise had to tell him. 'My mother-in-law is Jacob's mam. She's already lost her husband and her youngest son over the past few months, and I'm not sure how she'll take this news. Please, let me be the one to tell her?'

'Where will I find her?'

'We live down the street.' Louise gestured to her parents. 'This is my mam and dad.'

'I'm sure we won't have a problem with you telling your mother-in-law, but as I say, we've not yet confirmed the identity of the bodies. By all means tell her what you know, and I'll be along to see her shortly.' He took out his notebook. 'What's the number of the house?'

Louise told him, and he wrote it in his notebook. 'She's a frail old lady,' she warned. 'I don't want her frightened.'

He smiled at her concern. 'Don't you worry, miss,' he said kindly. 'Like I said, I'm a family man. I'm not here to frighten anybody.'

After he'd gone, the three of them sat silent and

stunned for a minute or two. 'I can't believe it,' Steve said. 'Jacob and his woman . . . *murdered*!'

Patsy was shocked to her roots for the second time that day. 'Who on earth could have done such a terrible thing?'

Steve had no doubts. 'Some poor bastard he'd rubbed up the wrong way at some time or another – though it's a pity the woman got caught up in it.'

Louise was quiet for a long time. She couldn't help but recall what Susan had said about both Jacob and the woman he was living with, and how at times she had threatened to 'make them pay'. Not for one minute did she believe her sister was capable of murdering anyone. All the same, it made her shudder inside. 'I'd best get to Sal,' she said. 'Before the police do.'

———⊰◦⊱———

S AL TOOK THE news without a word, her face and manner calm and stony. Then she sat in the front room looking out of the window. When, an hour later, the police officer came to talk with her, she confirmed, in the same expressionless voice and manner who she was and that she had not talked with her son for some long time, because she held him responsible for the tragic circumstances of the death of her other son, Benjamin Hunter.

Other than that, she had nothing to impart that might help them catch the killer.

After the officer had left, she went upstairs and there she stayed for the rest of the day, seated by the window, her hands folded in her lap and her eyes staring ahead. She came out once to use the bathroom, and a second time to make herself a cup of tea.

Both times, in spite of Louise's attempts to draw her out of herself, she didn't say a word, and realising this was Sal's way of dealing with the shocking news, Louise did not press her.

PART FOUR

FORGIVING

Chapter Twenty-one

ON A RAINY day in the early summer of 1953, some two months after the unsolved murders, Louise was called to attend a special hearing with regard to the baby girl, who she had called Virginia after Sal's mother.

Behind Louise came her parents, and Sal, all there to give her moral support and, more importantly, to bear witness to her good character.

'These are exceptional circumstances. We are fully aware of the ordeal it has been for you, Mrs Hunter, but you must see how we have to be certain to make the right decision. A child's future is in the balance and cannot be taken lightly.' The spokesman had a quiet and thoughtful manner.

'I understand that, sir.' Louise didn't care how long and arduous the ordeal was for her, providing that come the end of the day, she was given custody of her daughter; for she had already come to think of Jinnie as just that . . . her very own daughter.

He went on, 'We have taken everything into consideration. The fact that the child was fathered by your own husband, and that the mother was your sister, makes this a peculiar case. As I'm sure you're aware, one of our officers has traced your sister and she confirms her wish to have the child adopted by you.'

At this point his female colleague interrupted, 'Your sister's abandonment of the child was very, very wrong, and as a rule would be regarded as extremely serious, warranting a degree of punishment, but according to the doctor, she left while the balance of her mind was disturbed.'

The gentleman took up the argument. 'After consultation with the doctor who tended her, it has been decided that her misdemeanour will this time be overlooked. We understand the family, and your sister herself, had been through a very painful and worrying time.'

'Yes, sir.' Susan had been found in Blackpool, but when Louise went to see her, she refused to come back home, insisting that she wanted nothing whatsoever to do with Ben's child.

The officer's voice shook Louise out of her reverie. 'However, it is our duty to work in the child's interests, and in view of everything, together with verification of your own good character, we have unanimously decided to grant you the right to apply for adoption of your late husband's child.' He smiled at Louise and glanced at the child in her arms, gurgling and gazing up at her with adoring eyes, and he knew they had made the right decision.

After waiting for so long, and undergoing all the official business in between, Louise was overwhelmed with emotion. 'We've nearly done it, Sal,' she whispered brokenly. 'She's our baby now.' Her eyes filled with tears of joy. And when she could hold back her own tears no longer, Sal cried with her. 'It's only what you deserve, lass,' she told Louise. 'The child could have no better mother than you.'

While the others made their way home, Louise had one more errand to attend to, before following on. 'I'll catch the next tram,' she promised, and when they had gone she took the tram in a different direction, to the churchyard where Ben had been laid to his rest.

Taking the baby to where the newly laid stone was erected, she stroked her hand over the lettering there. Even the touch of her fingers against his name seemed to bring him closer.

She closed her eyes. In her mind she could see his face, a strong, smiling face before he lost the house and land, then, afterwards, a sad and bitter face, and nothing she could do made him feel any better. 'I'm sorry I couldn't help you, my love,' she murmured. 'And I do understand why you went to Susan. I failed you then, and I failed you again . . . in a way you never knew.'

Even now, she did not realise he had been told the truth about her and Eric, and that was part of the burden he could no longer live with.

The truth caught like a physical presence in her throat, but she forced it out. 'I made the same mistake,' she confessed. 'Me . . . and Eric.' Now that she had gone so far, she had to tell it all. 'It was not your fault, love, but you made me see him in a different light, and when you became so difficult to live with, I found a warmth with him that I had already lost with you.'

It sounded so cruel, but if she was to go on in her new life, she must tell it. 'I won't lie to you, Ben. I love Eric, with all my heart. But I won't go to him, not now. Not ever, that I can see. It would be too much of a betrayal.'

She held out the baby. 'Do you see her, Ben?' she asked softly. 'This is your baby girl . . . yours and Susan's. I love her so much, as much as I once loved you, and still do; not with the fire and passion that we knew before, but with a deep, abiding closeness that will stay with me for ever. I'll raise your daughter to be good and honest, and I will always be there for her. She's your daughter, Ben, and when she's old enough to understand, I'll tell her about you . . . and her mammy. Now though, with you gone and Susan denying her existence, she's my responsibility. I won't fail you.'

She said a prayer for him, and left.

Ben was her past. Jinnie was her future now.

As she ran for the tram, it was Eric who picked up her handbag when it dropped into the gutter. 'I heard the good news from Sal,' he said, tickling the baby under the chin. 'I'd been delivering some eggs, and saw Sal at the tram stop.'

Louise took her handbag and thanked him. 'I've been to the churchyard,' she said.

He nodded. 'Sal thought you might.'

She kissed the baby on the forehead. 'She's *my* daughter now.'

He was silent for a minute, then he surprised her with a remark that took her aback. 'The rumour is you lost a bairn of your own some time back?'

'That's right, I did.'

'*Was it mine?*'

This was no time for lies. 'Yes, but no one knows that. Sal thought it was Ben's child.'

'She'll not learn anything different from me.'

'I'm glad.' She knew she could trust him.

'I should have been there for you.'

'That wasn't possible.'

'Louise?' He spoke in a broken whisper.

'Yes?' She sounded so cold, when all she wanted was for him to take her in his arms and tell her everything would be all right.

'I love you.' His voice was laden with emotion.

'I love you too.' More than he knew.

'So . . . ?' He wondered if he dared hope.

'No, Eric. Not now.' The guilt was still there.

He nodded. 'When you're ready, I'll be waiting.'

'Goodbye, Eric.' It sounded so final.

He didn't answer. Instead he smiled, and walked away, and Louise had to restrain herself from calling him back.

With a heavy heart she boarded the tram and, going against her every instinct, she let it carry her away from him. She never remembered the journey home. Her heart and mind were still back there, with Eric.

When all the passengers had disembarked, leaving her and the baby the only remaining passengers, she gazed down at Jinnie's sleeping face; Ben's baby, and now *her* baby. She wondered at the cruel irony of it, and yet it seemed so right.

When the baby stirred in her arms, she kissed her tenderly, her voice heavy with love as she whispered against her little face, 'Oh my darling Jinnie, I hope you will never experience the heartache life can bring. So much has happened that you will have to know. One day, when you're old enough, I'll tell you everything. I'll tell you what a good man your father was, and how much he would have loved you.'

There were things though, that she would *never* tell – like how she had betrayed that good man with Eric. Even now, Eric was close, alive in her mind, in her soul; she would never need him more than she did right now, and the loneliness was suffocating.

Suddenly aware of the child looking up at her, she lowered her gaze and was overwhelmed by the beauty of those bright, intense eyes; it was almost as though the child understood what she was feeling. 'You'll never know what turmoil you were born into,' she whispered, 'and I'm glad of that. So much pain and badness, and yet out of it all *you* came . . . the most wonderful, beautiful little soul. I don't know if I can ever make it up to you,' she mused, 'but I mean to spend my life trying.'

In all the doubt, there was hope.

'I forgave your mammy and daddy,' she said sadly. 'Who knows? Maybe one day I'll be able to forgive myself.'

Then she smiled. 'Eric is a good, kind man,' she said, 'and I love him so much. The thought of spending my life without him seems like a terrible punishment to me.'

She looked out of the window and saw a glimpse of sunshine creeping through the clouds; it seemed to signify what she was thinking. 'We're lucky,' she told the child, smiling into Jinnie's blue watching eyes. 'We have each other, you and me. We've been given a second chance . . . and all the time in the world to put things right.'

Her heart lifted.

Sometimes, just when you thought things couldn't possibly get better, life had a funny way of proving you wrong.

Settling back into the seat, she thought on her life with Ben. In spite of all that had happened, there had been some very good times. And something told her there were good times still to be had – not with Ben, no. But it would happen for her, and Jinnie, and maybe somewhere along the way, Eric too, would feature largely in their lives.

She believed it with all her heart.

⇒➤◉◄⇐

IN THE FIRST week of August, 1953, Louise Hunter's application for adoption was granted.

In the same week, the police arrested Maggie's ex-husband. He was charged on a count of two murders, and expected to receive the severest penalty for what he had done.

The children, Hannah and Adam, were taken into the local authority's care; though they were not expected to be in care too long, before a new home was found for them.

At long last, Louise began to look forward to her new life with enthusiasm. Jinnie was her shining light, though always at the back of her mind she prayed that she and Eric would get together sometime in the very near future.

From a distance, Eric kept a protective watch over her. He had loved her for so many years without hope. Now though, he knew in his heart that one day, she was bound to come to him.

He would wait for the day, and meanwhile see that no harm came to her or the girl, for they both meant the world to him.

If you've enjoyed reading about the Hunters and the Holsdens, then look out for Josephine Cox's new novel, *Jinnie*, out now. To give you a taste, here's the first chapter . . .

Chapter One

Blackburn Town

Dropping her carrier bags to the floor, Louise Hunter kicked off her shoes and with a long, heartfelt sigh, leaned back and closed her eyes. It had been one of those days.

From the rear of the tram, a young woman caught sight of her and, knowing what she knew, found it hard to tear her gaze away. Her companion, a bright young thing called Helen with painted mouth and long, bare legs, was suddenly curious. 'D'you know that woman?' she asked.

Keeping her gaze on Louise, her friend nodded.

Impatient, Helen nudged her. 'So go on, Stell, who *is* she?'

'Ssh!' Shifting her gaze, the girl called Stella warned, 'Keep your voice down or she'll hear you.'

Offended, her friend slithered down in her seat.

'All right, all right – keep yer bloody hair on! I were only *asking*!' A moment or two passed, before her curiosity got the better of her once more. 'Well? Are you gonna tell me who she is, or what?'

Rolling her eyes to heaven, the dark-haired young woman cupped her hand to her mouth. *'It's Louise Hunter,'* she hissed.

'And who the devil's Louise Hunter when she's at home?'

'Ssh!' Stella said in a whisper, 'Do you remember when we were kids, there was a scandal about a big murder on Craig Street?'

'Oh, my God, *'course* I remember! A man was arrested . . . he killed that woman Maggie Pringle and her boyfriend.' Excitement trembled in Helen's voice. 'But what's *she* got to do with it?' She raised a wary glance to Louise.

'Everything.' Stella leaned close again. 'The murdered man was her brother-in-law, Jacob. There were them as said it were Louise Hunter's sister Susan who'd really killed them, on account of she was already having an affair with Jacob Hunter when the bugger went and set up home with this Maggie. Had a couple o' bairns, she did – a little lass, and a boy.' She shivered. 'After the murders, they found the kids hiding in the cellar . . . poor little buggers.'

'How old were they?'

'I'm not sure.' Screwing up her eyes she made a

calculation. 'From what our mam said, the lad saved his sister's life. He were about six year old then. That were ten years ago, so I expect he'll be coming up towards sixteen or seventeen by now. Adam, his name were – aye, and his little sister were Hannah. She were a couple of years younger than him.'

The other girl was both impressed and disappointed. 'You seem to remember a lot more than *I* do.'

'That's because you're three years younger than me, and you didn't listen at keyholes like I used to.' It was all coming back like yesterday. 'Besides, I used to earn money of a weekend, running errands for the women down Johnson Street. By! They never stopped gossiping about all the goings-on.' Stella chuckled. 'And I don't mean just the murder, neither. They were a randy bunch up that way! According to Mrs Newsom at number ten, she and her old man were at it every night o' the week!'

'Cor! That must be why she ended up having twelve kids!' Helen smirked.

'And not all of 'em her old man's, neither. She "couldn't get enough of it", that's what she said.'

The image of Mrs Newsom with her scary hair and bandy legs came into their minds; the idea of her cavorting naked with a man was all too much, and try as they might, they could not contain their laughter.

Wiping her eyes, the older one glanced up, relieved to see that Louise was not disturbed by their hilarity.

'Where's the sister now?' Helen said ghoulishly. 'The one they said might have done the killing?'

'Gawd knows. She disappeared off the face of the earth, and as far as I know, was never seen again.' Her gaze went back to Louise who, deep in thought, was oblivious to their interest in her. 'Happen *she* knows and she ain't saying.'

'She's not a bad looker, is she?' Helen remarked. 'How old d'you reckon she is?'

Another minute, another calculation. 'Hang on, there was summat else, as I recall.' The older one reached deep into her memory. 'Some time before the murders, there was a suicide.' She gestured to Louise. 'It was her husband,' she breathed.

'Bloody hell! She's had a colourful life an' no mistake!'

'According to our mam, Louise Hunter was about twenty-five when it happened, so she'd be what? In her mid-thirties by now.' Stella couldn't imagine how terrible it all must have been. 'Me and our mam were in the market last week, and we saw her then. Our mam said she'd never married again.'

'Bit of a waste though?'

They looked appraisingly at Louise, taking in the

straight, proud cut of her shoulders, and the long brown hair that fell loosely down her back, and just then as she turned to check the whereabouts of the conductor, the two young women were surprised by her warm, hazel-coloured eyes and her pretty smile. 'For all her troubles, she's managed to keep her looks and figure, ain't she?' The girl called Helen was impressed, and a teeny bit envious.

'Oh, I don't know,' said her friend peevishly. 'She's not bad, but I've seen better, even at her age.'

And that said, they got onto the subject of dating, and how they were sure to pick up a fella at the Palais on Friday night.

———⟫•⟨———

U NAWARE OF THEIR interest, Louise settled back and closed her eyes. She felt incredibly weary, anxious to get home to Jinnie. After a while, her thoughts inevitably returned to Eric Forester. It had been ten years since the tragedies, and for a long time afterwards, she and Eric had kept their distance, though there had not been a day when she hadn't wanted to go to him.

These past two years had been the worst. When Eric's handyman had moved on to pastures new, Louise had left her job at the factory and returned to work at Maple Farm, where she had once lived with Ben, her late husband. The farm had been in the Hunter family for generations, until it had been auctioned to pay for an outstanding debt. Now Eric owned it; Eric, the man she had loved, in secret and in torment, for so very long.

Louise was thrilled to be back, working on the land, but there had been a price to pay; working alongside Eric was tearing her apart. He didn't know that, and she could never tell him. *She wanted him, needed him like she had never needed any other man.* But the past would not set her free.

Some years ago, Eric had vowed to love her for ever. When she turned from him then, he never spoke of his love again, but she knew he loved her still, and always would. For didn't she see it in his eyes every time he looked on her, and didn't she love him in the very same way?

Theirs was a powerful love – but not as powerful as the guilt they felt over what had taken place all those years before. Oh, the times when she had wanted to reach out and touch him, aching for his arms to enfold her! But she never did; and for the same reason, he never made a move towards her. Because, like her, Eric was imprisoned by the past, and too afraid to grasp the future.

'Montague Street next stop!' The conductor's cry carried through the tram, shattering her thoughts.

'C'mon, ladies, let's be 'aving yer!' As he passed Louise's seat, he caught her eye. 'Sorry to disturb you, luv.' He gave a cheeky wink. 'I saw you deep in thought – or were you having a crafty little kip, eh?'

Louise smiled. 'A bit of both.'

'Had a busy day, 'ave yer?'

'Busy enough.'

Still chatting with Louise and not looking where he was going, the conductor was flung forward as he tripped over a young man's legs that were stretched out in the gangway. Composing himself, he straightened his unkempt hair and gave a little embarrassed cough. 'You'd best tuck 'em in, matey,' he warned, 'afore you cause a nasty accident.'

Disgruntled, the youth did as he was asked, albeit it with a sour face and surly manner.

'Young buggers these days,' the conductor chuntered softly to Louise, 'they think the world revolves round 'em, so they do!' As he continued forward, clanking his ticket machine and chatting to the other few passengers on the tram, it was just as well he didn't see the look the young man gave him.

A murderous glare if ever there was one, Louise thought to herself.

Collecting her bags, Louise made her way to the exit, at the same time helping an old lady who was jostled and unsteadied by the lurching of the tram as it meandered along the line. 'Thank you, dear.' Small and frail, with seemingly poor eyesight, the old lady leaned heavily on Louise's arm. 'I don't usually go out on my own,' she went on, happy that somebody should take the time to listen to her. 'My sister normally comes with me to the shops, but she's not been well lately . . . fell over and sprained her ankle, she did. I'm allus telling her, "tek your time, Annie, you don't have to *run* everywhere", but will she listen, No, she won't!'

At the thought of her beloved sister, the prettiest of smiles crossed her wizened features. 'She meks me mad at times, but I don't know what I'd do without her.'

Louise helped her off the tram. 'I'll be all right now, dear,' the old woman told her. 'I'd best get home and see what *she's* up to. Knowing her, she's probably up the chimney with a long brush, filling herself and the house with soot. She's done it before when I've been out. By! I'll have a word or two to say if she's at it again!'

With that she set off at a sedate pace, across the boulevard and on towards Ainsworth Street.

When she realised that the old dear was about to try and cross the busy road on her own, Louise set off after her. 'No! Wait a minute, I'll see you across!'

Unfortunately, as Louise made for the old woman, so did the bad-mannered young man – but with a very different intent. In the split second when the old woman turned to see why Louise was calling her, the surly young fellow from the tram came at her like a bull at a gate; the impact sent her reeling backwards, and her shopping bags went crashing to the ground. Sweeping up her handbag as it fell at his feet, the young man sped off, while from somewhere behind, the cry went up, '*Thief!* Grab the bastard!'

When a policeman appeared out of nowhere across his path, the young man skidded to a halt. He turned and ran in the opposite direction, almost colliding with Louise, who was running to help the old dear. She saw her chance, swung her shopping bag at him, and caught him on the knee with it. He went down, taking her with him, and in the scuffle that followed, she managed to swing her bag and hit him again, by which time the policeman and a pair of burly passers-by had him by the scruff of the neck.

'You did well, missus,' one of them told Louise.

'Lost all me apples though,' she panted, and groaned to see her freshly picked apples rolling into the gutter. When he offered to collect them for her, she laughed out loud. 'Thanks all the same, but no,' she said graciously. 'Every dog in Blackburn must have done his dirty business in that gutter. Never mind though.' She thought of Eric and how he had helped her pick the apples that very morning. 'There's plenty more where they came from.'

When the handbag was returned intact and the ruffian had been marched off to answer for stealing it, Louise escorted the old lady safely across the road. 'Are you sure you're all right?' she enquired. After all, she thought, the ordeal must have shaken her badly.

'I'm fine, dear,' the woman answered in sprightly manner. Then, to Louise's surprise, she laughed out loud. 'Wait till I tell my sister,' she chuckled. 'Tackled to the ground by a thief, and saved by a pretty young woman.'

Louise was flattered but realistic. 'Not so young these days. Too much water under the bridge, more's the pity.' It hardly seemed possible that she was coming up to her thirty-sixth birthday.

'You might not think so, but you're young next to *me*!' The old dear leaned forward, so no one else could hear. 'I'll tell you summat else if you like?' she confided wickedly.

'Oh, and what's that?' Louise was intrigued.

'You've got nicer legs than I ever had, *and* you wear prettier drawers than I do an' all.' She giggled like a naughty child. 'All blue and frilly. I saw 'em when you were rolling about on the ground with that devil.'

'Oh, did you now?' Louise had to laugh. 'They're nothing special . . . two and sixpence on Blackburn Market, but you're right – they *are* pretty.'

'It just goes to show, doesn't it, dear?'

'What does?' Louise had taken a liking to her.

The other woman wagged her finger. 'You must never go out without your drawers on. You never know when you might be suddenly upended, showing your bare arse to all and sundry.'

Before a shocked Louise could respond, the old dear was hobbling away down the street, singing to herself and clutching her bag so tightly it would take a steam train to wrench it from her.

Gripping her own bags more tightly than usual, Louise quickened her steps towards Derwent Street. By! She couldn't wait to tell Jinnie and Sal about her exciting escapade. No more than she could wait to hear what the two of *them* had been up to!

She glanced behind her to see the old lady rounding the corner and, recalling her *cheeky* words, she laughed out loud, instantly embarrassed when a fat lady with two children glanced curiously her way. 'It's been a nice day,' Louise said lamely, and without replying, the woman quickly ushered her children on before her.

'Please yourself,' Louise shrugged, but the smile was already creeping over her pleasant features again. Amazed that such a sweet little old lady could use such ripe language, Louise chuckled all the way home.

Looking Back

Josephine Cox

From the moment she learns of the stranger's visit, Molly Tattersall is filled with a sense of fear.

A short time later, Molly's mother disappears, leaving behind a letter in which she asks Molly to take care of her five brothers and sisters. Molly's wayward father rejects his responsibilities, leaving her to make a choice between the young man she has given her heart to and the family she adores, and who now desperately depend upon her.

Just eighteen, Molly is made to realise that, however hard it may be, she must put the children's happiness before her own. It is the cruellest decision of her life, with long-reaching and heartbreaking consequences. Only one thing is certain: Molly's life will never be the same again.

Josephine Cox is the author of twenty-four bestselling sagas which are all available from Headline.

'A Cookson by any other name' *Birmingham Post*

'Impossible to resist' *Woman's Realm*

'Driven and passionate' *The Sunday Times*

'As warm and affectionate as an old chair in front of a coal-black range, and as satisfying as a Lancashire hotpot, Cox's talent as a storyteller never lets you escape the spell' *Daily Mail*

0 7472 6492 9

headline

Now you can buy any of these other bestselling books by **Josephine Cox** from your bookshop or *direct from her publisher*.

FREE P&P AND UK DELIVERY
(Overseas and Ireland £3.50 per book)

Looking Back	£5.99
Rainbow Days	£5.99
Somewhere, Somebody	£5.99
The Gilded Cage	£5.99
Tomorrow the World	£5.99
Love Me or Leave Me	£5.99
Miss You Forever	£6.99
Cradle of Thorns	£6.99
A Time for Us	£6.99
The Devil You Know	£6.99
Living a Lie	£6.99
A Little Badness	£6.99
More Than Riches	£6.99
Born to Serve	£6.99
Nobody's Darling	£6.99
Jessica's Girl	£6.99

TO ORDER SIMPLY CALL THIS NUMBER

01235 400 414

or e-mail orders@bookpoint.co.uk

Prices and availability subject to change without notice.